THE QUEEN'S MIRROR

The Queen's Mirror

*Fairy Tales
by German Women,
1780–1900*

EDITED AND TRANSLATED BY
SHAWN C. JARVIS
AND JEANNINE BLACKWELL

University of Nebraska Press:
Lincoln & London

∞

Library of Congress Cataloging-in-Publication Data
The queen's mirror : fairy tales by German women,
1780–1900 / edited and translated by Shawn C. Jarvis and
Jeannine Blackwell. p. cm. – (European women writers
series) Includes bibliographical references.
ISBN 0-8032-1299-2 (cl.: alkaline paper) – ISBN 0-8032-6181-0
(paperback : alkaline paper)
1. German fiction – Women authors – Translations into
English. 2. German fiction – 18th century – Translations
into English. 3. German fiction – 19th century – Translations into English. 4. Fairy tales, German – Translations
into English. I. Jarvis, Shawn C. II. Blackwell, Jeannine.
III. Series.
PT1327.Q44 2001   833.009'9287–dc21   00-047949

CONTENTS

ILLUSTRATIONS

ACKNOWLEDGMENTS

We are grateful to the Stiftung Weimarer Klassik for permission to translate the following manuscripts: Gisela von Arnim, "Von der Geisterfrau," "Die garstige kleine Erbse," and "Von der Brautschaft," Stiftung Weimarer Klassik, Arnim Bestand GSA 03/995.

We would like to thank the many professionals who have assisted us in obtaining materials and information. For general help with their fine collections, we thank Dr. Peter Düsterdieck, Bibliotheksdirektor, Universitätsbibliothek der Technischen Universität Braunschweig, Hobrecker Sammlung, and Carola Pohlmann, Kinder- und Jugendbuchabteilung, Staatsbibliothek Preußischer Kulturbesitz, Wegehaupt-Sammlung, as well as the Europäische Märchengesellschaft, Schloß Bentlage in Rheine.

We thank the following scholars for sharing their expertise on illustrations and texts: Dr. Heinz Härtl, Stiftung Weimarer Klassik, Goethe-Schiller Archiv; Sven Lüken, curator, Staatliche Museen Kassel; Prof. Dr. Ulrich Marzolph of the *Enzyklopädie des Märchens* in Göttingen; and Prof. Ruth-Ellen Boetcher Joeres, University of Minnesota. For help in obtaining materials by interlibrary loan, we are indebted to Janet Layman and the entire staff of Interlibrary Loan, University of Kentucky; Christian Hogrefe and Gabriele Joeckel of the Herzog-August Bibliothek, Wolfenbüttel; Mareile Alferi, Diplom-Bibliothekarin, Martin-Luther-Universität, Halle-Wittenberg; and Dorothy Brenoel, Thiel College Library. Special thanks go to Manfred Buschmeier, Ruhr-Universität Bochum, for generous assistance with bibliographic research. We are indebted to Dr. Luise Pusch of Hannover, Germany, for help on portraits of Fanny Lewald; Ursula Hildebrand-Wehrli of Zollikon, Switzerland, for her enthusiastic support and the use of the illustration of Ricarda Huch; and Dr. Roland Specht-Jarvis for his invaluable clarification of thorny passages. We owe a special tribute for technical support to Neil Andersen, university photographer, and Joni Brown, CAD specialist, at St. Cloud State University for special photographic services. We especially thank Carolina Steup for her careful editing and proofreading of the manuscript and Mary M. Hill for her thoughtful copyediting. We thank for their comments on earlier versions of this project Dr. Linda Dégh of Indiana University, Dr. Jack Zipes of the University of Minnesota, and Dr. Lisa Ohm of the College of St. Benedict and Saint John's University.

Finally, we thank our children, Bettina, Alex, and Elly, to whom this volume is dedicated, for listening to our stories.

THE QUEEN'S MIRROR

Fairy tale splendor. Illustration by Carl Offterdinger.
From Luise Pichler, *Märchenpracht und Fabelscherz* (Stuttgart:
Wilhelm Nitschke, [1881]). Reprinted with permission of the
Staatsbibliothek zu Berlin, Preußischer Kulturbesitz, Kinder-
und Jugendbuchabteilung, Signatur BIVib, 131.

The Historical Context of German Women's Fairy Tales

Jeannine Blackwell

W HEN AND WHY did women in Europe start writing down the fairy and folk tales of their cultures? And why have modern readers heard so little about them? Since there is almost no lasting historical record of that moment of writing and its justification, we might think that women actually did not compose such tales until the late Victorian era of popular children's literature.

Yet the magnificent examples in the 1690s of the French women writers associated with Charles Perrault give us a clue that there is much to be discovered.[1] Investigations about the sources and methods of Jacob and Wilhelm Grimm have revealed that more than fifty women and girls contributed tales and tale variants to the Grimms' storehouse of stories from 1808 to the 1830s.[2] These clues to women's participation in narrative culture have been confirmed by our research: German-speaking women not only told but also recorded and wrote fairy tales, and their stories are different from those of their male counterparts.

We expand on previous research by presenting a cross-section of tales by German-speaking women. Some of our choices were associated with the famous tale-gathering projects, for women often had more access than their male friends and relatives to the *Volk* through the marketplace, the small shop, servants, and consumer providers such as tailors, shoemakers, and laundresses. Other writers we have chosen operated in different spheres: the Weimar court, German Romantic circles, children's educational establishments, the literary salon, the Kindergarten movement, and the women's emancipation movement.

The Queen's Mirror begins with the first known fairy tale written in German by a woman and moves on through each decade until 1900. To our surprise and even consternation, that first author was not a woman of the *Volk*, disenfranchised and powerless; she was Catherine the Great, empress of Russia. Why did she write her tales? If we are to believe her dedication, her purpose was to instruct her grandsons in how to become ideal rulers. In doing so, she relied on an old European genre, the *Speculum, Spiegel,* or *Mirror:* a handbook for etiquette, mores, and appropriate training for one's vocation or station. Catherine followed a tradition that began at the latest with Machiavelli's *Speculum, The Prince.* Toward the end of our anthology in the 1880s, we include a different kind of reflection on the burdens and loneliness of queenship written by Queen Elisabeth of Rumania.

Why did women lesser than queens write fairy tales in German? The reasons are as varied as the women themselves. Women clearly wrote some tales for the entertainment and delight of their children or pupils, as is the case with Maximiliane von La Roche Brentano's tale to her five-year-old daughter, Ludovica Brentano, and with the schoolteacher/governess Karoline Stahl. Some writers such as Villamaria (Marie Timme), Amalie Schoppe, and Elisabeth of Rumania followed the folklorist search for "authentic" regional tales, rewritten for a broad public. Professional women writers such as Agnes Franz tried to find a niche for children's literature in the writers' market. Others, like Sophie Tieck Bernhardi von Knorring, wrote stories for the men in their lives who demanded tales from them for publication. A chosen few could use them in salon life as the catalyst to conversation, inspiration, and humor, as did Gisela von Arnim, Marie von Olfers, and the members of their fairy tale circle in Berlin, the Kaffeterkreis.[3] For women writers who were essentially excluded from writing drama for public theater, fairy tale drama provided an outlet for stifled dramatic creativity;[4] we find such high drama in Karoline von Günderrode's tale "Temora" and Marie von Ebner-Eschenbach's "The Princess of Banalia." Women writers such as Fanny Lewald, Louise Dittmar, and Ricarda Huch had already used tales to comment on social problems, anticipating the political and socially critical tales of the twentieth century. Still others used the fantastic as a proving ground and mirror for self-presentation. In tales and fragments not presented here, Bettina von Arnim and Karoline von Günderrode describe their lives and the lives of their fictional alter egos in terms of flawed fairy tales, or tales that turn so sad they cannot be written to the end. Other writers claim or insinuate that the tales are composed for children close to them: a veritable cottage industry arose in those works by aunts (of real or assumed identity) who, having no children of their own, could simultaneously fulfill the maternal imperative and be successful authors: Tante Hedwig, die schwarze Tante, Tante Amanda, and many more.[5] The authorial pose provides a woman with justification for public writing while also creating the illusion for both mothers and children of a fictional familial intimacy in children's private reading, loosening the fetters of surveillance and supervision in the family circle.

When did women start writing fairy tales in German? To our shock, we could locate no other printed or manuscript German tales by women before 1782,[6] although we, and most eighteenth-century writers and critics, assume that women were certainly involved in telling stories in family and community settings before then. Then comes a veritable explosion of fairy tale composition by women writers. Between 1790 and 1810, Sophie Albrecht, Benedikte Naubert, Caroline Auguste Fischer, Frederike Helene Unger, Karoline de la Motte-Fouqué, Johanna Eleonore von Wallenrodt, in addition to the many writers included here, all published fairy tales or fairy tale collections. All this publication preceded the appearance of the Grimms' two-volume collection in 1812/1815 (the last authoritative edition appeared in 1857).

One of the reasons for this burst of activity was the success of the anonymous female author of more than fifty novels and the four-volume collection, *Neue Volksmährchen der Deutschen* (New folktales of the Germans, 1789–92). Benedikte Naubert, possibly the most prolific and popular author of her time, influenced not only women writers but also Clemens Brentano, Ludwig Tieck, and the Grimms, as well as Thomas Carlyle and Sir Walter Scott. Her tales set the standard for the genre written by women: realistic, moralistic, multilayered, often multigenerational, imbued with history, yet deeply fantastic. The Grimms admired her work but still criticized her dependence on historical sources and literary style. Naubert's work was part of a cascade of fairy tale printings in the 1780s and 1790s by Johann Karl August Musäus, Christoph Wieland, Ludwig Tieck, and others and of folk songs by Johann Gottfried von Herder and his followers, as well as Friedrich Bertuch's publication of part of the *Bibliothèque bleue* (older French and Arabic tales published as chapbooks in France from the late 1600s into the eighteenth century) in German translation, appearing from 1791 to 1796.

The shadows cast by Jacob and Wilhelm Grimm over the landscape of the nineteenth-century fairy tale are deep and long. Because the Grimms' collection of household and children's tales has so dominated research on European folk tales and fairy tales, it might appear that no other tales were being written or gathered in Germany during this period.[7] The Grimms' model of ideal naïveté and simplicity of narration by the *Volk* shunts aside the crafted literary tale and privileges the peasant woman as the ideal source of such oral tales. At the other end of the literary spectrum, authors of the artistic fairy tale of German Romanticism such as E. T. A. Hoffmann, Ludwig Tieck, Novalis, and Clemens Brentano in the early nineteenth century also seem to have excluded women writers from, or at least not to have acknowledged them in, their publications.[8] Between the naive, "anonymous" folktale and the Romantic literary masterpiece there has been little room for other tale-telling traditions, particularly for tales written by women.

As the Grimms' tales were accepted as part of the patriotic (Prussian) school curriculum and were anthologized and selectively translated in Victorian England, they came to dominate the definition of the folk tale, as Charles Perrault's slender production came to dominate the fairy tale. The model for the school and home gradually became the adaptation of the Grimms and other collectors/authors by women for children's consumption. Exacerbated by decades of Disney adaptations, that is still our model today: rewriting Perrault and the Grimms.

In the last three decades, however, three new directions of research have brought to light alternative tales by women (or by anonymous authors who were likely female) that bridge the chasm between the naive peasant tale and the high literary one.[9] First, research on the collection efforts and publication record of the historical French and German sources has explained women's role in the formation of the traditional tales. In addition to recent work by Renate Baader and Lewis Seifert on French tales by women and articles in *Marvels and Tales: Journal of Fairy-Tale Studies,* German scholars Karl Schulte-Kemmingshausen, Wilhelm Schoof, and Heinz Rölleke have clarified the sources of the Grimms' tales among young bourgeois and aristocratic women of their acquaintance. In addition, the 1980s brought more source studies and analyses of the Grimms' literary and ideological imprimatur on the tales by the American scholars Maria Tatar, Ruth Bottigheimer, and Jack Zipes, among others. The second development in fairy tale research has been the publication of feminist and multicultural collections of folktales from around the world, African American stories, and Victorian fairy tales, all of which expand our understanding of plots, tale types, and characters.[10] Finally, feminist adaptations of the standard tales by such authors as Angela Carter and Anne Sexton began to appear in the 1970s and have continued ever since.[11] *The Queen's Mirror* combines these three developments by presenting a historically based survey of female-authored German tales that give background and resonance to today's feminist fairy tales while critically revising the notion of the female tale-teller.

Our anthology ends in 1900, because the fairy tale itself changes so drastically at that time. The mass media of the early 1900s – film, comic books, children's theater, mass-marketed toys – changed consumption habits. The literary fairy tale moved to high art and movement politics at the beginning of modernism with the "new" fairy tale of expressionism and the workers movement. The end of the nineteenth century marks the advent of univer-

sal literacy in German-speaking countries and the final, permanent division
of the fairy tale–reading public into gendered youth and adult markets, a
change that had been developing during the course of the nineteenth century. Around 1900 early childhood professionals – the very kindergarten
teachers trained on fairy tale plays – and other writers began to create modern children's fiction such as Sibylle von Olfers's *Wurzelkindern* (root children) stories. Another ironic twist at the end of the nineteenth century was
the success of certain women dramatists such as Ernst Rosmer (Elsa Bern-
stein) and Adelheid Wette based not on their own works but on their opera
librettos adapted from the Grimms' tales and set to music by Engelbert
Humperdinck.

There is thus not only a change in readership at this date but also a similar permanent specialization of professional authors as well. The turn of the
century marked the entry of women into university life in Germany and
Switzerland and thus allowed certain women access to "high" academic and
literary culture as well as the literary avant-garde (the fairy tales and plays
of Isolde Kurz, Lou Andreas-Salomé, and Gabriele Reuter fall into this cate-
gory). Finally, Freud began to read fairy tales as part of the "family romance"
of ego development.

How did we choose these tales, and what did we count as a fairy tale?
We allowed the authors themselves to designate works as "fairy tales"; we
chose works from collections that included the words "fairy tale," "fantasy,"
or "magic" in their titles. We sought out tales that focus on women figures
in relation to the magical: female characters who play an active part in en-
countering the fantastic. A few examples are Amalie Schoppe's midwife who
assists at the childbed of a fairy queen, Bettina von Arnim's queen who learns
the language of the animals, and Gisela von Arnim's fantastic self-portrayal
in her *Märchenbriefe an Achim* (Fairy tale letters to Achim).

We highlighted certain recurring motifs that have resonated in women's
literary culture and in the dominant depiction of women, love, and family
relations in fairy tales. A central concern for us was the notion of girls'
maturation, learning and maturing as a magical-realistic process, as variants of the standard "Rapunzel" and "Mother Holle" tale types. Along with
Catherine the Great's early depiction of a boy's maturation, we include the
story of a girl's violent maturation in Anna von Haxthausen's "The Rescued
Princess" and a sequestering story by Agnes Franz, "Princess Rosalieb." We
include a number of tales about mother-daughter relations such as Benedikte Naubert's legendary tale of a superhuman maternal rescue and the
anonymous tale "The Red Flower," a poignant story of a daughter's rescue

of her mother. We feature several stories on water sprites, animal brides, and the motif of human/nonhuman transformation and transcendence. We chose Villamaria's "The King's Child," the transformation story of Pharaoh's daughter, a sea creature who loves a mortal; Fanny Lewald's merman story; and Louise Dittmar's stinging condemnation of women's status as society's apes in her "Tale of the Monkeys." Our last tale, Ricarda Huch's "Pack of Lies," tells a moving story of a man who covets a mermaid's poetic voice. Our fourth emphasis was on the multifaceted depiction of romantic relationships, which often overlap with the tales of maturation and transformation. Tian's (Karoline von Günderrode) "Temora" is a tragic *Liebestod* carried out by a king's daughter; "The Symbols" by Amalie von Helwig describes the stroll of the hero and the magical heroine through a cave symbolic of the female body; Marie von Ebner-Eschenbach's "The Princess of Banalia" tells of a well-behaved queen's love for a wild man and her suicide after his death. Our final important motif was the tension between public responsibility and private self, particularly in the depiction of self-reflecting queens. In these tales, magic is often the only means for resolving deep conflicts between these realms. Benedikte Naubert's victorious Queen Boadicea in "Boadicea and Velleda," Bettina von Arnim's queen who seeks refuge in the animal kingdom in "The Queen's Son," Carmen Sylva's (Elisabeth of Rumania) queen of the ants in "Furnica," and the little working-class girl of the anonymous "The Red Flower" are examples of the sad sacrifices suffered in the course of doing one's higher duty.

We included a range of tale forms that are representative of the variety in the genre during the period 1780–1900. Moralistic, even pedantic tales, the romantic fantastic, satire, tales intended only for private family use, fairy tale novels, dramatized tales, reworkings of tales for children's theater and puppetry, an early example of a socialist fairy tale, and transcribed oral renditions are all included here, so that the anthology is also a history of the genre as used by women authors. We have included tales with more complicated literary forms such as encapsulated narratives and narrators and intertwined levels of time, historicity, fantasy, and fantastic realism, for we have found that these forms are representative of the style of German women tale writers from 1782 to the present.

We selected the best and most representative works of certain writers because of other roles these women have played in European culture. We sought them out because of their later influence on women's literary culture in other areas (Karoline von Günderrode, Marie von Ebner-Eschenbach, and Fanny Lewald, for instance), because of their connection with the development of fairy tales by the Grimms (the Brentano-Arnims and the Haxt-hausens), because of their singular roles in European political life (Catherine the Great and Elisabeth of Rumania), and because of their contemporary fame as prolific and beloved writers and thus their unrecognized influence on later generations of readers and writers (particularly, Benedikte Naubert, Amalie Schoppe, and Marie Timme).

We surround our stories with a frame that is itself the frame of a frame. It is not the desperate nightly narrative of Scheherazade in *A Thousand and One Nights,* nor is it the frame of Charles Perrault's *Les Contes de ma mère l'Oye* (Mother Goose tales), nor yet *The Decameron* or *Il Pentamerone.*[12] We use instead Gisela von Arnim's narrative of her fictionalized foremother, who must tell the author stories to make her laugh, which Gisela in turn tells and illustrates to her real-life nephew Achim. In this, we follow a long tradition of female storytellers who weave their tales together, each reflecting on the other, inside and out.

Queens and mirrors: they form a deadly combination for women, according to contemporary feminist critics.[13] What we have found, on the contrary, is that mirrors are indeed truth machines for German women writers. They show girls their future so that they can act autonomously (Temora and Rosalieb), while mirrorlike surfaces reveal subterfuge, slavishness, and bad character in one's mate (in stories by Lewald, Dittmar, and Ebeling). They tell bitter truths about one's own worst emotions, as the princess of Banalia sees in her mother's mirror.

Princesses and queens, real and fictional, are no mere prizes, simple subplots in the hero's quest, in these texts by German women writers. These queens and princesses must learn to govern, to hate, to quit, to accept or refuse, to be torn between duty and desire. They must seek out love on their own terms, even if it breaks their hearts, for that might be the price of living in the harsh reflection of the truthful mirror. The princess of Banalia, for example, willfully chooses life and pain, and ultimately death, over the path of regal isolation and cold, unfeeling deeds. She leaves behind her heritage: "Here many of my forefathers ended their lives in ghostly silence, weary of battles and daring deeds. Far from life's intimacy, distanced from every mortal urge, they sleep here a dreamless sleep. They do not think, they do not feel. They live their death." Instead, she chooses life with all its pain, but she also chooses to die for her noble, savage love.

Use these stories for your own reflection. Imagine yourself to be Catherine the Great, Elisabeth of Rumania, or merely the princess of Banalia. And now step into the mirror, "back in the time when wishing still helped."[14]

NOTES

1. See Baader, *Dames de lettres;* Seifert, "The Time that (N)ever Was"; and the *Marvels and Tales* special issue on Charles Perrault (*Merveilles et Contes/Marvels and Tales* 5, no. 2 [1991]).

2. Schoof, *Zur Entstehungsgeschichte der Grimmschen Märchen;* Schulte-Kemmingshausen, "Annette von Droste-Hülshoff"; Rölleke, Anhang und Nachwort; and Bottigheimer, *Grimms' Bad Girls.*

3. Jarvis, "Trivial Pursuit?"

4. Kord, *Ein Blick hinter die Kulissen.*

5. A few examples are Hedwig Haberkern, *Tante Hedwig's Geschichte für kleine Kinder. Ein Buch für erzählende Mütter, Kindergärtnerinnen und kleine Leser. Mit sechs bunten Bildern von Louise Thalheim* (Breslau: Eduard Trewendt, 1869); [Amanda Hoppe-Seyler], *Der kleine Frieder. Erzählungen, Märchen und Lieder von Tante Amanda. Mit 8 Bildern von Th. Hosemann* (Berlin: Winckelmann und Söhne, n.d.); Clara Fechner, *Die schwarze Tante. Märchen und Geschichte für Kinder. Mit Holzschnitten nach Ludwig Richter* (Leipzig: Georg Wigand, 1848); and even an anonymous male author posing as an aunt, [Ulrich B. Celius], *Theater-Märchen. Erzählungen aus unseren Lieblingsopern für die deutsche Jugend von Tantchen Ungenannt* (Leipzig: Schloemp, [1920]).

6. We also located the following information. There is no attributed author for *Märchen für junge Damen, oder: Beyträge zur Mädchen-Philosophie* (Bern, Switzerland: Niklaus Emmanuel Haller, 1774), although some scholars have indicated the publisher himself as author; the moralistic stories do not have any magic motifs. Philippine Engelhard, *Neujahrs-Geschenk für liebe Kinder von Philippine Engelhard, geborne Gatterer* (Göttingen: Johann Christian Dieterich, 1787), has no fairy tales but does include an introduction in which Engelhard discusses open education with children on childbirth and how mothers suffer; Engelhard also published *Spückemährchen* (Göttingen: Johann Christian Dieterich, 1782), a ballad with motifs of the boy who left home to learn about the shivers.

7. There has been copious research on tale collectors; see Bolte and Polívka, eds., *Anmerkungen;* Rölleke, Anhang und Nachwort; Rölleke, ed., *Märchen aus dem Nachlaß der Brüder Grimm;* Rölleke, ed., *Unbekannte Märchen von Jacob und Wilhelm Grimm;* Schoof, *Zur Entstehungsgeschichte der Grimmschen Märchen;* and *Enzyklopädie des Märchens.*

8. The Grimms, for example, spoke of the tales contributed by the aristocratic Haxthausen girls as simply "from the Paderborn region" and those from the Hassenpflug and Wild girls as "from Hesse," rather than giving specific names. In this anthology, the tale by Sophie Tieck Bernhardi von Knorring was published under the name of her first husband, August Ferdinand Bernhardi, with no attribution to her.

9. Haase, "Feminist Fairy-Tale Scholarship."

10. Auerbach and Knoepflmacher, eds., *Forbidden Journeys;* Hamilton, *Her Stories;*

Phelps, ed., *Maid of the North;* Park and Heaton, eds., *Caught in a Story;* Rush, ed., *The Book of Jewish Women's Tales;* and Zipes, ed., *Victorian Fairy Tales.*

11. Bernheimer, ed., *Mirror;* Carter, *The Old Wives' Fairy Tale Book;* Datlow and Windling, eds., *Black Swan, White Raven;* Datlow and Windling, eds., *Black Thorn, White Rose;* Datlow and Windling, eds., *Ruby Slippers, Golden Tears;* Datlow and Windling, eds., *Snow White, Blood Red;* Sexton, *Transformations;* Walker, *Feminist Fairy Tales;* and Zipes, ed., *The Outspoken Princess.* Marina Warner's recent book, *From the Beast to the Blonde,* about the iconography and mythology of predominately female tale-tellers, builds on the research of all these scholars.

12. See Warner, *From the Beast to the Blonde.* Belcher, "Framed Tales," presents African examples.

13. See Gilbert and Gubar, "The Queen's Looking Glass"; Bernheimer, ed., *Mirror;* Rose, "Through the Looking Glass"; Yolen and Stemple, *Mirror, Mirror;* and Warner, *From the Beast to the Blonde.*

14. The first line of "The Frog Prince," the first tale in the Grimms' 1857 edition. Versions of this tale were contributed by the Wild daughters of Kassel, Marie Hassenpflug of Kassel, and the Haxthausen family, which consisted of six daughters, two female cousins, and one son.

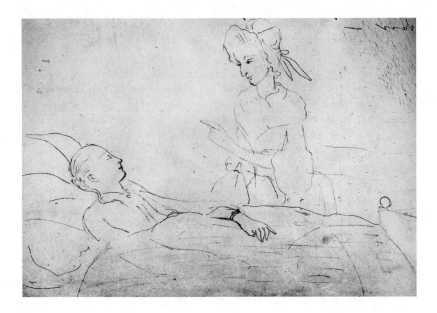

The Ghost Lady. Illustration by Gisela von Arnim.
Reprinted with permission of the Stiftung Weimarer Klassik,
Arnim Bestand GSA 03/995.

Prologue
The Ghost Lady
1853

Dear Achim,

You won't want to believe this – that this bracelet on my arm was dug out of a grave, where it was on the arm of a lady who appears to me every night at the stroke of midnight and tells me the most bizarre stories from her life, and so I will write it all down for you, and you will be convinced of it all.

Every night she comes to my bed and asks about her bracelet. "Good evenin' to ya, good evenin' to ya, give me back my bracelet," she says every time, and every time I say, "No! First you must tell me a whole bunch of stories, and if I laugh, then you get it back, otherwise never."

Then I asked, "What did the children do back in your day?" and she said, "Oh, goodness gracious, we weren't a thing like you; we had to behave very well. Goodness gracious, in the morning when we got up, we kissed Papa's hand, and the little boys were very different from Achim. They kissed Papa's hand every morning, had their lunch, and to make them sit up straight they were tied by their pigtails to the backs of their chairs.

"After the meal they went for a walk, one behind the other, close on the coattails of the first, like soldiers in single file.

"Then the good doctor arrived to give each of them a purgative for breakfast so that all their nasty habits would disappear. And then they ran away in fright and raced to the chicken coop behind the house, and then when he returned they ran again into the milking shed – and what a fright when he came there, too – and then farther, into the pantry, where they fell into a vat of syrup. That was a scare! The only thing to be seen of them was the pigtail of the youngest sticking out!

"Then they crawled out again, for the old geezer had left to go get a spoon to dig them out. Now they all licked each other off, which was quite tasty. Then the old man came back, and they ran away and climbed a big apple tree, and he came, and they bombarded him with apples.

"From there they climbed on to the roof, but the nasty old doctor came up out of the attic window and caught them, all except little Jacob, who was clinging to the bell in the tower.

"And that, of course, made the bell ring. People thought that there was a fire, so they all ran out together and caught little Jacob too, and then it was purgative time for them all!"

I almost laughed, but I stuck my head under the covers just in time, and the old lady said, "See, you almost laughed, and now I will run off, at least for today," and then she nodded, and disappeared, and now I want to see what she will tell me tomorrow.

TRANSLATED BY JEANNINE BLACKWELL

Catherine the Great in coronation regalia with the royal heir, Paul Petrowitch, and a copy of *De l'éducation du prince*. Joseph Lante after Stefano Torelli, 1762. Reprinted with permission of the State Historical Museum, Moscow, SHM Inventory Number 16116 E111-7847.

Catherine II, Empress of Russia

(*known as Catherine the Great*)

1729–1796

Born a German princess, Sophie August Frederike, princess of Anhalt-Zerbst, became Catherine the Great of Russia, one of the most important monarchs of her day. She was a strong proponent of Enlightenment thought and reflected this in her numerous plays and three published fairy tales (one in a bilingual German/Russian edition). Catherine was married in 1745 to the future czar of the Russian Empire, Peter III, and overthrew him in 1762 after his accession to the throne; she reigned as empress from 1762 until 1796. In addition to her legendary military and diplomatic undertakings, she fostered connections with the German and French intelligentsia throughout her reign.

"Fewei," the first known female-authored fairy tale in German, is the story of a young czar's maturation and path to an enlightened reign, led in part by a wise man. Catherine wrote this tale for her two grandsons, who were destined to become czars themselves. While it has little of the magic and wonder of the French and later German tales, it shows well how the Enlightenment used the fairy tale format for pedagogical, even pedantic ends. Readers can find the motif of the wise hermit and teacher in Sophie Tieck Bernhardi von Knorring's "The Old Man in the Cave" and compare the training and quest of the young man growing up in several of the Grimms' tales: no. 4, "The Boy Who Left Home to Find out about the Shivers," no. 121, "The Prince Who Feared Nothing," and no. 136, "Iron John," all in the 1857 edition. Fewei's princely quest for maturation reflects that of Prince Almansor in Elisabeth Ebeling's "Black and White"; see also nos. 326 and 502 in Aarne and Thompson, *The Types of the Folktale*. Modern tales include Jean Ingelow, "The Prince's Dream" (in Zipes, ed., *Victorian Fairy Tales*), and "Maria Morevna," a Russian tale of a woman ruler and her husband, whom she teaches how to govern (in Phelps, ed., *Maid of the North*).

Catherine, Empress of Russia, "Mährchen vom Fewei," in *Erzählungen und Gespräche. Von I. K. M. d. K. a. R. Zweyter Theil* (Berlin and Stettin: Friedrich Nicolai, 1784), 177–228.

The Tale of Fewei

1784

T HEY SAY that in Siberia there once lived a populous, industrious, and wealthy people. And once upon a time this folk had a czar whose royal line was of the Chinese name Toa-a-u, a wise and virtuous man who loved his subjects as a father loves his children. He oppressed no one with excessive taxes and spared them every chance he could. He disdained extravagance, pomp, and debauchery, and thus his court exuded dignity and moderation. Now this czar had a czarina whose face was as lovely as her heart and mind were sublime. She took great pains to please her husband and to follow his example. They had lived together in love and harmony for many years yet had no children, for it is always said that no happiness in the world is ever truly complete.

The czarina was often ill, and her many and varied ailments worried the czar greatly. He summoned doctors from near and far, from his own and foreign lands, to consult long and hard about her illness. Although they were often in disagreement, they still prescribed such large amounts of herbs and other plants and compounds as medications that simply to list their names and dosages filled entire rolls of the paper of that age.

The czarina and her ladies-in-waiting stared in horror and disgust at the vats full of medications brought for her to ingest. She complained that they tasted awful, the ladies maintained that they looked repulsive, and the czar doubted whether such a potion of so many different herbs and ingredients would have a positive effect. He confided his worries to his courtiers. It has often been said that clever rulers always have sensible advisors, and that was the case here as well. One of the worthy men of the court, Wiseworth by name, said to the czar, "My Lord, why are you so distressed? If you think that the medications will do the czarina more harm than good, it will take only one word from you. Have them thrown away, and I will seek out a man for you who has the gift of healing, and he will make the czarina well. He is not here but lives not too far away in the wilderness."

Wiseworth's words cheered the czar's heart and filled him with the hope of seeing his wife restored to health. A messenger was sent immediately to bring the gifted man to court. The messenger found his dwelling in the forest, a small cottage covered with straw, and knocked at the gate. A dog began to bark; someone peered out a small opening and asked, "Who is that knocking?" The messenger replied, "I am the czar's messenger. Is your lord at home?" "He is at home," answered the man and opened the door. When the messenger stepped in, the lord of the house was sitting at the fire and reading a book. When he heard from the messenger that the czar required him, he immediately arose, dressed, mounted his horse, and rode with the messenger to the czar's court.

When the czar saw him, he asked his name and origins. To the first question the man answered, "I am called Katun." To the second he answered, "I was once a courtier of the prince of Sengor, at whose court I was forced to bear unwarranted persecution from evil, envious people who besmirched my name. I lost my fortune and my friends," he lamented, "and suffered unjust deprivation. Since I did not grovel or lie, as was expected at the court of the prince of Sengor, I have chosen to live in solitude in the forest, and occupy myself with learning the properties of herbs, so that I may be of service to others."

When Katun had finished his reply, the czar led him to the czarina. They found her resting, her feet raised on a soft white pillow, covered in a blanket of red velvet lined with black fox furs. She looked very pale, her eyes were absolutely blank, and she complained of leg cramps, insomnia, and nausea when she saw food. Katun inquired about her habits and heard that the czarina lay day and night in a warm room, did not make the slightest movement, never enjoyed fresh air, and constantly ate little morsels of food. She slept during the day and chatted all night with her ladies-in-waiting, who rubbed her feet and told her fairy tales or gossip of what this one did or didn't do, said or didn't say. Our root doctor said to the czar, "My dear czar, forbid the czarina to sleep during the day, talk during the night, or eat and drink, except at noon and dinnertime. Order her to get up and only to lie down at night; absolutely prohibit her from using a coverlet in a warm room; have the czarina go walking, drive around, and enjoy the open air."

The czar tried to convince the czarina to follow the root doctor's prescription, but she raised all sorts of objections and said, "I am used to living like this. How am I supposed to change my ways?" Finally, the pleading of the czar won out over her usual routine. She was taken out of the bed from under the warm velvet and black fox fur covers. At the beginning she was supported under her arms, but finally she began to walk alone. Soon she was set in a sleigh harnessed to six reindeer with gilded horns and bentwood trim covered with ermine and set with ruby buckles. The czarina rode around for two whole hours, and when she came home she ate and slept right well; her color improved, and she became lovely again. Her eyes sparkled as before, and from pure joy the ladies composed a song that began with these words: "Let the joyous news be spread, without her pills, she's left her bed!"

And indeed, the czarina not only improved, she flourished. And after a year, God gave her and the czar a son, a beautiful little czarevitch who was named Fewei, that is, "Golden Sun." The czar bountifully rewarded the gifted man who had cured the czarina without any medicine and allowed his return to his chosen solitude again.

The czar began to concern himself with raising his son. He was given a nursemaid, an intelligent widow who knew how to tell if a child cried because it needed something, because it was sick, or because it was being contrary. The child was not swaddled or cuddled, he was not sung to sleep or rocked in any way, and he was given the right kinds of food at the appropriate times. The child grew so that it was a pleasure to see.

After six weeks, a large colorful carpet decorated with flower garlands, about two measures long and just as wide, was brought into his bedroom and spread on the floor. When the czar's little boy awoke, he was placed on his right side on the carpet, and he turned immediately over on his tummy. This was repeated several times a day. Gradually, the child accustomed himself to getting up on his hands and knees; soon he sat up by himself, and he began to walk before he was one year old, first along the wall and then around the room.

Next they began to play with toys with the boy, carefully chosen toys with which he learned about the world around him and that suited his naive understanding. Before the child could talk, he made signs for everything he wanted to express and even knew the names of the letters. When he was asked where this or that letter was, he pointed at it with his finger. When he was sick, he learned to be patient and stayed as quiet as possible, and so the sick spells were less severe and reduced while he slept. When he was three years old, he was inoculated for smallpox; after that he had even more desire to learn and know everything. Without anyone pushing him, he taught himself to read, write, and do arithmetic; his favorite games were the ones that led him to new discoveries. The czarevitch had a good heart and was sympathetic, generous, obedient, and grateful. He honored his parents and other superiors, was courteous, friendly, and benevolent to all people instead of quarrelsome, capricious, or fearful, and every time and everywhere he followed the good counsel of truth and common sense. He liked to speak and hear the truth, hated all untruth, and never prevaricated, even in jest.

Both in winter and in summer he was taken out into the open air when it did not endanger his health. When he was seven he was given a tutor, a venerable old man, who let him gradually learn to sit a short time on a horse, to shoot arrows and flints, and to hit a target with darts. In the summer the czarevitch swam and bathed in the river Irtisch. The only games chosen for the czarevitch were those that increased his body's strength and agility and gave his spirit courage and conviction. Books and teaching enhanced his innate intellectual gifts. The czarevitch grew and became stronger in body, health, and spirit.

When the czarevitch turned fifteen he grew tired of the quiet, peaceful, and tedious life in his father's house and desired things he could not even name. He wanted to see the wide world, and how things were in other lands, and everything he had heard tell of – this kingdom and that duchy, how affairs were arranged at various courts, what customs were practiced by this or that army, which entertainments and habits prevailed here or there, where anything stranger, or better, or worse could be found, and what actually constituted a well-run state.

When the czar and czarina heard of their son's plans, they could not easily agree to his travels. The czar weighed the question, but the czarina went to her room and began to weep and told her ladies that she did not want to let the czarevitch go and that without him her life would just be a burden. The court ladies answered, "Do not cry, Czarina, we will convince the czarevitch that he should not travel to distant lands." The czarina sent them off to speak with him. When the ladies arrived and were announced as having come from the czarina, he immediately gave them an audience. The ladies entered the czarevitch's room and spoke thus: "Dear Czarevitch, your mother, the czarina, has sent us to convince you to stay with us. Your parents will seek out a lovely bride for you, and make you a rich fur, a golden fur lined with sable. Here with us you will have a warm room in winter and lovely apples and green meadows in summer. What more could you want in distant lands? When you have children and our court is no longer barren, then you will be allowed to travel into the wide world, but as it stands now, you are your mother's only hope and joy."

The czarevitch answered, "My dear ladies, I regret that my mother is grieving, but I cannot always stay at home and fly kites. I want to see with my own eyes what people tell of in stories; I want to witness the things printed in books. I do not wish to know things only from hearsay; I want to see for myself the strength or weakness of neighboring lands; I want to see the mountains, forests, citadels, seas, harbors, and bazaars and bring you back handsome gifts." The ladies bowed deeply before the czarevitch, left the room, and returned to the czarina with his response.

In the meantime, the czar, accompanied by Wiseworth, entered the room and found the czarina in great distress and sorrow. The court ladies stood with folded hands along the walls and pondered what to do. Wiseworth stood deep in thought, and the czar asked, "What do you say, my lord?" Wiseworth said, "My lord czar, summon the czarevitch and tell him that because of his tender years, you cannot allow him to go to distant lands until he has proven through trial that he is obedient to you, that he has a steadfast soul, patience under duress, and moderation in times of good fortune, that he is loyal, brave, generous, and benevolent, so that he will win honor and fame among foreign peoples."

The czar was pleased on hearing this speech. He patted Wiseworth's left shoulder warmly and said to him, "Oh, my loyal advisor, you are an honest man. I will give you a large hat with a golden tassel, just as I myself wear on high festival days." Wiseworth bowed before the czar, touching the ground, and said, "I thank you and am forever your most humble servant." The czarevitch was summoned and informed of the czar's resolve. The czarevitch submissively heard his father's command and said, "Let the will of my father, the czar, be done. I will not thwart it, and I am ready to do everything he commands."

The next day, the czar went walking with the czarevitch in the gardens. The czar, seeing a dead branch hanging from a tree, took it down and stuck it into the ground. He ordered his son to take a watering can and water it twice a day for an entire year, morning and evening. The czarevitch went twice a day, morning and evening, and watered the dry twig with a watering can. His young companions found this ridiculous and told him in annoyance, "Water the dry old twig as much as you like; it will never become a tree. Your father has thought up a mean trick and is playing it on you." The czarevitch thought long and hard and finally said, "Listen, my good friends and good lords, whoever gives an order must be the one to think it through, and our only job is to obey and to carry out the command in submissiveness without complaint, and without much reflection." A short time thereafter the czar came into the garden to see if the dry twig had taken root; he shook it, pulled it out of the ground, threw it away, and ordered the czarevitch to stop watering it with the watering can.

In the autumn the czarevitch rode to the hunt on a white steed with falcons, sparrow hawks, and hawks to amuse himself for some days in the open air. He had hardly ridden seven leagues when the czar's messenger hurried to him and said, "Our lord, the czar, requires that you return immediately and has sent you a sumptuous robe. Kalmuckian ambassadors have arrived, and you are to appear in ceremonial attire."

The czarevitch immediately turned his white steed around and rode in full gallop back to his father. The horse had become quite winded and was sweating; the czarevitch dismounted and washed his face with a fine cloth of Dutch linen. When the czar saw him in common hunting attire, he asked, "Why are you not wearing your ceremonial garb?" The czarevitch answered, "The sweat of my brow, produced as I was hurrying to fulfill your commands, is more honorable than any sumptuous robe. If I had changed clothes, I would have perhaps come too late. The Kalmuck delegation should see with their own eyes how quickly your son does your bidding."

The Kalmuck delegation presented the czarevitch with a letter from a relative of the czarina, the Mongolian prince Agrei, inviting the czarevitch to visit. The czarevitch wrote in answer, as was his wont: "Czarevitch Fewei to the Mongolian prince Agrei. You no doubt know that I reside with my father, the czar; without his permission I am not allowed to visit you. By obeying him now, I am learning how I myself will later rule; about the rest, your ambassadors will inform you as is necessary."

The rest was this: the Kalmuckian ambassadors were importunate people. When they saw that they would not get the answer they wanted from the czar, they tried to win the confidence of the czarevitch. The Kalmucks wanted to appropriate a piece of land from the czar's holdings, along with its people and livestock. They thought they could deceive the czarevitch because of his youth, for they saw that he was friendly and open with them, as he was to all people. At the start they sought to move him with clever speeches and pleading, aiming to make Fewei put his signature on a letter allowing the Kalmuckian troops to cross the patrolled border. They tried to appeal to his sympathy and said, "We are poor people, you are rich, and what difference is such a small thing to you?" The czarevitch paid no attention to this and told them resolutely that he would never do such a thing, for the cities did not belong to him but rather to the czar, and that he would advise them to avoid burdening him with such requests in the future.

Thereupon they promised him and his entourage all manner of advantages and great gifts if he would attempt to convince the czar to allow them to graze their sheep on the meadows of the citadel. Fewei's answers remained unchanged. He told them with a derisive laugh, without raising his voice: "Poor people usually have nothing to give the rich as gifts. I myself do not accept gifts in any case, and those who are loyal to me know that this is also forbidden to them."

Since the Kalmucks could accomplish their ends by neither exhortation nor bribery, they began their journey home. On the way they met some Tatars from the great horde of those who travel around trading and told them this:

"The youngest son of our ambassador has run away. He is a young man; if you find him, bring him back to his father." The Tatars said, "Good enough; if we find him, we will bring him back." Back in those times the Tatars were a rough and uncouth people. After a few days of travel, they noticed a young man in the plains who was walking along with no companions, and they believed him to be the son of the ambassador. The horde surrounded him and tried to abduct him, saying, "You are the runaway we have been seeking." The young man answered, "You are doing me a great injustice. I am no runaway but the child of an honorable man."

Since they did not believe him and wanted to drag him away by force, he backed up to a tree, pulled his saber from its sheath, and said, "Whoever attacks me first will never go home alive." The Tatars were stopped short and could not figure out how to capture him; he stared them down and derided them thus: "I think I have made you all as fearful as you have made me brave." Just at this moment a guard of the czar came riding past, scattering the Tatars and overcoming those who had not quickly taken flight. The leaders of the guard saw with horror that the young man whom the Tatars had taken for the son of the ambassador was the czarevitch, Fewei, although he did not look anything like a Kalmuck. Since the czarevitch saw the naïveté, stupidity, and confusion of these people, he himself asked that they be released, after which the Tatars were allowed to return to their lands.

When Czar Toa-a-u heard this, he was very angry, because he considered it a violation of his own authority that such criminals were allowed to go free without his knowledge. These were, after all, the ones who had wanted to abduct Czarevitch Fewei Toa-a-u-kovitch. He therefore angrily told the czarevitch, "What call had you to speak on their behalf? You interfere in things, my child, that do not concern you; I alone have the power to pardon and punish. You are my son, but I am the possessor and upholder of the czarist rule."

Since the czarevitch saw that the czar was so angry with him, he said, "I have done wrong, my lord father, but it is my compassion that was the cause." Thereupon he stood silently and reverently before the czar, but the czar in his anger was not yet satisfied and asked him, "Why are you standing there so silently, as if you are criticizing my judgment in your heart? Did your tutor teach you to do so?" "No," answered Fewei in a quiet voice. "He taught me always to bear your rage with patience and not to be obstinate. I see my offense, and I am deeply sorry that I have provoked you to anger." These words softened the czar's fatherly heart somewhat, and he said, "Then you are dismissed." The czarevitch kissed his father's hand and went to his room.

Toward evening, Fewei began to feel chills, piercing pains, and heaviness in his head, and he could not sleep at all during the night. In the morning he had a high fever, and the czar and czarina were informed that he was ill. His parents came to see him, and even though the illness worsened with every hour, Fewei bore it all stoically and was so patient and calm that he only complained when the doctor asked him if this or that hurt. Finally, his youth and the loyal care of all those around him helped him overcome the illness. Fewei returned fully to health and had grown a foot in the meantime. The common folk call this illness "growing pains" or say, "His beard was growing." And indeed, the czarevitch began gradually to trim his handlebar mustache with gilded scissors.

The joy over his recovery was sincere and heartfelt, and the poets wrote new songs filled with exuberant praise about it. Fewei was no friend of flattery; he pondered it and told his courtiers, "Allow no pride to enter my heart, and repeat the following to me every day when I awake from my night's sleep: 'Fewei, get up from your bed and remember all day long that you are human, just like the rest of us.'"

The next spring the czarevitch rode out again into the country and unexpectedly stopped by Lord Wiseworth's house. He dismounted, went into the drawing room, and remained there while the lord of the house was told that Fewei had arrived for a visit. Meanwhile, a long time passed, and Fewei's companions began to get restless and said that the lord was being impolite to let the czarevitch wait this long. Fewei answered, "Lord Wiseworth has many tasks to accomplish for the czar; possibly I came at an inopportune time for him. It should not be hard for us young people to wait. Just recently Lord Wiseworth himself had to wait in my reception room, and he did not become impatient."

Soon thereafter the lord rushed in and apologized for his tardiness. The czarevitch embraced him and said, "It is easy to pardon the one whose loyal service has been praised by my parents for deeds I must always remember." Wiseworth bowed deeply and replied with tears of joy, "I am pleased to hear your kind words, for they will lengthen my days." The czarevitch breakfasted with him in an arbor near a large lake. From his seat on a bench, he looked out a window and spotted a boat with a fisherman in it gliding across the water.

The czarevitch decided he would like to ride in the boat. He stood up from the bench, went to the door, called the fisherman, and prepared to get into the boat. A group of people came rushing over. Some said that it was too dangerous to sail in such a small craft, others argued that the boat was too old, still others that it was not seaworthy, and yet another group that it rocked too much. A fifth group worried that its wood was rotting and the sixth that there would soon be a storm. In short, they all told the czare-vitch one terror after another. Meanwhile, Fewei took the rudder out of the fisherman's hand and said, "The fisherman is a man and sailed in this boat without mishap; Fewei is also a man and can sail in it without drowning. I have been raised with the fear of God, but I know no other." With these words Fewei sat down in the boat and sailed for some length of time across the lake, in spite of some bad weather. He landed safely, took leave of his host, put his left foot in the stirrup, mounted quickly, and galloped home.

Wiseworth, who was very pleased with Fewei's visit, told his friends later that evening, "Among his other fine gifts, Fewei has the ability to talk with all people as if he was seeking their favor, and there is no hint that he is talking with them just out of politeness. The czarevitch is not haughty; he loves his neighbor as himself, and since he knows that he is also human, he always remembers when he is speaking with another that he is talking with a fellow human being. But each of us, even when we speak with him for the first time, feels a certain encouragement, a confidence, which Fewei arouses by his innate modesty and courtesy."

Wiseworth's friends wanted to repeat his words of praise for Fewei precisely the next day but could not remember the correct wording of his speech. Nosy people usually catch the beginning, the middle, or the end of a speech but not its import. Wiseworth had detractors who had heard this conversation in parts and brought it, distorted, to the ears of the czar. They said that Wiseworth had told them that Fewei was haughty, among other statements that were not complimentary to the czarevitch. Fewei was unruffled by this and said, "I am always ready to improve my mistakes and failings, and I am grateful to Wiseworth that his words have given me a new opportunity to improve." And during it all, his behavior toward Wiseworth did not change in the slightest. Soon he discovered what had really happened.

In the summer Fewei came unexpectedly to a rich merchant to examine his wares. The merchant, who was overjoyed at the visit of the czarevitch, wanted to give him numerous gifts, as was the custom then. He had silver jugs on gilded platters, golden cloth bags filled with gold, costly furs, and woven Persian silk rugs brought into the room. At the same time the merchant's daughter entered, a young widow clothed in black with a sorrowful face, and she placed the gifts before him. The father offered the gifts but said of his daughter, "She is being pressed by her husband's relatives and creditors." Fewei replied, "I accept your gifts gladly and give them all to your daughter as a dowry, and hope that they will bring her a husband who will love her more for her virtue than for her beauty and her wealth."

When Fewei returned home, he heard that his squire had taken a fall from his horse and gravely wounded his foot. He went to see the squire and sent for the surgeon. While the man's foot was being dressed, Fewei filled his boot with money and said, "Give this to the squire; it will be enough for him to pay for his medications."

Around this time, or soon thereafter, the People of the Golden Horde invaded the czar's kingdom. They captured several of the czar's subjects and wanted to hold them for ransom. The czar called up his troops and armed them to repel the Golden Horde. The troops moved out in the spring, drove the Golden Horde back over the border, and sent the czar some prisoners from the Golden Horde, along with his freed subjects. Many people said at the time, "However badly the Golden Horde treated our prisoners is how we should treat them now." When Fewei heard these words, he said, "It is not fitting that we adopt evil behavior; let the People of the Golden Horde experience nothing but humane treatment toward fellow human beings and other virtues from us; let us be the model of everything good in the world."

A year later, the czarevitch took a wife and had children with her that were very much like himself. Some years thereafter, he traveled to distant regions and lands and then came home again. Fewei and all his progeny lived long and full lives, and he is renowned among his people still today.

TRANSLATED BY JEANNINE BLACKWELL

Ludovica Brentano Jordis

1787–1854

Ludovica Brentano Jordis, called Lulu, contributed two tales to the brothers Grimm; the first is no. 38 II, "Mrs. Fox's Wedding" in the 1857 edition. She wrote down the second tale for the brothers on 31 May 1814, reporting the following: "When I was five or six years old, my mother told me a fairy tale; I don't remember everything, but I will write down here everything that I still know." Her mother, Maximiliane Brentano, was the daughter of novelist Sophie von La Roche, the first widely known German woman novelist. Jordis grew up in Frankfurt, surrounded by the same influences as her more famous literary siblings, Bettina and Clemens. All three Brentano siblings took part in the Grimms' tale collection project.

This tale, "The Lion and the Frog," was included in the first edition of the second volume of the Grimms' tales (1815) as no. 43 but was omitted in later editions. The tale has similarities to the Grimms' tales no. 66, "Bunny Rabbit's Bride," and no. 135, "The White Bride and Black Bride," but is more closely related to other tales of violent transformation at or preceding a marriage, sometimes on the wedding night: Anna von Haxthausen's "The Rescued Princess" in this collection as well as the Grimms' tales no. 108, "Hans My Hedgehog," and no. 1, "The Frog Prince," in the 1857 edition. Ludovica's mother apparently based her tale in part on Mme d'Aulnoy's "The Beneficent Frog" (in Zipes, ed. and trans., *Beauties, Beasts, and Enchantment*, 545–63). She no doubt had heard or read it, possibly in its German translation, "Der Frosch mit dem rothen Käppchen" (in Bertuch, ed., *Die blaue Bibliothek*, 9:71–112). However, this version is considerably shorter, and the genders and family relationships of the frog, the lion, and the princess are changed, presumably to make them understandable and enjoyable for a five- or six-year-old girl.

The motif of the royal lion who returns to rule a kingdom has resonance with Bettina von Arnim's "The Queen's Son" and with "A Peaceable Kingdom." The story of a girl who takes off with an animal on a quest to disenchant him (no. 65 in Aarne and Thompson, *The Types of the Folktale*) has a long tradition, from the Greek legend of Amor and Psyche to "East o' the Sun, West o' the Moon" and "Beauty and the Beast." This tale is different from most of the animal bridegroom tales, for the violent transformation of the animal is brought about by his sister, rather than his wife.

Bolte and Polívka, eds., *Anmerkungen*, 3:58–60; Rölleke, ed., *Kinder- und Hausmärchen*, 3:538. See also a translation by Zipes in *The Complete Fairy Tales*, 695–97.

The Lion and the Frog

1792/1793; 1814

T HERE WAS ONCE a king and queen who had a son and a daughter who loved each other very much. The prince often went out on the hunt and sometimes stayed out late in the forest, but once he did not come home at all. His sister nearly wept her eyes out until finally, when she could stand it no longer, she went out into the forest to find her brother.

After she had gone a great distance, she was too tired to take another step, and as she looked around, she saw a lion standing next to her who acted friendly and looked so kind. She climbed up on his back, and the lion carried her away and stroked her with his tail and fanned her cheeks.

After the lion had gone quite a way they came to a cave. She was not afraid when the lion carried her inside, and she did not jump off, because the lion was tame. As they went deeper into the cave it became darker and darker, and finally it was black as night. After a little while they emerged into daylight in a wondrous, fair garden. Everything was so fresh and shining in the sunshine, and in the middle of the garden there stood a splendid palace. As they came to the gate, the lion stopped, and the princess climbed down from his back. Then the lion began to speak, saying, "You shall live in this beautiful house and serve me, and when you fulfill everything I demand, you will again see your brother." So the princess served the lion and obeyed him in every detail.

One day she was walking in the garden. It was so very lovely there, but she was sad because she was so alone and deserted by the whole world. As she was walking back and forth she noticed a pond, and in the middle of it there was a small island with a tent. Then she saw, seated under the tent, a grass green frog wearing a rose petal on its head in place of a bonnet.

The frog stared at her and said, "Why are you so sad?"

"Oh, my," she said. "Why shouldn't I be sad!" and she told it all her woes.

When she was done, the frog said kindly, "If you ever need anything, just come to me, and I will help in word and deed."

"But how will I ever repay you?"

"You have no need to repay me," said the croaking frog. "Just bring me a fresh rose petal every day for my bonnet!"

Then the princess returned, feeling somewhat consoled, and from then on, no matter what the lion demanded, she would run to the pond, and the frog would jump hither and yon and soon rustle up the thing she needed.

A little after that, the lion said to her, "This evening I would really like to eat a mosquito pie, but it must be very well prepared!" The princess thought, "How on earth am I to whip that up! That is totally impossible." So she ran to her frog and lamented her plight. But the frog only answered, "Don't worry at all! I can whip up a mosquito pie as quick as you please." And it set to work, opening its mouth left and right and snapping it shut to catch just the right number of mosquitoes. Then it hopped back and forth, gathering firewood together, and started a fire. When the fire was burning merrily, the frog kneaded the dough and put the pie on the coals, and two hours later the pie was ready and as tasty a dish as you could wish. Then the frog told the girl, "You don't get this pie until you promise me this: after the lion has fallen asleep, you must chop off his head with a sword that is hidden behind his bed."

"No," she replied. "I won't do it! The lion has always been kind to me."

But then the frog said, "If you don't do it, you will never see your brother again, and anyway, you will not harm the lion with this blow."

So the girl took courage, grabbed the pie, and carried it to the lion. "This looks tasty," said the lion, sniffing it and then taking a bite; finally, he ate the whole thing up. When he had finished, he felt tired and wanted to snooze a bit, so he said to the princess, "Come and sit next to me and scratch me a bit behind the ears while I fall asleep." And so she sat down next to him and scratched with her left hand while hunting with her right for the sword behind the bed. When he had fallen asleep, she pulled it out, closed her eyes tightly, and chopped off the lion's head in one fell swoop. But when she opened her eyes again, the lion had disappeared, and her dear brother was standing next to her. He kissed her warmly and said, "You have rescued me, for I was the lion and was enchanted. I was cursed to remain so until a girl's hand cut off the lion's head out of love."

Then they went together to the garden in order to thank the frog. But when they arrived, they saw that it was jumping all around gathering kindling and making a fire. When the fire began to burn brightly, the frog jumped into the flames. The fire burned a bit longer and then went out, and a lovely girl was standing there, a girl who had also been enchanted and was the beloved of

30

the prince. And they all went home together to the old king and his consort, the queen. There was a great marriage feast, and no one who was there went home hungry.

TRANSLATED BY JEANNINE BLACKWELL

Boadicea and her daughters. Etching by William Bond
after Henry Singleton. Reprinted with permission
of the Mary Evans Picture Library, London.

Benedikte Naubert

1756–1819

Benedikte Naubert was the most prolific author of fairy tales and magic novels of late-eighteenth-century Germany, producing more such works than her better known contemporaries Johann Karl August Musäus and Christoph Martin Wieland. Maintaining her anonymity until 1817 despite her incredible popularity, she lived apart from the urban centers of German literary culture. Her four-volume collection of *Neue Volksmährchen der Deutschen* (New fairy tales of the Germans, 1789–93) was an acknowledged source for the Grimm brothers. They discovered her identity, and Wilhelm Grimm traveled to interview her at her home in Naumberg in December 1807 before the publication of their tales; he preserved her anonymity.

Combining mythic, legendary, and fairy tale motifs, Naubert tells the story of Boadicea, or Boudicca, within her novel *Velleda, ein Zauberroman* (Velleda, a magic novel, 1795). Both Boadicea, the queen of ancient Britain, and Velleda, a legendary Germanic sorceress, were immortalized by the Roman historian Tacitus. Boadicea (d. 61 A.D.), the queen of the Iceni in Britain, led a fierce revolt against the Romans, as legend has it, because the Romans had raped her two daughters. While the Romans were conquering the Isle of Man, she massacred thousands in London. According to legend, she was killed with her daughters in a chariot while still fighting. In Naubert's tale, Boadicea, the widowed queen, must decide between ruling her nation, leading the fight against the invading Romans, and retrieving her nine daughters from the magic wise woman, Velleda. In telling the fates of Boadicea's daughters, Naubert connects the Germanic myth of the Brocken mountain, home of the witches' sabbath, to the occupation of Britain by the Romans. Velleda, a historical figure both revered and demonized in Tacitus's *De originie et situ Germanorum,* is a powerful sorceress in Naubert's work who offers the princesses access to immortality in the magical world of goddesses, while their mother draws them back into the mundane world of history and marriage. This struggle between two powerful and sympathetically

33

portrayed maternal figures – one biological, the other spiritual – introduces a theme that continues in later German women's fantasy literature.

The sorceress Velleda appears again in another story in this anthology, Amalie von Helwig's "The Symbols." Readers can compare this tale to other stories such as the legend of Demeter and Persephone, the search of a mother for her daughter in the underworld. Supernatural female mentors can be found in Gisela von Arnim's "The Ghost Lady," Agnes Franz's "Princess Rosalieb," and the aunt in Fanny Lewald's "Modern Fairy Tale." Other comparable stories are "East o' the Sun, West o' the Moon," with its quest for a loved one, and Anne Sexton's sorceress in "Rapunzel" (in *Transformations*), a maternal figure who loved and lost a daughter. A contrasting story of a girl caught between enemy tribes can be found in Lisa Goldstein's "Brother Bear" (in Datlow and Windling, eds., *Ruby Slippers, Golden Tears*). Mme d'Aulnoy's "The Bee and the Orange Tree" tells of heroes and heroines transforming themselves into animals and objects.

[Benedikte Naubert], "Boadicea and Velleda," in *Velleda, ein Zauberroman* (Leipzig: Schäferische Buchhandlung, 1795), 1–124.

Boadicea and Velleda

1795

A N ANCIENT KING of the Iceni had nine daughters, and this king was perhaps one of the wisest men, but by no means the mightiest, who had ever worn a crown.

You, my dear readers, no doubt know that in times long past, when the Romans first visited Britain, it was ruled by a score of petty princes. Dimly remembered names – Brigands, Britons, Picts, Silurians, Iceni, Trinobants – once designated the people we now call one nation, and Britain has achieved a power under this one name that none of its divided branches could have boasted of back in those ancient days.

Conflicting privileges, divisiveness, and jealousy made the many peoples of Albion easy prey for their formidable enemies, and our king with his nine daughters felt the impotence of his own scepter too much to think he could prevail alone against the superior forces of the victorious Romans.

His anxiety increased when he considered his unique situation, his borders, and his discord with his neighbors. Few of the neighboring princes were his allies, and he was too proud, too brave, and too wise to be in their thrall. He hated the timidity and slavishness with which some had capitulated to the Romans and lamented the impotence or hypocrisy of the others. If the king of the Iceni had been as powerful and great as he was wise and brave, Caesar would not have conquered Albion so easily. But as it was, even the great Caractacus had long been the triumphal prize of a Roman general; Cadallanus and Vellocatus bore Roman chains at home; and others had been forced to give Rome the dearest thing they possessed, their children, to vouchsafe to Rome the allegiance of their homeland.

That was what this good king most feared: surrendering his children. Legend often forgets the names of the wisest and best of humankind, and so this good king was named merely the King with the Iron Crown, for he refused to wear a golden one. His valor would keep him from the Romans' sword, his honorable death would prevent his enslavement, but his worst fear was that his children, daughters of innocence that they were, might be dragged to Rome and raised in the immorality of Nero's court. What a thought for a prince who was cut from the cloth of kings and fathers long past and who was mightier and happier with his dull diadem than the Tiberiuses and Neros who sank under the burden of jewels plundered from every corner of the world with blood-drenched laurel wreaths on their brows.

The King with the Iron Crown also had a queen who shared his concern about the royal house, and we must admit that hers is the name that this story bears. Boadicea was not yet, however, the heroine who was to be acclaimed by friend and foe alike; it was misfortune that later made her great. Back then she still lived the quiet life of queens in ancient times, not unlike the life of good, common housewives, and it never occurred to the king of the Iceni to seek her advice on matters of importance.

In the matter that now lay before him, the king would have been well advised to consult her, for it lay too much in her realm as queen and mother for her voice to be left unheard. Boadicea's husband, who was deeply worried about his daughters in these times of approaching doom, made certain arrangements to their benefit, and his greatest mistake was doing so without speaking with the best of women, the kindest of mothers.

The Iceni princesses were accustomed to blind obedience toward their parents, and so one day, when a parental order (which we will hereafter communicate to you) came from their father, they did not question it, although the eldest of these ladies, who had reached the age of understanding, might have had disturbing second thoughts about the tone of the stern command. The king's secret order directed them to prepare for a long journey without taking leave of their mother; they were to leave before dawn on the following day.

"Will Boadicea not be coming with us?" asked Bunduica, the eldest, with tears in her beautiful eyes.

"No!" was the abrupt answer from the stern king.

"And when will we see our dear mother again?"

"Only the gods can decide."

"Cannot one of us at least, our youngest sister, her darling, stay with her?"

"None of you may!"

"Father! Good Father! Where are we going?"

"Wherever my fatherly love and paternal rule might lead you."

As you, my dear readers, well understand, there is no saucy retort to answers such as these. As the first morning rays dawned in the sky after an uneasy night, the daughters of the King with the Iron Crown, who commanded them to make haste, crept to their beloved mother's bed, kissed her robe and her fingertips, and scattered flowers around the sleeper's bed. Deftly, Bunduica grabbed little Velleda, the youngest of the sisters, who in her naive pain was about to break out in loud sobs, and covering her mouth with kisses, swept her away to where their father beckoned their departure.

You should not, dear readers, imagine the journey of an ancient king and so many princesses as it would be today. Here there were neither state pomp nor ceremonial carriages, neither handmaids nor many servants, and the legend does not even report if the trip was by horse or on foot. You may believe it or not, but the whole company consisted of not more than ten persons, and the sparse baggage was arranged so compactly that it could be handled without wagons and horses. Rome's luxury had not yet been embraced by the peoples of Britain, who scorned the yoke of the Romans, and the few necessities these simple children of nature required did not need to be transported from one region to the next; they could be had anywhere.

Regardless of how many days, or how many miles, regardless of their moods as they traveled by land, there came a time when the king's will compelled his obedient daughters to travel by sea. Like willing, patient lambs the nine sisters boarded the ship, and the king after them, as he gripped the rudder with his own hands and piloted the vessel, since no one other than those in their party was allowed to accompany them.

The trip was short but full of peril. Thunderclouds blackened the skies, waves stormed the ship, water swirled in a thousand maelstroms and threatened to drown the small party in the deep. The youngest princesses wept and wrung their little hands to heaven; the older ones choked back their anguish and gazed hopefully at their father, whose face remained calm as he performed the duties of a seaman with cold determination and who brought the ship to the approaching shore.

"Never fear, my children, never fear!" he constantly shouted. "Soon we will have it behind us. To avoid great disasters, sometimes we must not shrink from small ones, and wise are the ways of fate when it surrounds safety's refuge with terrors, so that all but the bravest are kept out."

As reasonable as the king's words were, still his listeners understood hardly half of what he spoke. Most of his words were swallowed by the raging storm, and the rest glanced off the hearts of those who had given up almost all hope. If anything could console these young seafarers, it was the courageous stance of their pilot, not his words. They did not know the dangers of which he spoke, did not know the refuge toward which he led them, and did not know why they needed to be seeking for it outside their father's house.

Princess Bunduica had already reached the ripe age of fifteen and thought she knew a thing or two about the ways of the world. She alone had perceived from things her father said that he trembled before the growing might of the Romans. She did not tremble before these glorious strangers about whom she had heard so many rumors; she only wished to know them better. She knew that many of the British kings had surrendered their power and sovereignty without resistance and made friends with them. Everything that the world could say about these feared rulers revealed their greatness and nobility. Even the lot of the vanquished was brilliant. Caractacus followed the chariots of his conquerors in golden chains. The virtues of this mighty captive were honored in Rome, his children were playmates of the young Caesars, and even though Bunduica was too sensible to wish the same fate for herself and her family, she could find nothing abhorrent in her abiding fantasy of one day seeing the capital of the world as the daughter of a friend of the Romans and thereby experiencing a life more sumptuous than her rough fatherland offered.

Bunduica expressed nothing of these thoughts that could only bring about her father's disapproval. Nor do we know if she entertained them exactly at this moment in our story. For lo, the dangers of the journey were behind them, the ship touched land, and the seafarers no doubt felt nothing but the delight that thrills those who see the raging waves behind them and solid land before them. They threw themselves into its lap like children into the arms of their loving mother.

The Isle of Man was the spot where the king and his daughters landed, an island surrounded by rugged cliffs, seemingly formed by nature as a secret and secure refuge. Verdant plains rested in the wide lap between towering crags, and celestial temples in the valleys promised protection to virtue, even if such virtue were exiled from the rest of the world. Here it was that since time immemorial the most hallowed secrets of British religious ritual were kept, mysteries that may have been closer to the truth than today's world might think; then again, perhaps they were nothing more than a thick cloak around terrors that today would outrage humanity.

The good King with the Iron Crown, who was as pious and devoted as he was virtuous, knew nothing of the latter, and for his benefit, we will choose to believe that here the Druids never performed human sacrifices for the propitiation of a cruel god, never put innocent youths and maidens of blinding beauty through fire at their secret ceremonies.

Although this pious prince knew nothing of such atrocities that, according to legend, were committed here by superstitious priests, he did consider it advisable not to enter the large temple standing in the middle of an oak forest at the heart of the island. Safety dwells in solitude and serenity, and a treasure is best hidden when it is placed in a single pair of loyal hands.

Night had fallen as the father turned with his children to the high cliffs that looked toward Ireland. The landscape was more terrifying as the moon rose. The little princesses trembled, and even the older sisters could not hide their fear.

"Father! Dear Father! Where are we going?" Bunduica repeated again in a melancholy tone the long-unanswered question.

"I have to hide my fair milk white lambs in the arms of a loyal shepherdess," he answered in a sweeter voice than was his wont, "so that no wolf can tear them to pieces, so that no impure breath can harm their beauty. This is the home of Velleda, for whom our youngest was named. She is of the race of the Aurinians and came to this shore from Germania, to the great good fortune of this land. But also for my own good fortune, my children, as well as for yours! Through her I was told of the pending doom of my royal house, the first portent being my own demise. Soon you will be left as orphans, my children. Your mother cannot protect you, for she is merely a woman. Boadicea will die with me, as she has lived with me.

"Do not mourn for us, my beloved. Children whose parents have been torn from them are children of the Divine, and She has given you wise Velleda as a second mother. Sleep in her arms! Sleep away the evil days until the good days dawn again. It means much to me that I heard happy tidings of your future from her lips. Your happiness will be secure if you practice blind devotion to her commands as you would to my own and fidelity in virtue to the death as you have been taught. Fate has taken such happiness away from your mother and me, in order that it might be your legacy instead."

The king of the Iceni could have continued talking to his daughters in this way without interruption, for long before he finished they were all weeping at his feet, felled by his powerful words. A few grabbed his hands and covered them with kisses, others embraced his knees as if to beg him not to desert them. Little Velleda, who had hidden herself in a fold of his regal cloak, cried out from her hiding place: "I'll be safe here until you can take me back to Mama to die with her."

It broke the king's heart. He kissed his daughters and wept with them. Parting seemed impossible, and who knows how long this scene would have lasted if a figure had not emerged from the shadow of the cliffs and brought it to a close.

"Why are you here, King of the Iceni?" called out a woman of superhuman size who stood opposite the father and daughters in the moonlight and whose sudden appearance gave the young girls a fright nearly outweighing their grief.

"If you have the courage to die," this apparition said, "then you must have

39

the courage to leave your daughters. And if you do not trust me enough to leave them in my hands, how can you then trust the One in whose hands my destiny as well as theirs now rests?"

The stranger's rebuke was so gentle, the expression on her face as she raised her eyes to heaven so beautiful and expressive, that the princesses little by little grew accustomed to her extraordinary figure and viewed her with less dread than at the outset. Their father spoke: "This is the wise Velleda, the shepherdess who will protect such innocent lambs from the wolf and from the impure breath of the world."

The Aurinian kissed the young girls one after the other. Little Velleda, her namesake, crept out of the folds of her father's cloak where she was still hiding and wrapped herself in Velleda's instead. "You shall be mine," she cried as she hugged the child to her breast, "mine alone, my sweet. Your name already makes you dear to me! And even if all your sisters are abandoned by both me and good fortune, you will still stand firm, a paragon of immortal wisdom and everlasting fame in times to come."

The astounding woman's words took their breath away; the moment she spoke she had already won their hearts. Velleda continued to speak with the king and the princesses to ease the pain of his departure, but it seems to us that the wisest thing she did was to quiet them with the tone of her voice and rain sweet slumber over the inconsolable girls so that their father had the chance to leave unhindered.

"They are all sleeping now," she said as she gave her hand to the departing king, "and when they wake, they will be consoled. Do not worry about them; they will grow fond of me and love me as a mother. Soon they will be inseparable from me. But before we part, allow me to ask you some questions. Speak: why have you hidden these children in my arms?"

"I hoped to leave them in the arms of virtue."

"And you would rather have them die than lose their virtue?"

"Rather death than that."

"Allow me one last question. My power is great, but not unlimited; my knowledge is vast, but even I am not infallible, not omniscient. I have lived long and may live even longer, but I am not immortal. Speak: what will become of these poor girls sleeping peacefully at our feet. What will become of them when fate overtakes me?"

"Then you must decide their fate and give them over to hands as true as your own."

"And if I can find none?"

"Then death rather than the danger from which I have just saved them."

"Very well. So go now, for you have settled everything that you had to arrange on this side of the grave. Go where your fate beckons you. Henceforth you will have few cares, and the trip back to your fatherland will be short."

So they parted, and alas, wise Velleda was all too right. Brief was the journey of the king of the Iceni, and few his cares, for indeed soon he would feel none at all. Since he believed his dearest loves were now safe, he could calmly face his future.

On his return from the Isle of Man, storms raged and waves crashed against the ship even more than on the journey out. He was either more careless with his own life than with the lives of his children, or else he was so preoccupied with a future he was destined not to see that he overlooked his own present. Enough, the seaman's luck shifted, the wind overcame him, the sail tore, the rudder was lost, the deep opened its jaws to swallow its booty, and the Iceni saw their good king no more.

Words cannot describe Boadicea's heart, the heart of a wife and mother, when she was certain she had lost both her husband and her children. Wives as well as mothers will perhaps read these pages; let them explain to the rest of you what I conceal here now. If Boadicea shared one thing with every other woman in her situation, it was her almost annihilating despair. But in one respect she was far beyond thousands of her sex: she did not falter where they faltered. Misfortune did not destroy her; it gave her new strength. She had never considered herself an extraordinary woman, never felt she was the sort to be a heroine or ruler. In those times, no flatterers set such ideas in the heads of queens. But later events show what stores of courage and determination the Divine had placed in her soul.

On the same day that her husband's iron crown was brought to her, miraculously recovered by the tide, and thus his death was confirmed, she received the terrifying news: the Romans, for whom Icenia had previously been sacred and untouchable, were now approaching its border. A choice had to be made: either a quick resolve to a courageous defense or else servitude, which many British kings had already accepted without raising their swords.

"Ha!" said Boadicea, holding her husband's crown a few moments in her hand and gazing at it intently. "You did not sink where the best of kings sank into the deep, so you will not sink now, even if I must fall. Arise, my people! I am your queen. The Iceni crown now graces my brow! Into the fray against the murderous foe! This diadem will bring victory, even if it bedecks a head accustomed to floral wreaths."

Boadicea placed the king's iron crown on her head, and no one disputed her claim to this gem. It was made of iron, and such diadems weigh heavy but are never coveted. They also terrify, and fear cleared the path for the new heroine and conquered the Roman foe before the weapons of the Iceni could reach them: the fear that a woman had steeled herself to meet the rulers of the world before whom all others bowed – and might best them. And here Boadicea was as clever as she was brave, using the superstition of her people to her own advantage and thereby winning a glorious victory. Before battle, custom demanded that an omen presage the outcome: the most timid animal of the forest was to determine which side would know victory and which would lack resolve and suffer defeat. And lo, as the hare was let loose between the armies, it pushed its way into the close ranks of the Romans and indeed brought death and destruction to the unvanquished, while giving the courageous Iceni the triumph, since they were renewed by this favorable sign. It was a victory that even the scribes of the enemy could not deny.

It has often been suspected that human strength is not broken by a doubled burden but, rather, can be spurred on to a quicker pace because of it. This was the case with the queen of the Iceni. The loss of her husband and children, the danger to her fatherland – either one of these misfortunes alone might have depressed her into an ordinary state of mourning, even despair; together, however, they made her a heroine, a victor.

Oh, but what a sad, joyless victor she was! With whom was she to share her happiness and the glory of victory? The thrill of danger was past. The loud acclaim of the people and the fame heaped on her even by the enemy did not follow her into her desolate home. Here was deadly silence; the resounding names of Queen and Victoria were sorry substitutes for Wife and Mother. Ah, but all from whose lips those sweet words once sounded were gone!

In contemplating the cruel fate of a tenfold loss in a single day, a clear intellect like Boadicea's had to consider the circumstances and the improbabilities connected to them, and these improbabilities gave her consolation.

By ever more careful probing, the queen finally was convinced that although she was a widow, she was perhaps not a childless mother. The path Boadicea took to arrive at this conclusion is unknown to us; enough, she found the path and, drunk with delight, she dared to find a way to happiness. She followed the trail of truth until she was certain that her children were on the Isle of Man. Because she knew the wise Velleda (it was no secret to her how much regard the deceased king had for her), there was no doubt in her mind about whose hand guarded the princesses.

The queen of the Iceni, as great a lady as she was, had several weaknesses in common with the meekest of her sex. Among these was a jealous coveting of her husband's affections and refusal to share them with any other creature. The uncommon regard with which the king honored the stranger Velleda and the devotion with which he heard her pronouncements had always made her unpalatable to the queen; she did not love Velleda, she could not. Yet interference in their happy love could not have been a worry caused by Velleda, the aged Aurinian, who indeed had never been beautiful; only on the wild Brocken mountain of the Harz, her homeland, would her gigantic figure hold no terror. But the king's gentle wife wanted to share his regard with no one else. Since wresting the king's regard away from Velleda was impossible, and since Boadicea was incapable of stooping to unworthy means to achieve that end, she tolerated what she could not change, but she tolerated it only as long as she played the subservient role of the king's wife. As queen, she thought she could behave differently than before. Did it never occur to her that perhaps her obstinacy might have cost her a share of her husband's trust, and that she might otherwise have been consulted in the secret escape that now made her so unhappy? Might it have stood in her power to hinder the impetuous step that robbed her of husband and children?

Boadicea knew now with certainty that the princesses were under the sway of the despised Aurinian. To wrest them from her control was her main goal, but how? She, the victor over the Romans, could not stoop to beg from the woman whom she hated and who seemed to have proven her malice by her blameworthy abduction of the queen's daughters. Inquiries could possibly have cleared this up, but that path was rejected, and no other means were left but force, which for the devout Boadicea was too great a sacrilege to the sacred island, or subterfuge, for which she, as an upright Nordic woman, had little talent.

In her last battle Boadicea had taken among other booty a young Roman girl whose thousand pleasantries so pleased her captor that she wore her chains only one day.

"You are free," said the queen of the Iceni to the charming Flavia. "Take what you will from the booty of my warriors, take back all that is yours. If you like, take more, take all the prisoners of your tribe whom you love and return to your family, but go quickly before you take my heart away, and the gods take revenge on me for my affection for one of my enemies."

Flavia did not go. She begged the queen on her knees not to be sent back to a fatherland that she protested was not her own. She proved that her parents had been of the British tribe, that she had been abducted as a child during one of the defeats of her people and given a name that was not her own and thereby made a Roman. She had returned as a servant to the wife of the Roman Consul, whose residence was London, to the womb of the Britain that bore her, and she never wanted to leave again. What Flavia related was more than probable. Boadicea could no more deny her credence than she could reject an innocent soul who sought refuge in her arms.

43

The girl with the Roman name stayed in the house of the queen of the Iceni; she knew how to exploit her constant presence and thereby win the queen's heart. If anyone could have consoled this sad mother about the loss of her children, it was Flavia, and console she did, though without becoming a substitute for her lost daughters. The queen did not want a substitute, nor could she find a place in her heart for one. She still harbored hope in her heart that she would see the lost girls again, but since she herself was lacking in schemes for accomplishing this, no day passed without Flavia presenting her mistress with new plans for saving the princesses from the sorceress's power.

"How would it be," she said one day, "if we loaded a ship and went to the aid of the captives? The craggy Isle of Man is of course inaccessible, but hard work and luck often find paths obscured by the dark cloud of mystery."

"The Isle of Man," answered the queen, "can only be approached from the coast facing Ireland where two black cliffs hide it, and it cannot be found by effort or happenstance. It is protected by the hand of the gods, who will never reveal their most hallowed secrets to profane eyes."

"Or," said Flavia another time, "what if we won over the servants of the Divine, the Druids, to our side? They cannot possibly be in connivance with this she-devil, this abductor of your children."

"The same difficulty!" answered Boadicea. "Access to their island is forbidden to us."

"And is there no holy day in the year when the temples of their gods are open to Britain's peoples?"

"How can you as a British woman not know that? Of course, the holiest day of the year, the day the sun begins her spring rotation anew, gives us and all the peoples of the earth certain privileges."

According to her own account, Flavia had fallen into the hands of the enemy at a young age, and so she knew very little of Albion's customs and ways. The queen instructed her patiently, and so she learned how one can gain access to the Isle of Man on Britain's great holy day. Among a thousand significant and insignificant terms and conditions, Flavia also learned that on this one day of peace with the whole world, any use of weapons on the Isle of Man is forbidden, and thus the island would be easy prey for its enemies if it were known to them, as it now was to her.

Flavia never tired of making plans, and every time the queen demonstrated the impossibility of each proposal, something always remained that the rebuffed girl kept in mind to use at a later time.

The British peace and spring festival was approaching, and the queen, who, like the lowest of her subjects, had access to the isle of hallowed secrets only on this day, was actually scheming to use it for a personal negotiation with the Druids of the Isle of Man to seek their assistance in wresting her children from the sorceress. But the increasingly restless Roman legions, who seemed to have slumbered as if dazed by their last defeat, threatened again, and the presence of the warrior chief was required; her duties as mourning mother took second place to those toward the fatherland.

"Flavia," said Boadicea when the servant embraced her for one last time on the eve of setting up the warrior camp, "you know everything we've decided for that fateful day; you know the obstacles to our undertaking, and you know the means to remove them. Act not only wisely but faithfully, for know this: no one whose goal is not completely pure and blameless before the gods ever returns from the Isle of Man alive. Alas, the best of kings had to pay for that trip with his life; how could the Divine approve of his wrenching these children from the arms of their mother to sacrifice them to Velleda! Go, Flavia, go! No more tears, no more vows! I know what you wish to say, and you must surely know from this task how much you mean to me. You are the only one I would trust, for the nature of our secret makes collusion with others an unwise choice."

Even though Flavia was forbidden to make her usual oath of unquestioning loyalty and silence, still she swore at the feet of the queen: if she returned home triumphant, Boadicea would find her daughters at the hallowed hearth, where now only the mourning household gods stood watch.

The Iceni forces found more resistance than ever before, but still Boadicea returned victorious to her quiet hearth, which she protected with pious devotion when the welfare of her land did not demand her scepter or her sword. But what greeted her as she approached home this time were not the shouts of her daughters as promised by Flavia or the reflection of a cheerful fire. A cricket, chirping sadly, had taken up residence at the deserted hearth in her absence – a creature that, as legend has it, foreshadows doom. Drops of blood seemed to run down from the smoky images of the household gods.

Since the beginning of time, the quiet gods who protected the house had performed the same service among all the tribes and races, and they were pictured in similar ways by all nations: as pilgrims, with walking sticks in their hands and broad-brimmed hats on their heads. Every nation has a legend of gods being taken in as friendless strangers by a hospitable house, a house that they then rewarded with protection and manifold blessings. This kind of divinity has always found the gentlest and most loyal disciples. For a person in need like the queen, given her constant feeling of weakness, it was natural to turn to a higher guiding hand. She was not drawn to the exalted inhabitants of golden temples, however, but sought out the old, unassuming guardian spirits of her house at whose feet her forefathers had wept and rejoiced. The quiet witnesses of her most secret devotion, they shared the home's sorrows and joys, celebrating with rich offerings before their eyes and on their altar, the homely hearth.

Pious Boadicea carefully closed the door in order to pray there. "Good spirits of my home," she pleaded with quiet tears, "can you reward me for my offering of the victory wreath with nothing better than these sad portents? I know it is not one that a woman often brings. Oh, where are my daughters? And where is their rescuer, Flavia?"

"You would have received the answer to this first question," came a whisper from the cold ashes, "if the second had not passed your lips. The mention of unholy names never goes unpunished before the ears of the gods. Dry the bloody tears from our cheeks and be prepared to weep even more bitterly than we over your blindness."

The queen was too accustomed to receiving answers to her questions at this place to be shaken by the voices of the gods, but the content of their message made her start, and what she heard did not satisfy her. She wanted to hear more.

"O gods," she cried, "you who watched in consolation over my tears as I wept for my husband! O gods, you who gave me the courage to wear this crown and the advice that brought about a victory over your and Icenia's enemies! Do not leave me now without counsel, care, or consolation. Instruct me, since now perhaps every moment is precious, and help me use each moment to act."

Boadicea wept and pleaded for naught. Occasionally, to be sure, a wisp of white ash would rise in circles as if moved by an unseen breath, and a soft whisper would seem to rise, yet in vain she strained her ears toward the faint sound. The chirping of the cricket drowned out the voice. The words "You asked too seldom to expect answers now. Yes! Moments are precious! Lost is lost!" were more the call of her own conscience than the pronouncement of the gods, who, as she now saw to her horror, had turned their faces from her toward the wall, as if they did not even want her to see their closed lips.

Nothing could be sadder than the hours the queen spent at her lonely hearth while her people jubilantly celebrated the latest victory outside. As evening came, the stillness outside her door was the harbinger of the death the words of the house spirits had foreshadowed.

It was midnight. There was a knock at the door, and the queen opened it.

"What news do you bring, messenger?" she asked the man as he stormed breathlessly into the room.

"Have you not yet heard the rumor from Man?"

"From Man? What rumor?"

"Ha! The people lament in horror and scream to heaven about this blasphemy, and you, the queen, have not heard?"

"Speak! Boadicea commands it."

"The Isle of Man! The Romans have overrun it!"

"Man is protected by the gods. You are delirious!"

"Man was once protected by the gods but was betrayed by humans to the Romans."

"Betrayed? Man betrayed? You are mad!"

"The whole nation is raving. Do you not hear their roars? Some are calling you the betrayer, for who but you knew the secrets of that holy place? They will demand revenge from your hands or else will tear your flesh to pieces. I came here to warn you. Flee! Your repute as the victor over the Romans will not save you, so save yourself and flee!"

Boadicea listened with horror to what the messenger said, but she did not flee. How could she, she who knew her own innocence as well as her invincible courage?

Just as the house of the heroine Deborah rested under palms, so stood Boadicea's, sheltered among the oaks. Their shade could have hidden her, but why hide? Because of the victory she brought her people? Because of the simple poverty in which she lived in their midst? She owed the gods alone an explanation for trespasses of which she herself knew nothing.

The cry of the raging people of which the messenger had warned rang out toward her. She emerged from her oak forest like a goddess from a temple. The iron crown, which the waves had carried as the king sank down, was her only sign of majesty. Yet she did not need even this, for each who saw her walking in her natural-born grace and majesty had to say, "There walks the queen of the Iceni, the victor over the Romans, or else a goddess."

The people fell silent as they drew close enough to discern her figure by the torches' glow. Those in the front ranks called to those in the back that the queen was present. A mere quarter of an hour earlier they had demanded the undoing of the queen by their hands, as such rabble is wont to do, but now they could not find the words to speak of it to her. Those who demanded that she either take revenge for the desecrated Isle of Man or be its scapegoat now whispered to themselves, "We must let the queen's will be done; she must not be made to account for anything. She has advised the land too often to be mistaken now."

Boadicea was in more despair than her people when she finally heard what she had only suspected from the words of the messenger and the prophecies of the gods. Man, the holy Isle of Man, the protectress of the deepest secrets of the Divine, the mother and teacher of the wisest among mortals, of the holy Druids, and (her mother's heart sighed) the dwelling place of the lost princesses, was in Roman hands! Somehow they had found access to the inaccessible. On the day of the great festival of peace, which took all weapons from the hands of Man's defenders, they had crept in as a wolf among the unsuspecting flock. According to British legend, the gods had encircled the island with monsters to have them guard the seven portals of the great temple, the heart of the island; they had not stopped the victors. And everything already swam in blood. The priests were already dying in their own sacrificial fires as people asked what was happening. Where had the enemy entered? Had some god of revenge poured them from the sky or given them wings to soar over the cliffs?

Boadicea rushed with astonishing haste to avenge these deeds that turned every heart to stone. The people's rage came to the aid of her zeal, but yet – came too late. Man had been deserted by the enemy. They had fled less because of a mounted defense than because of the screaming lament and horrific curses of the outraged priests of the island's gods. A group of women armed with torches, led by a towering figure, had frightened the great Sveto-nius Paulinus, the Roman consul, back to his ship. And thus they found no enemy to repel; they were already gone. But what did that accomplish? The beautiful temples of the island, the wonders of their world – and per-haps of ours as well, had they been saved – were destroyed. All the hallowed groves, the sites of miracles – there were so many of them – were turned to ashes, and alas, far worse, thousands of innocents had been slaughtered, thousands more taken into captivity, and every true-hearted British woman would choose death over such infamy.

We need not describe Boadicea's desperation as she sought her daugh-ters in the midst of all this devastation; what was astonishing was her loving search for Flavia as well. For it never occurred to her that this traitor, who understood how to charm her way into the queen's confidences and into all the secrets of the land, was responsible for all the misfortune. Alas, the queen was a model of how a great soul can still be blind.

While Paulinus, shaken by the terrors on the Isle of Man, hurried to London to confront the outraged people whose secrets he had desecrated, and while Nemesis Boadicea likewise prepared for battle to exact bloody retribution – publicly for her gods and privately for her daughters, who she thought had been abducted by the Romans – the last living beings on the nearly devastated Isle of Man rose up to leave it as well.

At sunset on that ghastly day, from atop the highest crag surrounding the island there soared a powerful eagle. First it gazed into the ball of sinking fire that dipped into the sea of night, then peered down with those penetrating eyes that can bear any earthly gaze into the field of bodies below, as if it sought some prey. It spied a female body in the bloody mess, soared quickly down, and tore her flesh to pieces without drinking her blood. Then it rose into the air anew and called out three times in that tender tone that every species uses when it calls its young. Momentarily, from the same cleft the eagle had just left, there rose into the air nine silver white doves. They followed the route over the sea inscribed for them by the eagle and finally landed on the coast of Ireland on the beautiful foothills of Bangor. They nestled underneath the wings of their foster mother, who had already prepared them food and a nest.

Among you, dear readers, there are some who with a special gift need only be given a hint in such probable and believable stories as this to guess immediately where it is headed. Have not at least some of you children of the fairy tale muse already surmised that we have old acquaintances among the travelers to Bangor and in the mutilated corpse on the Isle of Man?

Be that as it may, this much is certain: after Boadicea had assured the peace by once again conquering the Romans and could turn once again to her own affairs, she continued her search and received reliable information. Although Flavia had really been found among the massacred on Man, the queen had no reason to believe that her daughters had met the same fate or, worse, had been taken captive by the Romans. It was certain that the sorceress (after the tale of the eagle we can surely use that name without reservation) – it was certain that the sorceress Velleda had successfully gathered the princesses from Man and had hidden them on the distant coast of this island, where passing seamen had spotted them on the shore.

What tidings for a tender mother! It would have taken far less certain news of the life and whereabouts of her daughters than these witnesses provided to prod her on the path to find her lost girls. She wanted to see them with her own eyes and herself arrange the rescue of her children. Flavia, whom rumor and serious reconsideration had brought the queen to mistrust, was the one who had instilled in her suspicion of every other human soul whom she might have trusted with this precious burden.

Boadicea saw no serious difficulties in carrying out her plan except one: How could she secure the peace of her people and not endanger them? But when this concern was satisfied by means of a truce with the much-feared enemy, too noble to break such agreements, there lay before the good queen many more complications than she had imagined.

There are people who have seen everything in the world, and then, when they are asked in more detail, cannot really say exactly where they actually saw it. The travelers who had first given notice of the probable location of the princesses were long gone from that region; they were bold seafarers who continuously plowed the waves and who were seeking out the unknown Atlantis or were headed for the Isle of Taprobane, just as the queen needed their counsel. There is nothing in the world to do with such adventurers: just when you need them in the West, you can be certain that you must seek them in the East.

The queen had even more trouble with those who had simply repeated the message of the first ones. They had all sorts of excuses for backing out of their claims, and when they were to be detained and forced to take the queen to the spot where her motherly hopes were drawing her, they disappeared without a trace and left the woman who had depended so on their help nothing but the prospect of a long and dangerous journey with no guide. Meanwhile, month after month had passed since the truce had been reached, and Boadicea feared that these dearly purchased days of peace would dwindle without her having accomplished her heartfelt desire.

Among all the experienced seamen whom the queen brought into consultation, there was one old sea pilot who declared himself ready to help her. "Your Majesty, it is not my place to praise myself for accomplishing things I cannot do, even though I could paint a rosier picture of my own feats than most could. I have seen many a thing in this world, and if I wanted, I could gather up all the wonders of North and South which I've seen and easily make a blue mist of dreams to delude you with vain hopes and reap your gratitude and reward. But now hear my advice. Of course, I do not actually know the place where your daughters were allegedly seen, but I think that we should simply sail off in the Lord's name along the coast of Ireland up to the great embankment, and there let heaven help you further. This much is certain: if there is one place where magic can work its spell, it is surely in that desolate part of the sea where sailors are loathe to go. What you cannot find there you will seek in vain in all the nearby waters."

Boadicea was glad to have even this faint ray of hope, and she bravely began a trip whose duration and direction we cannot know. Seafaring back then was by no means like today, and the old designations for places as well as the changes that more than one thousand years have brought to land and sea would confuse even better geographers than we fancy ourselves to be.

In short, the queen finally arrived in those regions whose appearance matched her anxious expectations of extraordinary things. The ship navigated into waters that seemed to pull it forward with the languid tide. Everything breathed a monotonous stillness; no ship met another, no living thing stirred from the deep, no bird soared through the air, no wind rippled the waves, and the coast that retreated in the distance completed the picture with its smoke gray tones. It gave no joy to the senses, no refreshment to the spirit, but lent a certain anxiety to the heart that no one could bear for long.

"This is as far as I can bring you," said Boadicea's pilot. "Were I ready to dare more, I would not find one mate on the whole crew who would agree to come with me. All that I can do is make it to one of those small bays and lay anchor there. The sloop is yours to use as you will. If you can use your formidable powers of persuasion to convince a mate to join you or if you want to dare it alone, that is your choice. I would have gladly accompanied you, but I cannot leave my ship without putting both you and myself in extreme danger."

Not since Isis took to the sea to find her lost husband has a seafaring queen been in such a quandary as Boadicea was at that moment. Probably – her heart convinced her and some of the clues mentioned by the sailors who first claimed to have sighted the princesses confirmed it – probably she was in the only place in the world where she could fulfill her fervent wish, but that place could be seen only in the distance. How could she bring it nearer? From the bay where they had dropped anchor she could spy the prospect of the coast where her children perhaps dwelled. She gazed into the wild blue yonder and strained her eyes in the dawn and moonlight. But she would have needed the eye of an eagle to find anything but black basalt cliffs, with an aura of superstition making them more terrifying than even their melancholy uniformity.

Boadicea had the courage to attempt anything to bring her children back into her arms or, better said, the courage to seek the possibility of finding them here. But what is resolve without resources? The vessel offered her by the seaman was a sloop that her arms were too weak to steer. And no amount of gold from the Roman booty was enticing enough, no promise of hers tempting enough to win a sailor for the voyage.

When she sat on deck and gauged the ocean's breadth, longing to fly over it to fulfill her desire, often a sailor would join her and, moved by her misery or tempted by the chance to get ahead, would listen attentively to her promises and entreaties. But soon one of those fantastic legends about the basalt coast would circulate again, and the poor queen would wind up once more a thousand miles from her hopes.

"Do you see that bridge with brass pilings?" someone would say, pointing to a spot in the black foothills that are called the Giants' Dam. "In the olden days, when the giants who wanted to storm heaven were banished to this island by the gods, they planned to build a bridge to the mainland by undertaking this huge project that only their hands could accomplish. A thunderbolt from heaven, though, stopped their rash undertaking and turned them into stone themselves. That row of colossal columns that rise above the others is made from the transformed sons of the earth. Those who approach them to look more closely at the scars left by the bolt will be turned into stone themselves. A number of daring or ignorant seamen have met this fate, and neither their ships nor anything on them could escape the same punishment. If you look closely, you can still see the forms of ships, sails, and masts amid those crags."

What all can the imagination craft from undefined forms? To please one storyteller, Boadicea let herself see ships, sails, and masts; another showed her human and animal shapes; a third saw the ruins of a splendid city, transformed by fire from heaven in payment for its sins and now the scarred blackish stone covering the entire opposite shore. The threat of being turned into stone, struck by lightning, or buried under monstrous rubble was always woven into the story, and finally Boadicea realized that every word, every promise, every gift was spent in vain; her fellow voyagers would never dare to do what only a despairing mother could.

The worst thing was that finally the seamen and crew began to weary of the useless waiting in this rocky cove and wanted to weigh anchor. It could not be denied that the air was heavy and constricted the heart; it was natural to want to leave the place. Even the queen felt it, and she did not even need to think of her truce running out to fan her desire for a quick resolution to this tedious adventure.

After Boadicea had spent half a moon like this, she convinced herself that she had to do it herself or else return home with nothing accomplished. She made her plans secretly so that she would not be hindered in their foolhardy execution by her friend the pilot – and foolhardy is what any frank person would call a plan to throw oneself into the waves and swim through the waters at the very spot where they break on the rocks, so perilous it is, even for sturdy ships.

This loyal mother, ready to follow her heart or else die, became secretly acquainted with a fisherman who often cast his nets in the bay where the ship was at anchor. After she had tried in vain to convince him to sail to the basalt cliffs in her sloop, she bought his small skiff, whose sides were almost even with the water's surface. Its only virtue was that it was light enough to be steered by a weak feminine arm in calm weather.

Boadicea did not tarry in trying out her dearly purchased vessel, and the moon shone on her journey. She had to make use of the night, because her friend the pilot protected her with such generous care during the day that she could not venture into such a rash undertaking under his watchful eye.

The sea was calm, and the sky was mirrored in the clear tide, yet the trip held terrors that only Boadicea's fearless soul could bear. When the royal seafarer emerged from behind the bay, from which the length of the basalt coast could not be seen, and saw it in its full breadth with all its strange gigantic shapes, almost doubled in size by darkness and shimmering moonlight, when she saw the terrible wildness of the huge hills in whose shadow her skiff now glided and heard the uncanny roaring of the ocean at their base, it would have been no wonder had she lost heart and let the rudder fall into the wild waves. But Boadicea was courageous enough to make the trip not once but several times and not to be discouraged by the fruitlessness of her repeated crossing.

She had already accomplished something: she had learned the lay of the land. If at the beginning the wild majesty of the objects she sailed past had made her pulse beat faster, this disquiet grew ever more moderate and eventually dissipated as she made the trek again and again.

This much the seafarer saw ever more clearly: just as she had always thought, there was nothing to the fabled dangers of this coast, and the waves seemed to respect her little boat, for maternal love, the truest, bravest passion, directed it. The wind shied away from blowing on it, and more than once there seemed to be an invisible hand carefully steering the vessel past the numerous whirlpools and the many hidden cliffs.

Finally came the seventh day after Boadicea's first attempt. The moon was full that night, and the pilot informed the queen that he had bargained for only three days more with his mutinous crew and that then the futile waiting in this hole would have to end. "There are more of these kinds of places in the world," he stated, "where you can hope to find what you are seeking! Regions that are more easily approached, where you can more likely expect to reach your goal. From watching this spot so long, you will have discovered that nothing living can survive here; there is not even a place to land. You would know this all the better if you had come nearer the coast, as I once did by accident."

No one knew this coast better than the queen, and the pilot could tell her the whole story of the doomed voyage during which he was thrown onto it without really telling her anything new. While he spoke, she thought of other things, such as repeating the trip that night, for in the previous night she had noticed something that astonished her.

Yesterday, as she sailed past the closest basalt cliffs, she had entered a region that she had not yet seen at so close a range. The rows of black columns that lined the coast rested on reddish stones, giving the forbidding rocks a pleasant appearance, and they ended on the seaward side in a broad plain covered with soft grass – the only place in the region boasting any vegetation.

What astonished the queen even more than this was a group of silver white swans bathing here in the moonlight, some of them appearing to dry their feathers on the green lawn. These lovely creatures, glowing with pure, heavenly light, made a charming sight, mirrored in the clear tide. The seafarer wanted to enjoy it at closer hand, for the image of living things in this barren region was too pleasant to her, too unexpected not to raise her hopes. She hoped for a landing nearby, possibly even a sighting of humans, but hardly had she sailed her boat closer when the birds of Cytherene, frightened by the splashing of the approaching boat, flushed out of the tide and sought the shore. Their companions resting there also took flight on outspread wings, and it was strange that the seafarer counted nine of the birds in flight. Nine, the blessed number that was sacred to the mother who had just lost the same number of daughters.

People like our adventurous queen have their own minds, and that helps them in times like these. Why exactly nine? she thought on the trip home, and for the whole day, and also during the pilot's long narrative that we have omitted here. "Why exactly nine?" she said almost aloud, as she boarded her boat. Might something behind this number mean future happiness for you, poor maligned mother? This is the basalt coast to which you were directed to find your children, and this is the time of the full moon, which the soothsayers always say is the most favorable time to break evil spells.

Boadicea's fantasies ran wild; she had never begun a trip with such upheaval, not even the first one. Her heart beat loudly, and she could hardly wait for the time when her slowly drifting skiff, which no rudder could hasten, would reach the region where the swans had bathed the night before.

She was firmly determined to attempt to land on the coast. Its steep slope and the impossibility of tying up the boat suggested some of the difficulties, yet at her approach everything looked more favorable. And lo, the peak of the beautiful foothill, swathed in charming green, jutted out from its rough neighbor; no swans, however, bathed there that night.

The seafarer approached the shore ever more bravely. She could have touched the soft grass with her hand, and the temptation to disembark was great, but she had doubts about the return trip and even greater doubts about where the pleasant green hill might lead. At its top were two lines of black columns whose capitals must have been forty feet high and so close together that no entry appeared possible.

Boadicea had never seen the wonders of this coast so closely; she convinced herself that these columns were neither the play of natural forces nor yet a group of transformed giants but, rather, the rear wall of a building made by human hands, still occupied by humans, and misapprehended and avoided by others merely because of ignorance.

The queen's eyes sought an entrance, and in her searching she almost forgot the tottering boat in which she was now only standing on one foot, while the other was already touching the shore. Her eyes shone with curiosity and keenest anticipation. She forgot herself and her boat, which the tide threatened to carry away at any moment. Her eyes measured the heights of the wondrous edifice yet were drawn back to a lower locale, for there one of her other senses found delight and occupation. The soft, melancholy strains of a flute floated from a grotto formed by the water at the edge of the cliffs about twenty feet from her. Soon thereafter a female figure stepped out of the shadows, and Boadicea almost ran to greet her with a cry of joy, for finding a human being in such a desolate place was a welcome sight for an adventuress like the queen of the Iceni.

The flute player reclined on the grass, taking no notice of the lady in the boat, and soon placed the pipe to her lips for a new melody. She looked back at the cliffs she had recently left, and slowly and quietly a number of milk white lambs gradually stole up behind her. They settled down around the shepherdess, and after they had listened some time to the sweet melody echoing from the cliffs, their eyes began to close. One by one they fell into slumber.

"Slumber on, you gentle creatures, slumber on," called the shepherdess as she put down her flute and stroked the closest of her dear lambs. "Be refreshed by the night, for I do not take you out in daylight for fear of the wolf."

Thus she spoke and probably would have said more, but Boadicea, who had looked the shepherdess carefully in the eye and counted the number of lambs, gave a loud cry. The vision disappeared, and the rocking boat was seized by the wind; the startled seafarer was reminded to find firm ground and to use her rudder, which had lain idly in her hand as she strained to hear and see.

"O heavens, heavens!" cried the queen, who could not have cried at a less propitious moment. "The same blessed number nine, and more important, the guardian of the flock is a being I recognize! O Velleda! Velleda! Your name brings back the most vivid memories! But why are you leading my flock? These lambs are mine! The mystery is solved; the enchantment has been revealed. Heaven help me break its spell!"

To be sure, Boadicea had no other witness to her lament than the heavens that covered her in clouds and the sea that pounded its waves more fiercely below her than before. The shore that she was leaving was just as desolate and still as if lambs had never grazed there nor flute tones whispered; even the coast disappeared from her gaze, and she was lucky that the power of the tide drove the boat back toward the ship. A storm chased after the vessel, and if it had attacked on the open seas, the ship would surely have been buried in the deep.

The pilot was on deck directing the mates to batten down for the coming storm. He saw the foundering boat and ordered its rescue. Boadicea's secret wanderings were discovered. Nothing more could be kept secret, and after the storm had blustered to an end, the storm of chastising friendship broke loose over her head. She was chided for the insane journey she had undertaken, one that could have killed her.

The queen could do nothing but confess to her friend, the honest pilot, that this was not the first time she had risked her life. The pilot listened with astonishment to her tale and the events of the last night. Deep in thought, he finally said, "My queen! The hand of the gods holds sway over you with a special power. No one other than they could have steered that boat on your first journeys; only they could have rewarded your last trip with the signs of the long-sought little ones, signs only a blind man could ignore. Yes, it is undeniably true: the sorceress is holding your daughters captive on this shore, in manifold transformations. Now that we have certainty of this, I cannot, indeed, I may not withhold my help from your undertakings without being heartless and inhuman. Be assured, you will make the trip once more, but not *alone* in your pitiful boat. Rather, I will steer you there myself in a better craft. The passing storm promises a fair day for tomorrow, and the night will be calm. I will arrange it so that I am not missed on board, and if the gods will it, we will weigh anchor tomorrow to take you and your lost loved ones back to their fatherland."

"Oh, that would be wonderful," sobbed the queen as tears of grief and joy poured from her eyes. "That is too wonderful to think of. For if all this is true, and we were to find my daughters again in their transformed state, who would disenchant them? Or who can free the victims from the power of their abductress and bring them back into our own?"

"I have great hopes," said the pilot, "for you should know that I still wear the ring that, as I told you yesterday, I once miraculously found on this basalt coast. It breaks every magic spell, as I explained to you in detail. The princesses, your daughters, will be delivered to us, but only if they desire it, for no power can break the force of human will."

The queen knew nothing of the antimagical force of the captain's ring, for unfortunately, as you may remember, she had paid as little attention to the captain's story as we did. Yet she was content to know that such a jewel was at hand without worrying needlessly about its provenance. We hope, my dear readers, that you will emulate this great queen's discretion and not trouble us with questions for which we have no answer.

The day following this adventure, which was exceptionally fair as the captain had predicted, was spent preparing the ship for departure from the unpleasant waters. The pilot and the queen also made their secretive preparations; everything was set, no one suspected them, and at midnight they boarded a seaworthy, fully rigged vessel that could have held many more than nine princesses, a queen, and a helmsman. Soon they set sail on what would be Boadicea's last journey to the basalt cliffs. Oh, if only she had been more fortunate! But we must tell the tale one thing after another, without spoiling it for you by giving portents of misfortune to come.

The queen knew the route of the ship better than the helmsman. Having carefully navigated seven times to the Irish basalt coast was of course different from being tossed there once by a storm, even if one did find a magic ring on the trip. Boadicea's eyes led the way, while the arm of the pilot steered them, yet her eyes seemed strangely weaker than the helmsman's as they sailed.

"My queen," cried the helmsman suddenly, after Boadicea had pointed out the green peaks of Pleaskin and looked around with a keen glance to see if anything promising was visible. "My queen, what do you see?"

"I believe I see a number of white summer birds, like the ones lured by the thousands into the moonlight on sultry July nights. They are dancing on the surface of the sea!"

"Summer birds," laughed the old man. "May the gods protect your eyes, my queen! There are nine girls bathing there, and perhaps they belong to your kin. Take this ring and place it on the thumb of your right hand, and you will see what I have seen."

The queen did not tarry in accepting the offered jewel; she put it on and shouted for joy. "It is they!" she cried with outspread arms. "It is my children. O Caedismanda, Bunduica! Cynobelline! And my youngest, whose name I cannot speak. Come, come to my arms! O all of you, come to me! How the years have changed you all! You have all grown so beautiful and tall. But my eyes still know you, and my heart, calling your names so loudly, will soon be beating next to yours."

The boat was still far from the shore when Boadicea learned of her happiness through the ring's magic. While she spoke, a gust of wind speeded the journey, and the ship sailed among the laughing and bantering girls, who believed themselves protected by their guise as birds, which had first confounded Boadicea's gaze. They felt no need to withdraw but rather teased and frolicked around the boat, just as white summer birds have always done on sultry July nights.

Boadicea continued to call out the names of her children and to stretch her arms out to them. The captain, an unassuming man, no longer possessed the magic ring and so could see nothing. He retired to the stern of the ship in order not to disturb the reunion of mother and children. It was completely one-sided and did not last long.

The princesses listened at first and finally could no longer doubt that something, somehow, had torn the veil of magic that protected them and that they were exposing themselves to these travelers in a state in which neither princesses nor farm girls like to be caught unawares. They were even more horrified to hear their own names being called out; alas, they did not recognize the dear lips, the loyal heart that uttered those words. Their modesty, and the fear of abduction inculcated by their protectress, made them flee; they flashed out of the water to the shore like lightning, shrouded themselves in their veils, and vanished.

You can imagine the horror that overcame the queen as the most charming vision she had ever beheld dissipated into thin air, and the green coast with its black crown of cliffs lay more lonely than ever before her. In the end, she fainted, and the captain, who had never learned how to revive a woman of status, made do by first removing the ring and then throwing a paddle full of water on her and waiting for her to come to.

While he sat holding her hand and listening for the queen's pulse to return, he noticed in passing that something was stirring on the shore. His eyes were again opened because of the magic ring, and he saw quite clearly that the being was a lovely maiden who emerged slowly from the cliffs and with piercing eyes sought an object that she soon found. A gust of wind had driven the ship back a little, but now it floated closer, and the girl from the cliffs also approached as close as the terrain would allow.

"Travelers!" she cried in a clear voice. "If you are coming from Britannia, and are sailing back there, please tell Queen Boadicea that her daughters are being held captive here by magical means and await rescue!"

When an enchanted princess utters words like these, they demand as rapid a response as rescuing a soul from purgatory. The captain knew what he must undertake.

"Maiden!" he replied. "If the queen of the Iceni were present at this moment, what could she do to release you from the sorceress Velleda?"

"Oh, now," answered the princess, "now is the hour that all is possible. Velleda is not at home. There is a festival of the Aurinians that called her back to her homeland in the Harz Mountains. We are all alone, and only my fear of falling into disloyal hands could keep me from –"

"Awake, my queen!" cried the captain, interrupting the princess. "Awake and gaze on the fulfillment of all your wishes. Reveal yourself to your daughters. Your name, your face, will accomplish more than all my words."

Boadicea had revived by the end of the conversation. The captain landed the boat, and she ran to shore and into the arms of her daughter Bunduica.

Imagine this scene of reunion; we cannot describe it. Bunduica finally tore herself from her mother's arms and hurried to the cliffs in order to lead the rest of her sisters to these motherly kisses. They appeared, and nine heavenly figures pressed around the happy queen. They embraced again and again; they spoke of a thousand magical things. The night turned to dawn, and the captain, leaning on his rudder and holding watch, finally called that they must come to an end, for they did not know how long they were still safe.

"Safe," answered Bunduica. "We are safe until the rising of the moon on the morrow, but I share your opinion that we cannot leave this sad shore too soon, to breathe purer air and live among humanity again. Arise, my sisters! Here is our mother. For her sake, you will surely give up your advantages, will you not? You will surely not have reservations about leaving this forsaken desert, where we blossom and fade unseen, where we see nothing of the beautiful world but this dreary corner that the gods in their wrath must have created as our prison?"

On hearing these words from their sister, the princesses let go of their mother's hands and stood pale with downcast eyes, as if they had no answer. A deep silence followed, and the queen could break it no more than anyone in the company. Finally, Boadicea recovered enough to say the following words: "What is this? What do these downcast looks of my children mean? How can I explain this blanching, this cold withdrawal? Is it possible, O heaven, that there is any question whether my children should follow me or stay in the thrall of an evil sorceress?"

"Mother," interrupted young Velleda with an eagerness that made her feel much better, "do not wound our hearts by calling our foster mother such awful, unfair names."

"And you, Velleda," replied Bunduica, flushing with anger, "do not betray the small amount of love of your mother and of your fatherland by your silly attachment to this person, who, no matter what she has done for us, has harmed us greatly by taking our freedom."

"Freedom, Bunduica?" cried the little philosopher. "What is freedom to people who like us do not yet know how to act?"

"Here is our mother," cried Bunduica, as she embraced Boadicea. "We will place our freedom in her hands; she is better able to protect it than a Germanic woman who is a stranger to us."

"And is there only one voice here," interjected the queen into her daughters' argument, "that will defend the rights of a mother? Will no one stand on Bunduica's side? Are you all silent? I am not surprised that Velleda is against me; her name is her excuse."

Velleda broke into tears at this bitter accusation. She could not justify herself, but she embraced her mother's knees and pressed her to her heart. "I can't act differently!" That was all she could say.

After the queen again challenged them, the eight recalcitrant daughters began, one after the other, to stutter out that they would never leave this shore, even on the hand of their beloved mother, without the approval of their guide, and each was able to explain the reason for her refusal. Velleda's more than motherly kindness, her superhuman wisdom, the heightened understanding her young pupils gratefully heard from her lips, her warnings of the dangers of the world, thousands of proofs of her loyalty and infallibility, everything was mentioned. With one voice, they defended the Aurinian and denied their wounded mother her rights.

"Sisters," Velleda finally said, "I am the youngest among you, but the preference our foster mother always showed me enriched me with knowledge that none of you possesses. Allow me to use it, as the great Aurinian so often said, according to my own convictions and to confirm it with visions into the future she taught me. We have no choice other than separation from virtue and from her, the great Velleda. Our wise father saw this as clearly as I see it at this moment, and that is why he tore us from the world and gave us to her. The events on the Isle of Man reveal how angry the gods become at any attempt to take us from her. Oh, I do not condemn the dear hand that unwittingly brought such suffering over the sacred island, but I weep for the misfortune that, in a desire to tear us from Velleda, desecrated the dwelling of the gods. Bunduica! Bunduica! Even then you would have been the easy prey of the treacherous Roman girl who presented herself as our mother's messenger if Velleda's punishing hand had not annihilated her attempts! You agreed with Flavia, and since we have been on this island you have never missed a chance to call out our names to passing sailors and thereby to bring on our heads the most dangerous of all snares, the snare of a mother. She does not know, this blinded mother, what she is about to do by tearing us away from safety and leading us into danger. We will not follow her, we dare not! Your will is free, my sister! Do as you will. But if I could only hold you back! It is not the excess of tenderness for your mother, whom we all respect, that makes you thankless toward our benefactress, no! Ask your conscience: is it not the disgust at solitude, the fear of wilting here on the vine unseen, and the curiosity about the brilliant life of the enemies of our fatherland, which I fear you will soon learn well enough to hate?"

Listening to the preaching of such a young person as little Velleda is unpleasant because it is unnatural. No one other than her seven sisters was pleased to listen to her. The captain wished she would stop; Boadicea did not deign to respond to her when she finished; and Bunduica, who clung even tighter to her mother, pressed for departure. After one more question from the seaman about whether any of the other princesses wanted to join the travel party, and after they refused in one voice, he pushed off with the rudder, which moved the ship a great distance out to sea and took it far from the gaze of Velleda's loyal charges.

They stood with outstretched arms on the shore and asked only for a motherly kiss, for an end to her suspicion that they acted against their duty, and for only one blessing to alleviate the anguished battle between the love of virtue and love of their mother. For naught! They had not hearkened to Boadicea, and so she did not hearken to them now. The last shimmer of the sail disappeared over the horizon. Young Velleda sat weeping with her sisters on the shore; morning found them there, weeping still, and still weeping they were when the moon rose from the sea and announced the Aurinian's return.

Venerable Velleda was accustomed to making her trips on bird's wings. In the region where the sun dipped into the evening sea, there rose an eagle. The ray of the sinking day star reddened its feathers, and its fiery eye sank with it into the tide. Then it looked around in the twilight sky, soared higher, and approached the basalt coast, and the princesses recognized their foster mother, who quickly stood among them in her natural shape and held them in her arms.

"So you are all mine once more," she cried triumphantly. "You belong to me and to virtue! You all battled bravely, young heroines, and many among you will be rewarded in eternity for it. Do not be angry with me, my children. It was not I who made this battle a duty; it was fate. I would have gladly allowed you to go with your poor mother; she has a greater right to you than I, and it was your choice! You are blessed that you did not use this freedom as your sister did! Have pity on her, and forget her!"

Young Velleda stopped her sisters from seeking more information about the Aurinian's words. She herself asked, in order to wake the wise old woman out of the reverie in which she sat musing, what good deeds she had opportunity to carry out while under way.

"On its flight," answered the sorceress, "the eagle met a warbler that had stolen one of the eagle eggs lying in its nest hidden from the vultures. The victim of the theft warned her, for the thief was flying directly toward the real thief, and luck to her if she escapes him!

"Further, I saw a lost vessel that sought in vain to find a larger ship in which disloyal sailors had set sail in the absence of their pilot. I showed the lost ones the surest route by which they could avoid a warship under enemy flag. The Roman truce expired while unimportant issues were being negotiated. The Iceni again encounter the enemy when they encounter the Romans, even though they are still wearing the countenance of friends, and the unsuspecting are easily fooled."

Velleda understood more of these words than any of her sisters, and so she was not happier than they; she wept without pause and wrung her hands to heaven. "O my child," said the Aurinian. "Are you so soon feeling the pain that higher wisdom brings? Woe to you if wisdom does not compensate you with her secret joys for the wounds that she inflicts! Your heart will break, for you are destined to see everything you love sink; and it will break twice over because you do not possess the happy gift of ignorance of the future."

After a time the Aurinian gathered all her charges around her. "My children," she said, "everything under the sun is fleeting. I have thwarted my lot long enough, and now I feel that I must finally surrender to it. Yes, children, I feel that I am mortal like you! I must admit to you that since Bunduica tore herself from me and exposed herself to destruction, peace has almost completely left my soul. My body's health has suffered for a long time; when I was overtaken with wrath at the seductress of my children, and took such unnecessary revenge on Flavia's corpse that time, some of her venomous blood must have entered my own veins. Even heavenly souls are sometimes overpowered by an earthly passion, and fate requires a stricter atonement from them than from others.

"I cannot keep you in this unpopulated region any longer. If death should overtake me, what would become of you? And Bunduica's desire to make her dwelling known to the world will threaten our safety here; I cannot keep your hiding place here secret from the treacherous world to which I surrender you so unwillingly. You must follow me to more populated regions."

The princesses were all prepared to do as their foster mother bid them. They were somewhat surprised that the trip would not transpire in the usual quick and comfortable way. This time they did not soar on wings; a boat, just like the absolutely mundane kind used by mortals, brought the travelers not in moments but after a number of days and hours to the Orkney Islands. The Aurinian chose the smallest one to settle on with her children.

The wise woman's increasing weakness caused the princesses much concern and showed in the visible decline of her body as well as in the powers of her mind. She seemed not to have known that the Romans already dominated this region and that only the ruins of a few ancient Druid temples were still in place to offer sanctuary to the refugees. The dangers were clearer to Boadicea's daughters than to their guide. Many of the princesses seemed to lament that they had not followed the call of their mother, until the young

Velleda, who had never once said anything about the affairs of her family, opened the book of the past and the future for them and spoke to them the following words: "My sisters, never regret the sacrifice you have made for virtue's sake! We would not now be happier if we had obeyed the queen. She and Bunduica (grieve for the fate of the misguided girl) missed the ship that they had thought to board and that the unwilling sailors had already taken into different waters without their captain. They were warned, yet they met Roman ships to which they, at Bunduica's urging, all too easily surrendered. There is a legend that in his dying moments, our father commended us to the protection of the Romans. People used this brash lie to deceive our mother and sister. Oh, this unhappy girl wanted all too much to get to know this people with their superficial splendor, a people who offered the queen of the Iceni and her daughter nothing but shame, revenge, and death. The truce had ended, and this gave the enemy the excuse for their actions against their former victor. Berated and scorned, Boadicea and Bunduica escaped Roman hands.

"A well-fought battle brought the queen revenge against her enemies for this disgrace. Bunduica died as a heroine at arms, and our unhappy mother – I will weep eternally for her – took a sleeping potion to sleep away all her suffering and to awake only in the land of eternal oblivion. We will see her again, and you all sooner than I, for long is the sad path that fate has set out for me."

The sisters looked sadly at each other when Velleda had ended. They did not speak, but their eyes betrayed their thoughts. The deaths of their mother and sister, the loss of their mentor, the fear of what would become of them after her demise – what a swirl of despairing thoughts! Their long silence was finally interrupted by a loud, unanimous oath. Whatever would befall them, they would first sacrifice life before virtue and even choose voluntary death over the risk of losing it.

The Aurinian kept their dwelling on the tiny island, today named Westray, so secret that no one could surmise it. This island was considered by the nearby Romans to be deserted; the ruins of the temples filled them with dread; the legends of evil spirits dwelling there found believers even among the enlightened lords of the world. Only the plenteous game, which was multiplying by leaps and bounds, could now and then entice a daring young warrior to undertake a hunt in these dubious environs.

Two of the noblest Romans (the world would later speak their names with cautious respect) convinced each other one day to sail over to one of these deserted islands to seek not so much the enjoyment of bagging roes and bucks but relaxation in the solitude of the place after the atrocities of war. We will call them Flavian and Julius, names they had in common with thousands of their time, when only a few of their deeds set them apart from their peers, over whom they later excelled so much.

The youths found the island beautiful, and they built huts from the branches of wild apple trees, which grew to unusual size there. They lived from these fruits, fish, and bird song; occasionally they bagged game. The beauty of the animals and the serenity in which they went through the forest without fearing hunters or their mortal shots disarmed the good-natured warriors, who on principle never attacked a defenseless opponent.

Many a brave Englishman who would rather die than surrender when he had lost his weapon to a superior opponent had honorable Flavian to thank for his life. Gentle Julius, who made it his special calling to protect the weaker sex, could be certain that if Albion had to cry for revenge against all his brothers, it would have no tears to shed on Julius's account. Julius had often assured Britannia's daughters the sanctity of their virtue, and he was therefore so highly regarded by them that they used to call his name as a charm when danger approached. Sadly, this did not help in all events; there were many soldiers who bore the same name as this good Julius, but not many were like him. His power was limited; he commanded only a small number of men at the time, yet his bravery was greater than his power, and he knew how to rule in places where he really should have obeyed. If he had always been at hand when danger threatened virtue, Boadicea and her daughter would not have died as martyrs of innocence.

A man who treats people with respect in war is incapable of cruelty to animals. Flavian and his friend lived in peace with the residents of the forest and got to know them. As they supped or sat in the evening in intimate conversation, it often happened that a milk white roe with great gazelle-like eyes would sneak up to partake of their meal or lie down next to them as if it wanted to hear their conversation. Two of these creatures especially had obvious trust in these hunters, and when Flavian and his friend believed themselves to be most alone, they were certain to have one or both of these tame little creatures at their side. Nothing could frighten them off except the attempt to catch them; they seemed to consider the lightest touch of the hand an attempt on their freedom. Once, when Julius in a moment of excess enjoyment of his lovely companion took out a golden band to adorn her slender neck, the confidence was suddenly destroyed; the shy roe disappeared like feathers on the wind, and many days passed before the creatures were seen again, even at a distance.

The youths had brought some fire with them to the island to cook their food. A sudden rain had extinguished it down to the last coals, and since there was neither fire stone nor flint on the island, and the art of robbing a bit of fire from the sun's rays was not in their hands, our warriors were actually at a loss about what to do. Even if they could have decided to eat everything raw and cold, the nights were beginning to get chillier, and without the warmth of a comforting flame they could not hold out much longer. The strangers had almost decided to leave the island that they had come to love in all its sweet solitude before they actually wished and the call of battle demanded their presence.

In deep discussion about this, they sat once at sunset at the entrance to their ever brightening bower. Fall storms had blown its leaves away, and the heavens threatened a rainstorm, which in this season usually meant an extended rain. They needed to think seriously about seeking a warmer abode or to consider vacating the place altogether. The youths had the forest, the centerpiece of the island, in view as they deliberated. From the middle of the wood on a hill rose the ruins of one of the temples destroyed by the Romans' martial wrath or religious fervor. The visitors had not yet extended their outings into that region; a secret dread held them back from the place where the gods had dwelled and where so much innocent blood had been spilled on the altars. But the principles of youths in that day were still primitive and unrefined, and every place was sacred where one worshiped the Great Mover of nature. If the fate of the ruins had depended on them back then, they would have taken care of them as piously as the temples of Rome. They were occupied discussing thoughts like these when suddenly Julius, who had turned his eyes directly toward the destroyed Druid shrine, gave a start. He turned quickly to his friend, who was speaking and had not seen what his friend saw, now again for the second time.

A bright flame rose toward heaven from that distant hill and joined with the rays of the setting sun that reddened the whole surroundings, a sight that could not have been more beautiful. The deep silence of nature and the gradually deepening twilight increased the solemnity of the display that Flavian now saw as well, and it repeated itself several times within a quarter of an hour.

"What is that?" said one to the other after a long, astonished silence. "Reflection of the setting sun, or some other play of nature? Sorcery? Effects of subterranean powers that still reign here in secret when people try to drive them away from this place, and perhaps bide their time until they can wreak vengeance on their slanderers?"

Each of the youths had his own opinion about all this, yet they did not tarry long arguing about it; they soon decided to investigate more closely what they had seen from afar. The discovery was no small thing: they had seen fire, and fire they needed. Flavian's astute idea was most likely: some of the exiled Druids might still have a secret dwelling here, and the jets of flame that rose every minute could be signals for their compatriots on other islands or means to frighten the daring away from this desolate region. But this idea confirmed the youths' resolve instead of undermining it; Julius merely noted that even if the supernatural were at work here, they had nothing to fear from the spirits reigning on this island, since they would know that he and his friend were totally innocent of all violent deeds, capricious cruelty, and desecration.

Night had almost fallen when they reached the forest, and the path they followed to the ruins would have been obscured by the thickening shadows had they not found the inside of the groves illuminated by a wondrous light. This led one of the youths, who still partly believed in the supernatural, to turn around often to his friend with a look that said, "See, Flavian, the portent of things that await us!"

The light was not bright or blinding, only like the pale shimmer of dawn or the first rays of the new moon, and thus made the path visible to the wanderers. It lighted the way sufficiently, and as they walked through the forest, the jets of fire rose periodically from the mountain so that they could not lose their way.

The forest was behind them; they saw the ruins much closer now, situated on two larger hills amid many smaller ones overgrown with delicate greenery. They seemed to be the remnants of two temples; a huge cleft separated them, or it seemed that the hand of a higher power had split open this abyss to keep these shrines apart, each perhaps the dwelling of a single god.

While Flavian, who was skilled at clever speculation, shared his thoughts about all this with his friend, they came so close to the object of their quest that they almost lost it in the shadow of the trees that surrounded its base. The path inclined steeply, and overhanging branches and thick underbrush made the going difficult. It seemed that no foot had treaded this path for years, except the light step of wild game.

As the region became more frightening and as twilight gripped the hearts of the wanderers, they fell silent, lips sealed. The quiet, barely interrupted by their soft breathing, gave them space to sense what was happening around them all the more clearly. As they climbed higher, they seemed to hear the sound of soft human voices. Some of them were wonderfully melodious (the youths heard them with delight), and they signaled silently to each other to avoid any noise, since they could now hear words and did not want to miss a syllable.

"And why, my children," asked a voice that rang out louder than the others, "why is it harder today for you to obey the call of your mother? Nine times, nine times the fire rose from the altar to call you back home out of the wilderness, but only your two younger sisters appeared, and now that I count you all, you are all mine once again, except for the lost one. Now I see so much distress in your countenances, so much fear at being at my side, so much impatience to leave again! Speak, my dears, what is the meaning of this strange behavior?"

"What is this?" answered a different voice, "the wisest of the wise, who can otherwise read everything in our hearts as in the book of fate, needs our instruction? O gods! Is this yet another sign of the weakness that troubles us so about you?"

A deep sigh was the answer to this question.

"Hush, sister!" The eavesdroppers, who could not see through the thick foliage where the voices came from, heard another voice say, "Hush? Mother wants only to hear from us what she already knows. I can already read in your hearts, and I can provide the answers for you, if you allow it. You are silent? Well, then, I will speak!

"Mother! The gift of future sight that you gave to your daughters is a source of bitter pain for many of us. We see that you will soon be taken from us; we see that we will soon depend on strangers for help and support, and where can we find this help?"

"Have you forgotten, my darling Velleda, what I have told you so often about this?"

"No, Mother. I know well the arms are near that will reach out to us when yours can no longer support us. I also know that they are good hands in which you can leave us. Boada and I know our future friends; we listen to them every day, and we find no fault with them. But our sisters? Bunduica's fate makes them all shudder just at hearing the word 'Romans'; they cannot believe that these two strangers are an exception to their degenerate race. They would rather die than surrender themselves to them."

Flavian and Julius looked at each other and squeezed each other's hands harder; they realized that they were being discussed. They moved closer in order to catch every word, and even if they knew less well how to understand the situation than you, dear readers, they still heard this much: that a group of women was gathered to hold judgment over them and that they faced a number of accusers and, as they could tell by the voices, only two defenders. Each of their most secret activities on the island was brought forward and then pardoned. The one side considered the attempt on a certain Boada's freedom, which the youths could not recall, an especially high crime. The other side had no adequate response and passed over it in silence. Only the judge – the voice that had spoken first – decided favorably that the Romans had intended no harm and that they must wait to let fate determine the final outcome. It was to be decided today – a pronouncement that caused the majority of those present to swear loudly that the Romans were not to be trusted and that they would rather choose death than fall into their hands.

The youths were certain from the beginning of this discussion that it was a female court that was being held, and they bound up the melody of these judgmental voices with so sweet an idea of all their other corporeal charms that Flavian and Julius would not have been Romans had they not felt the liveliest impatience to see what they had until now only heard: a gathering of young beauties under the aegis of an elderly judge who took pains to consider Flavian's and Julius's every action and to weigh feminine suspicions against the Romans' good faith.

Julius, who was the more eager of the two to find a path to the shimmering light they had spotted through the underbrush, was the first to have luck finding what he sought. A few bent branches revealed an opening where they could comfortably climb, and he waved to his friend, who stood behind him. Suddenly, they stood on a small ledge bordered on one side by the venerable ruins of the temple; the other side looked out toward the island and the surrounding sea, to which the pale, all-engulfing twilight lent a magical, shimmering charm.

As beautiful as all this was, the new arrivals had no eyes for any other sight but for those who had just spoken. But a powerful noise, erupting as they stepped forward, revealed that the majority of the company had fled. They had become aware of the strangers before the men, who had been busy with the arduous climb, could see them, and the only person who was within their sight was the one who could or would not flee. She was also the one who offered the least delight to their eyes.

A small woman, apparently as ancient as the building at whose crumbling gate she sat, as pale and shadowlike as the virgin Echo, rose from her seat and stepped toward them.

"Welcome, Caesar Augustus," she said as she turned first to Flavian, "and you, great Julius, Albion's sire and protector!"

The youths stared in amazement and assured her with the humility that their respect for her demanded, despite her small stature and wraithlike demeanor, that there was neither a Caesar Augustus nor a Julius who deserved such praise as this but, rather, only a pair of obscure, low-ranking men of the Roman army, brought by adventure to this hilltop.

"Names do not matter here," smiled the old woman, "but your activities in this holy place do. It is not adventure that brought you here but your free will, as I know well. Speak; name your desire!"

"We saw fire on your hilltop," answered Julius, "and we need fire to warm us in this cold clime and to prepare our food. We have climbed up here to obtain fire."

"And fire you will receive," answered the old woman as she swung the torch she carried in her right hand in wondrous circles around the youths. "Heavenly fire for great and noble deeds. If you ever reach the exalted goal set for you, remember the old woman from the temple's mount!"

Even though Flavian had an inkling of what she meant, he still considered these events to be little more than the sorcery of some elderly British soothsayer. He solemnly repeated the request for true earthly fire and reached for the torch, which then promptly extinguished and left them in total darkness.

"It means nothing," replied the old woman serenely. "There will still be embers on my hearth, and I must have fire when I call my family together again. You will dine with us tonight. Stay here until I have prepared the meal."

The young Romans heard their hostess distance herself with a soft sound, and as their eyes became accustomed to the dark, they thought they saw her floating toward the interior of the nearest temple. Soon thereafter the blaze of fire that had drawn them there arose again at some distance from them, brighter and more brilliant than it had been when they were down in the valley, and with each burst it spread enough light for them to see the old woman below the crumbling vault of the decrepit shrine, standing at an altar with one hand full of incense that filled the place with sweet scents, conjuring up a magnificent vision that rose for the seventh time toward the heavens. They heard a soft rustling in the bushes and saw the company that had been foretold approach the dinner table.

It was not what they expected, to say the least. They had hoped to see among the old woman's family some of the maidens whose voices still rang sweetly in their ears. Yet what they saw was nothing more than eight white deer of the sort they already knew. Julius thought he recognized among them the two who customarily joined their company. These two rested at the spot on the hillside where the old woman had previously sat and where they had not been noticed before due to the darkness. They seemed not to have left the spot and sat gazing at the youths like old friends, while the newcomers held themselves shyly at a distance from the strangers. The two retreated only when Julius approached them to renew this old acquaintance by softly stroking the shiny coats of the beautiful creatures.

"You are causing me a lot of trouble today," said the old woman to her astonishing family as she emerged from the temple. "Come, let us take our meal, for you know that tonight may be the last we sup together."

The old woman took her place at the temple gate. At her feet rested the guests from the forest and across from her the two Romans. On the tender grass wine in earthenware jugs, bread, and fruit stood prepared, and from the fire shooting up on the altar inside the temple there came enough light so that the table company could see well enough to eat their simple repast.

The meal was eaten in absolute silence, and the youths soon rose to take their leave. They were filled with terror at what had transpired and wished for a speedy departure. Even Flavian had noticed things about the old woman that made him question his belief that everything there was totally natural. What disconcerted him the most was the human reason that shone through even the most minute movement of the gathered animals in the dinner company and the profound distress that clouded the glances exchanged between them and the old woman.

When the old woman noticed that the youths wished to depart, she turned to her so-called daughters. "My children," she said, "you know the things I have often discussed with you in recent days. Do you allow me to pose to these strangers the question that I agreed upon with you, not considering that only two of you gave full agreement? You know that your answer determines your fate. Good enough, I expect no answer from you, and therefore I turn to you, brave youths, and ask: Have you no other request from me other than for fire, which I have already granted?"

Julius looked at his friend and exchanged a few quiet words with him, and when he appeared to have obtained his permission, he spoke thus: "We did not come here to demand gifts or to pillage either you or this temple. If, as you say, our first request has been granted, then we have no other desire except possibly that you would let us have one or two of these white roes."

"You may have all eight," answered the old woman with a pleased countenance. "And I wish to heaven that I could have given you the ninth as well, yet she is gone, and no amount of wishing will bring her back! My daughters, do you accept what these strangers offer here? For know this: they swear to you to protect you from this moment on. They swear never to fetter your freedom and are to expect only your voluntary submission. They swear, should they later learn more of you, to do everything on your behalf that your own mother would have done if fate had not taken her from your side at this moment. Pray tell, Romans, do you swear this?"

"We swear," said Julius, "whatever you demand of us."

"And whatever you perhaps do not yet understand," added the old woman, "will come with time. Your eyes will be opened, and if then your hearts give us proof of your untarnished loyalty to your oath, then take it as a pledge for the great things that the future holds for you and that you now, in your modesty, consider impossible."

A deep silence followed this pronouncement. All sides seemed to be lost in thoughts that could not or should not be expressed in words. The Romans stood withdrawn, leaning on their swords, and the old woman sat with her family. Both parties shed tears, and it is said that since that day, deer and roes have had the gift to weep as humans.

"Why do you grieve, my children?" began the old woman finally. "Leaving me – is that actually leaving virtue behind? Could you really mistrust these men? True, they are Romans, but you heard what they have sworn. They will break their oaths as little as you yours; they would choose death before vice. If you tremble before the danger of becoming slaves to the latter, then the choice is still open to you, but you must decide quickly, for my moments are numbered. You yourselves see that time has left me barely a shadow of my former self, and there is perhaps only one more step to take before the total dissolution of my earthly shell. Decide quickly before my departure subjects you unconditionally to the power of strangers."

It seemed to the youths that the old woman became ever more shadowy as her emotional speech continued, and she had hardly finished when six of her listeners sprang up and, casting fearful looks at the strangers and a glance filled with melancholy tenderness at the speaker, fled. Meanwhile, their two sisters approached the strangers and let their slender throats be adorned with golden clasps that the youths had taken from their arms. The six bolted with lightning speed through the adjacent temple toward the abyss that separated this temple from the more distant one. They appeared to plunge into the chasm that was too wide to be leapt over; flames shot up and engulfed them. A rush of noise concluded the whole scene, and in a flash everything was buried in total darkness. The youths fell unconscious.

The next morning, when they found themselves in their usual camp, the most natural thought that came to them was that it had all been a dream. The only amazing thing about the whole affair was this: that when they each told the other of this night vision, their versions were identical, down to the smallest detail. There had to be more to all this, and Flavian agreed gladly with his friend's proposal to retrace their steps of the previous night and to find out if anything was left there that could clear up their confused thoughts about the affair.

Since they had never before taken this path through the forest to the temple region, except during the real or imagined pilgrimage, it was astonishing that they could recall it step by step from the previous night. They soon passed the underbrush in which there glimmered no supernatural twilight this day; only the pale light of a misty autumn day barely penetrated the thick canopy of leaves above. The small mountainous area beyond the forest lay before them. Amid the lower green hills, veiled with white gossamer and strewn here and there with silver meadow saffron, there rose up the higher temple mount and, on its peak, the ruins looking, stone for stone, exactly as they had on the night of wonders. They climbed up and found they knew every inch of the place. They identified the spot where they had overheard the strange conversation of the old woman with her family, as well as the opening where Julius had bent back the branches to see what he had heard. If this had been a dream, then no one has ever dreamed more realistically. Julius, whose belief about the events is easy to guess, given what has already been said about him, stopped trying to counter what Flavian had said, and they strolled in deep stillness across the plain to the temple gate and through it into the inner sanctum.

While Flavian amused himself admiring the various architectural wonders of the monument of ancient British worship, Julius continued his wanderings to the chasm that separated both temples and found it impossible to cross.[1] He peered down into the abyss and thought of the previous night. He still saw the snow white daughters of the old woman plunging down and being consumed by flames, and here actual fire seemed to have been present a short time before.

On the way back through the foremost section of the ruins, he found glowing coals on a stone that seemed to be the remnant of an altar. An earthenware bowl with some incense stood beside it, and when he scattered the incense on the flames, a miniature apparition of the events of the previous evening emerged. Flavian, who saw this, was even more shaken by it than his friend; he signaled their speedy departure, and Julius did not hesitate to follow him.

As they passed through the outer temple portal, they noticed a grayish stone representing the figure of a small, seated old woman. Travelers can still find it there today, but not with the emotion of these two youths. At that moment, as its meaning and a number of other ideas connected to it became clear, they were struck with such terror that remaining on the spot was absolutely impossible. They left hill and forest behind in a haste that a later historian might call flight, had he no reservations about saying that these two heroes of the ancient world actually ever fled, even in a fairy tale.

Their stay on the island did not last much longer. They had found fire in the temple, to be sure, and it probably would have smoldered a few hours longer after their adventure, but they had no desire to go fetch it, and ever

---

1. Newer guidebooks describe the chasm between the two Druid temples on Westray as merely a large trench.

harsher weather served as an excuse for not spending one more day on the island.

The youths told no one what had befallen them, but when they later spoke together about it in private, all the objections Flavian made to his friend's opinions were contradicted but one: there had never been a trace of that last gift presented to them by the old woman of the temple mount. All the game of the deserted island seemed to have been frightened off. When they tried later to find out more about it thirdhand, about whether two white roes with golden clasps on their necks had been seen, clasps the young men were actually missing from their arms, the answer of the hunter or fisherman was always a sympathetic, embarrassed no. Flavian and Julius finally asked no more, because they were ashamed. The whole affair would have been forgotten, at least by the young Romans, if certain things had not subsequently transpired that reminded them of their adventure on Westray. It is a pity that the legend is too vague on this point for us to speak of it clearly.

In later years, Flavian and Julius grew to be great in virtue and deed. Many of their former comrades whom they now commanded claimed that they were the favorites of the gods, perhaps to explain the ignominy of falling short in their own achievements. The augurs claimed several times to have seen two white eagles circling over their heads as battle approached, or people saw a pair of white doves, bedecked with golden neck bands just like the birds of Cytherene, guarding them in their sleep. Others spun the legend even further, as the heroes became more renowned and more ripe for flattery. Soon they were alleged to be in the forests of Italy or yet again on the plains of Salisbury in Britain strolling with heavenly white-clad virgins on their arms. Titus Flavian, whom the world would soon honor as Vespasianus, a good Caesar, was already then being called Caesar by the legions, in spite of the hated ruler of Rome – this man, who the people gradually noticed was reaching his potential, was hailed as the second Numa because of the similarity of their ghostly apparitions. We cannot say anything of this, except that if any of this was true, the nymph at his side was no Egeria but, rather, one of Boadicea's daughters, the wise Velleda, who had been given him as companion in life by the old woman that night at the temple. He would have surely made her his empress if the lady had allowed him any other affection than Platonic love. If and when she and her sister first revealed themselves to their friends or how it transpired has never been told.

Between Julius, later called Agricola, and his Boada there was a more tender affection than between her sister and Flavian. But the gods, who did not want to grant the daughters of unhappy Boadicea the blessings of love, did not favor this passion: a thunderbolt killed the lovely Boada as she walked at Julius's side. Later, when he became Britain's viceroy and the benefactor of this island, he had a glorious monument built to his wise and virtuous beloved, through whose teachings he became the man that all the history books still praise today. The monument's ruins are lost to posterity; time has destroyed the eloquent marble, and a green hill covers Boada's funeral urn, which has been excavated in our own times without knowledge of what it was. Julius, who was not yet rich or great when the fire of heaven took his beloved, placed with her in the grave the most precious thing he owned: part of his armor. Remnants of them were found with her excavated funeral urn.

Velleda wept long at the grave of the last of her sisters; she made many a pilgrimage to the island where the other daughters of Boadicea preferred death to falling into the hands of the Romans, to whom their dying protectress had wanted to commend them and whom they feared only because of prejudice. When the last of the nine Iceni princesses had lived out this sad migratory life, fate raised her friend Flavian to the throne of the Roman emperor.

He brought her lasting happiness. She lived as a queen in Britain; in the Harz Mountains in Germany, which she visited as had her foster mother before, they honored her as one of their first wise women.

She was almost deified by the ancient Germanic peoples, and they were so successful at making her their own that only a few who are as well informed as you know that she was not a German but a Briton by birth. In England the traces of her are to be found in the star watch on Salisbury Plain, as well as on the Gray Ram of Marlborough, about which I will tell you soon.

But Germany thanks the yearly gatherings that she used to hold with the women of her order in the Harz Mountains for giving it the legend of the witches' sabbath on the Brocken mountain. You know all too well that as soon as a legend comes to the mouths of the rabble, they chew around on it until they have reduced it to their own level, and it begins to resemble them. Clever students of the old traditions know what to think of such things.

TRANSLATED BY JEANNINE BLACKWELL

Sophie Tieck Bernhardi von Knorring

1755–1833

Sophie Tieck Bernhardi von Knorring, author of a novel, fairy tales, plays, and poetry, was a member of German Romantic circles in Berlin. Like other Romantics, she reworked medieval literature into modern romantic poetry; like her brother Ludwig Tieck, she wrote longer, mysterious fairy tales with developed, problematic protagonists. Romantic love relationships and family interactions play an important role in most of her tales.

"The Old Man in the Cave" reflects German Romantic interest in dreams, visions, and the protagonist's quest to explore realms shrouded from human understanding. In the process of this quest, the young protagonist and his elderly alchemist mentor learn that deepest understanding is gained not by achieving new intellectual heights but by restoring a lost harmony. The young man helps his mentor reconcile the dysfunction in his own family while reconstructing a world in which his dream love can become a reality. This rechanneling of the quest back on itself and its questioning the role of the magic helper make the tale an interesting revision of the fairy tale quest. Nevertheless, the story maintains the traditional marriage as happy ending and reinforces the role of the male hero in Romantic love quests.

The haunting nature of the hero's quest is reminiscent of Ludwig Tieck's "Rune Mountain," as well as Benedikte Naubert's "Die weiße Frau" (The woman in white). The German Romantics revived interest in stories and legends of magic helpers, such as Merlin in the Arthurian romances, the legend of "The Sorcerer's Apprentice" by Goethe (1797), and of course the legendary Peter Schlemihl, the man who sold his own shadow. Several stories in this anthology tell of resolving irreconcilable problems or repairing the damage done by a seemingly irreparable mistake ("Temora," "The Queen's Son," "The King's Child," and "The Princess of Banalia"); others narrate the quest for superhuman abilities and describe the dangers of hubris ("Black and White" and "Pack of Lies"). This story has similarities to the tale type no. 325 in Aarne and Thompson, *The Types of the Folktale,* and no. 68, "The Thief and His Master," in the 1857 edition of the Grimms' tales.

[Sophie Tieck Bernhardi von Knorring], "Der Greis im Felsen," in *Bambocciaden,* pt. 3 (Berlin: Friedrich Maurer, 1800), 149–80.

The Old Man in the Cave

1800

I N A T I M E long past there lived in the darkest part of the forest an old man whom no one knew. In the whole region thereabouts he was called "The Old Man in the Cave" or "The Kind Sorcerer," for everyone who came to him and sought his counsel went away consoled. Villagers and townspeople alike came to ask him about their problematic cases. If they brought him a small gift, he accepted it thankfully, but if one of the rich ones thought that he had compensated him sufficiently for his counsel by handing him a pile of gold pieces, then the old sage smiled and laid the coins to one side, and the next poor soul who came to him needing aid left happier and richer.

It was a pleasant morning, and the old man sat before his cave, smiling. He watched the sunbeams gilding each leaf and observed how only the gentlest breeze was necessary to chase the leaves out of the brilliant shimmering into the darkest shadows. "Oh, you image of human fate," he exclaimed. "A small wind can touch you, and then suddenly you stand with all your brilliant blossoms in sinister shadow!" While he was talking to himself like this, a youth approached him, a thoughtful expression on his face.

"Honor and greetings to you, ancient father," he addressed him. The old man returned his greeting and invited him to sit down on a stone before the cave.

"What has roused you from your slumbers so early?" the old man asked the youth.

"People tell me," he responded, "that you are a wise sorcerer."

"And so you require my help?" asked the old man, smiling.

"Yes, wise sir," cried the youth. "But do not think that I will bother you with those things that you hear all the time from rash young people. I do not ask that you support me in winning the love of some girl, and neither do I expect you to show me the path to fame and honor. No! My goal is much nobler."

"Well, then, what is it you seek," said the old man, "if these things mean so little to you?"

"Do you not believe that the most noble goal of humanity," the youth continued, "is knowing everything in its innermost and outermost essence, and particularly everything within one's own self?"

"I do, but only after one has truly comprehended it all," said the old man. "But continue; tell me your desire."

"I wish," said the youth, "that you would bestow on me the gift of seeing my own thoughts standing before me after I have crafted them, so that I might be able to judge what my soul is thinking and whether it deserves to be called good or evil, clever or naive. I know that this is much to ask, dear old man, but my gratitude will know no bounds."

"It is less than you think," said the old man, "but I do not believe that you will thank me for this gift. I will do nothing more than increase the strength of your vision so that you may see the images your soul creates and sends out into the world. But I repeat: you will not thank me. For one whole year you must bear seeing all your thoughts and resolutions. When the year is over, return to my cave again, and I will relieve you of this burden that you now wish upon yourself."

The old man rose and went into his dwelling; the door closed, and the youth was left alone on the bench. "Why on earth," he mulled to himself, staring at the ground, "would I ever regret receiving such a fine gift? What new wisdom will I attain using this new vision? I will examine everything with an incisive gaze, and I alone will be able truly to judge myself and all humankind."

He rose and was about to return to the city when at his feet he suddenly saw a small, short-sighted, misshapen figure wearing a huge pair of spectacles on his nose. Leonhard shrank back at the sight of this ridiculous monster and was about to run away when the creature disappeared into thin air. "What on earth!" cried the astonished youth. "Was that supposed to be the embodiment of my thoughts?" He thought the same thought again, and the ridiculous figure with the spectacles approached again.

"You evil sorcerer!" cried Leonhard. "You mock me and are trying to show me my thoughts all distorted." After he spoke these words, he saw near him a child who stared at him with an utterly stupid look, then hurried to catch up with and join the misshapen figure. "Well," said Leonhard with contempt, "I have to admit, my soul has sent a fine pair of replicas of itself out into the world." He had barely ended this speech when a young lout with black curly hair and fiery eyes stood next to the others and looked at them with hatred. "My search for wisdom seems to be off to a pretty bad start," said Leonhard. "It would have been better if I had not asked the old man for this gift." A young boy with straight blond hair and blue eyes, not handsome and not misshapen, stood next to him; his face was neither stupid nor intelligent. He looked indifferently at Leonhard and joined the others. "Well, this is a fine state of affairs!" Leonhard cried angrily. "Of my four thoughts so far, only one is even slightly tolerable, and even this one is a thought of regret, so what good is he to me? If I cannot summon up anything more sensible than this but can only mildly regret the stupid things I thought, then I wish that I could destroy the whole lot of them." He stepped into the midst of his thoughts and tried to shoo them away, but, far from being frightened of him, they closed in around him. "Is it not possible for me to think anything sensible," he cried, "so that this whole brood will leave me?" He put his head in his hands and was about to try with all his might to think something clever, but then he was reminded all the more of every previous thought, and even when he believed he had created something new and looked up, one of his four offspring approached him again.

In despair, he returned to the city, and his thoughts accompanied him. His path led through the deepest part of the forest; tall, ancient oaks rustled above him, and his heart was moved. His four thoughts left him, a devout awe flowed through his breast, and he totally forgot his request to the old man. Finally, he reached the path out of the forest. When he saw the towers of the city before him, he looked up and noticed a handsome youth fluttering away from his side, and the four figures floating off in the distance were now hurrying back to him again.

Leonhard tried to recall the thoughts that had accompanied him so well in the forest, but his efforts were in vain. The more zealously he tried to remember, the more eagerly his foolish companions rushed in on him. "So that means I can have good thoughts only when I am not aware of them," he said and went to his home, musing to himself. He did not have the courage to look up; he was afraid that he might have created a new figure similar to the ones accompanying him.

As he went through a narrow street toward his home, he heard a lament from the window of one of the smaller cottages. He walked up and looked through the pane. A young girl stood at the bedside of a sick woman, and two small children sat wailing on the floor. "Does no one take pity on this poor unfortunate woman?" said the girl and raised her blue eyes to heaven. At the same time she caught sight of Leonhard and shyly stepped back. Pity drew him inside; he opened the door of the house and stepped into the sparse room. Here he saw the mother of the children, a young woman, pale and close to death. Leonhard approached her, saying that the crying children had drawn his attention, and he asked her to accept some of his wealth. The ailing woman sat up and tried to thank him; she gestured to her children, who approached Leonhard. He looked around and turned toward the older girl, for he expected her to approach him with a touching outburst of thanks. Instead, she withdrew even farther and looked down at her hands. Her glances did not reach Leonhard, although it was her glance that had caused him to enter this house of misery in the first place.

Well, now, thought Leonhard, that is certainly strange. The look she raised to heaven seemed to ask so urgently for help for these poor people, and now that it has been given, she acknowledges my generous actions so little that she does not even give me a grateful glance. He saw this thought take shape next to him and shrank from his own incredible stupidity staring at him with dullard eyes. He became confused and took his leave, promising the family that he would visit them on the following day. He hoped to be rewarded with a friendlier glance from the girl for this promise, but in vain; she remained motionless and stared at the floor. As Leonhard left the house in a foul humor, she escorted him to the door. He wanted to make the most of the favorable moment and said, as he grasped her hand, "Who could remain unmoved by such human suffering when the prettiest eyes are weeping because of it?"

The girl gazed at him and smiled; she opened her mouth as if to answer but then disappeared before Leonhard's eyes. He still felt how her soft hand glided out of his own when he saw her no more. Dumbfounded, Leonhard looked at the closed door, and many thoughts floated before his eyes. They followed in rapid succession, none of them thought to completion, and each was clasped to the other so that the most wondrous thoughts floated before him and seemed to form a mysterious dancing circle. His befuddlement about the vanished girl gradually faded as he considered these phantoms, but that only increased their number. Leonhard could not compose himself; he became enraged by the visible thoughts, which only resulted in the formation of new ones without the elimination of the old.

"What a fool I am," he finally cried, "that I begged for such nonsense. This worthless flimflam will cause me to lose my mind. I have to bear this curse for a whole year, and already on this very first day it is unbearable." He ran home and could scarcely discern his own dwelling from the others, so deeply had the mysterious horde confused his mind. He threw himself on his cot and hoped to find rest, but here, too, he had to fight long and hard with his cursed spirits before the relief of slumber removed them from his sight.

As Leonhard closed his eyes, he found himself again in the cottage and saw the girl with the sky blue eyes. He spoke with her and revealed his love for her, and she answered so sweetly that he dared to embrace her. He awoke and looked around disgruntled, for the dream had tricked him. He tried to fall asleep and conjure up that fair image again, but in vain.

When the first rays of the sun spread out over the heavens, it occurred to him that he might again visit the old man in the cave and lament his many sorrows to him. He did not look around at all; he was afraid that even this thought would not take a favorable shape, and yet he still wanted to carry it out. After half an hour he was already under way and hurrying toward the city gate. As he passed through the narrow street, and as he saw the house where he had experienced such strange events the previous day, he stood still and observed it carefully. He went up to the window, but the shutters were closed, and everything inside was so quiet that it seemed to be utterly without occupants. "It is still early in the day," said Leonhard, "and the unfortunate folks are still sleeping, forgetting all their woes, which will be there again when they awake." He was still standing lost in thought before the small door when he spied a little old lady creeping laboriously through the street with her cane. She bade Leonhard good morning, and he returned her greeting, asking if she lived in this alleyway.

"Just a few houses from here," said the old woman.

"So you might be able to tell me," Leonhard continued, "who the people are who live in this house?"

"The people who live in this house!" cried the old woman. "Dear sir, nobody! This house has stood empty for many years; the owner boarded it up. He left, as I said, many years ago, and no one has set foot in it since. You can tell by the high grass that has grown up around the doorway." Leonhard was astonished, for he had not noticed the high grass before. The old woman left, and he stood pondering, his eyes still fixed on the grass that swayed in the morning breeze.

"Did I just dream this?" he finally cried. "Is the whole episode simply a child of my imagination? I will gain nothing from this," he cried, "no matter how I torture myself. The old man will tell me whether this event really happened or was a dream."

He hurried to reach the forest, raced along the dark paths that led to the old man's cave, and felt half fearful, half relieved when he finally saw the old man sitting again on his stone bench. He approached him, but the old man took no notice of him; deep in thought, he was drawing figures with a stick in the sand. Leonhard did not want to disturb his contemplations, but finally the old man looked up.

"You come to me at an inconvenient time," he said harshly to Leonhard. "You are disturbing me at an important hour in my life."

"Venerable sir –" Leonhard began.

"I know what brought you here," said the old man. "If you had loved her, she would not have disappeared."

"I did not love her?" cried Leonhard. "Her vision follows me incessantly. From the moment her glance first met mine, my heart was eternally hers."

"Possibly someday you will learn what love truly means," said the old man, "but for now you do not know what that feeling is." He rose and went into the cave, leaving Leonhard alone on the bench.

"And if this is not love," he said to himself, "what emotion is it that forces me to think of her constantly?" He immersed himself in thought and unwittingly drew figures in the sand, as the old man had done before him. When he looked up sometime later, he saw the old man standing next to him again, weeping uncontrollably. Leonhard was terrified and asked, "What troubles you?"

In a melancholy voice the old man asked him to erase the figure he had just drawn; taken aback, Leonhard did so, and when the last traces were gone, the old man looked at the youth smiling. "I thank you," he said. "Without knowing it you have done me a great service."

Astonished, Leonhard asked what the service could have been.

"The signs," the old man replied, "which you absentmindedly drew in the sand forced all the images of my suffering and my unfairness before my soul and made you the master of all my actions. At my request, you erased all this sorcery; you have now forgotten the symbols. You will never be able to retrace them again, and fate will never be so favorable a second time."

"What!" cried Leonhard. "I had magical power all along and never suspected it?"

"Everyone has it," said the old man, "and real magic actually consists of knowing the wondrous power of the magic symbols. How amazed people would be if they knew what connection their trivial undertakings had to the most wondrous events of nature. But come with me and accompany me to my dwelling. For although your mastery over me has been eradicated, that symbol still forces me, by its very existence in the past, to love you forever, just as a few words often bind two hearts for all eternity." He opened the door to the cave, then turned once more to Leonhard.

"You should not be surprised at the company I keep, whom you will meet inside," he said, smiling, "and you must promise me not to annoy them with any questions." Leonhard promised and followed the old man. When he had carefully bolted the door of the cave, he bade his guest sit down. Leonhard did so and was surprised to find the cave empty, since the old man had spoken of some company. He was still thinking about it when he saw that the old man was arranging chairs around a table that was already laid with bread and fruits. The old man glanced lovingly back into the darkest part of his cave, and a faint white shimmer began to move. It floated closer to the table, and Leonhard saw to his astonishment how the figure of the woman he had seen in the cottage emerged out of the darkness. She carried her youngest child in her arms. The other followed, holding the hand of the girl who had directed her sky blue gaze at Leonhard. Silently, the company took places at the table, and the old man indicated to Leonhard that he should also take a seat. Astonished, he did so. The old man served his guests and with friendly gestures encouraged them to eat.

Leonhard's eyes were fixed on the girl, and for the first time he saw how lovely she was: the blond locks that fell about her shoulders, her slender frame, her delicate limbs, and the inexpressible grace that accompanied all her movements. The small repast was soon finished, and everyone rose from the table with a serious demeanor. The old man folded his hands and glanced down for several moments; a slight trembling seized the stately figures, and they withdrew into the darkness. A dull shimmer remained for a few moments, but soon this too dissipated. A wreath of fresh roses had hung in the blond locks of the girl; when she stood up, Leonhard noticed one rose fall from her hair to the ground. He approached the chair she had vacated and to his great joy saw the lovely fresh rose on the ground. Quickly, he bent down and picked it up. But how astonished he was when the bloom, which had just shown all its resplendence, withered immediately in his hand.

The old man watched him, smiled, and opened the door of the cave. Both men stepped outside, and Leonhard hid the flower next to his heart. He remained a long time with the old man, but he did not dare to ask him at the outset who the girl was. Finally, he remembered his thoughts and was astonished to see none of them. "How is it possible," he said, "that in speaking with you, whom I esteem so highly, I had absolutely no thoughts at all?"

The old man smiled and said, "I hid them from your eyes while you were talking with me. I know that it confuses you when you see that not everything you think is as excellent as you might like."

Leonhard then asked about the girl. The old man replied gravely, "Perhaps the time will come when it is useful for you to know her origins. Now please spare me from having to tell you things that sadden me, only to satisfy your curiosity."

Leonhard tried to assure him that it was not simply curiosity but, rather, the most ardent love that compelled him to ask. The old man looked at him and said, "You do not know what love means, and very few people in the world do. All of you speak of it so often that everyone believes it must be something very pleasant, and therefore you believe that you have often experienced it because you have wished it so."

"You have a cold heart," said Leonhard, "and are numb to all the emotions of youth; that is why you judge so harshly."

"That is not so," replied the old man, "for all your thoughts are visible to me, and I will leave it for you to observe them again." He went into his cave, and a horde of colorful figures abruptly surrounded Leonhard. He now saw the whole conversation he had held with the old man and was astonished when he saw that one thought that he had rejected as too common and had not uttered walked hand in hand with another one that Leonhard had considered the best and most sublime his soul had ever produced. The two of them had embraced each other so ardently, and looked so much alike, that their close kinship was apparent.

Vexed, Leonhard rose and began walking through the forest. As the oaks and beeches rustled over his head, he recalled the gentle feelings that had moved his heart on the previous evening as he had walked in the shadows of these trees. He thought of how he had seen the girl in the small cottage, and all her movements appeared so vividly before his soul that a deep longing filled his heart. The more he thought of her, the deeper the magic crept into his soul. He stared up at the treetops, and a blissful joy rushed with all its sunbeams through his heart. His gaze fell to the ground, and, strangely moved, he looked at the grass and flowers swaying. Small blue forget-me-nots grew on the ground, and it seemed as if they looked up at him with innocent, loving blue eyes. He bent and plucked one from its stem to press to his lips. Then he remembered the rose he had hidden next to his heart; he drew it out, and it blossomed again in his hand in its most ineffable beauty. He kissed it in ecstasy, and it seemed to him as if the lips of his beloved returned the kiss. He looked up and saw several charming children with golden hair romping in innocent games around him.

This was the first time that Leonhard had been at peace with his thoughts. He returned home, and longing seized him anew as he found it empty. He thought about the bliss of having his beloved share his earthly possessions, share all his joys with him; he imagined with what delight he would rush to fulfill any new wish he saw in her eyes. All these images swirled around him until sleep overcame him. He dreamed that his house stood in flames. He strained and struggled to save some of his valuables from the fire, and no thought of his love occurred to him. Finally, he rested from his exertions and felt exhausted. The sun shone cheerfully in his rooms; he thought of his beloved and could no longer call back the image of the loveliness that had delighted him so the day before.

He rose, dejected, and dressed. "Am I so unhappy," he said to himself, "that I cannot embrace her anymore with true love, and I must therefore lose her? Oh, all my happiness would then be lost; nothing could console or gladden me!" He hurried to the forest to hear a comforting word from the old man's lips. He found him in front of the cave, smiling cheerfully as the youth approached. Leonhard was melancholy.

"What is troubling you?" asked the old man.

"Ah!" replied Leonhard. "I was so happy last night. I felt love, and now my heart is cold again, and you will judge me harshly and say that I should not be happy." He told the old man how the feelings in his heart, along with the rose that he kept close to his breast, had blossomed, and how the same emotion had raced with its sunbeams through his soul.

"Never mind," said the old man joyfully. "You are in love, and you will be happy. Not every person who feels love is happy enough to feel it every moment in his heart with the same intensity. Petty cares often banish this divine gift, but when it does return, receive it with all the glory of your heart."

"You say that I shall be happy?" exclaimed Leonhard with delight. "But pray tell, where can I find my dear beloved?"

"Now I will tell you who she is," spoke the old man. "I want to speak now of my own sorrows, for they are now past. Once even I was young and loved and was happy. The girl who had won my heart became my wife. I had dedicated myself early in life to the magical arts, and many of the powers of nature stood in my thrall. I could have amassed much gold, but our contented hearts disdained all splendor and show. My wife and I lived in the small cottage where you first saw the girl, and we lacked for nothing. My wife bore me two daughters; I lost her with the birth of the second. My grief was indescribable. I felt deserted and forgot for a time all the consolation the arts of alchemy could give me. Finally, I recovered enough to be able to think things through again, and I was comforted, for it stood in my power to continue my contact with my beloved Elvira. Every noon and every midnight my beloved would appear and bring my heart comfort and peace. She watched with purest love over our children.

"Thus passed several years of my life in this happy state. Finally, a young man won the heart of my eldest daughter. I advised her to put this love behind her, for I saw that his love did not deserve hers in return. She was beautiful, and it was only her beauty that attracted him. Against my wishes, she left my house. The ingratitude that repaid my love and care so badly made me angry, and I swore I would never forgive her. I saw my wife as often as usual, but she never mentioned the daughter who had left us, and she seemed to pour all her love into our second child. After several years had passed, she accused me of nursing my anger for too long and counseled me to forgive our eldest daughter. For the first time ever, I refused her something, and for the first time, her beloved shadow turned away from me indignantly.

"Several days later I took a walk in the forest and among the cliffs found this cave, which no one had ever noticed. I tarried here for a long while and then hurried back home, so as not to miss the hour when Elvira visited me. As I entered my home, I saw an ailing person lying in the bed; two children sat on the floor and wailed, and my second daughter stood next to the bed. I approached with great sympathy, but this benevolent feeling turned to rage when I recognized the sick woman as my eldest daughter. 'What!' I exclaimed. 'You dare to enter your father's house again, the father whose love you scorned and whom you deserted so shamelessly?' As I was about to say more angry words, my darling Elvira stood before me.

" 'You are abusing love, the most sublime feeling of all humanity,' she cried, 'in hatred. And for that reason you are not worthy of love. Go! Leave this house, which was the only abode of love, and live among the animals of the forest. You will not see me again, until love and compassion have repaired what your hatred and harshness have ruined.'

"She was the one who lulled my children into a gentle sleep and who kept them from losing the years they were dreaming away. Each year, for one hour on the day that I insulted heaven with my rash act, my children take on the shape in which I found them, and they are visible to the eyes of a mortal. No one before you, however, had ever noticed them. After a time, my wife's spirit forgave me, and I was allowed to see my children at the time of day in which I had before enjoyed their company. With all my arts, I was able to make my younger daughter invisible from any man who desired her without truly loving her, for I wanted to protect her from a life of misery such as her sister had experienced. The unhappy girl very quickly lost the bloom of novelty for her husband, and he left her. She finally became so sick and miserable that she had dared come to me to beg for my pity. She became so weak before my arrival that her sister prepared her a bed, and I was cruel enough not to welcome her with love." Tears flowed from the old man's eyes as he spoke.

"Now it is all past," he finally said. "I hope that from now on we will be happy. Follow me. It is noon, and you will find my children in the cave. Embrace your beloved, and if she does not disappear before your eyes out of your embrace, she will be yours, Elvira will be reconciled, and I will live in her company again."

The two of them went to the cave, where the table was prepared as on the previous day, and when the old man had set the places, the figures approached. Leonhard's heart trembled with delight and fear. He went to the girl, and she looked gently at him. He took heart and wrapped her in his arms, pressing an ardent kiss to her lips. Still he saw her there before him. He could not believe his happiness, and he kissed her again and again. Kindly, the old man joined them and took her from Leonhard's arms. "I am happy again," he said, "and both of you are as well."

Now the eldest daughter approached them with her children. "Forgive me, Father," she said.

"Oh, my daughter!" exclaimed the old man, "please forgive me." They all embraced and welcomed one another, and the most joyful of conversations enlivened the whole company, which on the previous day had held such a silent meal.

"Are you not contemplating your thoughts?" said the old man laughingly to Leonhard. "The ones that were supposed to float visibly all around you?"

"Where have they gone?" asked Leonhard and looked around for them.

"I have freed you from that curse," replied the old man, "for it seems to me that you have given up studying yourself so much."

"What did I accomplish," said Leonhard, ashamed, "with that special gift that seemed so important at the time?"

"Nothing," answered the old man, "just as a person does not really achieve anything through too great introspection except great confusion."

"Oh, what a fool I was," cried Leonhard, "when I called it folly to wish for a girl I could love. Love – love is the greatest happiness that heaven has bestowed on its beloved children."

"That is true for you," said the old man, "and thus you have spoken a universal truth – about yourself. Be content, for even the wisest man can do nothing more than that."

Leonhard stayed true to his resolve to live in wisdom, for now he called love the greatest truth of all. He saw his thoughts no more, and so they appeared to him to be as reasonable as they had before, and he lived with his wife as happily as any human can.

TRANSLATED BY JEANNINE BLACKWELL

Anonymous

The anonymous author of the collection *Feen-Mährchen* (Fairy tales; Braun-schweig, 1801) was both praised and belittled by the brothers Grimm in the first edition of their fairy tales, for this collection contained several "real" fairy tales, as they called them, but also tales reworked from the French tradition. Some scholars have considered the author of this collection to be a woman. Albert Wesselski bases his assessment on the author's introduction, in which she presents "her" aunt, the original source of the tales, in the role of Goethe's "beautiful soul." The elderly aunt is a powerful mentor who tells the children tales to escape the sadness of her own tumultuous life. The author herself, the darling of this aunt, becomes a tale-teller as well, refashioning her aunt's tales from her own childhood fantasies. Now in her old age, she tries to remember and record those imaginings in print. Fairy tales, for her, make troubles pleasurably distant and offer a space for reinventing her own life.

If the introduction is credible, this collection is the first to document the passing of the oral tradition of (predominantly French) fairy tales from one generation to next and their reworking into "literature," that is, written, au-thored fairy tales. These stories reflect the full range of fairy tale possibilities, good and bad: sea adventure, rape, romance, marital infidelity, cannibal-ism, cruelty, and even anti-Semitism. The Grimms cited four of the tales as sources in their collection.

"The Giants' Forest" bears a similarity to Mme d'Aulnoy's "The Bee and the Orange Tree" but changes the venue from a desert island (originally based on a shipwreck story in the New World) to an isolated spot on a river apparently in Europe. A young princess lost in a storm is rescued by an ogress, who raises the princess as her own child and who plans to marry the foundling to her son. The ogress is softened from the French version into a threatening helper who is later integrated into the domestic life of the saved princess; she bears a distant resemblance to the superhuman female figures of Benedikte Naubert. This story presents significant variations on the "chase and transformations for escape" plot found in "The Bee and the Orange Tree" and the story of the ogress's children with their switched crowns. It also gives the heroine a more active role, for she saves her rescuing prince herself and takes her ogress back home as a nanny for her own children.

Other tales that have strong giant women or cave women who befriend a young person are no. 327a in Aarne and Thompson, *The Types of the Folktale*, "The Giant's Daughter" (in Phelps, ed., *Maid of the North*), and "Jack and the Magic Beans." Ogre bridegrooms also abound, such as Juliana Horatia Ewing's "The Ogre Courting" (in Zipes, ed., *Victorian Fairy Tales*). The Grimms themselves saw this tale in connection with their tale no. 70, "Okerlo," in the 1812 edition, provided by Jeanette Hassenpflug, as well as no. 113, "The King's Children," in the 1857 edition, provided by Ludowine von Haxthausen.

"Der Riesenwald," in *Feen-Mährchen zur Unterhaltung für Freunde und Freundinnen der Feenwelt* (Braunschweig: Friedrich Bernhard Culemann, 1801), 44–72.

The Giants' Forest

1801

For ten years King John had wished for a son who would maintain the glory of his throne and solidify his reign, but all his wishes and hopes were for naught. The otherwise so beautiful, clever, and virtuous Mathilde, his beloved consort, remained barren. Each day the royal couple grew unhappier; each evening found the fair lady in tears. To make their suffering even more exquisite, the king received news that his brother's wife had given birth to a son. From that hour on, all peace left the royal castle. The king treated Mathilde, the loveliest of her sex, harshly, and his accusations tore her heart more every day, until she finally determined to make a pilgrimage to Palestine and to try with her splendid sacrifices and contrite prayers to touch the heart of the Holy Virgin. She had hardly revealed her plan to her husband when he joyfully gave his approval and arranged for all her necessities in the most splendid way imaginable. She was given a large, magnificent retinue and regal gifts, and thus she departed after a few weeks, richly outfitted with her old husband's best blessings.

After her long year's journey she arrived in Loreto happily and without incident. Already during the first days of her stay her beauty and modesty won each and every heart, and the sly priests, before they noticed her costly gifts, singled her out of the crowd of gathered pilgrims and supported her pious prayers with all their might.

It was her custom to spend the first hours in the morning, before any other pilgrim awakened, in front of the image of the acclaimed Virgin. There she poured out her heart in sighs and tears, and there it was that the Blessed Virgin softly promised to hear her supplication. After having that vision, Mathilde spent one hour in the evenings in the lonely chapel. At the end of her pilgrimage, she parted sadly from a young cleric who had accompanied her for her morning and evening devotionals. With full certainty that her petition had been heard, Mathilde returned home.

On the return trip, Mathilde became certain that her prayer had been answered, so she doubled her pace and sent the joyous news ahead to her husband. A few days after her arrival she gave birth in his arms to a baby girl, who was as beautiful as the day and as charming as the sunrise. This new bolt from the blue would have clearly broken the spirit of her parents had they not immediately harbored hopes of marrying her to the son of the king's brother, King Philip, thus uniting the two kingdoms. As soon as they had agreed on this, a delegation was sent to King Philip to inform him of his sister-in-law's lying in and to present him with the proposal of an engagement between the two children. The king received the delegation graciously, bestowed fine gifts on them, and gave them a sealed message for his brother in which he asked formally for the hand of little Aurora for his son, Frederick. As soon as the parents on the other side had made all the required arrangements, great peace reigned in the royal castle, the most tender affection and harmony flourished between the sublime royal couple, and little Aurora grew, to the great delight of her parents, to be one year old.

But alas, a new disaster interrupted this bliss for many years! Not far from King John's castle there flowed a great river in majestic waves. The closer shore was delightful and inviting, and an island not far from the shore was exquisitely verdant and lush. There was no more pleasing spot in the whole kingdom, and the king often went to this lovely place in small boats with his entourage. He felt that the birds there sang more sweetly, the flowers smelled more fragrant, and the cooling breezes were like gentle zephyrs. The far shore could not be seen, for the distance was too great, and since no mortal had dared to cross the terrible waves of this rushing river in a small boat, it had thus remained unexplored. Since the residents of the closer shore imagined they saw huge trees across the river when the weather was clear, they called it the Giants' Forest in jest, and lived happily ever after, unworried about its inhabitants.

On a beautiful, if somewhat sultry, summer day, the king again organized a small excursion on the water. He mentioned it to the queen, who was more than willing, since he also suggested that darling little Aurora and her nurse should come along. Toward evening the royal couple boarded a beautifully decorated vessel and were followed in a second one by the nurse with the little girl; then came the rest of the entourage in more than twenty small boats. They came ashore safely and savored the cooling breeze and the fragrant shade of dense forests. Suddenly, the skies became overcast with dark clouds, in the distance rolling thunder could be heard, and bluish lightning appeared from time to time. Since the boatmen were concerned about the rising winds, everyone quickly boarded the boats and gave themselves up to the restless waves of the river. In vain the rowers used all their might; in vain the king offered substantial rewards for their efforts. Before they were able to reach the shore, a frightening gale arose, scattering all the boats so that one flew here and another there. The king's vessel landed first, and in the course of an hour, the rest had been gathered. Only the one carrying the princess and her nurse was missing; the courtiers insisted that they had seen the boat capsize and Aurora's little cradle disappear in a flash from their sight.

Her poor mother fainted from grief, and the sorrowful king tried every means to pull his beloved child from the waves. Alas, it was all for naught. The deep darkness of the night and the ever increasing storm made every attempt at rescue impossible. The violent, driving rain soon forced them all to flee to their homes.

While the city and the castle rang with cries of grief and woe, the wind pushed little Aurora's cradle to the far shore, and a wave threw her without injury on land. The sweet little child would no doubt have been a tasty morsel for the wild animals had not the queen of the giants, Tertulla, strolled past at exactly that moment. She rushed over on hearing the little girl's cries, and, since she and her people belonged to the race of flesh-eating ogres, she was about to take this tender tidbit to her children. But upon observing Aurora more closely, her heart opened with compassion, and the child's darling smile won Tertulla over completely. She took Aurora in her arms, cuddled her, and tried to quiet the terrified little child, who looked around fearfully but found neither her loving parents nor her good nurse. Tertulla carried the child and her cradle to her cave, and the next day when the king of the giants, Anak, and his eight sons returned from the hunt, she pleaded with them for Aurora's life. They acquiesced to her request all the more easily since the ogress had eight sons but no daughter. From that moment on she cared for the child as her own. Tertulla was a giantess, to be sure, but she was also a good woman who did not live in complete harmony with her monster mate; she planned to raise Aurora to be her support in old age.

The little girl repaid Tertulla daily for her pains with thousands of kisses and hung on her so exclusively that Tertulla could convince her only occasionally to be friendly to her husband and sons. Seldom was she able to accomplish this, for Aurora had such a strong aversion to these residents of the Giants' Forest that she avoided all company with them. Under some shady trees on the bank of her river of misfortune she built herself a little hut, where she spent many a day, staring longingly at the far shore. She didn't realize that her loving father and her tender mother were grieving for her there, for Tertulla had left her with the illusion that she was the daughter of a poor giantess who had commended the little one to her with her dying breath. Tertulla had visions of making Aurora happy by marrying her to her youngest son, who was both her favorite and, according to the custom of their land, the crown prince.

As much as Aurora loved her foster mother, she still shuddered at the very thought of being united with Oglu. She had now reached the age of fifteen; her heart often beat restlessly, and she was filled with constant longing. Yet she had not found an object that could reduce, let alone still, that yearning. Every day she became more pensive; she often fled for days into the deepest solitude of the forest, climbing cliffs and crawling through caves and underbrush. She was so happy to find at last a hidden cave in the cliffs where she could pour out her emotions and weep, hidden from every human eye.

Oglu had often crept after her, for he loved the charming girl. He had found her every time, but in the cave she remained undisturbed; neither his footsteps nor his hated eyes followed her to this lonely refuge. She decided to make the cave her dwelling on the day she was to become Oglu's bride; she would flee here, and so she gradually furnished it completely. The inside of her cave was as pleasant and gay as the outside region was rough and wild. Every day she covered the bare cave walls with daisy chains and strewed her bed with soft moss; unnoticed, she brought in animal skins and a supply of dried roots. As soon as she was finished with these preparations her cheerfulness returned. She spent more time with Tertulla, stayed more often in her hut on the riverbank, and delayed the approaching day of her marriage with utmost cleverness from day to day.

Tertulla shook her old white head, but she was unable to do anything to hurt her beloved daughter; she herself asked Oglu to have patience. She visited Aurora more often in her little hut, always decorated with flowers, where she found the girl resting like a forest nymph on fragrant herbs. She loved to spend time with her, and she taught her the secret arts of magic. She taught her to foresee future events in the stars and showed her the hiding place of her wishing cap, which she could use only when direst need demanded it. The girl had a receptive mind; she understood the aged fairy's instruction quickly and well and put her into an awkward position by asking her questions about her own fate.

Tertulla had long ago applied her knowledge to foresee Aurora's future, but every time she saw several graves, Aurora in the arms of a handsome man, and herself as a beneficent mother, surrounded by unfamiliar objects. She carefully kept this from her daughter and assured her that one could never learn the fate of close loved ones, for no one was adept enough to master that difficult art. She strictly forbade her from trying and asked her sincerely soon to become Oglu's wife. Weeping, Aurora threw her arms around Tertulla's neck, and Tertulla kept silent, trying not to upset her further. More than ever, Aurora kept her distance from Oglu and his brothers, partially from her disgust at him, partially from a loathing of their way of life.

A violent storm had raged for several days. The storm was more terrible than any Aurora had seen, and the great dashing waves washed onto the shore many people, who were then eaten with great relish by the giants. One day when the giants had celebrated just such a wild feast, Aurora paced thoughtfully up and down the riverbank, weeping for the unfortunate castaways from the wreck who had found their death in the waves and then served as a repast for these monsters. Suddenly, the waves tossed a dead body at her feet. At first she was greatly alarmed, but then as she looked more closely at the dead man and found him to be a pale yet very handsome youth, she decided to drag and carry him as well as she could into her little hut, which luckily was nearby. She was filled with boundless joy when, following her vigorous jostling, a rush of river water gushed out of his mouth, and after a bit a pair of large eyes gazed at her with gentle exhaustion.

She knelt near him, beside herself with ecstasy, pressed his hand to her heart, and rubbed his cheeks and temples until his blood began to circulate properly again and her ardor brought the pale youth fully back to life. As soon as he had recovered sufficiently, he rose and knelt before Aurora and tried through gestures to show her his gratitude. Cheered by his appearance, happy because of her possession of such a lovely being to whom her heart was deeply drawn, Aurora leaped about as happy as a child. But as soon as she remembered that the giants would eat him, too, she became pale as death. Her joy was at an end, and she stood before him with tears in her eyes, on her face an expression of fear and pain.

Through her gestures she tried to make him understand. She led him before the hut and anxiously showed him that he should seek to return where he came from. He, in response, showed her the rushing river and the towering gray waves, and as he pulled back with a shudder, Aurora had a thought that restored her cheerfulness. She took up her bow, grasped his hand tenderly, and indicated to him that he should follow. She led him along isolated and dangerous paths to her small, hidden cave.

No person on earth could have been happier than Aurora then, for she had her darling in safety. She pulled him to a bed of soft moss, stroked his burning cheeks, disappeared for a moment, and brought him fruit and cool water in a mussel shell. As soon as the beloved youth was refreshed, she gave him to understand that she would have to leave him for some time but that he should not leave the cave. The youth understood her, and although he did not know what danger awaited him that so frightened the lovely girl on his behalf, he did promise her to stay and, deeply moved, pressed her hands to his lips.

When Aurora was gone, he examined the interior of his new home. He admired the simple yet appropriate taste of the beautiful savage, which was what he considered Aurora to be. While doing so, he noticed among the wilted and fresh garlands of flowers that adorned the cave's walls a long, silk ribbon, yellowed with age, on whose end there were still traces of gold lettering. Curious, he pulled it out. Who could describe his astonishment and joy when he found on the less worn side the full name of his long-lost betrothed and relative of sixteen years! For he was Frederick, Aurora's betrothed. He had been on a trip to visit his uncle when a violent storm tossed the ship against the rocks. The whole crew had perished in the waves, and he alone had been miraculously rescued on the shore of the Giants' Forest.

Deep joy overwhelmed him. He sank onto the grassy bank and was so lost in his thoughts that he did not notice Aurora until she stood smiling before him and spoke to him in his mother tongue. She had left him to use the wishing cap to wish for the ability to speak his language. Who was more delighted than Frederick! He watched her with utmost love, and as he drew her softly into his arms and pressed the first kiss on the blushing girl's lips, he said with a trembling voice, "Aurora, beloved! You are not a savage; you are a close relative of mine, the bride promised to me in your cradle!" He pressed her to his heart anew; his lips were silent, but his caresses convinced Aurora how great his ecstasy was, how deeply he loved her. Finally, she extricated herself from his arms, sat next to him, and said laughingly, "I have heard your words, but I do not understand them. I am the daughter of a giantess who is long since dead. Our queen, Tertulla, raised me herself out of compassion. But now I am to marry her son Oglu, and since I do not like him at all, I sought out this cave. It is hidden from all human eyes. Here I will seek refuge, if I cannot escape on the day I am to become Oglu's wife."

Frederick saw in one glance the extent of his misfortune. Yet in order not to distress his beloved, he did not let her see it; rather, he told her of her heritage, the misfortune of her youth, and finally of their family relations and of the sacred claim he had had to her since the cradle and swaddling clothes. He called her by her real name, Aurora, and had the pleasure of seeing that this name seemed familiar to her, and in truth hearing this name did seem to bring many memories together in her head that had until now slumbered in her soul. She was startled as if out of a dream. "Yes," she said happily, "you are my relative, and I did have parents! Oh, are they still alive? Oh, let us flee! Your dear life is in danger. I will tell you everything, but now I must hurry so that I do not give my foster mother cause for suspicion."

She pulled herself out of his arms, and, pleading with him not to leave the cave, she handed him fruits and plants for his dinner and raced with the speed and agility of a mountain goat from boulder to boulder toward her little hut on the shore.

Already from a distance she heard Tertulla loudly calling her by name, a name that echoed ten times through the valleys. She hurried all the more quickly and arrived breathlessly at Tertulla's feet. Tertulla reproached Aurora bitterly for straying so far and causing her so much worry. The charming girl easily pacified the old fairy, but then Tertulla told her that the family had decided unanimously that they would celebrate their son's marriage at the next human sacrifice. Every objection was dismissed, all Aurora's caresses were for naught. For the first time Tertulla was truly angry, for the first time intractable. She left Aurora in a terrible state with outpourings of rage that made her tremble.

Midnight found Aurora sunk deep in despair, but a ray of hope suddenly refreshed her spirit. She sought out some dried fish from her hut and found some cider in a barrel, and since she found the giantess with her sons in deep sleep, she hurried to her beloved, who was still awake, sitting on his pallet. She explained the proximity and magnitude of their shared danger, but she did not withhold an explanation of how she planned to use the wishing cap to save them – the same cap with which she had so quickly learned his language. The prince found this means to be most reliable, and after they had spent some time in sweet chatter, Aurora went back to Tertulla. Before going, however, she stressed to her lover that he must exercise the greatest caution.

Exhausted from the many events of the previous day, Aurora fell into a deep sleep from which she was awakened only at midday by Oglu's cries of joy. Tertulla knelt beside her bed as she awoke; in her face the unhappy girl read the news, and, full of horror, she heard that early that morning Oglu had found a white man asleep deep in the cliffs. He would now serve as the sacrifice to celebrate their wedding day. As deep an impression as this horrible news made on Aurora, she still pulled all her strength together and promised with great equanimity to become Oglu's wife if he came to her and did not refuse to grant her one small request.

Tertulla hurried immediately with this happy news to her son, and the young giant, who loved Aurora with all the passion that such a rough heart can achieve, came without delay to her side. She had hardly seen him enter her hut when she threw herself at his feet and with all the charm that stood at her disposal repeated her promise if Oglu would grant her this single request: to let her care for the prisoner and his needs until his death. Oglu lifted the pleading girl up, kissed her brow, and immediately gave the order to deliver the prisoner, bound with chains, into the hut of his beloved so that she could feed him during that day and eat the first morsel of him the next. Aurora swore even that, and in a few minutes the unfortunate fellow was in her hut. He had left the cave earlier that morning and had fallen asleep next to a spring and thus was easy prey for Oglu's snare. As soon as she saw him, she said a few words in his language, telling him to play along. She then treated him like a prisoner and joked all day with such glee that even sly old Tertulla was misled and took her cunning for the truth.

Only after the evening star was in the heavens, after the men were snoring in their beds, drunk from the sweet cider, did she leave Tertulla, at whose side she slept in a shared bed, and hurried to her beloved, who pressed her to his heart in despair. But Aurora was strong. She told him her plans and filled his soul with hope. Just as she was loosening his chains, Tertulla entered the hut. Terrified, the lovers parted, and the cunning old woman acted as if she had not noticed; she simply commanded Aurora to lead the prisoner to their shared sleeping quarters and to give him a spot next to her sons. With quaking knees Aurora followed her orders; she guessed her foster mother's intentions in this moment and decided half in despair to use every means to save her beloved. She tried to give him more courage than she herself had. While he lay down next to the soundly sleeping monsters, she took from the head of the eldest son the stone crown, which all the sons of the giantess wore day and night, and pressed it quickly onto her beloved's head. She then lay down next to the old woman and pretended to be sound asleep. What she had suspected came true. When Tertulla believed the girl was fast asleep, she got up quietly, felt in the darkness for the heads of her sons, and with a few stabs in the heart murdered the man whose head bore no crown.

Frederick took fright as he heard the moaning of a dying giant next to him. But since everything thereafter became quiet, he was about to fall asleep again when Aurora's silver voice called softly to him to follow her silently; she led him deeper than before into her cave and then fled back to the side of Tertulla, who was still sound asleep.

Hardly had she lain down again, and the first rays of sun fell into the cave, when a loud wailing began. The giants were grieving for their brother, whom Tertulla had killed in Frederick's stead. The mother was beside herself and declared herself the murderer of her own son; she surmised Aurora's sleight of hand and would have doubtless taken bloody revenge on her had not Oglu taken the trembling girl under his protection. Meanwhile, the others stormed out, looking for the stranger, and after Oglu reconciled mother and beloved, he hurried after his brothers to make the unhappy youth feel the magnitude of his pain. Aurora trembled before the return of the giants.

While Tertulla was weeping beside her son's corpse, Aurora got hold of the wishing cap, and she had barely put it safely away when the sons of Anak returned. They lamented their brother's death with horrible howls and made it clear to Aurora that she would become their brother's wife that day or else suffer the most terrible excesses of their rage. During all the sixteen years of her stay in the Giants' Forest she had never seen such fiery eyes or heard such ghastly voices. Trembling, she huddled close to Oglu, who was mollified by her tears and promised her total protection from his brothers and a postponement of the marriage until the next day.

During the first moment that she had no witnesses, she made use of the magic she had learned, conjuring the rosebush that stood next to their pallets to take on her voice and to answer Tertulla's questions. As soon as she had finished this task, which was fairly difficult given her inexperience, she hurried back to the hut, where she stayed until nightfall; only later, in the shadow of the night, did she flee with her wishing cap to her anxiously waiting beloved. He had heard the roaring of the giants all around him, and even if he did not understand their language, he had interpreted their vehement howls to mean that he was the object of their search. As soon as they had recovered somewhat, the lovers wished themselves to be a thousand miles away from the Giants' Forest and instantly found themselves in a charming region where a dark green pomegranate forest invited them to rest in its shadows and refresh themselves with its lovely fruit.

While the lovers were resting there in total safety, whispering a thousand pleasantries to one another, Tertulla was waking up. She felt next to her and, because she found Aurora's spot empty, cried with a clear voice, "My little daughter, where are you?" And just as loudly the rosebush answered, "I am sitting at the fire, warming myself." Fully reassured by this answer and accustomed to Aurora's nightly wanderings, Tertulla fell asleep again. But as the rays of the morning sun awakened her anew and Aurora was still not in her spot, she jumped up hastily and cried anxiously, "My little daughter, where are you?" And just as placidly as before the rosebush gave the same answer. In vain the giantess ran to the fire; in vain she sought the missing girl everywhere. Aurora was gone, and Tertulla trembled for her own life, for she knew the rage of her sons. She hurried to the secret spot where the wishing cap was hidden, the treasure with which she had weathered every storm, but what a shock! It also was missing. What choices did she have? Her last and only hope was a pair of fairy boots, in which she covered one mile for every step. She put them on without much thought, and before her sons had awakened, she was already many thousands of miles away from them.

Something – the mysterious twinge of sympathy for Aurora, for she still loved her, or perhaps just chance – led her along the same route that the lovers had taken. She had almost reached them when Aurora sensed her presence. She informed her beloved immediately and wished herself into a peach tree full of lovely and delicious fruit, wished the cap into her treetop, and wished her lover into a bee. Just as the transformations had taken place, Tertulla came panting past them and disappeared from sight. But in the same instant a whirlwind rose up, grabbed the magical cap, and carried it off. It finally stopped, landing beneath the window of the lovely daughter of the king who owned this park. She, who was already familiar with magic objects such as the cap, took it in and kept it carefully until the true owner could be found. The fate of the lovers was horrifying: Aurora was totally frozen in place, and Frederick, with only a small amount of energy and unable to speak, was able to help neither her nor himself.

Chance did its part. On the evening of the same day the king's daughter took a walk in her park to enjoy the lovely fragrance of the trees. She noticed the magnificent peach tree and approached it to eat of its fruit. Suddenly, she felt the pain of a bee sting on her lovely hand. Petulantly, she chased the bee away, but it flew off only until she approached the tree again. The bee was relentless in its attacks, and in a few moments the princess had been stung several times. Full of bitter displeasure, she finally pulled a leaf off the tree. Great drops of blood flowed from it, and she surmised an enchantment. She hurried back to the castle, picked up the wishing cap, and threw the cap up into the treetop. Seconds later, she had the pleasure of seeing a charming couple who could not find words enough to express their thanks. The pain of the bee stings was wished away, and so all three cheerfully went to see the father of the clever and beautiful rescuer. The lovers told him their amazing story, which brought him unending pleasure, particularly the description of the Giants' Forest. He remembered that Aurora's father had been his friend in his youth, and on the next day when the lovers wished themselves to be back with their parents, he sent all his best wishes and promised to attend the wedding with his daughter, if they gave them enough notice and could make the trip pleasantly short for them by means of the cap.

Aurora's parents' joy was inexpressible as Frederick led their beloved, long-lamented daughter to them. His own father was immediately summoned, and the good king and his daughter were transported in the most comfortable fashion to the wedding. Happiness and celebration abounded. The castle rang with cries of joy, drums, and trumpets. The hands of the early-betrothed, early-separated pair, reunited by fate, had already been joined together when suddenly the doors opened and Tertulla stepped in, out of breath. She sank into Aurora's arms and asked for protection from her evil sons, for a quiet little spot where she could live out her remaining days.

Aurora was touched; she introduced her parents to her childhood guardian, and they thanked Tertulla warmly for all the goodness she had bestowed on Aurora. She was esteemed by everyone. The bridal pair welcomed her fondly, and as soon as the honeymoon was past, Frederick left with a substantial army with which to fight Tertulla's evil sons. He almost annihilated them, and the few who escaped his sword fled into the deepest recesses of the cliffs where no one could reach them and where, now and then, their progeny may still be spotted. Tertulla stayed with Aurora. She loved her more than all her sons, and she rocked Aurora's children in her lap until they were grown.

TRANSLATED BY JEANNINE BLACKWELL

Karoline von Günderrode

1780–1806

The Romantic poet Karoline von Günderrode is best known for her lyric poetry and letters, published posthumously in 1840 by her friend Bettina von Arnim and partially translated by Margaret Fuller in 1842. A member of the poorer nobility, Günderrode lived in a Lutheran cloister in Frankfurt am Main until she committed suicide at the age of twenty-six.

During her brief lifetime, two volumes of her *Gedichte und Phantasien* (Poems and fantasies) were published under the evocative, exotic, ungendered pseudonym Tian. Among those fantasies were adaptations of the elegiac works of Ossian, allegedly ancient texts actually written by James Mac-Pherson. "Temora" is one of those Ossian fantasies.

Although the German title, "Timur," seems to point to variations on the name of the infamous Mongolian ruler Tamerlane (or Temür, ca.1320–1405), Günderrode's actual source was MacPherson's *Temora, an Ancient Epic Poem in Eight Books* (London: T. Becket and P. A. de Hondt, 1763). It tells of Thia, who falls in love with Duth-Carmor and yet takes up arms to kill him in war. He dies alone in a distant land.

The older prophetess in this story reminds readers of Velleda and her visionary gifts, while the problematic love of the heroine, Thia, finds resonance with the mermaid's plight in Ricarda Huch's "Pack of Lies." A similar tale of poignant and ill-fated love of a magic girl and the man who enters her realm can be found in Susan Wade's "Like a Red, Red Rose" (in Datlow and Windling, eds., *Snow White, Blood Red*). The underground journey through which a heroine/queen leads her lover appears here, as in Amalie von Helwig's "The Symbols" and Marie von Ebner-Eschenbach's "The Princess of Banalia." Father-daughter dysfunction, a standard motif in fairy tales, is featured here as well as in "The Old Man in the Cave," "The Rescued Princess," and "The Fragrance of Flowers."

[Karoline von Günderrode], "Timur," in *Gedichte und Phantasien von Tian* (Hamburg and Frankfurt: J. C. Herrmann, 1804), 15–31.

Temora

1804

ERMAR HAD TOPPLED the house of Parimor from the throne. Parimor himself, his wife, and his retinue had fallen under the sword of his conqueror; Temora alone, his only son, fell, still living, into Ermar's hands. The land was loathe to bend to the will of the victor, who occupied the fortress of the unfortunate Parimor on the northern coast of the island and who shared absolute power with his brother, wild Konnar.

None of the friends of the deposed royal house knew where Temora was or even if he lived. The prophetess alone knew, the silent seer who lived in a cave at the entrance to the earth. She saw the approaching fates, the depths of the human soul, and the shackles of the unfortunate Temora. The prophetess lived apart and accomplished secretive tasks, and of all the mortals only Thia, Ermar's lovely daughter, knew of her abode. The seer loved the girl and taught her many secrets. She often revealed to her things yet to come.

Once the prophetess spoke thus to the daughter of Ermar: "Child! Fear for your father's fate! His cruel deed has awakened the ghost of revenge. Look here!" And in a mirror she showed the terrified girl a deep dungeon in the fortress; lying on rotting straw in the dungeon was a youth with burning eyes and thick brown locks. Thia could not feast her eyes enough, gazing at the prisoner. But the seer spoke: "This is the king of this land. He languishes in chains, and your father wears the crown that is his by right."

Deep in thought, Thia rushed to her father's fortress and searched all around for a door leading to Temora's prison cell. To the north the fortress was surrounded by craggy cliffs that stretched to the sea, and in these cliffs, hidden between underbrush and nettles, Thia discovered a grate that covered a dark abyss. She had seen the grate in the magic mirror, and every morning before the inhabitants of the castle awoke, and every evening when the mild twilight cloaked the deeds of love in its veil, she went forth, sat mourning beside the grate, and sighed, "Temora! Temora!" And it seemed to her as if invisible loving arms came up from the grate and embraced her so that she could not leave the spot, and she did not seem to care that the raw night wind blew around her and the dew of heaven drenched her.

Temora had languished for two years in the dungeon. His wild thoughts of revenge had already paled and diminished, and his dreams of salvation and rescue had all been dreamed out. He already felt himself forgotten by the whole human race when he thought he heard a sweet voice whisper his name, and every morning and every evening thereafter he heard the same voice calling, "Temora! Temora!" And when he slumbered on his pallet, he thought an angel with shining locks and rose-colored cheeks bent down to him, pressing gentle kisses on his lips and sighing, "Temora!" When he awoke, the rosy cheeks vanished in the black of the dungeon, the brilliant locks faded, and the kisses cooled, but the sweet voice whispered on, and he knew not whether the dream was real or whether what seemed real was a dream.

Days and weeks had thus passed when the girl spoke to Ermar: "Father! The prophetess has proclaimed calamity and ruin for you because of the son of Parimor, who languishes innocent in your chains. Your injustice will awake the ghost of revenge. Fear him!"

"Temora's power is shackled," responded Ermar. "Where is the arm that will carry out this revenge?"

"Fear for the future," spoke Thia, "and fear the seer's unerring words. I have seen Temora. I love him. Give him his freedom, give him to me, shackle him to yourself through a holy band of wedlock, or fear your daughter as well."

But Ermar was unrelenting until his daughter threw herself at his feet and swore to make her beloved a true son and friend to her father or else, should he prove ungrateful, to betray him and to stab him through the heart with a dagger during their embrace.

Temora lay in restless dreams; the ghost of his father appeared to him in a bloody shroud and spoke, "Avenge me! The time has come!" Temora awoke, with the words "The time has come!" still in his ears. He was still pondering this as the grate opened and a soldier entered and bid him follow. Silent, filled with strange forebodings, Temora followed his guide. When they arrived on the cliffs, the soldier withdrew, and Ermar approached the youth. "The time has come! Avenge me!" whispered a voice in Temora's soul. An invisible force compelled him; before Ermar could speak, the youth seized him and flung him down the cliffs so that his blood smoked down into the sea.

The castle dwellers gathered. They recognized the son of their king and jubilantly declared him their lord and master. But when night came and the king was alone, Thia approached him and spoke: "I loved you. I stood watch at the door of your prison cell, and entrusted your name to the night and the stars. Your freedom is my own deed, but you have murdered my father. You have laden my soul with blood guilt. I must flee from you!"

The girl left and did not return. The king became sad. The noisy hunts brought him no cheer, nor did the well-filled cup. He stood alone on his cliffs and looked out and saw nothing more than the terrors of approaching winter. The sky was covered with heavy clouds, icy rain began to fall, and the north wind ripped through the forest and drove the pale yellow leaves about in wild, winding circles. The surf surged on the shore, and the cawing raven answered its echoes. Thus passed the months, and the cold rain and snow kept falling, and the sky stayed as dark as Temora's soul. Then his friends gathered around him and spoke. "It is not good, Your Majesty, that you mourn in solitude! Let us do deeds; Konnar stills rules with an iron scepter over the folk on the other side of the mountain. Come! Reconquer your birthright, vanquish the traitors!" The youth obeyed; he pulled himself out of his dreaming and plunged into the fury of battle for victory and fame.

The outcome of the fight between Konnar and Temora hung in the balance. Temora was brave, and Konnar was resilient and clever. One battle was in Konnar's favor, and Temora had to withdraw into the mountains. The day passed in the roar of fighting, in thrusts and parries, but when night fell, and Mars was lulled into slumber, Temora's retinue gathered around him. In the ravines of the lonely mountains and the thick forests of the night where no spying enemy could find them, they set up a colorful tent. A hundred torches lit up the wilderness, cups of cheer were handed round, sweet music accompanied by the voices of brown-haired girls sounded forth, and Temora reveled in fame and lust and love, his company exulting in wild pleasures.

But once, when Temora was alone on his cot and sleep escaped him, he thought he heard the sound of soft feet, and as he listened, he suddenly felt the embrace of tender arms and hot, yearning kisses covering his lips. But when he awoke, his cot was empty. Three nights the mystery lover visited the king's bed; when she came for the fourth time, he held her in his arms and begged her not to leave until she had revealed her name so that he could share his throne and his eminence with her. "Let me leave once more, unknown to you," spoke the girl. "When night returns and the stars gleam again, a black steed will stand before you. Trust it; it will lead you to the place where all will become clear." The king let the girl go.

When it was night, he did indeed find the horse. A strange shiver ran through his body, but he mounted the horse, and it carried him through mysterious and tortuous paths, through ravines and forests, stopping before a splendidly lit palace. The gates opened, and two boys emerged. They held the reins for Temora and led him into a great hall. Mild twilight enveloped the place, for over a pool in which sweet balsam water splashed, only a half moon illuminated the room with shimmering light. The moon gleamed purple, then pale pink, then again blue like the heavens, then finally the lush green of a verdant meadow.

Astonished, Temora watched the play of changing colors. Then the door opened, and several lovely girls wearing all sorts of foreign and exotic finery entered. A flower wreath encircled one's blond hair, and a delicate white robe flowed around her. Another exuded Arabia's balsam, the costly dew of the Orient surrounded the brilliant rows of her black locks, and gold-wrought Persian silk veiled her voluptuous limbs. A third, dressed in delicate silver gauze, resembled the ethereal daughters of the air. The loveliest creatures of every clime seemed to gather around the youth. Suddenly, the water glowed like the sun and poured forth streams of light into the hall. Music like organ tones sounded in the air; a sweet voice accompanied the murmuring harmonies and hovered above them as a light spring zephyr floats over the roaring sea, but the notes grew louder and louder and drowned out the voice in melodious waves. The girls surrounded the youth and spoke friendly words to him, and each sent ardent glances his way as if she alone were the nightly lover. The king watched them intently; each seemed to him lovely and charming, but none moved his heart. "The one I seek is not here," said his innermost soul.

Then two doors flew open, and a splendid hall was revealed by lights of torches that glimmered on the marble walls. In the center stood a table. All the company was seated. The wine pearled into golden drops. The girls sipped with rosy lips from the goblets and offered them to the king. But Temora's soul was sad; he lowered his eyes, and all the magnificence and all the beauty were lost on him. As he raised his eyes again, however, he saw a figure in the opposite corner of the hall leaning on a column. She was cloaked in black and did not stir. Temora watched her long and often; a deep yearning drew him to her. The feast seemed unending to him, and he felt better only when they rose from the table.

The girls left the hall, still sending him inviting glances, but he did not follow them, and finally he found himself alone with the black figure. The torches were extinguished; a single pale light glimmered through the hall. The black figure approached him and spoke: "Follow me!" He obeyed, and she led him through strange underground passages to the top of a cliff. The full moon beamed, and Temora, shivering, recognized the cliff and the sea into which he had flung Ermar. His guide pulled back her veil. It was Thia. "Ghost of my father!" she cried. "Let this sacrifice avenge you." And with that, she threw her arms around the king and plunged with him down the cliff, so that their blood mingled and smoked down into the surging sea.

TRANSLATED BY JEANNINE BLACKWELL

A bacchante drunk with wine's fragrance. Drawing by
Bettina von Arnim. Undated. Reprinted with permission
of the Stiftung Weimarer Klassik, GSA 10-33/201.

Bettina von Arnim

1785–1859

Bettina Brentano von Arnim embodied in her life and works the great spectrum of fairy tale production in Germany. Her mother, Maximiliane von La Roche Brentano, told stories and tales to Bettina and her eighteen brothers and sisters, six of whom were stepsiblings from her father's first marriage. After her parents' deaths in 1793 and 1797, Bettina was raised by her grandmother Sophie von La Roche, the most renowned woman novelist of her time in Germany. Bettina cast her childhood as an autobiographical fairy tale in a letter to her older brother, the Romantic author of fairy tales Clemens Brentano. This story was first published by Bettina in *Frühlingskranz* (published in English as *Clemens Brentano's Wreath of Spring*) in 1844. "The Queen's Son," her first fairy tale, was penned for her fiancé, Achim von Arnim, in 1808. It was to be published in his journal, the *Hermit,* which folded before the tale could appear. A close friend of the Grimm brothers, she, her brother Clemens, and her husband, Achim, were deeply involved in the first collection of the *Tales* from 1805 to 1812, and the Grimms dedicated the collection to Bettina and her young son Freimund, one of the Arnims' seven children. Because of her continuing support of the Grimms and their family during their political struggles, they continued to dedicate later editions to her.

In Berlin, Bettina and, later, her daughters Gisela, Maximiliane, and Armgart held salons that attracted the best minds of Europe: Karl Marx, Heinrich Heine, Hans Christian Andersen, the Schumanns, the Grimm family, and many intellectuals and radicals. Gisela married Herman Grimm, one of Wilhelm Grimm's three children, completing the long family friendship.

Bettina's untitled fairy tale was first printed in *Westermanns Monatshefte* 113 (1913): 554–58 and given the title "Königssohn" at that time by modern editors; neither of the two manuscript versions, located today in the Goethe-Schiller Archives of the Stiftung Weimarer Klassik and the Freies deutsches Hochstift in Frankfurt , has a title.

This tale, like several others from the Arnim women and the Kaffeterkreis, shows the marks of a source in oral narration. It recaptures the immediacy of an oral version in its repetition of key words and shifts in tense when the action intensifies. It provides a commentary on the chasm between "man" and nature, male and female, and the powerful and the powerless.

"The Queen's Son" can be compared to tales of "The Peaceable Kingdom" and Maurice Sendak's "Where the Wild Things Are." The queen on a heroic quest in nature, as found here, appears in many other tales, such as Benedikte Naubert's "Boadicea and Velleda," "East o' the Sun, West o' the Moon," and Marie von Ebner-Eschenbach's "The Princess of Banalia."

The following translation is a slightly revised version of "The Queen's Son" that appears in Blackwell and Zantop, eds., *Bitter Healing,* 450–54. Used by permission of the University of Nebraska Press. Copyright © 1990 by the University of Nebraska Press.

The Queen's Son

1808

O NCE UPON A TIME there was a king who had a magnificent land, and from his castle on a high mountain he could see far into the distance. Behind the castle, beautiful gardens had been laid out for his pleasure; they were surrounded by splendid rivers and dense forests full of game. Lions, tigers had their dwelling there, wild cats crouched in the trees, foxes and wolves roamed in the thickets, white bears and also ones with golden fur often swam across the rivers in pairs and came into the king's garden. In the treetops nested eagles, vultures, and falcons. The forests were like a true kingdom of animals that encircled that of the king, and it was seen as theirs alone.

But then the king took a wife for her beauty and to have children. When she was with child, the common folk rejoiced that they would have an heir to the throne, and they held the woman in high esteem for it. But the time for the birth passed without her bearing a child. This made the king very sad, for he believed that his consort was ill and would soon die, yet she kept on taking food and drink like a healthy woman. The queen stayed with child for seven years. The king grew angry at her deformity and thought that she had sinned against God, since He was punishing her so. The king had her rooms separated from his own, and she was forced to live in the rear part of the castle. There she carried her heavy burden slowly and sadly through the lonely gardens and saw the wild animals coming out of the forest to drink on the far bank of the river. When springtime came and the old lions and tigers came with their young and suckled them, she would often wish in deep despair that she, too, was a beast of prey in the forest, wresting her food from life in a raging fight, just to feed her young. "But like this," she said, "I must wander here through the garden with heavy pace and heavy care. Every year I see you bearing your fruit, and I see how you raise your young ones in your wild, rough way. But I, a king's daughter, the queen, shall never raise my own noble progeny and be happy but rather be hated by the king, my husband."

Then one day, as she sat in a lonely spot under a palm tree, she felt pains, and she bore a son. He seemed to have the strength of a seven-year-old boy, for as he came into the world, a wild she-bear had ventured across the river, and he was barely out of the womb before he chased after her, catching her by the pelt; the bear swam back across and carried him off with her into the forest. Then the queen cried out in a powerful mother's voice: "My son, my only child, is in the forest and will be devoured by wild animals!" The king's guards came running and charged into the river toward the forests with bludgeons and bows and arrows to recapture the son of their lord. But when the animals saw these violent men invading their kingdom, they rushed from the woods onto the shore to defend themselves. The bears sat up erect and stretched out their claws, the lions bared their teeth and twitched their tails, the tigers roamed back and forth on the shore with fiery eyes, the wolves howled, the elephants stirred up dirt and pushed boulders into the water, the birds flew from their nests and filled the air with horrible shrieks so that none of the brave knights dared to climb up the bank. Thus they swam back to the deserted queen, for they believed that the king's son was indeed lost. But when they came to her, they found that she was again in labor, bringing six more children into the world, each of them happier and stronger than the last, so there was little grief for the lost son. The queen was brought before the king with the six babes as a glorious mother, and he received her with honors and jubilation.

The children grew, and the queen cared for them with great patience and gave them nourishment, but when evening came and she had put them to sleep, she would go behind the castle to the spot where she had sat and the she-bear had taken her child. She would go down to the water to try to lure her son out of the undergrowth. Deep in her heart she worried very little about her other children, only about this one, and she could not convince herself that he was dead. She was like a shepherd who cares more about the one lost lamb than about the whole flock and believes this lamb to be the best and only one. She is no longer afraid of the wild animals whenever she hears them howling in the night, and whenever one animal wanders into the garden, she runs up to it and asks about her child, but they don't understand her. Then she becomes impatient and desperate, she threatens and pleads and grabs the bears by the fur and says, "You have stolen my son from me!" They seem to care nothing about it, though, and act like animals do. They recognize the woman and do her no harm.

When she returns to the castle, she wipes away her tears and bends her face over the restless children, thus hiding her tears, and says, "My poor children are restless and cold, I must warm them and feed them so they will quiet down." Thus she hides her sadness from people the whole day long and never turns her face to the sunlight, for she is ashamed that she feels more love for her lost son than for the others. She raises them, to be sure, with great patience and wisdom during the day. But in the evening, when the children are asleep, she searches after her son. She tells the great hawks that glide high up in the sky, flying back and forth, to take her boy some food. She says, again and again, "O you winged creatures, if only I could float in the air and look down into the thickets to seek my son. Oh, tell me please if he is still alive, or if you have seen him dead?" When the birds scream incomprehensibly in the air, she thinks she can understand them and pushes back her hair the better to hear. She thinks the birds are calling to her that he is alive and will come to her soon. She tries hard to interpret their cries. She even speaks to the bees and the buzzing insects that hover over the water. They swarm around her, humming and buzzing, each in its own way, and then they fly away again. Oh, poor queen, not even one wild, ignorant animal will give you counsel. They know nothing of human lament! For humans persecute them and have no communion with them at all. Humans stalk after them to get their skins or to eat their flesh, but never did a human turn to them in sorrow, asking for consolation. Many a noble beast has grieved for the freedom that cunning humans have robbed from it. They have grieved that they must serve as slaves, which was not their task and which went against their very nature, and they have gotten only dry hay to eat for their pains when they could have eaten fresh, tender leaves in the forest. They have grieved that they had to be bridled and be ruled by the whip. So animals do not trust humans and avoid their path. And when they are cornered and helpless, they attack people and tear their bodies horribly, just to protect their freedom or their young.

Meanwhile, the children were growing up and were raised in wisdom; they were peaceable in spirit and noble in every respect. The king could not decide on which to bestow the crown, for it could not be said which was the firstborn or which would be better at ruling. When they competed in a game for a prize, it often happened that they all won the same prize or that they all excelled in their own special way. The king could not love one of them more than the others, for each was handsome, and their demeanor was like the iridescent feathers of an alluring bird in the sunshine: if it turns this way, then the red or green shimmers most splendidly; if it turns that way, then another color shines forth or yet another; if it struts and moves its wings, the colors change as fast as lightning, one as beautiful as the next. One cannot decide which is the most breathtaking of all. Or they were like a rainbow, where all the colors are beautifully combined, spanning the distant sky, so that each seems to grow out of the other. But the king did not have the right to divide his land or to give it to more than one ruler. So he had a large crown made from pure gold that would encompass the heads of his six children, and he said to them, "As long as your hearts stay as pure as this gold and you hold together as one, so that all your heads are encompassed in this ring, and you embrace each other in love, I will be able to say, 'My land has only one lord, and although it has many bodies, it has only one spirit.' "

Then he had a great feast prepared at which the people could see the new kings. All the nobles gathered at court. Out in the open air there was a great throne of gold where the king's sons sat, and the king placed the crown on their heads. The quiet, lonely mother was dressed in jeweled splendor, with golden veils and robes, and there was jubilation at her appearance. People called her the glorious mother and played splendid music on all the instruments to honor her. But she hides her face behind the veil and weeps bitter tears for her lost child. Then her sons step down from their seats, fall to their knees, and ask for their mother's blessing. She stands up and, with her right hand, blesses her children, but she holds her left over her heart in memory of her son.

The wild animals had heard the celebrating throughout the land and had grown restless; they swam across the rivers in great hordes. When the guards brought this horrible news, all the people fled to their homes, but the mother would not leave, for she had no fear. Her sons did not want to desert their mother when she did not heed their pleas and stayed to protect her. The horde of animals came onward, and among them appeared a beautiful face that looked upward toward the sky and seemed to be a human, only more beautiful and noble. He rides on the backs of the lions and tigers, jumping gracefully from one to the other. When his mother sees him, she says, "This is my son," and goes bravely to meet him; she embraces him and feels a stone move from her heart. The animals recognize the woman and do her no harm. But the boy had no human language, he could only express his will through signs. Therefore, he takes the crown and turns it seven times around his head, and with a strong hand, he tore an olive tree out of the earth, and gave each of his six brothers a branch while keeping the trunk for himself, to mean: "I am the master! But you shall all live with me in peace." And he became king of the animals and of humankind in spirit, without language.

TRANSLATED BY JEANNINE BLACKWELL

Amalie von Helwig

1776–1831

An important contributor to the literary enterprise of her times, Amalie von Helwig participated in the intellectual debates and high society of Berlin in the 1810s and 1820s and was named to the court by Amalie of Weimar. Like Benedikte Naubert, von Helwig used her knowledge of classical Greek, French, and English when compiling her collections of legends and sagas; her most famous works include several epic poems about traditional Greek myths like *Die Schwestern von Lesbos* (The sisters from Lesbos, 1801), *Die Schwestern auf Corcyra* (The sisters on Corfu, 1812), and *Taschenbuch der Sagen und Legenden* (The pocket guide to proverbs and legends, volume 1, 1812, volume 2, 1817).

A highly complex narrative consisting of a dedication, a fairy tale text, and a scholarly codicil, *Die Sage vom Wolfsbrunnen* (The saga of Wolfsbrunnen) is a nine-chapter novel that continues the story of the younger Velleda (here "Welleda") from Benedikte Naubert's 1795 novel *Velleda, ein Zauberroman*. Ostensibly about the history of Heidelberg, the tale describes Welleda's solitary life as a sorceress and her fatal attraction to a well-intentioned lover from the real world. Because of a curse on her father, Welleda's conflicted love leads to her own demise. In this chapter, "The Symbols," Welleda guides her lover, Ferrand, into a cave on a thinly disguised tour of the female reproductive system.

Von Helwig's text clearly reflects the Romantic writers' interest in classical mythology (she likens Welleda, for example, to the three Greek moon goddesses: Hecate, Diana, and Selene). This chapter also participates in a discussion that engaged Romantic circles: the nature of the elements and the spirits that reside in them. There is an examination both of the Greek concept of the four elements – earth, fire, air, and water – and of Paracelsus's (1493–1551) theory of the "Tria prima," the three primary elements – sulfur, mercury, and salt. Paracelsus allied the elemental spirits with the elements themselves: undines with water, sylphs with air, gnomes with earth, and salamanders with fire.

Veleda's popularity as an object for artistic interpretation took form in other works such as Friedrich de la Motte-Fouqué's 1818 novel *Welleda und Ganna;* E. H. Maindron's 1843–44 marble statue *Velleda;* Franz Sigrist's drawing *Veleda, the Prophetess of the Brukteri;* and Sobolewsky's 1836 opera *Velleda.*

Other tales to read with von Helwig's piece include the story of Cupid and Psyche and Marie von Ebner-Eschenbach's "The Princess of Banalia" (compare the cave scene).

Amalie von Helwig, "Die Symbole," in *Die Sage vom Wolfsbrunnen. Mährchen* (Berlin: Realschulbuchhandlung, 1814), 35–52.

The Symbols

1814

T HE STARS were already fading in the morning twilight, and an amber glow dawned in the eastern sky as Ferrand, on the last steep precipice of the mountain, pressed on toward the place that he had carefully noted, despite the darkness of the night. Now he skirted the hedge where flowering cypresses intertwined with wild cherries and towered up to a bushy crown. Luxuriant periwinkles wove an azure carpet across the glen from which the iron blossoms, together with the dandelions, peeked their resplendent heads, while dainty buttercups seemed to sprout from the edge of the folded veil that surrounded like a palpable mist the maiden who reclined in sweet slumber.

The youth had arrived here with a pounding heart, but this unexpected vision forced any wild hopes back into the depths of his soul. No greater happiness could befall him than this moment, now that he espied his mysterious beloved in such natural sweet slumber, like a dear, innocent child on the bosom of its mother sharing in the succor sleep brings to mortals as it dispels pain and sorrow into tranquillity and oblivion. Her pristine features, delicately circumscribed by a veil, retained the charm that had captured Ferrand's heart; only her majesty had retreated to the inner chambers of her soul, and lashes shaded the eyes whose gleam so dazzled and enamored him. To be able just to watch her as in this moment seemed to one so reverently enamored a rapturous pleasure, and even if he had suspected how much he would sacrifice, a cautionary voice seemed to warn him how much more would he risk for even greater bliss.

In the meantime, the morning breezes wafted more strongly over the mountaintop, and a pair of tall, golden yellow blossoms poised on slender stems stood as on guard at the sleeping woman's head. Now they whispered to each other and then into Welleda's ear, who suddenly awoke, sat up, and blushed demurely as she became aware of the hunter leaning over a whitethorn at her feet. He looked as if he wanted to inhale her beloved image into his very soul.

"You are very punctual, fair friend," she said. "For that you deserve that I keep the promise I silently made to you." Upon saying this she leaped up quickly, like a deer who sees the hunter take aim from behind a bush, and without waiting for Ferrand's reply, she hurried toward the desolate rock face.

For the first time the stone seemed foreign to the youth's gaze, like a huge edifice that, although touched by time, was still imposing and serenely majestic. Among the pillars he could clearly make out towering images of deities, and, above the architrave, he saw a row of sinuous gargoyles whose graceful gestures and expressions spoke to him of other, heathen times.

By now the morning wind had seized the thin veil the maiden delicately held as she stepped out from between the pillars with a torch in her hand. As the ethereal mantle fluttered over her beautiful head in a play of lovely folds, dark, mysterious impressions of luminous Selene, stern Diana, and mighty Hecate merged into a mysterious constellation before Ferrand's agitated imagination. He seemed to himself a figure from that magical world of fables. No longer knowing if he waked or dreamed, he awaited in mute anticipation one of the transformations that, according to tales of yore, was the punishment of unwitting intruders.

Welleda smiled faintly and, sweetly beckoning, entreated him to follow her to the portal, where the torch's flickering flame played about the dusky pillars. Meanwhile, the sunrise cast a rosy glow in the eastern sky. Uncertain what he should do, Ferrand looked over to the friendly heralds of day as the maiden called, "Do you want to part from me before knowing me?" The recollection of her promise to satisfy his burning desire for enlightenment, but even more the tender look in her eye that floated in a dew of wistfulness, drew him inexorably into the mysterious portal.

Wordlessly, the two entered the narrow, vaulted passage, where the jagged rocks left only enough room for two wayfarers, and a precipitously narrow footpath dropped off into endless depths. The dizzying precipice made him feel that the maw of death was ready to swallow him up in a never-ending fall. Trapped in the dark, steep pass, he abandoned himself in sensuous dread to the powers of his guide. In order to lead him, she had slung her left arm about his neck, while with her right she carefully held the torch toward the sloping ground. As a miner in the deepest shaft keeps his eye on the rope that fatefully intertwines annihilation and salvation, so Ferrand surrendered himself utterly to discovering the magical creature who held his fate in her hands.

The sorceress had wound the soft veil around her head, burying her great mass of curls, and in the glow of the torch a magical diadem shimmered on her high forehead. In the veil Ferrand now imagined he recognized delicately entwined calyxes, then various animals, and then again mysterious symbols of a foreign tongue. Meanwhile, the diadem, no longer illuminated by the flame, transformed itself into midnight black, confounding her friend's probing gaze. As the delicate figure herself often seemed to vanish into the surrounding cloak of darkness, solitary sparks flickered ever and anon across her robe like shooting stars, while Ferrand struggled in vain to interpret the symbolic import of their strange glimmering.

Then, as if she had guessed what thoughts raced through his mind, Welleda placed her lover's hand on her heart. He felt its steady, rhythmic beat and trembled no more as they wandered among the masks of a make-believe world.

They must have been deep inside the earth when the narrow, dark chasm widened, and the two, now accustomed to the darkness, were blinded by shafts of light from the widening vault. Rich veins of gold and silver coiled along the walls; pillars of salt crystals stretched their length in gigantic prisms that shone and sparkled in rainbow hues, depending on the angle from which flitting will-o'-the-wisps approached them. Sometimes the creatures slithered on the ground like iridescent snakes; at other moments they illuminated the mortals from on high like glowing beetles. Yellow sulfur erupted from dark chambers and gleamed mysteriously next to the hard, glinting iron as if, in ruinous league with one another, they threatened to vanquish the upper world. But the unpredictable, confusing movements of the will-o'-the-wisps hindered a more thorough observation of the surroundings as they flitted teasingly about. Amazingly high-pitched voices swirled around Ferrand's ears, repeating meaningless, jumbled words in confused tones. Darting back and forth, they surrounded the wanderers, uttering the following words in shrill tones:

Will-o'-the-wisp goes through the night,
Making now the dark shaft light,
Teases the wanderer ever faster
While he loyally serves his master.

We quickly follow your command;
Call to us, with you we'll stand.
We show the trail to hidden treasures –
Leave us to our little pleasures.

We did it all at your behest,
Obedient, but ne'er at rest
For we, a strange and motley breed,
Obey your command, it's you we heed.

"Listen to those earth-bound shooting stars," cried Welleda. "They're being importunate today, because, for once, they would like to be helpful despite their trifling size; usually they'd gloat over spreading confusion. Away with you, afterbirths of light that air and earth produce to ridicule the pure elements!

"To my side
From far and wide
With your mistress you shall stride."

The darting flames withdrew far into the darkness. The youth felt a sudden chill as his guide so imperiously scolded the murky images, and he was almost more terrified by their shy obedience than by their intrusive closeness.

By the constant light in the sorceress's hand the two wanderers beheld the surrounding cave into which they steadily descended; it appeared wrested from another element. The walls, spiked with coral, were formed from layer upon layer of snails and shells, the deposit of millennia and the decay of innumerable deaths; they bore the eons and the duration of an entire world's existence. Above these mystical vaults Ferrand gradually perceived a faint rushing sound that, swelling, rumbled over his head as if an angry river wanted to tear itself loose from its constricting vale and flood everything in its path. Just as the sides of a flimsy ship tossed by a tempest creak and groan in every seam, it seemed to the stunned man as if the walls threatened to cave in at any moment and become a watery grave.

Overcome by such impending terrors, Ferrand stood transfixed. Then, taking his icy right hand, Welleda spoke, "Love is nature's most potent power," and enlivening warmth, radiating in a ghostly flame from the maiden's mysterious diadem, coursed through his veins as hand in hand they hurried on together, while the raging torrents of the river Neckar rushed overhead.

Finally, the path seemed to lead upward, but the vault grew narrower again and darker. The will-o'-the-wisps disappeared into the recesses, and only the trusty torch in the maiden's hand illuminated the difficult, narrow track spiraling upward.

Suddenly, they entered a large underground hall dimly illuminated by five golden lamps hanging from the cupola. The light fell on a black marble slab that stood elevated in the middle of the room; its entire surface was engraved with mysterious symbols that mesmerized Ferrand's gaze in a labyrinthine tangle, drawing him ever deeper into a narrow circle, as if luring him with endless space. Hardly had he spied the lines that spiraled together at the center than they stood out in relief and sprang to life as characters that mockingly leaped about him, leering and grotesquely aping humans in their contortions. These characters held out a profusion of beautifully minted gold coins to the youth; each gnome repeated the word for the symbol from which he had just sprung.

"Have you nothing more to offer than your filthy lucre?" Ferrand shouted scornfully at the band of gnomes. "And is there no more sublime import to the magical curves of those lines? Away with this foolish trickery that confuses my soul and is but a lie."

"You have passed the final test valiantly," cried Welleda, beaming at her lover, who was still seething with anger and had turned his back on the gold-touting gnomes. "Now you shall observe nature in its eternal hieroglyphics."

Then the dark wall opened before his feet, and a broad stone staircase as smooth as glass sparkled in a play of colors, leading the way into the upper world. It slowly grew lighter around the two wayfarers as they ascended; the delicate white of the Pentelic marble diffused the blinding daylight and reflected it softly off the high walls. As his eyes became more accustomed to the light, he beheld in the crystal dome a brimming sea of light that spread life-warming waves around him. Rapturous, the young man greeted in the dawning of a new day his existence as a new creature of love.

By turns exhilarated and exhausted by such overpowering sensations, Ferrand collapsed at the foot of the golden griffins standing at the head of the topmost stairs of the entry. A mysterious breeze brushed his fevered brow like a kiss and awakened him from the daydream in which he had observed himself and his activities as if from afar. As he looked up, Welleda stood before him, smiling sweetly. She held a golden goblet in her milky white hand; he immediately recognized it as the one with which she had stilled Hinrich's thirst the night before. "You look surprised to see the familiar goblet," she said, "that your father's impetuous toss momentarily tore from me. It returned quickly to me together with the spirit that resides in it. Ingratitude or error shall never destroy the wondrous power my hand commands, and that, often desecrated or rejected by human folly, still retains its purity and potency."

Fixing his lover in his gaze, Ferrand emptied the goblet and immediately felt a new life force surging through his veins. Now he confidently followed his guide, who, with a delicate arm, already held aside a heavy drape laced with gold, revealing to him the entrance to the inner halls. There, in that space, the primal forces of natural creation intertwined, in eloquent symbols, into a crown.

Here fire and earth – polar opposites – seemed united in wishing to re-

123

veal their deepest secrets before the astonished observer. Resting on great granite pillars, a golden crown, studded with priceless jewels that sparkled in the dazzling hues of the flames within them, encircled the perimeter of the room. The animals who wander the Earth paraded in pure gold on the jagged ring of the diadem; innumerable plants that seek their sustenance deep within the earth snaked along the green carpets joining the mighty pillars, while crimson fruits, scattered across the colorful surface, glowed as brightly as the jewels above, and overflowing masses of grapes towered up from the basalt floor.

Pure fire, as if animated by an inner spirit, slithered in flickering waves amid the many creatures of the Earth, animating the figures and illuminating them with a gentle glow. It swept, purifying, through the ruby and jasper bowls in which healing herbs fermented, searing away all impurities and leaving the essential essences behind in greater potency. Glorious swirling flames shot up all around, from the ground, through the metal crown, and up into the starry dome.

"Here, my love, in the manifestation of matter, you may recognize the blueprint for corporeal existence," said Welleda, "just as fire, flowing around us here in its elemental purity, is the light of the elements and mirrors your spiritual existence." Now, as Ferrand looked at her beloved figure, he recognized on the yoke of her dress the same earthy hues and images of flora and fauna he had seen before, but now their order became meaningful. A brooch of brilliant rubies fastened the shawl laced with gold before her breast and swirled around her comely arm rising gracefully from its many folds. She seemed to float before him like a blossom of those images, the embodiment of pure elements. Such a fantastic image might inflame a painter's imagination, just as in Italy artists had depicted the young and earnest Sybil as the personification of the depths and heights human nature can reach.

An indescribable, soothing coolness now enveloped Ferrand's senses as he, on the maiden's arm, entered another bright room. She instructed him lovingly: "Now, just as earth and fire appeared to you in the greatest contrast, so now air and water will reveal themselves to you as spiritual and physical aspects of the elements, the primal creations that arose from Chaos. As the intermediaries between the other elements, they are at the center of planetary life, and breathe life into the organisms unfurling in churning space. Observe how the flower bud fills with sweet dew, while the mild west wind gently rocks it. The bird, an unfettered breed, sings on wing through the flower stalks toward the heavens. The air, unhindered by gravity, carries its bright tones on gentle wings over broad regions. Bright fish swim in crystal pillars of water, enjoying the transparent element of light.

The Symbols

"For only water and light experience the orbit of the sun and such beautiful animation from the spirit of the universe. They express their joy in the sublime chords of the dawn, in the melancholy shades of twilight. And borne by both, the constellation Lyra climbs into the ether and fills the universe with melodically pristine tones. But now as sun, air, and water caress each other in a searing kiss, behold the rainbow shining over us in a perfect play of colors, a beacon of peace and divine reconciliation."

As the maiden spoke, the dancing images called forth by her words transformed into enchanting music, while she herself, the bountiful flower wreath on her lilting curls, the silver robe around her rosy limbs, seemed to float away in the wafting strains of celestial harmonies streaming from her as they called her back to their resonant ocean. The entranced mortal, sensing the sublime, was overcome by the inexpressible and closed his blinded eye before the reflection of Isis unveiled.

TRANSLATED BY SHAWN C. JARVIS

Anna in her workroom. Sketch by Ludwig Emil Grimm, 1827.
Others present in the scene: Therese, Gräfin von Westfalen; in
the gallery: Ludwig Emil Grimm, his sister, Lotte Grimm
Hassenpflug, and others; behind the easel, seated: Ferdinand von
Droste-Hülshoff and August von Haxthausen. From Peter
Heßelmann, *August Freiherr von Haxthausen (1792–1866).*
Sammler von Märchen, Sagen und Volksliedern, Agrarhistoriker
und Rußlandreisender aus Westfalen. Ausstellung der
Universitätsbibliothek Münster 24. Februar 1992-25. März 1992
(Münster: Regensberg, 1992), 64. With permission of the
Universitäts- und Landesbibliothek Münster.

Anna von Haxthausen

1801–1877

Anna von Haxthausen was a girl of ten in 1811 when she first met Wilhelm Grimm and he asked her if she knew any fairy tales. The youngest of the eight daughters of a family of the landed aristocracy in north-central Germany, she and her older sister Ludowine were among the most active contributors to the Grimm collection. Among the more than fifty tales she and her family contributed are no. 133, "The Twelve Dancing Princesses," in the 1857 edition of the Grimm brothers' tales. She and her family, including their cousins Jenny and Annette Droste-Hülshoff, have been the focus of recent research on the formation of the Grimm collection.

The tale of this bedeviled princess presents some of the classic motifs of the fairy tale. First, it depicts the enchantment of a daughter through the thoughtless or greedy dealings of her father with the devil, as is found in no. 31, "The Girl without Hands," in the Grimms' 1857 edition. In this version the salvation of the daughter follows not from her own loving self-sacrifice or her passive acceptance of her plight but from a much more violent presentation of female evil, which can be "cured" only by religious exorcism. The salvation of this vampire bride shows how graphically violent and unrefined the oral tradition was. The presentation of this tale by Anna von Haxthausen in 1818, when she was seventeen or eighteen years old, about a girl of twelve to fourteen, shows that it was not necessarily the gentility of the Grimms' contributors that made their tales fit for the parlor but rather the Grimms' own editorial choices. This story fits in with other violent stories of pubertal transformation such as the Grimms' story no. 1, "The Frog Prince," as well as the French tale of "The Green Serpent" (in Zipes, ed. and trans., *Beauties, Beasts, and Enchantment,* 477–500).

Bolte and Polívka, eds., *Anmerkungen,* 3:531–37. Contributed by and in the hand of Anna von Haxthausen. Original found in the Grimm cabinet, "Zweifelhaftes, Fragmente, Spuren, Einzelnes 23/36" [Doubtful pieces, fragments, clues, isolated items].

·······································

The Rescued Princess

1818

O NCE UPON A TIME there were a king and a queen who had no children at all. This made the king so angry once that he said, "I just
wish I had a child, even if it were the very Devil himself!" And soon
thereafter, the queen had a daughter who was as black as a raven and so ugly
that people were actually afraid when they saw her. She roared like a beast
and was very stupid.

When she was twelve years old she told the king to have a tomb built
for her in the church. At first he did not want to do this, but she began to
roar so loudly that he agreed out of fear. The king had a tomb built for her
right behind the altar. She lay down in it, and the cover was placed on top,
but she could throw it off herself if she so desired. Every night six soldiers
took turns guarding her grave by her command, but every morning, when
people came into the church, they found that she had murdered them all.
The next night another six had to stand guard, and she murdered them in
their turn, and so it continued for two years.

Then one day while the king was out for a walk he met a young man. The
king said, "My son! Where are you headed?" The youth answered him, "Oh, I
wanted to go into service with a cobbler or a tailor." The king answered, "Tell
me, what is your name?" "I'm Frederick." The king spoke, "You shouldn't
apprentice yourself; you should become one of my soldiers. You can become
an officer or whatever you would like, but you must do one thing: spend the
night standing watch at the tomb of my daughter." Now Frederick had absolutely no desire to do this, for he knew what always became of the soldiers.
But since the king kept badgering him, he finally agreed.

When he reached the church that evening, he felt so much terror in his
heart that he ran out again. As he reached the city gate, there stood a little
old gnome, all wizened, who said, "Where are you headed, my son?" And
Frederick answered, "Oh, I just wanted to take a little walk." Then the little
man said, "I know well that you wanted to desert, because you are afraid

that the princess will murder you. But go back in there again! She will do you no harm, and I will now tell you what you must do. As you come into the church, you must spread out your arms and then kneel at the altar and pray and think constantly of God; and whatever happens to you, you may not look up or leave that spot."

Frederick did as the wizened little gnome told him. When it was eleven o'clock, the princess rose from her grave and took a saber and struck Frederick with it so hard that blood ran down. But he felt no pain and kept on praying to God. She began to roar so terribly that people in the town could hear her. And she ordered him to please leave the church. But he did not rise, and so the princess kept striking him until it was twelve midnight. And then she climbed back into her tomb.

When the king came into the church the next morning to see how things were going with Frederick, he was still sitting before the altar and praying. The king was amazed, and the whole land rejoiced. The next night six soldiers had to stand watch again, but the princess again murdered them all.

The third night Frederick was to stand watch again. When he entered the church, however, he felt so much terror in his heart that he ran out again. At the city gate, he again met the wizened old gnome, who told him he should not be afraid at all, but tonight he should lie face down on the altar and not look up at all and keep praying. So Frederick returned and did everything the white gnome had ordered him. As the clock struck eleven, the black princess returned and began to roar horribly and to strike him, but he kept praying to God until it was midnight, and then she returned to her tomb.

The king couldn't believe his eyes when he saw Frederick still alive. He promised him mounds of gold and silver if he would stand watch one more night, but Frederick did not want to at all, for he thought, Tonight she will kill me for certain, and I would rather run as far as my feet can carry me.

So he stole away. When he got to the city gate, however, the white gnome appeared again and said, "My son! Tonight you must stand watch at the grave once more, and then you will receive your reward. When the princess arises tonight, you must immediately lie down in her tomb and keep praying and think always of God, and no matter how much she begs you to get out of her tomb, you must not do it until she turns white as a snow angel before your eyes. When she starts to cry, you may arise."

When Frederick came into the church, he prayed to God in all devotion. When it was eleven, the princess arose, and Frederick lay down quickly in her tomb. She began to curse and roar so that people thought the church would sink into the ground. But Frederick kept on praying to God, and finally she began to plead with him and ask him to get out of her grave, saying she wouldn't hurt him. Then he peeked up just a bit toward her and saw that she had a white spot above her eyes, and when he peeked again, her whole forehead was white and then her whole face. He kept praying to God, and when it was almost midnight, she stood there before him, white as a snow angel and shining like the sun, and she began to cry and said, "Please rise, dear Frederick! I will do you no more harm, for you have redeemed me." And as she said this, the clock struck twelve, and he arose.

Then she told him that she had been bewitched for fourteen years because her father had said that he wanted to have a child, even if it were the very Devil himself. And as she told him this, all of the tombs opened up and all the soldiers whom the princess had murdered were revived, but their beards had grown so long that they dragged on the ground. And when the king came into the church, it was filled with soldiers, and he was met at the door by Frederick and the princess. She was so lovely that he could not believe she was his daughter. When she told him that Frederick had saved her, the king gave him his daughter as his wife, and he had a great feast prepared on the very same day to which all the soldiers were invited, for they were very hungry. And after the death of the king, Frederick became king.

TRANSLATED BY JEANNINE BLACKWELL

Karoline Stahl

1776–1837

The contribution of Karoline Stahl to the German fairy tale tradition lies in her mediation of French models for German readers. As a governess in Livonia, Russia, and Germany for several decades, she developed didactic tales for juvenile audiences. Her works were highly regarded by the Grimms, who referred to her collections in their 1857 edition and incorporated her story "The Thankless Dwarf" (in altered form) into their 1837 edition. In the tradition of the French tales that she in part emulated, her fables and reworkings of earlier fairy tale and saga motifs included moral instruction for upper-class children, enjoining them to avoid her catalog of the seven deadly sins of childhood: envy, tattling, vanity, prattling/gossiping, unhealthy snacking, dangerous play, and haughtiness.

In "The Godmothers," Stahl's penchant for using the fairy tale as modus for didactic purposes presages the Grimms' use of the fairy tale as an educational primer. The godmothers appear as four animal benefactors to the four royal children; when the father refuses to invite the fourth godmother to the fourth child's christening, the magic spell of benefaction for kindness to strangers in animal form is broken. The three eldest daughters, who had been blessed with beauty and magical gifts, commit Stahl's deadly sins and become haughty, vain, proud, and coquettish. The fourth child, Princess Merry, denied her christening gift by her father, remains virtuous and is ultimately rewarded for her spiritual goodness.

Stories to read with this piece include many of Mme d'Aulnoy's tales with an uglification plot (e.g., "The Green Snake") as well as christening stories such as the Grimms' story no. 1, "The Frog Prince," and "Sleeping Beauty." Spunky heroines like Merry appear in the tales of good and bad sisters like the Frau Holle stories, as well as Maggie in "The Red Flower" in this anthology.

Karoline Stahl, "Die Gevatterinnen. Ein Mährchen," in *Erzählungen, Fabeln und Mährchen für Kinder* (Nuremberg: Friedrich Campe, 1818), 19–27.

The Godmothers

1818

A KING who was very good lived happily with his wife, and their only wish was to have children. One day, as the queen was walking along the banks of a river, a portly frog caught her attention, and she stopped on the shore to watch him. "Why are you staring at me like that?" croaked the frog. The queen, amazed at hearing him speak, gave a start and replied that she was admiring his big belly, because his comrades were the very opposite of him, all skinny and scrawny as they were. "I'm pleased," said the frog, "that you like me so. I like you as well, and so I'm going to make you a proposal. You will soon bear a little daughter, and all that I ask is that you take me as her godparent." "It would be my pleasure!" replied the queen, who was feeling quite light-hearted and gay. "But how shall I find you again?" "Just have the lord chamberlain bring me an invitation," said the frog. "He can toss it in the water right here, and I will certainly come."

At that the speaker dove into the depths and disappeared from sight. The queen began to laugh and simply couldn't stop; she even started up again at the palace. Her old nurse looked very grave as she heard the event recounted and explained to her majesty that she was laughing inopportunely, because it was, as one could certainly imagine, no ordinary frog but rather an enchanted one, or perhaps even a fairy. Shortly thereafter the queen did indeed bear a little daughter, and as the preparations were being made for the baptismal celebration, the old nurse, ever cautious, reminded the queen to invite the godparent. She even managed to convince the lord chamberlain to toss the invitation into the water at the appointed spot.

The guests had already arrived when a portly frog as big as a cat appeared and joined the ranks of astonished godparents. After the ceremony, he went over to the cradle, looked in, and then hopped away again. The king was not happy about this particular godparent, but, for the sake of his wife, he kept his feelings to himself. When they went over to the little princess, everyone cried out in wonder – she had become quite lovely, and her hair shone like spun gold. If a strand fell out, it turned into real gold, and from then on the Jewish merchants rushed to the castle every day and bought these strands. Over time, this small fortune grew into a sizable one.

A year later the queen went for a stroll in the woods and spied an owl perched serenely on a branch. "Do I please you?" screeched the bird. "Yes, indeed!" replied the queen. "You please me, too," was the answer. "And after a number of moons, when you again bear a daughter, invite me to the baptismal feast as godparent." The queen vowed to do so, and the old nurse didn't fail at the appropriate moment to remind her of her promise.

All preparations were complete when an owl flew through one of the crystal windows into the hall and took a place among the baptismal sponsors. It fluttered over to the cradle, looked at the princess, and started back through the same window. This child, too, became quite beautiful and had dark eyes that glimmered like coals. Every teardrop she shed turned into a pearl from the purest sea, and, when she was older, two beautiful pearls glistened on her cheeks every morning when she awoke. They, too, fetched a great fortune from their sale.

Some time later the queen once again went out for a stroll, this time across a field. There she spied a mouse of ample proportions chewing on an ear of corn she held on the ground between her paws. "It's tasty, as you can see," she said, "and I am pleased that you are watching so kindly as I eat. I want to do you a favor and serve as godparent to your future daughter. Just have the appropriate invitation brought to this field." The queen felt somewhat awkward, because her husband had not seemed overly enthusiastic about the older princesses' strange godmothers, but she kept it to herself. The old nurse held fast to her view, and the invitation was extended when the queen bore the third girl. This time a stout mouse appeared at the baptism and decorously joined the sponsors. As a baptismal gift the child received not merely beauty but another gift as well: every time she spoke, a magnificent diamond tumbled from her dainty rosebud mouth, and she grew as wealthy as her older sisters.

Almost a full year had passed when the queen, who had pretty much stopped taking walks, was picking flowers at a brook. A charming goldfish swam up and struck up a conversation with her. Shortly thereafter it offered its services as godparent and then swam away merrily. The queen was very distraught because she feared a disagreement with her husband if she invited the fish, so she asked the old nurse for advice. She begged the queen to keep her word but suggested that it would be best to tell the king of the affair beforehand. He flew into a rage and expressly forbade the sponsorship. "Haven't we already entered into a kind of kinship with a frog, an owl, and a mouse, to the great astonishment of our subjects?" he said. "And now a fish on top of it? If this keeps up, all sorts of snakes and salamanders and other monstrous creatures will slither their way to our children."

The queen wept, but to no avail. At the baptism everyone was splashed with water, and their lovely garments were ruined. Even the little princess in her cradle wasn't spared, and as beautiful as the child had been, it suddenly became just as ugly. The old nurse had warned of the retribution that would be exacted for not following her advice, but it was all too late. "That's precisely why I will love this child so dearly," said the king, "because she's not beautiful and rich."

So all four princesses grew up. Because of their beauty, the three eldest attracted countless admirers, and many foreign kings, enticed by rumors of their beauty and their riches, came and asked for their hands in marriage, but the youngest had no suitors. The elder sisters, Golden Hair, Pearly Eyes, and Brillicinta, became vain, proud, and coquettish from the many flatteries they heard every day. The youngest, Princess Merry, so-called because of her cheerful nature, was instead good-natured, charitable, industrious, and clever. Because her sisters always made fun of her for her lack of looks and riches, she didn't become haughty, and since she was always ignored and overlooked at the royal galas, she stayed in her room instead and occupied herself with useful pastimes.

Once, when she went for a walk with her sisters, they heard a frog croaking pitifully as a nasty boy was about to put a skewer through him. Princess Merry begged the boy to let the poor thing go, but he just laughed in her face. Then she begged Golden Hair for a single golden strand to ransom the frog, but Golden Hair chided her and flounced away. Pearly Eyes and Brillicinta were no better, and Merry stood there completely distraught. At last she came up with an idea: she gave the boy her very pretty handkerchief and then carried the frog away to a marsh. Shortly thereafter several children came by carrying an owl tied to a pole, with lots of little birds fluttering and screeching around the captive. The children said they wanted to nail the nasty bird to a hen house. Princess Merry turned again to her sisters for help, but once more in vain – they just laughed at her. This time she had to sacrifice her earrings and necklace to ransom the owl.

A bit later some boys showed up dragging along a mouse on a string; they planned to give it to a cat. Merry pleaded with her sisters, but they wouldn't relinquish anything, and she ransomed the mouse with her straw hat and rings. Soon they came to a brook where some boys wanted to kill a goldfish they'd captured. Merry pleaded with them and had to hand over her shoes and socks. And so she arrived barefoot and without hat or jewelry at the castle, where the ladies-in-waiting reprimanded her and scolded her about attire unbefitting a royal princess. Her parents were informed, and the king commanded the foolhardy child to present herself before him, where he gave her a stern warning. Merry listened without interrupting, as was befitting, and she showed her father the little fish she had rescued, now swimming in a goldfish bowl. Suddenly, it began to grow bigger and bigger, and at last there stood before them a lovely woman who sprinkled water on the princess. In a flash the uncomely girl was transformed into a great beauty, and every drop of water that had been in the bowl turned into a magnificent diamond. "You see," said the fairy, "I wanted to be your godmother, but I was turned away, and so I punished you. You saved my life. As a mouse, and owl, and frog I was the godmother and benefactress of your sisters, who are hardhearted and vain. But they shall reap their reward and become as ugly as you once were." Instantly, Golden Hair was a nasty, red-haired thing, Pearly Eyes turned sooty brown and weepy-eyed, while hunchbacked Brillicinta sported a mouth full of black teeth instead of jewels. The riches they still had did not make them happy, because the mirrors that hung all about the palace reflected their hideousness a thousandfold. But Princess Merry remained as good and modest in her beauty as she had always been.

TRANSLATED BY SHAWN C. JARVIS

The kind and diligent housewife. From Amalie Schoppe, *Kleine Märchen-Bibliothek oder gesammelte Mährchen für die liebe Jugend,* vol. 2 (Berlin: L. Mathisson, 1828), facing 44. Reprinted with permission of the Sammlung Hobrecker, Universitätsbibliothek Braunschweig, Dr. Peter Düsterdieck, Bibliotheksdirektor.

Amalie Schoppe
1791–1858

An extremely prolific and popular writer, Amalie Schoppe was the editor of
Iduna, a journal for young people. Schoppe prided herself on the scientific
and encyclopedic variety of her works and presented moral instruction as
well as basic knowledge, stressing duty as one of her main themes. Widowed early, Schoppe supported herself and her one surviving son by writing
children's books, novels, and biographies as well as books on cooking, gar-
dening, and theater costumes, producing over two hundred volumes in total.
Her works were extremely well received, many appearing in two or three
editions and translated into French, English, Dutch, and Serbo-Croatian.
Emigrating to America in 1851 to join her son, she wrote stories of the New
World until 1858, when she died, honored but impoverished, in Schenectady,
New York.

"The Kind and Diligent Housewife" is a typical example of Schoppe's
work, in which she outlines for the reader the hallmarks of the ideal citizen:
responsibility, obedience, fear of God, industry, punctuality, modesty, fru-
gality, cleanliness, and politeness. Her work also typically shows women's
nurturing community and the preservation of family, sometimes at great
personal expense. The consequences of the good housewife's son's travels
and his quest for fame and fortune are seen from the perspective of the value
to his family and community. The tale shows that the quest is not accomplished by separation and conquest but, rather, by reintegration into and
understanding of the home base.

Other stories to read with Schoppe include "Fair Exchange" (in Phelps,
ed., *Maid of the North*), the story of a girl who works hard to raise a changeling, goes to a fairy queen to exchange the changeling for her real child, and
wins lifelong favor for herself and her family. Tales of supportive community
between human women and fairies include Benedikte Naubert's "The Cloak"
(in Blackwell and Zantop, eds., *Bitter Healing*) and, in this anthology, Agnes

Franz's "Princess Rosalieb: A Fairy Tale" and Fanny Lewald's "A Modern Fairy Tale."

Amalie Schoppe, "Die fleißige und mitleidige Hausfrau," in *Kleine Mährchen-Bibliothek oder gesammelte Mährchen für die liebe Jugend von Amalie Schoppe, geb. Weise, Verfasserin der "Bunten Bilder," "Lust und Lehre," u. a. m.*, 2 vols. (Berlin: L. Matthisson, 1828), 2:1–55.

The Kind and Diligent Housewife

1828

1

O N THE BALTIC SEA, which is often also called the East Sea, just off the coast of the beautiful, blessed land of Holstein, lies a small island separated from the mainland by a narrow strip of sea called a strait. Fehmarn is the name of this happy little island, and its inhabitants have preserved scores of the loveliest folktales and fairy tales from olden times, passed down from generation to generation and retold even in our own times. Right now I will tell you, precious children, one of those tales, and maybe even more, because they're quite charming and pleasant to read and hear.

I called Fehmarn a happy island and want to defend this claim. Imagine, dear children, a tiny land, completely flat, whose soil is so fertile that the most wonderful and bountiful crops abound; the grain grows so tall and profusely that a fully grown adult, standing, could hide in it. The sea surrounding the island gives forth the richest bounty of delicious fish and shellfish, which sell at incredibly low prices; the innumerable gardens are full of fruit trees and flowers; and the seashore teems with edible fowl. This prosperous island produces all earthly necessities in plenty, except those where excess would lead to human misery. Indeed, people have advanced their husbandry so far that every year a large amount of grain is exported to less prosperous areas, and the profits are used to satisfy other needs.

But what is more important than all the rest is the islanders' honesty and purity of heart. Even today people in the country don't lock their doors at night, because they've nothing to fear, although that's surely different by now in the little town of Burg. Energetic industry, thrift, moderation, orderliness, and hospitality are the virtues of the islanders; no pauper, no pilgrim is scorned and sent away unconsoled. On the contrary, he is welcomed with open arms into a very tidy and often spacious dwelling and sent away with a gift and encouraging words after having been a welcome guest for many days or weeks.

The diligent, never-resting housewife attends without respite to all the necessities of life. She makes sure the flax necessary for the household is planted, tended, prepared, and spun, and she usually even weaves it herself. On long winter evenings she sits surrounded by her daughters and maidservants and spins flax, wool, hemp, and, in recent times, cotton, too. When the snow white material is taken out of the bleach, all members of the household receive the amount they need, even the man- and maidservants, who are counted as important members of the family. Life is quite lively at harvest time. Joyous songs resound everywhere, colorful garlands flutter, and the housewife shows off her baking skills with appetizing cakes that are carried out to the happy reapers and sheaf binders in the fields. With the cakes they drink a healthy and hearty home-brewed beer, for wine is a great rarity in these northern climes.

The winter here is often harsh; the sea around the island freezes over, storms hang in the air, and mammoth mounds of snow darken the horizon. The low-lying houses are often snowed in so that people have to dig themselves out in the morning with spades and shovels. At such times, everyone usually stays at home; man and wife, children and servants sit assembled around the hearth, where a flame burns bright and warm, and then they tell all kinds of lovely sagas and fairy tales while the household listens attentively and enthralled, although the stories have all been heard many times before. On this island you can see the amazing phenomenon of the aurora borealis, which even natural scientists have yet to explain fully. You, my beloved children, must certainly have heard or read about it often; if not, have your parents, teachers, or well-read friends tell you about it. I myself was born on that island, so on many occasions I felt moved and touched by that strange phenomenon. I hope you all someday will be able to experience the northern lights; the impression will never leave your hearts, just as it still pleasantly glimmers from my happy childhood into my old age.

My great-grandmother, a wonderful woman of sublime virtues, used to tell us great-grandchildren the following fairy tale. It was passed down from generation to generation in our family when the raging storm outside shook the mighty oaks and beech trees, and the freezing rain beat at the windowpanes. That was when our great-grandmother, near ninety, sat in the padded armchair at the great oak table, on which a single light burned, and looked at us, her flourishing descendants, with her pious, clever eyes unclouded by age and still sharp-sighted, while our mothers, aunts, and great-aunts spun diligently or lovingly busied themselves with infants on their laps. At those times she was happy to satisfy our insistent pleadings to tell us a tale. Her robust good health, the result of moderation and a strict regime (in general, a trait of all the island's inhabitants) had preserved her clarity of mind, and she narrated as well and pleasantly as she had done in her youth.

Once, when we were gathered at the house of our great-grandmother, whose husband was the mayor of the town of Burg, a man still admired and praised by the residents, she told us to our great delight the following little story. It was all the more interesting to us because it was supposed to have happened in our very own family.

2

A long, long time ago (our great-grandmother began), our foremother lived on the spot where we now live, for although the house that we now call ours was rebuilt approximately seventy years ago, the land has belonged to our family since time immemorial. At that time our forefather was a simple but industrious and virtuous peasant who fed his family by the sweat of his brow, and his faithful wife stood loyally by his side. Heaven blessed their union with many wonderful children, and when the table was set for lunch, fourteen settings had to be laid, for there were twelve children. Of course, it was difficult to provide the bare necessities for so many every day, but what can stand in the way of constant industry and the love of order? Nobody went to bed hungry, and a cheery disposition and good health accompanied the sweet little ones, some of whom were already helping their father in the fields or their mother in the household. Heavenly blessings seemed to be showered on the virtuous home, for the crops thrived, the cows, who produced plenty of milk, stood content and round in the stable, every bread and brew of the housewife was a success, and no illness befell the parents or the children.

Every once in awhile something very strange happened, an unusual good fortune that no one could really explain, for while all the others gave themselves up to sweet, refreshing slumber, the diligent housewife, who was known all around as a model of orderliness and tidiness, stayed up late into the night to polish and clean the great copper kettles or the heavy pewter bowls and plates, an activity in which she took great pleasure. The next morning, when she stepped to the hearth to prepare breakfast for her husband and the children, she would find a lovely, gleaming gold piece of a casting unknown to her, and no one knew whence it came. These gold pennies (as these gold coins were called back then) were carefully saved and never spent with the other money. They were something sacred to the family, because no one knew their origin.

Once, when our foremother was sweeping the loft long after midnight, a task she hadn't had time to do during the day and still had to do because they were going to put the freshly threshed grain on it the next morning, she saw by the weak glow of the lamp something strangely shimmering and sparkling in a far corner. She tried to reach it with the broom, but when she started to sweep that area she heard a clattering noise. As she drew nearer with the lamp, she saw ten or twelve gold pennies like the ones she had occasionally found on the hearth. Amazed and pleased, she bent over to pick up the precious discovery and collect it in her apron. Suddenly, she heard something rustling and bustling behind her and at the same time very, very quiet footsteps. Startled, she spun around; since everyone in the house was sound asleep, it couldn't be anyone in her family moving about. As she lifted the lamp toward the area from which the sound had come, she saw a tiny little gray manikin of unusual build who gave her a friendly and pleasant look.

Her first reaction upon seeing this specter (whom she took for a fiend or demonic delusion) was to make the sign of the cross, but the little fellow didn't budge; he just smiled sweetly. She plucked up her courage. Since the sign of the cross hadn't sent him fleeing, he couldn't be an evil spirit, but the sight of him was strange indeed, and she couldn't help feeling a bit frightened despite her daring and her piety (which always go hand in hand). The little gray man had a disproportionately large head with long, straight hair falling over half his face and down his short neck from under a pointed cap. His large, shining eyes sparkled from the shadows behind his hair like two bright stars. His nose was broad and somewhat flat, but his mouth was pleasant, and a slight smile danced on his lips. The rest of him, hardly two feet tall, was wrapped in a large, plain gray cloak held together at his waist by a wide leather belt from which a little silver whistle hung. In his hand the little fellow held a long wand that appeared to be made of pure gold and seemed to gleam in the semidarkness, which the dim lamplight could only partially dispel in the expanse of the loft.

"Greetings, pious and diligent housewife!" spoke the little figure in a soft whisper. "You have often pleased me with your untiring efforts, which I, like all my brothers, love and appreciate. We have in the past also rewarded you for them, for the gold pieces you found on the hearth today and on earlier occasions were from us; they will bring you and yours good fortune." At this he amiably stretched out his hand to her, and she, having regained her courage and lost her fear of the fellow, reached out hers, which he gently squeezed.

"You could have more," he continued, "if you decided to follow me. We possess great riches and would give you a share of them, so much that you'd have enough for your entire family forever, but you'd have to do us a service and stay with us awhile, long enough to put our underground dwelling in

order, as yours is above ground. Our women are not as diligent and energetic as you, so many things in our household have fallen into disarray. That
irritates and displeases us, since we love order and tidiness and can't get our
wives to attend to matters. If you were to stay, say, six months with us and
were an example to them with your diligence and industry, I don't doubt
that it would bear fruit for them and for us, because our womenfolk also
admire and revere you humans. So, agree to my proposal and be certain of
a rich reward."

"How dare you suggest such a thing, little man," said the righteous housewife with indignation. "What would become of my own household if I
agreed? What would become of my own children, who couldn't survive an
hour without their mother and nurse? No, I'll have nothing to do with it, and
if you gave me that shiny gold just to tempt me into doing my own family an
injustice, take it back and everything else you gave me in the past! I know
that shimmering metal is a great temptation for many and has been many
a person's undoing, but he who trusts in God and is diligent and pious will
never overestimate the value of gold so that he neglects his duties or does
something against his conscience."

"Now, now, don't get so upset!" said the little man as Mistress Mary (that
was our foremother's name), outraged at his suggestion, shook the money
out of her apron at his feet. "What we gave to you already is rightfully yours
and yours to keep, even if you don't want to do us even the smallest favor,
for it is the reward for your virtue and your diligence. But what we would
give you if you could bring yourself to grant my request, that gift is beyond
imagination. Listen: neither you, nor your husband, nor your children, nor
your children's children would have to work and toil ever again. You would
always have the tastiest morsels, would sleep on eiderdown, and would look
on in leisure as hired hands and maids worked for you. Doesn't that tempt
you in the slightest to follow me?"

"And would we, if I were crazy enough to pay your temptations any heed,
be so healthy, happy, and content with God as we are now, when we earn
our bread by the sweat of our brow?" she asked.

"If you remain modest," was the response, "then why not? I know," he
continued, "that the work is often hard for you, actually, a great burden. Just
this evening, as everyone else laid themselves to rest and you picked up the
broom to sweep the kitchen floor, didn't you heave a great sigh and say, 'I,
too, would like to rest after the long day's work, but I still have to sweep the
floor. Such a life is truly a burden!' "

"Yes, I did foolishly utter those words with an ungrateful heart toward
God," she interrupted him, "but when I passed by the children's beds and

saw them there so dewy and rosy-cheeked, enjoying the refreshing slumber that my diligence so late at night made possible, then I deeply regretted my dissatisfaction and asked for forgiveness from the Lord, who has certainly forgiven me because of my repentance. But it's quite indelicate of you to admonish me about my transgression. I swear you'll never hear such words from me again. So take your gold back and leave me in peace, because instead of working and being able to rest sooner, I'm wasting my time talking nonsense with you." With these words she picked up the broom she'd let fall in her fright at the apparition and busily started her sweeping again.

"My!" said the little man, watching her in amazement. "You are far too bent on your zeal and sense of duty and could go at it a little less fanatically!"

"That's your evil side speaking, little fellow, for whoever deliberately neglects even the smallest of his duties will soon end up neglecting them all!" Mary replied vehemently.

"Are you hoping to become rich with such efforts?" he asked.

"Rich? Did I ever ask to be rich? Our hard work provides our daily bread, nothing more, and that's all we ask of the good Lord in our prayers," she said.

"You are a righteous woman, Mistress Mary," said the little man with emotion. "I'd admire and respect you if you just weren't so stubborn! But I don't want to pester you any longer since I've heard your views. Out of fairness I'll help you today, because I've shortened your rest with my idle chatter. Keep these pieces of gold and know that as long as you keep one of them, it will be in your power to summon me should a time come when you need my help and might be in a state of mind to consider my offer. For that eventuality, take one of these gold pieces up to the hill that you can see from your window, dig a little hole about an inch deep in the grass covering it, and say these words, which you must repeat exactly:

Come Piper, come Piper, come to my aid.
I'm ready to follow; it's you that I've bade.

Then I will appear and take you with me into the world underground and not withhold the promised wages from you. Now go to bed. I'll call my brothers, and when you awaken in the morning, your loft will be cleaner and shinier than you could have gotten it in ten sleepless nights."

"I accept your proposal," said Mary. "But promise me that when I get up the loft won't look like it does right now, or else I'll be very angry, because the grain's to be brought in at the crack of dawn."

"You may rightly call me a liar," said the little man, "if I don't keep my promise, and so that you'll sleep peacefully, watch how we get started." At that he grabbed the little silver whistle hanging at his waist, put his lips to it, and blew into it. A shrill, piercing tone issued three times. At that very instant a horde of identical little men shouldering brooms and shovels appeared, and, as if they had known in advance what was needed of them, they busily set to work. Soon dust flew everywhere, and they scurried and crawled about, while the gnome who had been there first – for a gnome he was – played the role of a passive bystander. The other gnomes seemed to be underlings under his command.

"Now go to your room and think over what I told you," the gnome said to Mary, who was watching the goings-on with amazement. She immediately followed his instruction and took her leave. On the stairs she could still hear their hustling and bustling. She said a fervent evening prayer, stretched out on her bed, and was quickly enveloped in a deep sleep.

3

But soon things looked quite different in the happy dwelling of our foremother. Her husband took a massive blow to the chest from the hind hoof of a newly purchased, headstrong horse as he tried to hitch him to the plow. They had to carry him into the house, bleeding and on the brink of death, where he struggled to stay alive. When, through the constant nursing and loving attention of his wife and children, he returned to the land of the living, his health was so ruined that he couldn't attend to things and work as before; instead, he had to sit most of the time in the house and conserve his energy. That filled the formerly so active and industrious man with such bitter grief that his sorrow sapped his strength even more, and he became a mere shadow of his former self. Mary did everything she could think of to console and cheer him, but in vain; his physical condition affected his spirits, and often the pious woman shuddered when she heard him utter these ominous words: "The Good Lord shouldn't have done this to me; the Heavenly Father has done me wrong!" She tried to suggest to him that such un-Christian thoughts were sacrilege, and she reminded him of his earlier faith and trust in God, which, had it been genuine, should only increase in adversity. But no consolation bore fruit with him, and he sank deeper and deeper into melancholy and despair.

Although Mary worked tirelessly with the children day and night, the blessings of heaven seemed to have left them. Besides the major misfortune that had befallen the father, numerous smaller incidents occurred that further diminished their prosperity. One cow after another fell in the stable, the sheep got mange, and two horses went lame and were practically useless. According to an old saying, the master's eye fattens the cows. Since the master of the house could no longer attend to affairs, he had to take on a stable boy, but the boy was terribly negligent and lazy, and so one mishap happened after another. Finally, they figured out that the feckless servant was at fault and dismissed him. To add to the family's misfortune, the oldest son, who could have pitched in, had absolutely no interest in farming and did all his assigned work in the fields with the greatest reluctance. While his parents thought him hard at work in the fields, he stood for hours at a time at the seashore near his family's property, gazed out on the blue expanse, and sighed dreamily. If he saw a ship with fully drawn sails glide by or one disappear over the distant edge of the horizon, he was seized with terror that he might remain forever fettered to this clod of earth on which he had been born, while his restless heart continually yearned for distant shores.

This change in mood of the otherwise so upright and sensible lad Johannes had been brought about by an old seafarer who had achieved great wealth through innumerable voyages and now, in his old age, had bought the land adjoining that of our ancestors. Johannes often visited the jolly, zesty old man, who took a special liking to the handsome young fellow and told him stories about distant lands, peoples, customs, and traditions. He showed him all sorts of amazing things the young man had never seen before, so that gradually he felt the desire to see all these things with his own eyes. Constantly fed by the old man's stories and descriptions, this wish became an uncontrollable passion in him that even his characteristic common sense could not subdue.

He couldn't help subtly mentioning this wanderlust in conversations with his parents, but his mother always shooed him away, saying, "And if you, the oldest son, now the mainstay of the family given your father's frailty, if you were to go away, what would become of us?" Johannes blushed crimson at the reproach and fell silent, but the more carefully he hid his desires, the louder they grew in his heart, and the more uncontrollable became his longing for distant shores.

One day, when they were not expecting any guests and were quite disconsolate because of the father's deepening illness and new mishaps in the household, the old seafarer appeared at the door. After kindly greeting all the family and taking a seat in the padded armchair usually reserved for guests, he started in.

"I've heard, good neighbor, that you've lost a lot recently because of your stable boy's carelessness and negligence. All that could be amply recouped if your granary were full, for I have it on good authority that famine has broken out in the distant country of Spain, and those who bring in grain can make a fortune. If you have any extra, don't pass up the opportunity to send it there with a trusted person, and I think your son Johannes is just the one; he's already hankering for adventure. I still have a fast sailing ship in the harbor. It's currently unrigged, but it could quickly be put in order, and I'd lend it to you for a trip to Cádiz – that's the name of the place in Spain to which the grain has to be brought. Your undeserved misfortune distresses me sorely. I'd like to help if I can."

Caught off guard by his remarks, the couple listened to the old man, while Johannes sat there with flaming red cheeks. The pounding of his heart was almost audible, for now the moment had come when it would be decided if his greatest and sole wish would be realized or forever dashed!

Circumspect as always, Mary spoke after a bit.

"Even if we did have some excess grain and wanted to send it to the famine victims for their and our salvation, the only one we could entrust with this business is our Johannes, and he's no sailor. He's only been out fishing a few hours on a restless sea; he has no experience with seafaring and its dangers. If we were to accept your offer, which under certain conditions is probably a good one, we might lose him, your ship, and our last worldly possessions; it will come to naught."

"I didn't mean," said the old man, "that we would put Johannes in charge of the ship. We'd find another captain – why, he's already here! It's my former boatswain. He's just arrived and brought me the news about the famine in Spain. We'd send Johannes along with the shipment as the broker, and I'll also send along grain that I'll buy for this purpose. He'll represent our common interests, and when he's completed the transaction, he's certain to bring back a tidy sum – money isn't so scarce in that land as it is here."

"I like the sound of that!" cried the father, cheered for the first time by renewed hopes. "But what do you say, Mother?"

"I say," she replied, "it would be wise to follow the proverb: 'Stay at home and earn your living honestly.' How could we entrust our son to turbulent seas and dubious far-off shores when right now we only have enough bread for him and ourselves? Wouldn't it be tempting God if we sent him off under these conditions? There is greater suffering than the loss of earthly goods, which are easily replaced. Who knows if we're not endangering his eternal soul if we let him sail off to distant lands at such an early age? No, I'll never give my approval. Our current losses are great and painful, but they are bearable because they came from God's hand, and we can recoup them because we work hard and save. Heaven can replace with one hand what was taken from us with the other. But if I had to blame myself for the death of my beloved son or his moral undoing, I could never be happy again, even if I got Croesus's treasures for it." Thus spoke the upright and sensible woman, but she hadn't convinced the men. They gave each other a sign that they wanted to discuss the matter further when she'd left the room, which she soon did, since she wasn't used to sitting idly in the parlor but instead went to attend to things in the house.

As soon as she had left the room, the two men continued the conversation while Johannes listened enraptured from the corner of the room. Finally, they parted after Curt – that was the father's name – had shaken hands with the seafarer. They agreed that Johannes, despite his mother's protestations, would take a shipment of grain to Spain. The seafarer promised to equip the ship as quickly as possible and to put together a competent crew so that the voyage, from which they expected large profits, could proceed apace. Overjoyed, the youth followed behind the old man as he left and squeezed his hand at least ten times in gratitude.

"I was actually thinking of you when I made the suggestion, my lad," said the warm-hearted old man, smiling. "You're old enough and impetuous; why should you keep hanging around on dry land? There's a great wide world out there to explore! Once you've tasted freedom, you won't be able to stand being confined anymore. I know from experience. You'll turn into a fine and worthy seafarer, as I was in my youth!" And so they parted.

But Mistress Mary simply couldn't accept her fate, no matter how much her husband expounded on the advantages they'd have from their son's trip. As a good, obedient wife she didn't argue anymore after her husband had announced his decision, but her heart was heavy, and as she made preparations for the journey, great, heavy tears cascaded to the floor. She sought refuge in prayer so as not to fall into complete despair.

4

Finally, the ship stood fully manned and ready to set sail in the harbor (called the "Spot" on the island), and all the excess grain had been loaded. They had even used almost all the gold pennies to buy up grain from others, so that the ship held all the family possessed.

With a flood of tears and a broken heart, Mistress Mary bid her firstborn good-bye, and the other children wept as their beloved brother took their hands in his for the last time. Despite his yearning for far-off shores, he still found it hard to leave them. Although he put a brave face on it, even their father had to turn away a number of times to hide his tears, and then their beloved son was off, and his family watched with tears in their eyes as he sailed away.

All good fortune seemed to have left them with Johannes's departure;

there was one mishap after another. The crops, the best hope of support for the family for the next two years, were so ruined by wet weather that they didn't bring in half the harvest, and that half soon rotted. It all foretold a very sad winter if Johannes didn't return by autumn with money he'd made from the sale of the grain, but they continued to feel confident, because the old sailor had assured them he could be back in as little as two months.

The two months passed, and the harsh autumn storms that make seafaring so dangerous set in, and still Johannes was not back. The sea was soon covered with a thin sheet of ice, and thus ended the sailing season for the region. Poor Mary's heart sank, and in a sea of tears she broke the little bread they had left for the children. Since the situation was beginning to get desperate, she herself often took nothing in order to give them a bigger portion. Besides, she was so dismayed about Johannes that she couldn't have eaten anyway. Soon she lost the rosy glow in her formerly pretty face. The younger children noticed the difference with heartfelt distress; the older, wiser children were simply heartbroken.

Curt, the father, sank into deeper and deeper melancholy, for although there was never a reproach or even a hint of one from his wife's lips, his conscience told him that he alone bore responsibility for the misfortune they were now experiencing. Racked by this guilt, he lost all peace of mind and the last remnants of his health, so that even though before he had been able to get around a bit, now he was bedridden and for days often never spoke even a word to his family.

Under such circumstances the happy banter in the house died away and was replaced by gloomy looks and pale, careworn faces. In addition, the winter was exceptionally hard and stormy, and the worries about the still missing Johannes only increased with each storm. "Right now he might be lost at sea and in mortal peril and raising his arms to heaven; maybe he's being swallowed up by a fiendish wave!" These and similar thoughts troubled his mother's heart when a storm howled outside and the icy wind beat against the windowpanes.

Only the most fervent prayer managed to restore a sense of peace in such moments, and peace is what Mary desperately needed. Slowly but surely real hunger settled in, and many an evening the children had to go to bed hungry. The neighbors, who knew of the family's plight, often secretly left bread and other food at the door at night; openly giving charity to people who had been wealthy offended their sense of propriety. But the donations were not enough to feed so many hungry mouths, and the seafaring neighbor, who certainly would have been happy to help, had to everyone's amazement suddenly disappeared, and no one knew where he had gone.

Only one of the gold pennies was still in Mary's possession. She had always avoided spending this last one. She'd been resolved not to use it, not because she was afraid of the gnome, for she would have dared anything for love of her family, but because she thought it ungodly to enter into communion with those spooky creatures. She also couldn't picture leaving her ailing husband and suffering children. And yet her hand constantly trembled whenever she reached out for the sole remaining gold coin to buy some necessity, and so it remained a long time untouched. But now their plight was too desperate; there had been no fire in the hearth for two days, and it was unbearably cold in the house. The smaller children complained loudly of hunger, while the older ones bore the torture in silence so as not to break their mother's heart, for she was already suffering immeasurably. The invalid father lay with a raging fever in bed, cried of thirst, and in his wild, feverish rantings begged to have it quenched. With that Mistress Mary went to the little chest where she kept the gold penny, took it, and ran out of the house to buy the most urgent things. On the way she said with folded hands, "Lord, I entrust my family and my destiny to You; don't desert Your pious children."

But soon the gold penny was all spent, and there was nowhere to turn for help. As hard as it was for her, as a person who had grown up in plenty, Mary had to rely on the kindness of others; this final feat, the most difficult, she could only accomplish with constant prayer. She begged God for humility and trust and knelt in fervent prayer in a secluded little chamber, and the Lord did not desert her! He filled her heart with His unfailing divine solace: Mary stood up, consoled and determined to accept the help of good people. There was suddenly a rustling next to her, and as she looked around in fright, she saw the little gray man standing behind a table in the middle of the chamber. He was holding a very small but bright lantern in his hand and looked quite agitated.

"You rejected our help, Mary," he said, "and even in your hour of need you did not come to us for help. Nonetheless, I'm here on an urgent mission. Our queen mother is lying in and has been for many, many hours already. If you, an experienced woman and mother of so many children, could come to us just long enough to deliver the baby, we would repay your kindness a thousandfold."

"If you promise that I may return immediately after the baby is born," the compassionate Mary interrupted him; she hadn't heard the last part of his speech but only the first. "I'll go with you and assist her if you really think I can be of help, but then I must be allowed to return immediately."

"I give my word on it," said the gnome. "But follow me now, for time is fleeting."

"In the name of the Father and the Son, I'm right behind you!" said Mary, making the sign of the cross. To her great joy she saw that the gnome, too, had made this sign that horrifies evil spirits.

The doors, which had been closed, opened wide as the gnome tapped them with his wand, and soon they were in the open air. It was a frightfully cold night. The wind howled and whipped the flags on the clock tower, huge masses of clouds announced a monstrous snowstorm and blocked out every star, and everything was shrouded in total darkness, except where the gnome tread – his path was paved by a single ray of light in the darkness. Mary followed at his heels and said several prayers along the way to muster her courage for the coming challenge of helping a sufferer out of love and sympathy, for that alone was what motivated her. She would not have gone under any other circumstances.

Finally, they arrived at the appointed hill; the gnome blew three times into his silver whistle, and immediately the hill cleaved open to reveal a large entrance illuminated on either side with brightly colored twinkling lights. Friendly chatter and the following words could be heard:

Piper is here, Piper is here.
The kind and hard-working woman is near!

Hardly had they entered the passage than the hill rumbled closed behind them. Mary found herself completely cut off from all her fellow creatures and at the mercy of mischievous little gnomes about whose many pranks she'd heard in her childhood. She couldn't help shuddering at the thought, but the knowledge that she'd come of her own accord and with the best intentions buoyed her flagging courage, and she hurried behind her guide, who was speeding along as fast as his little legs could carry him.

Soon gnomes came running from all directions, and their size made their urgency seem almost comical. They surrounded Mary and led her to a small, pure white bed on which lay a small woman wearing a golden crown. She moaned and whimpered pitifully and anxiously stretched her tiny hands out to Mary. The bed was of pure gold. A large red stone set in its canopy spread light; indeed, it was a ruby, which is said to have the power of illumination. At the head of the bed stood a gnome whose stature distinguished him from the others in this underground world. A long, snow white beard hung down to his belt, on his head he wore a crown studded with magnificent jewels, and in his hand he held a golden scepter. Otherwise he was dressed like the others, but Mary recognized by his crown that he must be the king. She bowed before him, and he cordially returned her greeting, but his face betrayed his intense concern, which seemed to mount with every cry of pain the woman let out.

"Welcome, dear lady," began the king, "and help my queen in her hour of need. You will be richly rewarded."

"I'm not here for the reward but only to help," replied Mary. "And with God's help I'll be successful. But I must ask you all to leave, and that includes you, Your Majesty. Having others present distracts me and distresses the patient."

At that the king tiptoed out, and the woman in childbed found herself completely alone with Mary, who proved herself so adept and experienced that in a twinkling of time a healthy little baby boy, hardly an inch long, lay at the breast of his thankful mother.

You should have heard the cries of joy that rang out in that underground world. Mary feared she'd go deaf, and she covered both ears to wait for the first wave of joy to die down, but she watched the leaps and comical gyrations of the gnomes as they hopped about on one leg, twirled on their heels, and somersaulted past each other. Piper, who had been her escort, stood quietly by and blew on a little golden flute whose pitch was so shrill and high that Mary plugged her ears again after the first notes. Finally, they formed a procession: the tiny piper continued to play, but the commotion and shouting ended, and their faces grew solemn again. Every gnome held a flower garland, and, with Piper in the lead, they moved toward the spot where Mary still stood next to the queen's bed, busy with mother and child. Before she knew what was happening, she found herself in a fragrant bower the gnomes had skillfully assembled from the floral wreaths. The gnomes then sang a solemn hymn that praised Mary's virtues, especially her diligence and her compassionate heart. When the song ended, the king approached her with a solemn face, grasped one of her hands, and said, "Today you have done us a great service, and our gratitude is endless. Let it be known that, according to ancient unquestioned laws, our queens can bear children only when a mortal, moved by compassion and not by the desire for material gain, enters our underground world to assist them. You have passed every test and came with a pure heart and out of true compassion; so, too, will our gratitude know no bounds. I'll lead you through our treasures so that you may make your own choice. In addition, we want to show our goodwill toward your descendants and bless them in all their activities as long as they remain worthy of your name."

Mary was very surprised by this speech and remained silent for a while before she said, "I know from my ancestors' stories that you possess many secrets of nature and know how to make all sorts of herbal potions and elixirs that can restore a person to health. If you could give me something that would restore the good health my poor suffering husband once enjoyed,

I would consider myself rewarded beyond measure for the small service I willingly performed here, and I would put my faith in God, who has the best interests of His children at heart."

"You have chosen wisely, Mary," responded the king. "For good health is a thing more precious than riches and treasures. Yes, we possess such healing potions and will give you a flask. Pour its contents into your husband's cup, and from that moment on his pain will diminish and eventually completely disappear. He will actually be healthier and stronger than before."

"Then blessed be the hour that I came to you, good spirits!" Mary said, clearly moved. "I will always remember you from the bottom of my heart and not allow others to ridicule your name, as often happens on Earth, since you are unknown to us."

"Come now and review our treasures," the king said. "It doesn't happen often that mortals have the chance, since they've so often deceived us and cruelly derided us after we've led them here and given them riches. We've grown cautious and timid and only traffic with humans when we perceive great and exceptional virtues in them such as yours. In any case, your business here is finished. You see that the queen has fallen asleep with the newborn prince and will stay that way for several months until she reawakens and receives our congratulations."

"Then I would like to get back to my suffering husband and children right away," said Mary. "They may just have awakened and be wondering where I am. But I'd still like to stay a moment longer to see your treasures about which I've heard so much; then please escort me back again, as Piper promised."

The king commanded her to follow him and pledged again a speedy return to her loved ones. The treasures Mary saw in the underground realm can barely be described: gardens with lovely flowers that emitted a spicy fragrance, trees on which golden and silver fruits hung and where rare and colorful birds perched and sang the sweetest of melodies from their tiny throats, brooks of sparkling molten silver, grottoes of the most colorful precious stones that emitted brilliant light – those and many other things unknown on Earth unfolded before Mary's eyes. But soon she had seen enough; without asking for any of the displayed treasures, she reminded the king again of the promised potion for poor, suffering Curt and asked that she be led back to her loved ones. The king nodded to Piper, who took up his little lantern and led her to the portal, which opened immediately upon his command.

Soon she felt a blast of cold night air and, after a short while, was back in front of her own house, where everyone seemed still to be asleep, since the dark of night still enveloped the earth. "I leave you now and forever, pious lady," said the gnome who was accompanying her. "For according to our laws, we are now banned in the coming centuries from trafficking openly with humans, but remember us in love and affection as we will always remember you and yours. As long as your line shall live, so shall they enjoy our protection; we will invisibly help and bless the efforts of the industrious and loyal heirs of your virtues. But whoever strays from the path you have paved with your example cannot rely on our help, for whoever betrays himself betrays our trust. You will find the gift our king promised on your night table; use it with a pure heart, and be assured that it will bring you rich rewards."

With these last words the gnome disappeared in the cloak of night, and Mary felt her way into the house, whose doors stood open. Since there was no light and no fire burning in the house, she had to find her bed in the dark. After the fervent prayer she always said before bed, she fell asleep, exhausted.

5

The sun was already high in the sky when she awoke. Shocked at having tarried so long, she jumped out of bed and immediately glanced at the table in the corner of the room. On it lay beautiful bouquets. Surprised, she reached to pick one up and found that she could barely lift it: they were of pure gold, and the flowers were fashioned of all sorts of precious stones. The flask with the magic potion to restore her husband's health lay in their midst. She fell to her knees in gratitude and could hardly pray through her tears. Now all of her worries were over, and she was richer than she had ever dreamed or hoped. But nothing made her happier than the flask. She immediately poured its contents into a cup and brought it to her husband; at her urging he willingly drank down the sweet-tasting brew.

Mary took a few leaves from her bouquets to a man who knew the value of metals, and he gave her what was a sizable sum in those days. She bought all kinds of food with the money and came home heavily laden, finding everyone up, hungry and thirsty.

"Here, eat and drink to your heart's content!" she said, eyes aglow. "But thank the Lord, who sent us such unexpected relief in our time of need."

They all crowded around her and wanted to know how she had come by such riches, but she refused to tell her children how she got them for fear that they'd become lazy, a vice she hated more than any other. She carefully locked away her treasures and told only her husband, who was feeling visibly better; he shared her view and swore complete secrecy.

Now everything in the household began to look different. The father of the family stood again with both feet at the head of his household. They bought new livestock and had an even larger herd than before; a few outlying fields were bought and carefully planted with the children's help and that of some loyal servants. The neighbors speculated that the family had found a hidden treasure in the house, because nothing else could explain their current prosperity, but since they were universally well loved, no one begrudged them this unexpected good fortune or was envious. Of course, the family did possess a treasure: Mary, the pious, diligent mother, a paragon of virtue and propriety. Not even the material wealth Mary had gotten from the gnomes and held in safekeeping could compare to the treasure she carried in her heart.

Despite the increasing prosperity of the family, Johannes's absence was still a gaping wound in every heart, and the probability that he was lost forever dampened all their spirits. If his name were accidentally mentioned, tears sprang to their eyes, and if they happened to be sitting down to a meal, the food remained untouched. The spring and summer were almost over, and still there was no news of him or the ship. Mary often stood at the shore and looked yearningly out at the sea, but the ship with her beloved son refused to appear. Even more heart-wrenching was the father's grief; he viewed himself as solely responsible for the misfortune that plagued his family, which otherwise could have been so content and happy. If he hadn't so insisted on sending his son out into the wide world, he might be with them right now, sharing in their good fortune. No one saw or heard of the old seafarer either; he seemed to have disappeared without a trace. His house was shuttered, and his usually lovely garden was now completely overgrown because it was untended.

Another two years passed, and the idea took hold in everyone's minds that Johannes must have perished at sea. Two of Mary's daughters had already found worthy husbands and were happily married, and a third was engaged. Then, one morning, to everyone's great surprise, they saw the seaman's house open wide, the windows unshuttered, and him in the doorway. But when he spied someone from the family, he stepped back quickly. He seemed to want to avoid seeing them.

Mary, hoping to find out something about her missing son, decided to ignore his strange behavior and went over to greet him. As she entered his house, he covered his face with his hands and cried, "Please don't reproach me; I've already reproached myself enough. I looked everywhere for Johannes, but in vain. He never arrived in Cádiz, where I went first. He and the shipment must have been lost at sea."

Mary could tell from what he'd said that the old man, driven by worry for the missing Johannes, had lost all semblance of peace and had gone looking for him. She was deeply moved and answered him gently, "We're all in the Lord's hands. I didn't come to criticize you, dear neighbor. I know you meant well."

"Thank you for your kind words, Mistress Mary," the seaman said, moved. "What else should I have expected from you – you are always so gentle and kind. I want to bequeath all of my money and possessions to your children and make them rich, very rich. Just don't look at me askance when I come over for a short visit to chat about my seafaring days."

"May the Good Lord keep us from looking askance at you, neighbor," she said to him. "Come as often as you like; we'll save a cozy spot for you, and you'll be welcome whenever you come. We don't need your riches to add to our good fortune."

"Yes, you yourselves have become quite wealthy," he replied. "So I really can't give you anything more to increase your happiness." They parted at this point, and, with a heavy heart, Mary headed home through the garden.

At the doorstep she saw a tall, gaunt man clothed in rags; he seemed to be paying a great deal of attention to the splendidly furnished house and the new stables around it. "Surely a person in need," she said to herself and reached into her purse to give him generous alms. But as she drew nearer, his features seemed so familiar to her, and good heavens! She recognized the long-lost, long-lamented Johannes!

Sobbing, he rested his head on his mother's breast, and for a long time neither of them could find words to express their feelings. Then she led him into the house and, shouting for joy, presented him to the other children and her rejoicing husband.

After a hearty meal and a change of clothes, he had to tell of his adventures, which we're saving for the concluding chapter of this tale.

6

"At the outset," Johannes began his story, "our voyage started under favorable winds, and we sailed far, far out to sea until we had only sky and water before us. My heart was light and gay as land disappeared from sight, for as long as I could still see land, it seemed to me that I still wasn't sailing away and that I might be drawn back by some unforeseen circumstance. Oh, but all too soon I had no more fervent wish than to see dry land again!

"We had already been sailing for a number of days when the boatsman announced we were not far from our destination. But suddenly such a great storm arose in the north that our sails tore and our mast toppled, and we were blown inexorably southward. Besides the perils the gale winds and flooding on deck presented, our ship was repeatedly tossed against an underwater reef and sprang several leaks. We tried with might and main to bail out the water rushing in, but soon our situation became hopeless, and the boatsman told me I should prepare to die. In the hopes of escaping with our lives, we had already jettisoned into the sea all the lovely grain we had on board, and we looked sadly on as it floated away in yellow streams. Oh, my heart was heavy, and I wept bitterly as I thought of all the pains and work we, and above all you, my beloved parents, had expended to plant the grain, to harvest it, and to bring it to the drying floor. I remembered how we had sweated in the scorching sun during the harvest, and how you, beloved mother, how you disapproved when we children ground even the smallest bread crumb into the sand. And now I watched it float away, all the rich blessings of the Lord, the fruit of our labors and savings, our last hope to help us out of our circumstances, hopelessly lost to any of God's creatures. My heart nearly burst, and I longed for death, because to return to you empty-handed, to see all your hopes dashed, seemed more ghastly than death!

"My wishes, as foolish and sacrilegious as they were, were close to coming true. Just as, to our great joy, we sighted land, our ship took a great blow and split from stem to stern. Everyone on board fell into the sea and presumably drowned, for I never saw anyone from the crew again. Only a few remnants of the ship washed up on shore, which I myself managed to reach with superhuman effort and because of my exceptional experience as a swimmer. Just when I thought I was about to die, which only moments before had seemed like the answer to my troubles, I realized how much I still loved life, and I knew that my desire to die had been a delusion. Why else would I try so hard to save myself?

"I finally reached the island – I verified that it was indeed an island as I traversed the entire area looking for any trace of human life – and lay unconscious for several hours on the shore. When I awoke, it was night, and I was surrounded by complete darkness, but the air was not cold, and my clothing had dried. I felt a raging hunger and burning thirst, both of which plagued me so that I began to moan and lament. The position of the moon suggested that morning was still far off, and I couldn't expect to find anything to satisfy my needs before day broke. At that moment I understood what it meant to be on a desert island completely cut off from civilization, and, because no one heard my suffering, no one approached me with compassion to console me or to offer me food and drink. In addition, I had an almost unbearable pain in my head, and when I reached up to touch it, I noticed that blood was running down the nape of my neck. I must have been injured by some debris from the ship and hadn't noticed it in my scramble to escape. I wrapped my neckerchief around the wound and lay down, and, exhausted as I was, I fell asleep again. When I awoke, the sun was already scorching hot; my hunger had given way to excruciating thirst, and my only thought was to quench it. I soon discovered a freshwater spring – I scooped up water in my hand and drank my fill. What refreshment! What gratitude to God filled my soul!

"After I had attended to this most urgent need and had bathed my head wound in the fresh springwater, I began looking for food. And what did I discover? The Good Lord had also laid a table for me in the desert. Luscious fruits and berries hung on the trees and bushes all around, so that I only had to reach out my hand to feast to my heart's content. After having refreshed myself, I knelt down and thanked the Lord for my salvation and for the provisions I'd received. Then I returned to the beach to see if anyone from our crew had managed to come ashore, but it was deathly still. Although I repeatedly called the names of the crew, no voice answered my call, and this convinced me that I was the sole survivor. This thought sobered me, as did the thought of you, my beloved parents, because I could vividly imagine your sorrow if I never returned or didn't return by the time you expected me. My heart was so heavy, especially when I thought of you, Mother, and how you had been against me going and all your misgivings. Your premonitions all came true: the wonderful grain, our mainstay and last hope, had been washed away by the sea, the neighbor's ship had sunk in ruins, and your son sat on a desert island where he could not even hope to find humans, since there was no sign of man-made structures. Your long-lost son was quite possibly forever lost to you and leading a piteous life while you mourned him. Yet in the middle of this anguish, your teachings, my dear parents, came back to me: 'He who forsakes himself forsakes God,' you used to say, and so I decided not to give in to the pain but to do everything in my power to improve my situation and to leave the rest in the Lord's hands.

"Several larger and smaller planks from the wreck had washed up on shore. With those I built myself a makeshift hut near the spring and from there roamed over the entire island; it was relatively small but uninhabited, although quite verdant.[1] The first year I worried about the impending winter, but it never set in, and that allayed my fears, both because of my clothing

---

1. Probably one of the Canary Islands, which include Madeira, the largest of the islands. They lie off the coast of Africa in the Atlantic Ocean; have someone show you where they are on the map, dear children.

and because of my food supplies. I had discovered absolutely no wild animals, and, in short, I might have enjoyed this place, for I lacked nothing but you.

"How long I remained on this island I cannot say, since I didn't keep track of the days. Since the seasons didn't change as they do here, I couldn't have kept track of them anyway, but I'm relatively certain that I remained there several years.

"I awoke one morning to hear voices near me. I couldn't believe my ears and thought it must be a dream, but soon men in sailor suits came over to me and spoke to me in a language I didn't understand. They were, as I found out later, Spaniards. Fortunately, one of them understood a little German. They brought him to me, and it was he who told me that the island, along with several others, had just been discovered and that they had come ashore here to take on drinking water and had found my hut. These people generously offered to take me with them to Spain, where they were heading, and I gratefully accepted their offer. Finally, I was to see Spain, which had been the object of my desire, but only as a beggar. Since I possessed absolutely nothing with which to eke out an existence, I had to beg my way back home.

"And here I am again in your midst, completely cured of my wanderlust. From now on I'll gladly till the ground that provides us with everything we need. He who seeks gold and riches and isn't satisfied with the fruit of his labors or who, like I, sets out into the wide world longing for adventure, let him experience what I did on my desert island, cut off from all human contact, and let him reform, as I did!"

With this Johannes ended his story, and everyone once again joyfully hugged the prodigal son. The entire family had come together as soon as they heard the joyous news that their brother was back, and they also sent for the neighbor so he could join in their celebration.

From this point on the family lived in peace and happiness and thanked the Lord for the material possessions they enjoyed. They spread out across the island and populated it. The little gnomes were never seen again, and exceptional strokes of luck of the earlier sort didn't reoccur. But if someone in this family was very industrious and competent, then it seemed that everything he put his mind and hand to succeeded. That was probably still due to the kindly gnomes, who had promised their support in such cases, even if it was unseen. They gave nothing to the lazy ones, and no one in this family received anything by chance; they had to earn everything through the sweat of their brow, which the better ones gladly did, for the tastiest bread is always homemade.

TRANSLATED BY SHAWN C. JARVIS

Prinzeſſin Roſalieb.

Ein Mährchen.

Erſtes Kapitel.

Roſalieb und die Fee Amarantha.

In einem ſchönen Lande, wo Wieſen und Haine ewig grün blie-
ben, und ſilberweiße Heerden Jahr ein, Jahr aus, auf blumigen
Triften weideten, lebte ein König und eine Königin, welche ein
einziges Töchterlein hatten, Roſalieb geheißen. Man hatte aber
der kleinen Prinzeſſin dieſen Namen gegeben, weil ſie mit den Roſen
an Schönheit und Lieblichkeit wetteiferte, aber auch gleich dieſen
manchen kleinen Dorn beſaß, nämlich mancherlei kindiſche Unarten,
wodurch ſie nicht ſelten ihre guten Eltern verletzte. Dieſe beſtanden
aus einem großen Eigenwillen, und einer Ungeduld, die ſtets augen-
blicklich die Erfüllung ihrer Wünſche begehrte.

Agnes Franz

1794–1843

Agnes Franz (pseudonym for Luise Antoinette Eleonore Konstanze Agnes Franzky) wrote for both young people and adults. She published folk legends, children's theater pieces, parables, riddles, prayers, and aphorisms. Schooled in German Classicism, Franz stressed bourgeois family virtues in her works as well as the traditional feminine traits of moderation, modesty, piety, love of children, sense of family, industry, patience, contentment, prudence, and cheerfulness. In her tales, striving for fame and fortune always takes second place to quiet and unassuming fulfillment of duty.

This sequestering tale presents one of the classical fairy tale punishments for female disobedience and curiosity. In contrast to the standard tower tales, this tale prepares the disobedient girl through her sequestration: she eventually writes the story of her life through learning to weave. Images of the tower, the spinning wheel, Pandora's box, and the forbidden key play out a complicated plot of maturation and self-discovery. Rosalieb plays an active role in her development and in the unfolding of her own life story.

Other stories to read with this piece include the Grimms' "Rapunzel" (1857 edition, no. 12), "The Three Spinners" (Aarne and Thompson, *The Types of the Folktale,* no. 501), and "The Pink Flower" (1857 edition no. 76), and "Rapunzel" by Sara Henderson Hay (in *Story Hour*). Stories of sequestered girls and women include Bettina von Arnim's "The Queen's Son" and Alfred, Lord Tennyson's "The Lady of Shallott." Tales of women's magical spinning are Benedikte Naubert's "The Cloak" (in Blackwell and Zantop, eds., *Bitter Healing*), "The Rose Cloud" (Jarvis, trans.), and the Grimms' no. 24, "Frau Holle." Modern Rapunzel stories are Gregory Frost, "The Root of the Matter," and Elizabeth A. Lynn, "The Princess in the Tower" (both in Datlow and Windling, eds., *Snow White, Blood Red*).

Agnes Franz, "Prinzessin Rosalieb. Ein Mährchen," in *Kinderlust von Agnes Franz* (Breslau: Ferdinand Hirt, 1841), n.p.

Princess Rosalieb

A Fairy Tale

1841

CHAPTER 1. *Rosalieb and the fairy Amarantha.*

In a beautiful country where fields and groves remained forever verdant and silver white herds grazed year-round on blooming meadows, there lived a king and a queen who had an only child, a daughter named Rosalieb. They had given the little princess this name because she rivaled the roses in beauty and loveliness, but, like them, she also had a thorn here and there, namely, many a childish bad habit with which she often wounded her parents. These bad habits included great obstinacy and an impatience to have her wishes satisfied immediately.

If her wishes were not fulfilled on the spot, she threw herself onto the ground and began to cry so loudly that the entire court came running, concerned and dismayed. If the king and the queen then gently uttered an admonishing word, or if they dared to give a serious reproach, the little princess behaved all the more badly and fell into a state that made her parents fear for the worst. Finally, the court doctor had to be called in. The doctor often expressed his humble opinion that a switch from a birch sprig would have a much better effect here than any medication, but that idea horrified the gentle queen, and she determined to consult instead with a neighboring fairy who had a reputation for great wisdom and insight.

Shortly thereafter the queen did, indeed, betake herself to the beneficent fairy Amarantha. She introduced the little princess to her, requesting her sage counsel about the princess's upbringing. Amarantha scrutinized Rosalieb and then, instead of all kinds of rules and admonitions, gave the queen two gifts for her little daughter that would assure the greatest success in her upbringing. The first was a ring designed to teach little Rosalieb obedience; the second was a little chest of ebony that was not to be given to the princess until her fifteenth birthday. Amarantha handed it to the queen with a gesture of great mystery and asked her to carry the key to it around her neck. Neither the queen nor anyone else was to open the little chest before the appointed time. What it concealed no one knew, but the tale circulated that it contained priceless jewels with the magical power to vanquish all of life's evils.

The queen, exceedingly pleased with these gifts, embraced the beneficent fairy and bid her to continue to look favorably upon her family. Rosalieb was very pleased with the pretty golden ring the fairy was kindly placing on her little finger while solemnly admonishing her to wear it at all times.

CHAPTER 2. *What came to pass with Rosalieb and the golden ring.*

After the queen had safely stored the small chest, she began to teach little Rosalieb all sorts of useful things. A tiny spinning wheel of ivory was fetched, and a golden loom, so that Rosalieb could learn diligence and dexterity and be an example to all the girls in the land. For a short time the little princess liked the new pastime. She even quickly grasped how to twist the golden threads and was pleased when the whirring wheel, commanded by her foot, danced around so merrily, but soon she asked for a different diversion, and her teacher was never able to get her to finish her tasks. "You could show persistence once in awhile, just for me!" the queen said one day, leading the impatient child back to her work. But Rosalieb angrily kicked over the little spinning wheel, stamped her foot, and yelled, "But I don't want to spin, and I never want to spin again!" At that the ring on her finger pricked her so that she winced in pain. "Ouch, ouch!" she wailed loudly and rushed back to her mother.

"See, see, my child!" began the queen after Rosalieb tearfully raised her smarting hand up to her. "The ring is reminding you to be obedient; you owe that to your parents. The fairy Amarantha saw your misbehavior and punished you!" At that Rosalieb looked timidly around the room, hurriedly righted the spinning wheel she'd tipped over, and began spinning so diligently that the queen was mightily pleased.

Another time the princess was supposed to learn how to produce a delicate tapestry, something in which she had shown special interest. She was given a pattern and colorful threads that had all been carefully arranged. But she insisted on doing the flowers and the designs according to her own taste and used such inappropriate colors for them that the queen became annoyed and ordered her to finish the flowers according to the pattern. "But I want to make the roses blue and the lilies red!" cried Rosalieb, snatching at the delicate threads in such a way that they all broke. All of a sudden she pulled her hand back, as if it had been sorely hurt. "The ring, that nasty thing, pricked me again!" she cried. "I wish that the fairy Amarantha had never given it to me, so I could do what I want and wouldn't have to obey anyone!"

"Rosalieb!" said the queen, deeply grieved. "Don't you love me and your father at all? Do you always need such a painful reminder to be obedient?" The little child regretted her bad behavior a thousand times over, threw her arms around her mother's neck, and swore improvement in such a touching way that her mother joyfully forgave her everything.

A long time passed during which Rosalieb brought her parents joy and sorrow by turns. Every time she resolved to be good, the old obstinacy surfaced again. She seldom could be brought to do tasks and useful activities, but she always had an insatiable appetite for games of all sorts, and she always wanted new and more splendid ones. She also craved things that were injurious or dangerous, and when her parents denied her them, she became indignant and furious, until the ring gave her the sign and she obeyed, at least for a while.

One day she took it into her head to see the little chest that the fairy had given her as a gift. In vain the queen explained to her that it had been the fairy's express order not to open the little chest before her fifteenth birthday. Rosalieb would not stop begging and cajoling, and she pleaded with the queen to show it to her from afar, so that the queen finally opened the cabinet in which the mysterious gift was stored.

Hardly had the little princess espied the small chest than she stretched out her hands toward it and demanded it be opened. In dismay the queen pushed the impetuous child back, hurriedly locked the cabinet, and hung the key around her neck again. Rosalieb was so livid that she ran out crying and vowed aloud that the little chest must belong to her without delay, cost what it may! Hardly had these words crossed her lips than the ring again did its duty. This time, however, the pain was worse than it had ever been before. In fierce indignation, Rosalieb rushed into the garden, looked carefully around, slid the ring off her finger, and shouted, "Off with you, you nasty ring! I don't want to have anything to do with you ever again. From now on you can lie wherever you want and give the frogs and toads your sage advice!" With these words she tugged the ring completely off and threw it over the garden wall.

CHAPTER 3. *How Rosalieb is spirited away to a secluded tower in the sea and what happened to her there.*

Rosalieb had already begun to rejoice that her little trick with the ring had succeeded when she heard a rumbling in the air as if a storm were brewing high above her. The sky darkened, and suddenly two phantoms of the night with broad, mighty wings descended on Rosalieb, grabbed her by her pretty blond hair, and, despite her protestations, carried her off high in the air over the gardens and fields, far, far away to the coast of the sea. There they set their captive down in an ancient, secluded tower that was built on cliffs completely surrounded by crashing waves.

"Here you shall remain and reap the fruits of your disobedience!" the spirits said to Rosalieb, leading her into a small chamber whose door was carefully secured with massive bolts. "Here is a spinning wheel, and there is a book you may page through and read when you have spun your measure for the day! If you work hard, the table will set itself for you daily, but if you don't finish your measure, then this switch will punish you, and you will go to bed hungry!"

Terrified, Rosalieb noticed a great briar switch, which the spirits were menacingly swinging to and fro. It accidentally glanced off her shoulders and produced such severe pain that she lost both sight and sound. She fainted, and when she awoke again, the spirits were gone, but everything else remained. She was horrified to realize that she was separated from everything she loved and was imprisoned in an odious, deserted tower.

"Oh, good heavens!" she sighed. "Who will rescue me? What a fool I was to disobey my beloved mother! Now I'm the prisoner of these horrible spirits, and no one can hear my lament on this cliff washed by the churning waves of the sea!"

With these words she ran frantically around the little chamber and tried getting out at the door and then at the window, but all these attempts were in vain. She couldn't budge the heavy bolts or the iron bars at the window, and she was overcome by the hopelessness of her situation. She threw herself on the ground and tore her pretty golden hair until, totally spent and exhausted, she finally fell into a deep slumber that shrouded her agitated spirit in soothing darkness.

The morning sun was already high in the sky when Rosalieb awoke. She looked about with a sigh and began to weep the bitterest tears all over again. "Why should I get up," she thought, "when no joy awaits me? My beautiful dolls and toys, everything is so far away! I'm not in the mood to spin, and I don't feel like reading, either. There's no breakfast ready the way I was accustomed to in the castle of my parents, so I think I'd rather just spend the whole day sleeping and dreaming in bed!" Then she remembered the spirits with the nasty briar switch, and in a split second she jumped up and rushed over to the spinning wheel, observing with a sigh the great heap of flax she was supposed to spin. She tried twisting a few threads, but she had hardly spun a quarter of an hour when her spoiled hands sank to her lap, and she lost all courage to finish the appointed measure. Instead of making further attempts, she rattled again at the lock and bolts. As the morning wore on toward noon, no set table appeared. Instead, the spirits suddenly materialized in the middle of the chamber, enveloped in a cloud of smoke.

"What did we command you to do? And have you completed your task?" they asked in a threatening tone, brandishing the feared briar switch over Rosalieb as she shielded her neck and arms in terror.

"Oh, I'll obey and do everything you say; just have mercy on me!" Rosalieb implored, sinking to her knees.

"So prove that you mean it!" shouted the spirits. "Remember this saying that we give you in parting to contemplate:

Distaff empty, spinning done,
Before the food for you will come."

With these words they led Rosalieb once again to her spinning wheel and then disappeared like a mist from the chamber.

Startled, Rosalieb watched them disappear and then began to spin faster than she had ever spun in her life. It was as if the menacing spirits were standing directly behind her with the briar switch, and she felt frightened and harried. Slowly the work improved. The threads turned pretty and round and the spindle filled so quickly that it was a joy to behold. Finally, everything had been spun from the distaff, and Rosalieb looked with satisfaction at the fruit of her labors. "What will happen now?" she wondered, because she felt a great pang of hunger. Suddenly, over her head she saw a folded cloth come floating down, just like a balloon. Immediately, it spread itself out on the table, and she saw an appetizing meal: roasted pigeon, fruits, cakes, a flask of clear springwater, and fresh bread. Quickly, Rosalieb pushed her chair up to the table, folded her hands, and sat down to her solitary supper. As great as her grief had been a short while ago, equally great was her pleasure now that the spirits had kept their word and provided so plentifully for her. She was also pleased that she had finished her work, and in high spirits she repeated to herself:

Distaff empty, spinning done,
Before the food for you will come.

After that she ate with the heartiest appetite and had to admit that no meal had ever tasted so good. When she finished and had said her mealtime prayer, she watched as the tablecloth folded itself up again, and she had to laugh as it ascended – with all the dishes – and disappeared into the gray vault of the chamber.

CHAPTER 4. *About the strange book Rosalieb found in the tower.*

Rosalieb decided to muster all her strength to satisfy the spirits and to assure their goodwill. That very same evening she opened the book they had left behind and took great pains to decipher its contents.

At first the reading did not go very well, because until now she had not concerned herself much with books, but when she by chance deciphered her own name, she was driven by curiosity to keep reading. She sat and read late into the night and soon had determined that all these tales were about her and that the book recorded her entire life up to this moment. At length, to her amazement she encountered a picture in which she immediately recognized herself. It showed the little princess receiving the golden ring from the fairy Amarantha. She laughed heartily at the accuracy of the likeness, but then she grew sad and said, "If I had become good and obedient, as Madame Amarantha wished, I wouldn't be sitting in this odious tower like a bewitched princess!"

She would have liked to continue paging through the book, but night fell, and she laid herself to rest. She soon slept as peacefully as in the bedchamber of her parents, and sweet dreams settled soothingly on her eyelids.

Rosalieb awoke with the sun and found her distaff already wound with new flax. She got up immediately to set to work without delay. At first her little hands almost failed her in their task, but she thought of the previous day and how she had nevertheless managed to finish her work.

"Nothing ventured, nothing gained!" she cried bravely, and soon the little wheel danced about and the spindle filled so fast that her eyes were hardly able to follow. To her amazement, she had all the flax spun before the rising sun announced midday. Soon she saw her reward – her little table most beautifully set again today. And – O joy! – a flask of wine was there too, as if a comforting hand wanted to provide a tonic for her exhausted limbs. That afternoon she leapt gaily as a deer about the little chamber, looked out the window with bright eyes, and thought, "Oh, if only my beloved mother were here and I could show her my work! How happy she would be!"

Immersed in this thought, she finally took up the book again, eager to learn more of its contents. "I simply have to see what has become of little Rosalieb!" she cried and applied herself once again to putting the words together. But woe, what she read did not bring joy to her heart. Here the little princess quarreled with her nurse, there she stood in mute defiance of the orders of her good parents, everywhere she saw her bad behavior. It was as if she were looking at herself in a mirror. To make her despair complete, she finally came across a picture that showed little Rosalieb, completely red in the face as she reached for the forbidden chest, stamping her foot.

"Oh, ugh! How ugly!" she cried out. "No, never again will I be so badly behaved and willful and make such an awful face!" She shut the book, rested her head on her hand, and stared in somber contemplation into space. Suddenly, she jumped up again and cried, "I'd like to know if little Rosalieb doesn't turn out to be very good and well behaved in the end!" She opened the book again and paged through it from cover to cover. But no other picture was to be found, and as she managed with great effort to read the titles of all the chapters, she noticed that the story ended with her abduction.

She stood up with a sigh and went to bed totally despondent. "Oh, how awful I am!" she said. "It's good nobody can see me in this lonely tower, because the way I look here, no one in the world could love me!"

CHAPTER 5. *How Rosalieb finds the picture of her parents, and how she is carried home in her sleep.*

Much time passed during which Rosalieb became more and more enlightened. The spirits visited her daily and taught her all sorts of useful occupations; they even brought her instructive books and showed their satisfaction when their pupil became more and more obedient, diligent, and skilled. If now and then there were little setbacks, when Rosalieb suddenly relapsed into her old unruly ways and did not obey the spirits, then the feared switch and the absence of the heavily laden tablecloth did their duty just in time, and Rosalieb became well mannered, obedient, and diligent, so that the spirits were satisfied.

One day, when she had done her task exceptionally well, they appeared with a large, magnificently bound book full of the most beautiful pictures. "We bring you this as a reward for your diligence!" they said. "Read it and see how satisfied you are now with little Rosalieb!"

Full of curiosity, she opened the book right away, and what did she see? The image of her very own self, crowned by long golden hair and sitting at a spinning wheel industriously spinning the delicate threads. Her countenance shone as fresh as the morning, and her little blue eyes looked so cheerfully back at her that she suddenly had to laugh. Full of inner satisfaction, she watched the sweet little picture and said, "My, if I look like that, I would prefer to go to my dear parents today rather than tomorrow."

As she continued to look through the book, she was surprised by the sight of two pictures in which she immediately recognized her father and her mother. It was as if the two of them were alive, their faces peering out of the book, so full of expression, so complete the similarity. They looked right at Rosalieb and appeared to wave to her. "Oh, my dear, dear parents!"

she cried, deeply moved. "Oh, if only I were in your arms again! Oh, how I would try to make good what I failed to do before! How I wish I could carry you in my arms and never disappoint you again!"

With that she showered the picture of her parents with a thousand kisses, rested her cheek on it, and then fell asleep with thoughts of her home. The spirits appeared and found Rosalieb sound asleep, bent over the picture of her parents. "The good child!" they said, watching her with satisfaction. "It's high time we take her back to her homeland." And they lifted Rosalieb gently up in their wings and carried her through the night, high over sea and land, through the air, to the castle of her father.

CHAPTER 6. *Rosalieb's awakening in her mother's arms and the celebrations given in her honor.*

The queen had just awakened from a dream in which she had rejoiced at seeing her lost child again. But who could describe her surprise when she really did find her fair Rosalieb next to her, older and more beautiful than ever, and the bitter time of separation vanished like a bad dream. She quickly called her ladies-in-waiting to convince her that her good fortune was real. She stroked the rosy cheek of the sleeping child and gently pushed the golden locks off her beloved face. "She's back, she's back!" she rejoiced, and she pressed her long-lost little daughter to her joyous heart.

Soon the king appeared too, drawn by the joyous tidings, and then everyone in the castle streamed in to greet the dear, beloved princess. Rosalieb now opened her eyes and, overwhelmed with joy, found herself with her parents. For a long time there was no end to the tender hugs, the questions and exchanges. Rosalieb related everything that had happened to her since she had taken off the fairy's ring, and everyone listened with great interest to the bizarre story. Finally, they all agreed that the spirits had surely been in the service of the benevolent fairy, and everything they had made to happen had been for Rosalieb's good. Soon one festivity followed the next to celebrate the return of the beloved princess. The entire land was to share the royal couple's joy. Even the poor and orphaned were invited to the royal table, and Rosalieb walked up and down and passed out costly presents among them, so that every heart would be happy and content. She wore a dress of the most sumptuous silver lamé and a garland of blooming roses in her hair. She delighted all who saw her, especially since she was as kind and fair as an angel to all her subjects and could speak with them about all sorts of useful things, as if she were their equal.

"Oh, my dear child!" the king said to her. "How happy I am that the time of our separation has borne such sweet fruit! Now our devotion should requite all the suffering you endured! From now on you shall have everything your heart desires, and I most solemnly swear to fulfill any wish of yours I can!"

Rosalieb kissed her father's hand and said that her only and most fervent wish would be to make her parents happy. The king drew her to his bosom and, taking a golden chain from his neck, said, "Now wear this, my child, as reward for your love and modesty, until the time comes when we can give you the most worthy gift, the precious little box the fairy Amarantha has set aside for your fifteenth birthday. That, we may hope, will joyously seal your fortune and ours!"

As the king spoke these words, Rosalieb blushed, because suddenly the old temptation welled up inside her, and she felt a burning desire to see the contents of the little chest.

"How old am I now, Father?" she asked quietly. "You'll be twelve this June, the month of roses!" answered the king, not noticing the sigh with which Rosalieb received this information. "Three more years!" she said to herself, and it seemed as if a shadow beclouded all her joy. She left the room disgruntled, thinking, "What good do all the treasures do me as long as I can't call mine the only thing that is supposed to make me happy?" And she brooded incessantly and puzzled back and forth what the treasure could be that lay hidden in the little box. "It's a gold crown for sure!" she finally decided. "And I'll be able to share my father's reign!"

She returned to her family and tried to amuse herself with all sorts of games, but although she was able to hide her distraction and restlessness on the outside, she wasn't able to control them on the inside. Over and over the wish welled up in her: "If I could just cast a single glance into the little box, I would be patient until that unforgettable treasure is mine."

CHAPTER 7. *How Rosalieb seizes the key to the little chest,*
and how she once again lands in the hands of the spirits.

A long time passed during which everyone believed that the young princess enjoyed total bliss, because everything that could embellish and brighten a life was lavished on her. She had a room hung with gleaming gold and silver wall hangings and filled with the most exquisite flowers and birds. Every day she could choose her playmates and engage in the most charming pastimes with them. Everything the kingdom had to offer in the way of costly fabrics and jewels was there for her choosing. Every day she could pick the most beautiful fruits and grapes and make others happy with them. But no matter what the king and queen dreamed up to make Rosalieb completely happy, there was always a slight hint of dissatisfaction on her brow, and she often sat for long hours engrossed in gloomy thoughts, as if a secret sorrow troubled her heart.

One day, as the queen was taking her midday rest, Rosalieb chanced into the chamber and noticed that the little chain with the golden key had slipped off the queen's neckband as she tossed in her sleep. Rosalieb recognized it right away. Her heart pounded as she stepped closer and stretched out her daring hand toward it. Without difficulty she undid the clasp, and the key fell into her hand. She hurried triumphantly with it into the adjacent chamber, quietly opened the cabinet, and, aquiver with joy, pulled out the forbidden gift.

Finally, it was in her hands, the beloved little chest! She admired it, she jostled it back and forth, she shook it in order to discern its secret contents from the sounds it made. In vain! Her curiosity was not satisfied in the least. Now she tried the key, just a tiny bit. A slight tap – and the little chest sprang open! But alas, what did she behold! With a clap of thunder a black tower of smoke billowed out of the chest, and she saw the two spirits, well known to her by now. As they seized her she cried out loudly, suspecting the spirits' intentions. But in the wink of an eye she was surrounded by the mighty wings, and they set off on the journey by air, over mountain and vale, over land and sea, until, to her horror, she found herself again in the secluded tower. All her good fortune was far, far away and perhaps gone forever.

CHAPTER 8. *How Rosalieb had to learn patience and what she once again saw in the fantastic book.*

"Oh, you foolish and rash creature!" rang out the spirits' scornful voices. "Haven't you learned patience and obedience yet?" And they pushed a great loom before her that was strung with such fine threads it looked as if the slightest breath would snap them. "Now weave and exercise patience!" they continued. "Mind our words! Whatsoever you sow, so shall you reap! You won't see us again, because you are old enough to know what's to your advantage!"

With these words they vanished and left the hopeless child, now feeling utterly desolate. For a long time Rosalieb stared blankly into space, unable even to think. Then she frantically grabbed the threads on the loom so that they hung in complete disarray.

"Kill me!" she shouted after the spirits. "I'd rather die than bear this despicable imprisonment again!" And she rattled the iron bars and locks, threw herself on the floor, and cried out in such heart-rending tones that even a stone would have been moved to pity. But the spirits did not return. The day passed, night came, and Rosalieb still wept, dissolved in utter despair. Finally, spent and exhausted, she fell asleep. A dream about her parents refreshed her. "Persevere!" her mother had said. "Persevere!" she repeated to herself as she awoke and raised her hands in prayer, asking for assistance in bearing this heavy burden.

"If only it were possible, and I could return to you again!" she cried out as she got up and, leaning on the iron bars of her window, looked into the distance. "Yes, then I could bear everything, everything!"

She went to the tangled loom and saw in horror what her temper tantrum had wrought. She tried to separate the jumbled threads and knot them together, but they were so delicate that they constantly broke. "Patience, patience!" she repeated to herself with a sigh and started the tedious work again. Often her eyes and hands failed while working at the arduous task, and she wept in defeat, but the thought of her parents always raised her spirits, and she tried again to think of ways to complete her task. Finally, she succeeded in knotting a few threads. Then she managed to get the other threads in order. After that, and after interminable effort, she finally had the entire loom back in working order, and she began weaving as diligently as she could.

Only after she had worked for a while did she notice that a delicate floral pattern was blossoming under her hands. It was as if the entire weaving was composed of roses and lilies, and it became more beautiful and more colorful the more quickly the little shuttle flew. "I thought this work would be much more difficult," she said, "but I see now that with a bit of perseverance you can accomplish anything, and that patience can transform even the most unpleasant task into roses!"

With this in mind she finished the difficult work before the day drew to a close. Then, to her joy, the familiar cloth floated down, full of refreshing things to eat and drink, and Rosalieb smiled and said, "The spirits haven't yet forgotten me, no matter how stern they seem!" With gratitude and joy she ate the tasty meal, and her heart was as content and happy as if she had eaten with her parents. With tender thoughts she wished her parents a good night and went to her lonely bed.

When she finished her work the next day and looked carefully around her little room, to her joy she again discovered the well-known book that had so often shortened her lonely hours. Cheerfully, she picked it up and began reading again. Since by now Rosalieb knew how to read, it wasn't hard for her to understand all the nice sayings and to read the many stories that she found inside. Every day she made new discoveries in the book, and often it seemed to her as if the pictures and stories in it changed overnight, because she was always surprised by a new illustration, and she never encountered the same story twice.

Thus passed weeks, months, and years, and Rosalieb still lived in the secluded tower and had no company other than the tiny birds and butterflies that occasionally came over from the shore, as if they wanted to tell her of the flowers and groves that she had not seen for ever so long!

One day, with her work for the day complete, she opened up the book to pass the time. She discovered a picture that brought back the fondest memories of her childhood. It was of a part of the park surrounding her parents' castle. Here, at the silver fountain, she had often sat with her nanny watching the little goldfish; there, in the shadowy grotto, was her father's favorite spot. Her mother walked along these paths every day.

As she continued to study the picture, she noticed two figures in the distance. They drew closer and closer. It was her parents! Without thinking, she reached out to them, but alas! They strolled by and did not even glance at her!

"Oh, my parents!" she sobbed. "What have I done, that you deny me your love? Don't you recognize your Rosalieb anymore, or has my disobedience so alienated you that you banish me from your hearts?" At this thought she wept the bitterest tears, reminded of all the attention and love she had received from her parents and her own unpardonable transgression! She felt they had every reason to be angry with her, and she felt the greatest remorse. "Oh, poor me," she cried, "that I can't make up for my failings! I could endure the worst punishment, if I could just reconcile with my parents!"

After Rosalieb had spent many days in deep despair, she once again took refuge in the book, as if to consult with her parents again. With trembling hands she opened it to a beautiful scene, one she immediately recognized as one of the glorious hayfields bordering the royal garden.

She had always loved this field best because of its many flowers. Her father's castle looked down upon it, and tall shade trees cast shadows and offered respite to the weary. Here she saw the colorful pastoral carpet spread out before the castle. Silver white lambs played in the swaying grass, and she heard a lovely flute. "That's the evening song of our old shepherd!" she cried happily, and then she actually spotted his venerable figure camped under one of the shade trees.

A feeling of indescribable longing awoke in her. It was as if she looked into a paradise full of innocence and joy and was being drawn over to kiss the cherished ground. "Oh, happy shepherd," she called out, "who always has the castle of my parents in sight! Oh, if only I sat, like you, under that shady tree and breathed in the spring air of home! How happy I would be to trade all my royal trappings for the shepherdess's frock, and I would be content to tend the flocks of my father, since I am no longer worthy of the good fortune to be called his daughter."

She bent over the beloved picture in mute melancholy, and the shepherd's flute continued to play, soothing her into blissful dreams. She fell asleep, surrounded by friendly images.

CHAPTER 9. *Rosalieb is turned into a shepherdess, the gift of flowers, and the happy end to the whole tale.*

Rosalieb must have slept a long time, because when she awoke she was able to open her eyes only with great difficulty. But, lo, what did she see when she did open her eyes? She was resting on the same meadow that she had seen in the book! Here stood the shade trees, and there, in the rosy dawn, was her parents' castle.

"Oh, good Lord!" cried Rosalieb. "Is it only a dream? Are my eyes worthy to greet my beloved homeland once again? Yes, yes! My heart's desire has been fulfilled! The shepherd's frock I'm wearing proves to which station I now belong, and I will joyfully perform my duties if I can occasionally see the countenance of my beloved parents from afar or sometimes strew a flower in their solitary path!" Upon saying this she hurried to the shepherd and asked him to entrust her with one of his flocks. He looked with amazement at the charming child and offered Rosalieb a place at his side.

The morning bell rang out in the royal palace. Rosalieb looked up, and tears of joys streamed from her eyes. She raised her hands, deeply moved.

"What's wrong?" asked the shepherd.

"Our king and his consort are going to chapel now!" she cried out. "Oh, could you, in my stead, put these roses on their prayer stool?"

"If you love our good king so, I'm happy to do you this favor!" replied the shepherd and took the roses that Rosalieb quickly gathered and covered with her tears.

As the king and queen entered the chapel and found the roses on the kneeler, they looked at each other, because today was Rosalieb's birthday, and each guessed the other's thoughts. So blushed the cheeks of our beloved child! both thought, but they didn't dare utter it aloud, because each respected the other's sorrow, and both had given up hope of ever seeing their child again.

After the service, the two strolled musing through the park and, from there, into the blooming meadow. The queen carried the roses at her heart, and it was as if they emitted a magical power, because she was able to smile today for the first time since the unhappy day when Rosalieb had disappeared. With renewed delight she greeted nature flourishing around her.

Then, as she passed by the meadow where the silver white herds were grazing, the queen suddenly spied a little bouquet of forget-me-nots at her feet. She picked it up. One bright dewdrop shivered on the bouquet, and it seemed to her as if the flower pleaded to her of love.

"Rosalieb!" she sighed again. Her little daughter's eyes were of the same blue, and an indescribable feeling of sadness and longing filled her heart the longer she looked at the tiny blue flowers.

But Rosalieb was hiding behind a bush. She had spied the royal couple from afar and had hurriedly strewn the flowers in their path. Carefully concealed, she ventured nearer to them, but the loud pounding of her heart almost betrayed her presence. But as the queen cried, "Alas, my beloved child! It's as if you yourself were looking at me from these flowers! Oh, if only you were alive and I could press you to my bosom!" Rosalieb could contain herself no longer. She stepped out and threw herself at her beloved parents' feet. "Forgive me, forgive me!" she cried, her head humbly bowed, while her astonished parents looked down in growing amazement at the beautiful maiden whose delicate and stately figure contrasted with the simple shepherd's frock. Then Rosalieb looked up, her golden hair fell back from her beautiful, beloved face, and her blue eyes spoke through her tears: "Oh, take back your repentant daughter with love!"

Both parents immediately recognized their daughter, and they lifted her up and drew her to their bosom. None found words to express the feelings in their hearts. Suddenly, a rosy glow surrounded them. The fairy Amarantha appeared in her celestial chariot and held in her left hand the little ebony chest.

"Receive today, on your fifteenth birthday, the gift intended for you," she said, facing Rosalieb. "It is neither jewels nor a crown that I offer you but rather a garland of evergreen that signifies the treasure of contentment. You thought you could seize it with guile before the time, but you deceived yourself, because only patience and humility lead to its possession! Now you have gained these virtues and have thereby reconciled with your destiny! Your innocent love made you once again worthy of this gift. So take it as your possession and wear this garland always. It will always unite material fortune with inner virtue, and whatever fortune shall come your way later, you will always possess enduring contentment!"

In gratitude and great emotion, Rosalieb bowed at the feet of her protectress, who blessed her and wove the meaningful garland into her hair. Joy and peace remained with the reunited family. The royal couple happily put their sorrows behind them, because Rosalieb became the star that brightened their days and shed sunny light on them, even in their old age.

TRANSLATED BY SHAWN C. JARVIS

Fanny Lewald. Portrait by Elisabeth Baumann-Jerichau, 1846.

Fanny Lewald

1811–1889

Fanny Lewald is best known as an important member of Berlin salon culture, as an emancipated supporter of women's rights, and for her copious and important production of novels and autobiographical writings. From an affluent Jewish family in East Prussia, Lewald converted to Protestantism in 1828 in order to marry a theologian, who died before the nuptials. She lived a sequestered life at home until she was thirty-two; then, moving to Berlin and with the support of her older cousin August, Lewald began publishing novels and stories. In Berlin she was acquainted with other female writers: Henriette Herz, Bettina von Arnim, Luise Mühlbach, and Therese von Bacheracht. Her works in the 1840s, like those of her fellow intellectuals of the literary and political movement "Young Germany," center on critiques of arranged marriages, divorce, and the social, educational, and legal situation of women. Along with Rahel Varnhagen von Ense and Henriette Herz, she is one of the most important voices of German Jewish women in nineteenth-century Germany. Later in life she married fellow writer Adolf Stahr and turned to German Classicism and the cult of Goethe, although she maintained her interest in and support of women's rights throughout her life.

"A Modern Fairy Tale" is her first published work, and it reveals many socially critical themes of the Young Germans. A young girl of marriageable age develops, with the help of her aunt, the ability to see the essences of people. At a dance she meets two charming gentlemen suitors; later, by dint of her "second sight," they are revealed to her as cold fish in search of a human soul. This tale stresses the notion of female mentors and female community, as do the tales of Benedikte Naubert and others in this collection. It is a reverse mermaid story, in which the male is the sea creature who is seeking out a mate to help him become a human being. Finally, like the tales of Sophie Tieck Bernhardi von Knorring and Ricarda Huch, it centers on a quest to see and learn the essence of things.

Among the many animal transformation stories, this can also be read with Juliana Horatia Ewing's "The Ogre Courting" (in Zipes, ed., *Victorian Fairy Tales*), the funny story of Managing Molly outwitting the ogre in marriage arrangements, and with A. S. Byatt's "The Story of the Eldest Princess" (in Christine and Heaton, eds., *Caught in a Story*), a girl who is not cut out for the marriage quest but has different gifts.

Fanny Lewald, "Ein modernes Märchen," *Europa: Chronik der gebildeten Welt* 2 (1841): 193–204.

A Modern Fairy Tale

1841

I N OUR FAMILY we had an old, unmarried aunt who was said to have been very beautiful and to have had hundreds of suitors, at least according to all the mothers in the family, but she had turned down even the most prestigious offers of marriage. That seemed to us young girls a complete puzzlement, and if any of the older women added, "Aunt Renate's fate has been strange, and she's a Sunday's child," then the curiosity with which we watched Renate was at its peak, and only the mysterious sound of the words "Sunday's child" kept us from delving deeper into the secret.

When a girl was to get married, Aunt Renate was always consulted, and her opinion often determined if the union took place. That was more than enough to instill reverent terror in us – you could never know how soon you yourself might be in the situation of trembling before Aunt Renate's pronouncements. I was the youngest girl in the family and probably didn't have to worry yet about anyone asking for my hand, but dear, sweet Renate inspired even in me a vague feeling of awe, besides a certain warm affection. I found everything about her terribly attractive: her stateliness, her aristocratic nose, her clear, dispassionate gaze, and above all her determined no-nonsense mouth with its classically beautiful lips. In addition, the odd, slightly nunlike garb and small lace bonnet she wore looked as proper as they were plain on her, and I pictured that Aunt Renate had never been anything other than eternally fifty years old and that she'd been born in that black dress. When I also considered that I was born on Sunday and therefore also a Sunday's child, it all became very eerie, and I would have loved to have known what it all meant. A hundred times over that question hovered on my lips when I was alone with Aunt Renate, but I could never find the courage actually to ask.

I was about fifteen when they began to take me along to get-togethers, although I had to play the unenviable part of a "small fry," as adolescent girls were inexplicably called in jest. Once, at the beginning of winter, all of the high society who had returned from their country estates and the spas gathered at my grandmother's house, and there was talk that a few foreigners who were spending the winter in Berlin were going to be introduced. There was music, people played cards, and the young people wandered about the various rooms in a fashion that is only possible at the start of winter before the various cliques have formed and little intrigues have begun. Suddenly, the doors opened, and our cousin Franz entered the room with two very handsome men. One, in a dashing foreign service uniform, was introduced as Baron von Salmon; the other, in elegant civilian attire, as Assessor Pike.

After a momentary pause for mutual introductions and greetings, the party suddenly livened up. Curls were quickly freshened up around pretty fingers, shawls were tugged into place, and all the little flirtations of which every girl is guilty began. The gentlemen who had been at the gathering all along took notice, while the two fortunate fellows who were the object of all these charms hardly seemed aware of them. They walked about chatting and finally went into the little parlor where Aunt Renate had taken refuge. They were soon engaged in conversation with her. I was leaning firmly against Aunt Renate's leather armchair, because I hadn't yet managed to move confidently and freely through the gathering and was therefore really content only when I had secured a place to stand next to the fireplace, in a window niche, or behind some chair or another.

At first the conversation was small talk. The gentlemen had traveled extensively, and people inquired about mutual acquaintances they had encountered. Aunt Renate praised the wonders of Berlin to them. Baron von Salmon was anxious to meet Berlin's famous men, particularly the literary ones, and soon they were discussing the latest works of literature, especially one book that contained a long discussion about the transmigration of souls. The gentlemen criticized the book harshly and stated the opinion that such nonsense shouldn't be discussed even in jest and that in modern times the transmigration of souls shouldn't be considered any more real than fairy tales.

At that Aunt Renate looked very grave. I thought she was piqued because the entire time they were speaking with her, these two strangers had been looking in my direction and seemed to address their comments to me, although I hadn't opened my mouth and probably wouldn't have answered much to a question directed at me anyway (that's how uneasy their attentions made me), but yet, somehow, I didn't mind them.

"So you consider the transmigration of souls akin to a fairy tale, Baron," Renate finally said, "but I have my own views. I, too, am very far from believing that any old gallant cavalier or beautiful princess could suddenly be transformed into a lion or a little bird – to what purpose? But isn't it possible that it could work the other way around? There I am not so certain."

Assessor Pike seemed displeased with the turn the conversation had taken and particularly with the discussion of the transmigration of souls. He had tried repeatedly to change the subject, but when my aunt began to explain her opinion in more detail, he practically heaved his chair to the side and left the room. Baron von Salmon seemed to disapprove of that immensely.

"But surely you don't believe, Madam," he said, "that there are, in truth, creatures able to change their form whenever they please?"

"Not whenever they please, but I do believe that a higher power may often so ordain it."

"But do you believe it is possible that a human could be condemned to a life as an animal?"

"Oh, Heaven forbid! That would be regression in nature, where such things are impossible. But I firmly believe that animals have a soul similar to ours and that this soul can, for a short period of time, leave its body and enter another, human one."

"That would certainly be an enviable advantage, Madam, if one could, whenever he pleased, admire his beloved in the salon and, an hour later as a nightingale, lull her off to sleep with the sweetest strains of love. Surely that would be an ability incomparable to anything in the human experience."

"Incomparable?" retorted Aunt Renate. "Isn't sleepwalking, when our spirit departs the earth while our body remains an empty shell, analogous? Who knows if our spirit can't float as a seraphim in the clouds and enjoy heavenly bliss just as much as the spirits of animals can appear in human form among us."

Baron von Salmon laughed uneasily, and I, too, felt totally uncomfortable, because Aunt Renate had never spoken this way before. She almost embarrassed me, and thus I was doubly happy when the band struck up a waltz, and Baron von Salmon offered me his hand. Dancing was the only entertainment in which I could participate in this company – and von Salmon was simply dashing.

I thought he would probably make some sarcastic comment about my aunt's conversation, so I was completely astonished when he remarked during a break that Mistress Renate was an exceptionally intelligent and astute lady whose opinion he valued highly. To me it seemed she had babbled utter nonsense, and I couldn't have listened much longer without bursting out in laughter.

The waltz with the baron had barely ended when the assessor held out his hand to me for a gallopade, and so I danced almost the entire evening with the two strangers. I was very pleased that somebody was finally courting me as my older cousins had been. I suddenly felt so grown-up and self-confident that I crossed the room without slinking along various chairs on the way. Indeed, I wasn't even irritated when I heard Franz say to the strangers, "What on earth do you see in Bertha? She is such a small fry!" This didn't faze me since I'd also heard the baron's answer – that he found this small fry very fascinating and that the assessor was of the same opinion. It was as if I had been transformed, and I was determined not to let myself be crowded into the background anymore because I – what was it? I myself didn't know for certain. Had I known that fine word back then I would have said I was, as I am today, emancipated.

What more can I tell? The strangers visited my parents the morning after the ball; after that they were invited over and came often. Even when we met somewhere else, they lavished all their attention solely on me, and soon the news spread everywhere that Assessor Pike and especially Baron von Salmon were seriously wooing Little Miss Einstädt. The young ladies purposely called me "Little" Miss Einstädt (although I certainly was not little) just to show they didn't consider me their equal, and they treated me like a baby. When I danced with my so-called admirers, they never asked, "What did you talk about?" but rather, "What did he tell you?" as if I wouldn't be able to participate in the conversation. But I got my revenge and didn't tell them about all the lovely speeches I heard. One thing I couldn't conceal: the gentlemen had such ice-cold hands that their touch chilled me to the bone, right through my glove. "So," laughed one of the young ladies, "the suitors of a small fry must be cold-blooded amphibians or fish. They're attracted to their own kind – that's what draws them to you." My blood boiled at that and my cheeks flushed, but what could I do? I was only courageous in the company of my dance partners; among ladies I was still a self-conscious child.

My parents watched all of this with the flattered pride of parents who observe the first conquests of an only child. Only Aunt Renate seemed concerned and often made very strange comments about my two admirers.

In those days I had to go once a week to read aloud at my grandparents' house, where Aunt Renate lived. Once I brought along *The Green Domino* and couldn't get enough of the wonderful piece. The listeners laughed, too, until I came to the passage: "It is a race of fish, condemned to live in human guise, lovers so brutal and men so gallant." I chortled with glee, but my grandmother looked over at Aunt Renate, who said with a sigh, "Körner is a true poet; his naive soul apprehends and senses what the reason of reasonable men cannot discern, and often he expresses the most astonishing truths, as if by divine inspiration, perhaps without even knowing it." I was completely puzzled by her solemnity and by the comment itself, and when Aunt Renate began to weep uncontrollably and went to her room, my grandmother, too, became upset and told me to stop reading. Everyone in the room fell silent. I felt anxious because it seemed to me I was on the verge of discovering some dark secret, and I decided to put the puzzle together right away, at any cost.

With a pounding heart I stole after Aunt Renate. Her room was completely dark; she was standing at the window, illuminated by the moonlight. I stepped over to her, kissed her hand, and begged her to tell me what was troubling her. She patted me and said, "I was just thinking of you, my dear, and I'm so pleased that you have come. I have to talk to you. Sit down next to me and listen." I did as she said, and she began.

"The two of us, my dear Bertha, are companions in suffering, if I may put it that way. We're both Sunday's children, and that's why I consider it my duty to tell you about my past and to share my experiences with you so that you might be spared the suffering that made my life a misery. You have probably noticed that my attitudes about the connections between the human and spirit world are different from those of others, and you yourself have probably accused me of being out of my head sometimes; a Sunday's child whose eyes have been opened sees everything differently and more clearly and thereby loses a certain connection to other people. A Sunday's child develops second sight when she has put an unhappy love affair behind her with a pure heart and without bitterness.

"Perhaps you have heard how a great philosopher, the sublime Spinoza, explained the secret of creation to us. The Almighty Supreme Being, the Godhead, fills the entire universe, and He reveals His presence and designs in different ways, depending on the perfection of the creations in which He resides. So blooms the Lord in the blossom, so play the rays of Heaven in the little goldfish in a bowl, so rises a heavenly cry of joy from the throat of the lark, and all the more beautifully and clearly does God reveal Himself in the smile of an innocent child, the pure countenance of a maiden, and the proud features of true manliness. Everywhere and in every form that the Lord has chosen, there are moments in which this divine power almost seems to transcend the form and is discerned by another creature with whom it resonates. That is the secret of affinities that suddenly draw us to strangers – that is the loyal look of a dog who understands our sorrow and shares it and whose empathy is a solace to us. Believe me, that is the only way the human love of plants and animals can be explained.

"For centuries, people, vaguely aware of these truths, had believed that the human spirit could be banished to the body of an animal, but that is lunacy. Everything in the world is progressing. That is why things may only evolve to higher beings, and that's why it is possible that the spirit of an animal can appear in human form but not the other way around. The transformation happens only temporarily, unless the transformed animal succeeds in winning the first love of a human heart. This love cements the animal spiritually in human form and secures its existence in that form. But this process often leads to the death of the person who has sacrificed everything glorious and sublime in spirit and soul for this first love, and, receiving no compensation for these gifts, at the very least succumbs to spiritual impoverishment if he or she doesn't try with might and main to connect to nature and other human beings and thereby come closer to the purest well of godliness.

"But I'm getting off the track of what you need to know. If you want to know more about the matter, read *Undine* by Fouqué, 'The Little Mermaid' by Andersen, and especially *Tomcat Murr* or *The Hound Braganza*. These stories have many amazing insights into the topic.

"But let me get back to my fate. When I was about eighteen years old, the time of the wars with the French, Colonel Belaigle came to our house. His bravery was known everywhere, his proud character and flattering ways – only toward women – attracted me to him, and he wooed me from the first moment we met. I was young and good and soon loved the imposing man body and soul; every fiber of my being lay open before him, and he seemed to feast with great pleasure on the riches that my soul exposed to him as it was laid bare for the first time. Although I was aware that the colonel appreciated all these feelings but that he did not share them, I put that out of my mind. I was so blissfully happy giving love that I felt no lack. Our relationship continued in this fashion for quite some time, until Belaigle asked for my hand in marriage, and my parents gave their consent. During the calm that ensued after our official engagement I began to have second thoughts about our relationship. I began to notice that we didn't understand one another at all. I grew sad because I had given myself to him body and soul but had gotten no response to the feelings that fulfilled me. To my betrothed, a scion of the revolution, religion was a fairy tale we had been liberated from by the philosophy of the century, and he treated decency and self-restraint as foolishness from which we also had to liberate ourselves.

"In my heart's desperation I turned to God and asked Him to stand by me and show me a way out of the situation, if that were possible. After this prayer I fell asleep and dreamt that my long-lost nursemaid came to me, took me to her quarters at the cloister, and let me rummage through her old trunks and closets as I had sometimes done as a child. I soon found an old hymnal in which the Lord was pictured as an old man with a crown as well as some small, faded shoes and pinafores I had worn as a child. In short, everything was there, just as it had been when I had visited her the last time. She also showed me a book of spells and dreams and recommended I seek help in them whenever I was in difficulty. Then I played in the small convent garden with children I'd never seen and picked buttercups and daisies, and when one of the children wanted to take my flowers away, Belaigle came with his regiment and seized my bouquet, swept me up in his arms, and flew away with me, while the regiment band played 'Où peut on être mieux, qu'au sein de sa famille!'

"In the midst of the flight I awoke and, remembering my earnest bedtime prayer, laughed about the dream, but suddenly I was stopped in my tracks thinking of the old book of spells – I had actually received it as a gift from the old woman and had put it away without looking at it. I felt like a fool for putting any stock in a silly book at this moment, but after I dressed, I looked all over for it and finally found it. Secretly, I sat down and read: cures for freckles, for the evil eye, for witches, and for hexes, horoscopes for every day of the year. Finally, I found something that took me aback: 'A girl born on the spring equinox that falls on a Sunday may experience wondrous things when the equinox and the girl's birthday once again coincide on a Sunday. If she is aflame in love and unhappy, so she should stand at a crossroads at noon and take careful note of what she sees. Let her not tell of it, however, if she values her life, except to warn someone in her family in the same situation, because an overabundance of knowledge produces headaches.'

"At first it all seemed like complete nonsense to me, but then I thought, What if there are things between heaven and earth that our philosophers can't even imagine? Besides that, my birthday, the twenty-second of March, was in a few days and on a Sunday. What harm could there be in happening to stroll along Frederick Street and waiting for the clock to toll twelve times where two streets intersect? Curiosity, a sense of adventure, and above all inner turmoil drove me to the attempt, because I was very unhappy. Enough said – I went!

"The weather was lovely, and I crossed a number of streets with a pounding heart because by now I was completely convinced that something unusual was going to happen to me. The clock tolled twelve; the first six tolls had not even died away when I suddenly felt I was bewitched. I saw a lady with a bird's head; later a man passed by with a physiognomy that was unmistakably feline; then I saw someone stride by blithely while the Angel of Death floated overhead. I took leave of my senses, and, as if whipped by the Furies, I hurried home, shuddering at the thought of seeing my family again. Pale as death, I entered the living room and was overjoyed to see my parents and family members – in their beloved and familiar forms – coming toward me.

But the terrible secret had been revealed to me too abruptly; my body suc-
cumbed to the terrible bewitchment, and, a few hours later, when Belaigle
came over, I lay in violent hallucinations. The doctor declared it was the
start of a brain fever. Belaigle, about whom I had been babbling the whole
time, demanded to see me, and they humored him because they hoped his
presence would calm me. But the moment I saw him I cried out wildly. My
betrothed was a huge eagle whose eyes glowed hideously and who seemed
about to devour me. 'Save me, save me!' I cried. 'Get that eagle out of here
or I'll die!' My mother thought it a new fever hallucination brought on by
my sick mind; Belaigle, however, became deathly pale and left the room.

"A long time passed about which I remember nothing, because I was either
delirious from fever or unconscious. When I finally regained consciousness,
the image of Belaigle turning into a mighty eagle hung before my eyes, and I
could not bring myself to ask about my betrothed, although I felt an empty
space in my heart and a deathly chill that almost killed me. My parents also
avoided mentioning the past until I was almost fully recuperated; then they
told me that on the very evening that I was taken ill, the colonel had written a
quick note in which he announced he would leave immediately to attend to
pressing matters, but that the length of the journey was yet undetermined.
No salutations to me, no mention of the past, no hope for a joyful future!
My parents simply couldn't make sense of it and searched in vain for information from the colonel's superiors, who were just as astonished about his
sudden disappearance and ascribed it to a mysterious misfortune. Only I
understood and knew everything. Of course, I had paid for this insight with
my peace of mind."

Aunt Renate fell silent, and a long pause ensued. I shuddered with fear,
and a premonition of the disaster that would have befallen me suddenly
welled up in me. My aunt pulled me over to her, kissed me, and heaved a
great sigh; then she held me as one holds a child on her lap and continued:
"Do you, dear Bertha, still remember the evening when Baron von Salmon
and Assessor Pike were introduced into our circle? I'll never forget my horror as I watched them enter the room and I saw them as two fish. I thought
of the misfortune that could once again plague our family. In growing fear I
watched their attentiveness toward you and your complete ingenuousness.
For a long time I felt compelled to tell you all this, but it was possible that
you would be indifferent toward the two, and I didn't want to destroy your
blissful innocence unnecessarily. Forgive me, my dear child, if I offend your
sensibilities, but it seems to me that for a number of days you were not en-
tirely indifferent toward the dashing Baron von Salmon. This evening, when
the line 'it is a race of fish' from Körner's poem reminded me of the unspeak-

able suffering in my life, I could no longer remain silent. You, my dear child, my poor Sunday's child! You shall never become the prey of one of those subhumans, you shall never experience the world in that naked, icy reality that freezes a warm heart!" And once again Aunt Renate fell silent.

I cried bitterly, because although I didn't love Baron von Salmon, it wouldn't have taken much to turn the pleasurable sensations he made me feel into love. I threw my arms around Renate's neck and begged her to save me and to arrange with my mother that I didn't have to see the gentlemen ever again. My aunt promised everything and wrote my parents that my grandmother wanted to keep me overnight as well as the next day and that she would send me home the following evening. She would take my place the next afternoon and would help do the honors at our little luncheon. She hoped that my mother would not be unhappy about the switch.

Of course, my mother was satisfied with the plan. I stayed at my grandmother's and waited impatiently for my aunt's return the next day. She arrived about seven in the evening and told me straight away that she had sat at my place between Salmon and Pike, who didn't seem happy about it at all. "I also spoke with your mother, dear Bertha," Renate continued, "and told her that I would like to have you as my companion on my trip to the spa that I will undertake in a few days. I think your parents will give us permission."

Later, when we were alone, she said to me, "Baron von Salmon seemed displeased about your departure, but I told him to consider that, at this time of year, when all the ice has melted away and the flowers are blooming and the waters flowing again, he and his friend must also find the residence tiresome. I strongly encouraged him to leave Berlin and go to the seashore or back to their homeland, which they curiously had never mentioned. Von Salmon became very alarmed because he probably suspected his secret was out. He explained that he and Assessor Pike had already decided to take a trip to the North Sea via Hamburg and that they were planning to take their leave of us today since they would be leaving Berlin at the break of dawn tomorrow."

And so it happened. The next morning we received their farewell cards – their *pour prendre congé* brought me to tears. I felt very strange and was dizzy again, like someone who has been pulled back from a precipice in the nick of time but, recalling the danger, experiences the vertigo again. Those were awful days! But my good aunt helped me through it all, and she and my mother, who knew as much as she needed to know about the secret, made preparations the next day for our journey. With the shopping, packing, leave-taking, and anticipation of all the things that were awaiting me on my first excursion, I found no time to contemplate the past.

The trip and the stay at the spa completely distracted me, since the impression that the baron had made on me was really only a fleeting one, and after my return I made the acquaintance of my present husband, in whom I possess an honest, complete, and wonderful person. Even Aunt Renate finds him absolutely magnificent. The past has retreated completely into the background, so that the episode with Assessor Pike and Baron von Salmon often seems to me like a dream or a fairy tale, although not more than three years have passed since this escapade.

TRANSLATED BY SHAWN C. JARVIS

Louise Dittmar

1807–1884

Louise Dittmar has been unknown to modern German literary history in spite of her politically radical writings in the 1840s. She was the seventh of ten children born into a Darmstadt family of modest means, but her parents had high educational and professional aspirations for their eight sons. Because her father, a government official, lacked the financial means for a dowry, she never married and lived out her life in Darmstadt. Louise and her family became politically active because of the exploits of one of her brothers, who was a collaborator of Georg Büchner in plots against the government during the period 1833–35. She and four of her brothers stood on the democratic side, while the rest of the family remained loyalist. Her democratic brothers emigrated after the failure of the revolution in 1848; she remained at home, silenced, but she never recanted her democratic politics. Dittmar is perhaps best known for her edition of selected theological works of Lessing and Feuerbach (1847) that stresses their deliberations on atheism. Her satirical poetry and prose criticize the petty bourgeois mentality of Germans and their political cowardice as well as their unfair and destructive social and gender relations.

"Tale of the Monkeys," taken from the satirical novel *Bekannte Geheimnisse* (Open secrets), is prefaced by a chapter of advice to the hero, Juste Milieu, from his mother. She tells him that he can have any girl he wants, since they are counted as worthless, extra baggage in modern civilization. Best he should try for a girl from the capital – that is, one whose father has political power – or one who has money. Before he sets off on his bride quest, his mother tells him this fairy tale as a lesson and a reminder about properly evaluating the "merchandise."

"Tale of the Monkeys" is no doubt influenced by Mme d'Aulnoy's French tale "Babiole," in which a princess is transformed soon after birth into a monkey. She is taken into a monkey kingdom to wed a monkey prince, but she escapes to find the prince of her heart. "Tale of the Monkeys" is not, however, a story of transformation but an emancipationist critique of marriage customs in the straitlaced Germany of the 1840s. Its animalization of marriage rites echoes Fanny Lewald's "A Modern Fairy Tale" and the anonymous "The Giants' Forest."

[Louise Dittmar], *Bekannte Geheimnisse, eine Satire* (Darmstadt: Carl Wilhelm Leske, 1845), 29–37.

Tale of the Monkeys

1845

ONCE UPON A TIME there was a merchant who dealt wholesale in monkeys. But after awhile the monkey trade began to decline, and the merchant went bankrupt. What to do with that huge stockpile of monkeys? The merchant knew of nothing else to do with them except buy and sell them. They were eating up his capital, but he thought drowning them would be a shame. Yet his warehouse was so overstocked that the poor monkeys couldn't even frolic around. What, then, did the merchant do? He started up a business in customized monkeys. He packed up each monkey separately, wrapped up some specialty item with it, and attached an appropriate label. One was marked "kitchen herbs," others were labeled "parlor greenery," "nest egg," "fashion items," "please expedite," and so on. Then he placed the packages on the counter with a sign that said, "Take one – free!" Once in awhile the labels enticed a customer to take a package home. But once the customer had taken it "as is," gotten it home, and then realized it contained a live animal that stopped holding still once the transaction was complete, it dawned on him that he had been duped. And even that retail trade was not working anymore, for monkey culture had developed to the point that the monkeys were catching on to their master's tricks, and they put up a life-and-death struggle to avoid getting crated up.

"If monkey culture continues apace," said the merchant in despair, "these monkeys will eventually learn reason from their masters, and that will be the kiss of death to my trade."

"Stupid monkeys," shouted the disgruntled merchant and his customers. "Nature has decreed that monkeys will be monkeys, and nothing else! If you ever come to true awareness of your own monkeyhood, and try to defend yourselves with reason against your masters, you will wind up driving both merchant and customer into bankruptcy!"

With this fairy tale in his pocket, Juste Milieu went out to seek a bride. He didn't think much about the monkey moral but remembered instead his mother's lesson about men never getting the heave-ho from any girl. Over and over again he found his mother's words not only confirmed but even understated. He hadn't been raised to think overly much of himself, but all the irresponsible praise he encountered on his bride quest made him so vain that he started to adore himself. He even demanded that the female suppliants kneel at his feet to ask permission to adore him. It went so far that he made his followers form an actual cult around him, acknowledging no other god than him and worshiping him as the *Etre Suprême*.

All this pleased Juste Milieu immensely, and he knew how to keep his followers in thrall. Everyone knows that the best way to keep people aching for signs of recognition is to parcel them out grudgingly. Mr. Juste Milieu, the vice-president for Unjust Taxation Adjustments, made himself at home like a rooster ruling the roost of a recently foreclosed barnyard.

Juste Milieu's mother had given him a magnifying glass that had the ability to show him every young girl as she would be if she became his wife. Occasionally, he would take out this curious instrument that every suitor should use instead of a monocle. With it, he saw that one of the goddesses worshiping him whom he had considered to be the epitome of innocence was in actuality the pinnacle of stupidity; another laughing girl became a weeping woman; a third gave her hand at the altar only to shout, "Checkmate!" A fourth embraced him while saying, "My darling lifesaver!" A fifth took away his pipe and made him dance around for it. A sixth girl actually turned into a spider who had caught him like a fly in her web.

Inexplicable transformations, thought Juste Milieu, shaking his head. But he kept remembering the historical development in the "Tale of the Monkeys," in which a real monkey eventually emerged from a retail surprise package.

That is what comes of an overdeveloped sense of enlightenment and overly sophisticated culture, he philosophized. They try to teach machines to talk and monkeys to think. Where will it all end? Eventually, the spiders will all insist that they are enchanted princesses and demand to be saved, and the heiresses of the heroines of the capital will expect to be idolized.

In his damnation of the whole female infestation, our hero did not learn a thing. As long as he was in love, he was convinced that the heavens would make an exception in his case, because he was his mama's boy. And his high-flown expectations were not any higher than the next man's. He simply demanded a simple, modest, virtuous, sweet, pleasing, domestic, educated, reasonable, talented, lovely, and rich wife whose whole heart he would fill completely, who would hang on his every word with undying love and loyalty, and who would think of nothing else but him. Under these conditions,

Juste Milieu prided himself that he would consider her his equal, assuming that she would never call his authority into question.

Finally, he made his choice cleverly and carefully, like children do at the fair: he picked a woman whom he believed possessed all those qualities. His wife believed it herself and prided herself on one particular virtue that was missing from all those women from foreign places who deceive their husbands in so many ways. Her best trait was that she had deceived her husband only once – when she married him. A deception to last a lifetime! The best thing about this sorry situation was that neither of them noticed it, and if they were ever disappointed in their hopes, they consoled themselves that these were the ways of a weary world and did not look further into the matter.

TRANSLATED BY JEANNINE BLACKWELL

Sophie von Baudissin

1813–1894

Countess Sophie von Baudissin was associated with some of the most important literary and artistic celebrities in Dresden, including Hans Christian Andersen, Clara Schumann, and Felix Mendelssohn-Bartholdy. Her husband, a diplomat and translator, became well known through his translation of Shakespeare's collected poetry and his collaboration on the Tieck-Schlegel edition of Shakespeare's plays. Her literary production for children falls into three groups: fairy tales and environmentally conscious texts for small children; anthologies of other writers and her own stories for adolescents; and a two-volume work entitled *Theater-Almanack für die Jugend* (Theater-almanac for the young). She also contributed to Thekla von Gumpert's *Töchteralbum* (Album for daughters).

Published one year after the failed 1848 Revolution, Baudissin's story of the doll institute infantilizes the topic of revolt, revolution, and emigration. Because of his daughter's obsession with dolls, the king pronounces an almost biblical decree that all dolls in the kingdom must be surrendered. When the girls of the kingdom protest that they will be robbed of a wonderful opportunity to practice their mothering skills by carrying around babies, nursing the sick, and keeping house, the king gives them a reprieve, but only if the dolls remain happy with their mistresses. Alas, the dolls are ill treated at the hands of their owners, and, after a protest to the king, they emigrate to another land, where they are well cared for and soon beloved. What on the surface appears a didactic and moralizing tale in the French tradition, "The Doll Institute" can actually be read as a poignant comment on the *Zeitgeist* of Baudissin's era.

Other tales to read with this piece include the socially critical "Tale of the Monkeys" by Louise Dittmar and Catherine Sinclair's "Uncle David's Nonsensical Story about Giants and Fairies" (in Zipes, ed., *Victorian Fairy Tales*).

[Sophie Gräfin von Baudissin], "Das Puppenstift," in *Kinder-Novellen-Märchen. Ihren Neffen und Nichten erzählt von der Tante Aurelie. Mit vier fein illuminierten Bildern* (Potsdam: Otto Janke, n.d.), 83–91.

The Doll Institute

1849

ONCE UPON A TIME there lived a terrible tyrant. He wasn't Nero, or Caligula, or Ezzelino, but he probably wasn't much better than them, for just imagine it: one day he cruelly decreed that little girls in his kingdom should no longer play with dolls and that they were to hand over all their loved ones to him within three days! Imagine the outcry throughout the land! Not only the little daughters but the mothers, too, were outraged. Since no one person dared disobey alone, they decided to plan and work together to see what could be done.

Perhaps never before had women put their heads together so often; in the meantime, the little girls played even more busily than before with their dolls. Many of them who otherwise would have preferred to play with their brothers' swords and guns dug out their neglected dolls, because there were only two days left before they had to surrender them. One of these little girls was Flora; she had the most beautiful doll in the whole city. The doll was almost as big as Flora herself; her face, arms, and legs were made of wax, and they were even jointed like real limbs. Her big eyes blinked, and every day of the week Flora dressed her in a new outfit – her wardrobe was simply fabulous.

Adelgunde – that was the doll's name – had lain for several weeks in a corner of the room. Her hair was uncombed, and she was still wearing the yellow crepe dress she'd had on for the latest tea party but no shoes or socks. So now she could hardly believe what was happening to her when Flora pressed her ever so sweetly to her chest and sobbed over and over: "O Adelgunde, my beloved Adelgunde! They're going to take you away from me."

In the meantime the mothers had found out that the king's cruel ban was the result of a certain prejudice against dolls: he had a daughter who had never really grown up and now spent the day trying on different outfits. Because she had often played with dolls in her childhood, the king assumed her obsession with dressing up came from this earlier pastime – hence his terrible decree. "Women should be useful members of my state," he said, "not vain fiends of fashion!"

Hardly had they discovered the king's reasons than the mothers assembled again, and this is the plan they devised:

On the day that all dolls were supposed to be handed over, the king happened to be standing at his window; from there he saw an interminably long procession of people moving through the streets toward the castle. Slowly, he began to make out hundreds of festively clothed little girls. Each of them led or carried her doll, and there were all different kinds. The girls in the front rows had jointed dolls made of wax; Flora led the procession with Adelgunde, who was dressed in a red satin dress and black velvet cap. Behind her came the unassuming members of doll society, who had wooden or porcelain faces and were dressed in nursemaid or maid attire. At the end came the baby dolls; many of them could let out a little cry if you knew the right spot to press. As the procession reached the castle, all the little girls fell in unison to their knees, their dolls with them, while the baby dolls joined the choir and let out their pitiful wails: "Mercy, mercy!"

Before the king had opened the window and could speak, Flora took Adelgunde by the hand, stepped forward, and delivered the following speech:

"Your Majesty! Obeying your command, we are prepared to sacrifice our greatest joy to you. We understand that you were only thinking of our welfare when you planned to take away the playthings with which you believe we have squandered our time." The king nodded approvingly as Flora continued: "But consider, Your Majesty, that this play is not mere trifling. Aren't we rehearsing our future responsibilities? Don't we learn to carry children, care for them, and practice the virtues of good housekeeping? Consider, Your Highness, which talents you stifle in us if you take our dolls away! What's learned in youth is practiced in age, as the saying goes, and as the twig is bent, so the tree is inclined. As much as we love our dolls today, all the more will we love and care for our children later. Would you rob us so early on of the chance to develop and nurture our enthusiasm for motherhood?" Flora halted while the king appeared to reconsider. He hadn't thought about playing with dolls from that point of view before.

The children quickly exploited their advantage; once again they fell to their knees and cried (this time to the tune of "Robert the Devil"), "Mercy, mercy!" The jointed dolls knelt down, the baby dolls wailed more pitifully than before. The king appeared convinced. "Silence!" he called out, covering his ears. Then he himself began to speak.

"I give my consent," he began. "Go home with your dolls in peace." A resounding cheer interrupted him as he continued. "But only on one condition: your fledglings must be pleased with the plan and not prefer their freedom." The little girls laughed to themselves; how on earth could dolls have an opinion, and how would they express it anyway? What they didn't know is that a despot always has ways to enforce his will.

Hardly had the king addressed the dolls than they were able to speak. "Are you satisfied with this plan?" he asked, and the dolls, who felt honored by the king's addressing them and quite smug in their finery, and who remembered the kind treatment they had enjoyed in the last few days, cried out in unison, "Yes, we are satisfied!"

"Good," said the king. "Then I grant you the right, if you are not treated well and well cared for or if you are subjected to bad treatment, to bring your grievances directly to me. If they are well founded, you need no longer endure them but will be at liberty to leave."

This time the dolls only nodded in response, but they took note of what the king had said. The procession headed slowly off, and at the central square every girl joyously headed off in a different direction, giddy with victory, and rushed home with her doll in tow.

Everything went well for a time, but then one doll after another turned to the king. One said, "I certainly don't like to complain, but enough is enough! They left me outside on a garden bench all night long and it rained the whole time. The next morning my rosy cheeks were all wet, and the color from my hair had blackened my forehead. Ever since, instead of feeling sorry for me, they look at me askance and hide me when company comes." Another lamented, "The game they play with me is that I misbehaved and should be punished, and sometimes they punch me in the nose or knock a hole in my head like the one Regina is showing you."

Adelgunde, who was wearing a veil, chimed in. "I haven't been put to bed for weeks, even though I was given to my mistress this past Christmas Eve. Back then I lay on lovely soft feather pillows with snow white covers, and there was a chest of drawers full of fine linens and fancy outfits. They even sang songs to me in the cradle. And what do I get now? Lying forgotten in the cinders while I have to watch my wardrobe being used to clean paintbrushes and pens. And the cat sleeps in my bed! Yet I would have borne it all in silence if I hadn't experienced an even greater disgrace today. Look, Great and Righteous Sovereign," the doll continued as she drew back her veil, "they let Flora's brother paint a mustache on me, and he wasn't even punished. And she laughed while he did it. She just laughed!" Adelgunde fell silent, and the king, stunned by her terrible tale, showed her the greatest respect. He offered her and all the other dolls who had registered grievances with him a former institute for young ladies as a place to live, and every day more refugees sought asylum there. Only the baby dolls stayed true to their mistresses, either because they were still too young or because they couldn't walk on their own.

For a while the dolls enjoyed their freedom, but the joy soon subsided. They didn't get along with each other: everybody wanted to be in charge, and the gossiping was just terrible. (Probably they had learned this behavior from their young mistresses; a bad example lingers.) Then they heard about a child in town named Agatha whose doll was supposed to be faring well. Agatha hadn't just taken care of her and kept her neat and tidy for years on end, but she even tailored outfits for her and bought her a new head every Christmas, and that's no small matter (even if the old one is still pretty). She preferred her old doll over any new one.

Now all the dolls wanted refuge at Agatha's. Adelgunde said that no one would turn *her* away. She forgot that she had lain in the ashes, but even if she had been as pretty and fashionable as before, Agatha had room for only one doll at home, and no new one could take the place in her heart that Blanche, her doll, occupied. She took such good care of her that even now that she's grown up and married, her own daughter can still play with Blanche.

In the meantime the dolls had grown tired of their independence and bickering in the institute, but they didn't want to return to their former mistresses. They were afraid they would be laughed at. So they set out toward Nuremberg for a large toy warehouse where they were welcomed and received new heads and new attire. There they weren't allowed to quarrel in the presence of so many big and small tin soldiers, so slowly but surely they forgot how to speak at all. You can lose all interest in talking when you're forever on the shelf.

Finally, they were all sent off to other countries. Go out and buy one, but treat them well, and heed Agatha's example!

TRANSLATED BY SHAWN C. JARVIS

Gisela von Arnim

1827–1889

The daughter of the Romantic writers Achim von Arnim and Bettina Brentano, Gisela von Arnim spent much of her childhood in the company of the people who shaped the canonical German and European fairy tale tradition, from Wilhelm and Jacob Grimm to Hans Christian Andersen. In 1857 Gisela married Herman Grimm, Wilhelm's son, and together they kept up a correspondence with leading intellectuals of their times, including Ralph Waldo Emerson. Together with her sisters, Armgart and Maximiliane, and Marie von Olfers, Gisela founded the Kaffeterkreis, an (almost exclusively) female literary salon in the 1840s. From those beginnings, Gisela began a long path as a writer of fairy tales and fantasy pieces. In the 1840s she published a few of the tales she had written for the Kaffeterkreis and wrote (together with her mother, Bettina) the novel *The Life of High Countess Gritta von Ratsinourhouse* (translated by Lisa Ohm [Lincoln: University of Nebraska Press, 1999]), a fairy tale in the style of *Robinson Crusoe*. In later life Gisela produced numerous lengthy but not particularly stageable historical plays. Her contribution to the fairy tale tradition lies in her intimate reception of the Grimms' tradition and her protofeminist revisions of that tradition.

The works by Gisela von Arnim presented here form an especially interesting chapter in the German female fairy tale tradition because they were not initially written for publication but instead were conceived to be read aloud in familial and social salon settings among friends. One example of von Arnim's works for the salon is "The Nasty Little Pea." A story that problematizes the fate of the disenfranchised and highlights the virtues of community and self-reliance, it tells the tale of two outcast peas who find happiness in their lives together. In several pieces from a cycle of short epistolary tales written for her nephew Achim ("The Ghost Lady," "Wedding Day," and "About the Hamster"), von Arnim uses the fairy tale as a way both to mystify and demystify the mundane: the ghost lady is a deceased family member who explains the family's history, while real-life burglars at the Wiepersdorf family estate are explained away as an enchanted hamster who is vanquished by a dashing fairy prince. Von Arnim's story cycle with the ghost lady and her attempt to make her listener laugh harks back to the medieval female-narrated frame of Basile's *Pentamerone,* in which the storyteller attempts to inspire laughter from the never-laughing Princess Zoza.

Good comparison tales to read with "The Nasty Little Pea" are Hans Christian Andersen's "The Ugly Duckling" and "The Steadfast Tin Soldier."

Gisela von Arnim, "Von der Geisterfrau," "Von der Brautschaft," "Vom Hamster," and "Die garstige kleine Erbse," Stiftung Weimarer Klassik, Arnim Bestand GSA 03/995.

The Nasty Little Pea

ca. 1845

I'M A LITTLE PEA with a little black nose; I can't help it that I've got a blue tinge. Only the other peas think I can and look at me askance. I was stuck in a sack with them – they were all so round and yellow, and they threw their weight around and clattered when the cook came into the pantry, shook all the sacks, and looked for something to put in the soup.

I had only one little friend in the sack; she was a Moor, in other words, black and a girl by nature – she was an outcast, too. We ran into each other occasionally and recalled our only happy time, that of our youth, when we sat in the green pea pod with the sun shining through it and slumbered in our little beds side by side with our brothers. I had been the smallest, and she too; that brought us closer. She also had great intellectual qualities, but she was a Moor through and through.

One time we peas were in line to make up the soup; the old cook dumped us out. How we slipped through her chubby fingers! These big guys stood watch like gendarmes and didn't let any blue ones through and no black ones, either, and I was a blue one. The rest laughed among themselves and at me because they were to become soup, but I wasn't. I flew through the open kitchen window, flung by the cook's hand. There I lay with a few other blue ones. I could see nothing. The green blades of grass stood around and made fun of me, and the sun glinted through them. I had feelings, of course, and would have liked to speak.

Next to me was the gutter, and it saw my nasty blue face. Oh, I was so full of longing, I didn't know what to do. Suddenly, something flew through the air and cast a shadow over the sun. It came to rest, and I saw its gold and green plumage. It was a pigeon with fiery red eyes, preening itself. The wind carried off one little feather after another as the pigeon plucked them out with her curved red beak. Finally, she started picking up grains of sand around me, and suddenly she picked me up too. I vanished. It was very dark. The pigeon flew up onto the roof and chewed and I turned into music: "Cooroo, cooroo, cooroo!"

It went on that way for a while – very melodiously. But it was so dark inside, so very, very dark, and all sorts of odds and ends of leftovers and sand came and laughed at me. As she slowly but surely softened up, an old bread crumb said I was taking up too much space and couldn't even talk! "Come on, let's squish him. Squish! Squish!" And so the others squeezed, and I entered a dark canal. We moved forward slowly; I got very dizzy and plummeted into the depths.

I lay still for a while. I felt like I might be able to speak, but not quite. I lay on the ground and had started to sprout and pretty soon I grew through the green grass and flowers. The sun shone so warmly, but I couldn't speak yet; I heard all the flowers talking so sweetly. Then one morning a flower unfurled, and I could speak, much more sweetly than anyone, for I had a fragrance.

Not far from me there was a slender blossom, and she shyly bowed her little red head – it was the girl, the Moor. She had landed here by chance too and was no longer black but had become very beautiful. We shared our scent with each other – that's a sign of love for us. And soon we grew together around an old thorn bush under which we made our home, and our offspring unfurled in the sun and stretched toward the heavens.

TRANSLATED BY SHAWN C. JARVIS

About the Hamster

ca. 1853

Dear Achim!

Last night the lady finally appeared again. She told me that she had heard a very strange story being told by a hamster here in the garden as she was floating through, the way ghosts do.

It had to do with the murder of his cousin by an elf. He said that a giant had trapped an elf fairy under his fur cap, torn her wings off, and set her on his nose when he slept so that she could scratch the wart he had there.

A giant with a fairy on his nose. From "Vom Hamster," illustrated by Gisela von Arnim. Reprinted with permission of the Stiftung Weimarer Klassik, Arnim Bestand GSA 03/995.

The poor elf cried there so bitterly that the flies, who had gotten really strong from the sugar Grandma fed them, took pity on her as they flew around the nose, and they twisted a net from wisps of cobweb and carried her off.

Just as she saw her groom, the prince of the elves, off in the distance, the net tore in two as the lady of the house was passing by below, and the princess disappeared, nobody knew where to. At the same time a hamster was running away off in the distance, but because a strong wind was blowing, the prince thought, after looking for her for a long time, that the hamster had grabbed her, and he went after him, really mad.

He wanted to battle him, but the wind got nasty and blew so savagely that the prince flew away into the wide, wide world and finally through a wizard's window and right into a distillation flask he had put in the sun on the windowsill.

The wizard bottled him up in the flask and thought he was a fire spirit, but the prince bored around so long with his dagger like a corkscrew that finally he was free and could fly off. The water in the flask was a magic potion to produce clairvoyance, and since the prince had flown directly into it, he suddenly saw the princess falling out of the net and the hamster swallowing her as he ran by.

The prince went forth and battled with him, and when the hamster was dead, he not only fetched his beloved bride out of his cheek pocket but also lots of jewelry and gems that the hamster had stolen from the Wiepersdorf castle, and so then they were very rich people.

TRANSLATED BY SHAWN C. JARVIS

Top left: Fairy in a bee basket. From "Vom Hamster," illustrated by Gisela von Arnim. Reprinted with permission of the Stiftung Weimarer Klassik, Arnim Bestand GSA 03/995.

Bottom left: The fairy king battling the hamster. From "Vom Hamster," illustrated by Gisela von Arnim. Reprinted with permission of the Stiftung Weimarer Klassik, Arnim Bestand GSA 03/995.

Above: Fairies in front of the hamster. From "Vom Hamster," illustrated by Gisela von Arnim. Reprinted with permission of the Stiftung Weimarer Klassik, Arnim Bestand GSA 03/995.

Das Kind war ganz ſtarr vor Ent-
zücken und ſperrte immer weiter-
Mund und Augen auf, murmelnd:
„Ich will Prinzeß werden!"

Little Princess: "The child was transfixed. Her eyes beamed and grew
wider and wider, and her little mouth dropped open and kept murmuring,
'I want to be a princess.'" From Marie von Olfers, *Drei Märchen* (Berlin, 1862),
facing 30. Illustrated by Marie von Olfers. Reprinted with permission
of the Sammlung Hobrecker, Universitätsbibliothek Braunschweig,
Signatur 1006–2821. Dr. Peter Düsterdieck, Bibliotheksdirektor.

Marie von Olfers

1826–1924

A child of educated and polite society, Marie von Olfers grew up in a milieu of privilege. Her father, Ignaz von Olfers, was the director general of the Berlin Museum and entertained the intelligentsia of that city in the famous Yellow Salon that he hosted at his home. Her mother, Hedwig Stägemann, herself the child of a poet, stressed artistic accomplishment in her children: Marie developed her early interest in and talent for music, drawing, and writing into a lifelong occupation. A close friend of the Brentano/von Arnim family, Marie von Olfers was a founding member of the Kaffeterkreis with Gisela von Arnim and maintained an enduring friendship with her and Herman Grimm. Later in life she enjoyed great popularity for her drawings of costumes published in the *Frauenzeitung* (Women's journal) in Berlin. Many of her works for children were beloved by her contemporaries because of their charming illustrations. The family tradition of writing and illustrating children's literature continued with Marie von Olfers's niece Sibylle, known to Americans as the author and illustrator of the *Wurzelkindern* (root children) stories.

Part of a triad of stories von Olfers wrote "to benefit a poor orphan," "Little Princess" is a type of prince and pauper story. The young heroine lives in a loving, though extremely poor, miller's family. The nix, or water sprite, she befriends offers to exchange homes with her. Little Princess descends to the watery world, while the nix basks in the loving attentions of her newfound family. When Little Princess begs the nix to change roles again because life under the sea, as glorious as it seemed at first, is too cold and too distant from her real family, the nix agrees only because she has learned to love as humans do. After a brief visit back home, the nix returns to her new family and joins them as a foundling daughter to be loved equally with her adoptive siblings. Von Olfers's tale, in keeping with the orphan to whom it was dedicated, is a carefully crafted statement on the ills of society at the time and the simple but enduring message that beauty is found in simplicity, that love and affection are more important than wealth and riches, and that ultimately home is where the heart is. Like Bettina von Arnim's story, "The Queen's Son," this tale uses both present and past tenses in some narration, showing its roots in oral presentation.

Other stories to read with this piece include "The King's Child" by Villamaria and "Pack of Lies" by Ricarda Huch in this collection as well as Friedrich de La Motte-Fouqué's *Undine* and Mary De Morgan's "A Toy Princess" (in Zipes, ed., *Victorian Fairy Tales*), in which a princess changeling wins a place in a fisherman's family.

Marie von Olfers, "Prinzeßchen," in *Drei Märchen. Zum besten einer armen Waise. Mit sechs photo-lithographischen Bildern in Buntdruck* (Berlin: In der Rauck'schen Buchhandlung, 1862), 26–40.

Little Princess

1862

C AN YOU HEAR the mill? The water's roaring. I think it looks grand – stately and majestic – compared to the decrepit little house. The drops splash brightly on the rumpled straw roof and splatter onto the dirty windows that looked all cockeyed, half plastered over with paper, half tinged blue with age. A horde of rowdy boys cavorted on bales of hay, seven all told, all brothers. They looked like brothers, too, with their thick heads, straw blond hair, and bright brown eyes. On the highest bale sat the glorious girl, the youngest child, on her sunny throne. She looked so stately and majestic compared to her brothers, like the water compared to the mill. Her beauty sparkled as brightly in the sun as the glistening drops. The water and the child – they looked like enchanted princesses in the midst of all the ugliness, and in the village Little Princess was what they called the wee girl. When one of her brothers offered to play with her in a dirty puddle, she turned up her nose in disdain, hoisted her tattered skirt, and, in a dignified fashion, stepped down and over the muck to the brook that skipped clear and pure in glistening ripples between the green leaves and the blue forget-me-nots.

The child knew full well that she wasn't supposed to play at the water's edge, but it simply was too pretty there. First she sat down quietly, her dewy little face in her pudgy hands, but by and by she dipped one foot in and then the other and laughed so that her little teeth sparkled like pearls. She was becoming more and more taken with this beautiful element: now she was splashing around to her heart's content, just like a little water sprite. She shimmered all over – it was glorious! She admired her pink little arms and legs; how they glistened and how the water dripped like diamonds from the tattered woolen frock. The child splashed ever more wildly, the water leapt higher and higher, the rags shimmered more and more. Ecstatically, she shouted over and over, "Now I am a princess, now I am a princess!" And then a burly, ruddy woman comes out of the mill, weary and shabbily clothed. She grabs the little creature, shakes her so hard that all the glistening droplets scatter, and says, "Just wait, Princess, I'll court you!" And she gave her a smack. But then she wrapped her rough arms tightly around the child, kissing and cuddling her practically to death. "Little Princess, Little Princess!" she cried. "You could have drowned! The water nix might have come and taken you to her palace. You silly thing, just imagine, taken away from your mother to her palace. You're pretty enough already, you gorgeous girl, you lamb!" With that she carried her inside, undressed her, warmed her up, dried all her rags and her little socks, dressed her again, kissed her, hugged her again, and sent her out anew with one of the seven towheads in charge, out again into the glorious sunshine.

Little Princess had become very thoughtful – the water nix might take her to her palace? She would like that a lot! She wanted to live in a palace. Once she'd looked into a palace and had seen little princes and princesses, everything so beautiful and charming! The mighty coach, the magnificent dolls, the dazzling clothing, the servants who looked even more splendid than lords! My, she'd like to be in a palace right now! Everything in the mill was ugly, her brothers rough, coarse peasant boys, their home a hovel, the bed a sorry heap of straw. Sometimes she even found her mother ugly when she waded around in the manure with the pigs or walked around in her rags, her gray hair matted and tangled, her nose like a fat red potato and wrinkled like an old witch's. The boys, her brothers, could never become princes with their fat heads, but she could easily be a princess, she thought. The only things missing were the clothes and the palace.

She wasn't free of her fraternal guards until evening. She left her millet porridge untouched in disgust. Now they were all lying in the hot room and sleeping. Her mother and brothers were snoring. The millstone sang them a lullaby, but to the little one it kept singing:

> *Come, Little Princess, come on, do!*
> *Leave the mill's dross far behind you.*
> *It's lovely here to live below.*
> *Many a pearly crown does glow*
> *So that your beauty here might show.*
> *Come, Little Princess, come on, do!*
> *Leave the mill's dross far behind you.*

The child felt like she was on fire: she couldn't sleep. She watched how the moon gleamed and beamed, and from time to time the mill wheel sprayed a shower of silver stars across the little window. It was simply too pretty – she had to go out. Quietly she got up – everyone was asleep. She tiptoed out and away, through the sleeping flowers and birds, to the incessantly babbling brook. It was so oppressive in the house – now she could breathe! Wild with desire, she splashed around in her little white nightshirt, bathed like a little bird on a hot day, and called out now and then, "Water nix, come take me to your palace! I want to be a princess!"

Suddenly, a little nix did appear, beautiful and glistening like a silver moon, more shimmering than regular princesses, and said, "I can't. When they can't find you, they'll come looking for you. They'll churn up the waves and then – you'd get homesick, just like all the other human children who've come to us. But wait a second! I can still show you our treasures." At that she shook herself so that droplets of water trickled down, and these droplets were real pearls. And she built a palace of amber and coral, and then she called all the creatures of the sea, the clams, together – well, these were glories not to be described.

The child was transfixed. Her eyes beamed and grew wider and wider, and her little mouth dropped open and kept murmuring, "I want to be a princess, I want to be a princess!" Suddenly, they heard a cry from the mill: her mother came running, all her brothers in nightshirts in pursuit; they searched in panic for the child. Practically beside herself with joy, her mother pressed her to her breast. There was lots of hugging and kissing! The spanking was forgone out of relief and love, and the angels in heaven looked down through the firmament and smiled with pleasure.

The little nix saw all of that, too, and couldn't see enough of it, and as the mother carried the child home with the cheering brothers in tow, she heaved a great sigh. She had hidden in the reeds so that no one would see her. Now, as the moon illuminated all the treasures they had discarded like debris along the path, she gathered them all up, threw them in the brook, sighed again, and dove into the rippling waves. Because of her mother, Little Princess had forgotten it all and had fallen asleep in her arms.

But in the morning when she awoke, everything came back to her. She was quarrelsome and out of sorts; nothing seemed right, everything seemed twice as ugly and dreadful after the splendors of the previous evening. As she went to tie on her apron with the patch her mother had sewn on with such care, she wept bitterly. She wasn't allowed to go to the water at all, and at night her mother stayed next to her bed until she was sound asleep. Then she, too, went to bed.

For her part, the nix didn't like it any more below. She didn't like playing anymore. She'd asked them all – her uncle Fontainebleau, the mermaids, the merchildren – "Can't you love me, hug me, like the humans do each other?"

"Do you understand what she wants? I don't, and if you don't either, it's probably just nonsense." With that they flitted on past.

Then it occurred to the nix that she could switch places with the child from the mill. There was nothing more that one wanted than to be a princess, to have beautiful clothes and a palace. If they traded places, nobody would be missed, and everything could go on as usual.

She spent many a long day peeking out at every chance to catch the child, but they were keeping an eye on her. And the nix saw a thousand times over again all the love and affection that surrounded the child, how her mother took care of her, how tender her brothers were to her at every turn, and she envied the child all of this as much as the child envied her her palace. She peeked longingly through the dull panes into the shabby little house as if it were a fairy palace. Today one of her fat-headed brothers had flown through the paper pane and left a gaping hole. The little nix couldn't bear to stay outside when the door she wanted to enter stood open, so she quickly slipped on in. She crept over to the rosebud ear of Little Princess and whispered:

Listen to the water's cascade!
Let's our places, Princess, trade!
Your life of want you will forsake,
My life of plenty's yours to take.
Your little bed here shall be mine,
You'll sleep in my bed so divine.
Let me have this house rundown.
Take my palace, take my crown,
Take my realm and all my treasures.
Let me have these needy pleasures.
Give me all your woes so sweet
For confections, royal treats.
Give me all your want and need.
You'll get riches in the deed.

The child nodded sleepily in response, sat up in her tattered nightshirt, and said, "Have you finally come to take me to your palace?"

"Yes," answered the little nix. "But then your spot here will belong to me. I have to have a home somewhere. I'll give you my spot in the palace, and you give me your place here with your mother."

"She wouldn't take you for her child," the little girl said. "She knows her Little Princess too well."

"Well, we'll just see about that!" cried the nix. "I can turn into Little Princess! Just watch!" And she really did! Suddenly, a second, identical, blond-haired, rosy-cheeked, impudent girl stood there. The real Little Princess grew wide-eyed and looked somewhat unhappy, but as the crown gleamed ever so brightly and as the nix put her shimmering pearl necklace around her neck, she asked again, "Well, are we going to go to my palace?" And down they went, down the silvery water stairway into the golden hall of amber.

Everything shone and gleamed majestically. The little nix led the child to a crystal throne, placed her tiara of pearls and water lilies on her head, and said, "She is now your princess." Then thousands upon thousands of nixes came in throngs, and all of them bore gifts. Some blew merrily into beautiful conch shells – it was just too splendid. Nothing was ugly, everything was pure beauty. Little Princess hardly noticed that the little nix had disappeared. Now she was living in a real palace, was a real princess, had more beds than she could sleep in, more playthings than she could ever play with, more servants than she could ever need, more clothes than she could put on, and much more food than she could possibly eat. Now she was content.

The little nix for her part slipped into the ragged frock, laughed joyfully to herself, found the humble little bed, kissed the youngest brother sprawled across it, and cuddled in. The next morning she didn't let go of the mother's apron strings and ran after her like a puppy. "I don't know what's wrong with the child," said the mother. "It's like she's bewitched. She was always such a will-o'-the-wisp, and now she's sticking to me like a fly to flypaper." The little nix just smiled, and the mother and seven brothers cuddled and kissed her, and she just couldn't get enough of it. She didn't find them ugly at all. She stroked their ruddy brown cheeks and their straw hair, and she looked at them adoringly. Things went on like that for many weeks.

One night there was a knock at the window; everyone was asleep, only the little nix sat bolt upright. She knew it was Little Princess. Little Princess peeked in, all pale and skinny. She said, "Listen, I want to trade back. It's too cold for me down there."

"Oh, that won't work," said the little nix. "I like it here a lot."

"Let's switch," said Little Princess. "I want to stay up here, too."

"That won't work," said the little nix. "In no time at all you'd want to have your mother back all to yourself."

"Oh," said Little Princess, "nothing makes me happy anymore; nobody down there loves anybody. They laugh and play, but I can't laugh along. I want my mother. She's still my mother."

"You don't look anything like Little Princess anymore. She won't even recognize you." So the child went to her mother and cried and cried, and then she crept away again. The little nix pulled the covers up over her ears so she wouldn't hear the weeping anymore.

The next night it happened again – Little Princess came and cried. She sang,

On soft crimson pillows I'm freezing to death,
Without Mommy there I'm feeling bereft;
I was much better off in rags all atatter.
More cared for and loved, even shoes didn't matter.

The little nix acted as if she heard nothing, but she had of course heard it all, and the love that she had just gained, spoke to her: "Give her back her mother. You've learned how sweet it is to have one, much sweeter than palaces, lavish clothing, pearls, and gems."

But she couldn't bring herself to do it. Every morning she hugged the rough woman so ardently and so long that she'd say as she loosened her little arms: "All right, that's enough now. We don't have time for cuddling, even if we do love each other. But just look here – I've sewn you a pretty Sunday frock and knit you stockings, because you're the darling of my heart." The nix lowered her arms, and I think she wanted to cry – she wanted so much to keep her dear mommy. She had traded fair and square with Little Princess for her and had given Little Princess her golden palace in exchange.

The third night the child came again and sang:

That place far away still makes me sad
Despite the blossoms there I had.
That foreign land remains so cold
Despite the gold the sands there hold.
Sad, forlorn it looks to me,
Painful could this glory be.
In the hall that glimmered bright
I'd long in that cramped room to be,
Where to a meal so meager, slight,
The mother calls her brats, her boys,
The darlings of her sweetest joys.

"I won't come again," she said and bent over her mother. "I'm not allowed to." Gently she kissed each of her brothers; the little nix saw it all, and her heart melted. Suddenly, she pulled the child over to her and whispered, "Listen: if your mother still recognizes you, you can be together, and I'll go back to my cold palace." With that Little Princess cried so loudly for joy that she woke everyone up. Of course, her mother recognized her; how could a mother not recognize her own child, no matter how she looked? Now everything was recounted – the boys stuck their fat heads together and sat wide-eyed, listening to the amazing story. They were so happy to see each other that they completely forgot about the little nix. She sighed and jumped through the window into the mill stream. As the silver waves leapt up, they remembered her again. They ran to the window and called, but everything was still: the stream babbled, bubbled, and glistened in the moonlight as if nothing had ever happened, and the mill wheel rattled on.

The next morning by the light of day they all went to the front door; a little girl was sitting on the stoop and crying. When she looked up, they knew immediately that it was the little nix. The woman grabbed both her arms, swung her into the air, and gave her a big, fat kiss. But she was very sad and sobbed. She said, "They don't want me down there anymore because I've become a human child, and you don't want me up here because you have your own child back. Where can I go? Where's my house? Where's my home? Who loves me? Where can I find a mother?"

"Here!" the woman said. "You can be Little Princess's sister and my child. We love you, and you love us!"

Whoever seeks such a home will always find one, whether in Heaven or on Earth.

TRANSLATED BY SHAWN C. JARVIS

The daughter of palms with her father. From [Marie Timme],
Fairy Land Tales and Legends of Dwarfs, Fairies, Water-Sprites, Elves, etc.
From the German of Villamaria (London: Marcus Ward, 1876), 147.

Marie Timme

1830–1895

Almost nothing is known about the life of Marie Timme, other than her birth into the family of the officer and later civil servant Jeserich and her marriage to the Rhenish clergyman Timme. Her collection of fairy tales, *Elfenreigen,* was immensely popular and saw eight editions in German and two contemporaneous editions in England and America with the title *Fairy Land: Tales and Legends of Dwarfs, Fairies, Water-Sprites, Elves, etc.*

The basis for the story of "The King's Child" is the tale of the married mermaid in *Keightley's Mythology of Fairies and Elves.* (Timme would have read the German edition, *Mythologie der Feen und Elfen vom Ursprunge dieses Glaubens bis auf die neuesten Zeiten/J. Keightley.*) The saga of the selkies is an Icelandic belief that after the parting of the Red Sea, Pharaoh and his people transformed themselves into seals. The sealskin was the preferred means for the underwater sea dwellers to travel to the surface. The merfolk, attired in sealskins, could swim to shore, where they would then discard the skins and take on human form. They had to make certain they did not lose or misplace their skins. Each merperson received only one, and if the skin were lost, the merperson was forced to remain forever in the human/upper world.

This tale is part of the voluminous gathering of folk legends about merfolk, but it also reflects the influence of literary tales such as the legend of Melusine and Friedrich de La Motte-Fouqué's *Undine* and Hans Christian Andersen's "The Little Mermaid." Other merfolk stories end with the union of merfolk and human, as this one does; see the folktale "Finn Magic" (in Phelps, ed., *Maid of the North*) and "Russalka, or The Seacoast of Bohemia" by Joanna Russ (in Zipes, ed., *Don't Bet on the Prince*). A film version of the Celtic-Irish legend, *The Secret of Roan Inish (Island of the Seals),* was made in 1993 by John Sayles.

Selkie stories often show the tension between the harsh demands of civilization on women – domestic confinement, loss of status, painful childbirth, poverty – and their yearning for a different self, with a proud heritage, freedom, creativity, movement, and expressive language. The stories often depict deluded or deceitful human males who use and betray love to get the girl; she loves and is caught between conflicting worlds. See our last tale, "Pack of Lies" by Ricarda Huch, for such betrayal. The stories almost always end in tragedy or loss, whether on land or in the sea.

[Marie Timme], "Das Königskind," in *Elfenreigen. Deutsche und nordische Märchen aus dem Reich der Riesen und Zwerge, der Elfen, Nixen und Kobolde. Der Jugendwelt gewidmet von Villamaria* (1867; Leipzig: Otto Spamer, 1909), 40–58. Our translation is a thorough revision of "The King's Daughter," in *Fairy Land: Tales and Legends of Dwarfs, Fairies, Water-Sprites, Elves, etc. from the German of Villamaria* (London: M. Ward, 1876), 129–55.

MARIE TIMME *(Villamaria, pseud.)*

. . . .

The King's Child
1867

ATOP A STEEP CLIFF on the coast of one of the Shetland Islands, where the Atlantic dashes its blue, foam-crested waves, there sat, one lovely summer evening, a youth with an ancient and worn book on his lap. His hands were folded reverently over the yellowed pages, and his eyes rested on the sea below, which seemed to be receding farther north in the splendor of the setting sun to mix its gleaming waves with the gray waters of the icy sea.

The veil of the past was raised before the young man's mind; he looked back into bygone centuries and saw once again peoples who had long since mingled with the dust, enduring the misery of slavery and the lash of the slave driver.

Then he saw the prophet of the Old Testament, the man whose mighty word had changed the course of nature. He saw him standing on the bank of the Red Sea stretching his hand out over the waves, so that they rose up like walls, and the fleeing Israelites passed between them dry-shod. Behind them in hot pursuit came the Egyptian host, with Pharaoh at their head. His look was stern and haughty, and a golden band adorned his proud brow, so lately bowed in sorrow for the slain firstborn sons of Egypt. Beside him in the purple canopied chariot sat his beautiful daughter, who had never been permitted to leave his side since the Angel of Death had entered the king's palace.

On they moved, proud and menacing, while the sea still stood right and left in foaming walls. Then, as the foot of the last Israelite touched the distant shore, the Messenger of God beckoned once more, and the walls of water rushed together, burying the enemies of Jehovah's chosen people in a crash of waves so that not a single one escaped.

Such were the scenes that the yellowed pages unveiled to the young man, and he gazed at the sea below as if he saw, still raging beneath the waves, the deadly strife that had ended thousands of years before, far, far from that northern shore.

But was that really where it had ended? No, he had heard more. His mother had told the tale, and she had gotten the story from her mother, and she again from hers. Thus the mysterious tale, familiar to every child on the island, could be traced back from generation to generation. Pharaoh and his host had not found rest at the bottom of the Red Sea; no, they had to pay a heavier penalty than that to the God of Israel, whose might they had come to know. They had been changed into seals, or selkies, as the islanders called them, and were sent – they, the children of a more genial clime – to the cold waters of the North.

There they toiled down deep at the bottom of the sea, but often on moon-lit nights they rose out of the waves and tossed aside their sealskin robes. They then embraced on the sandy beach for graceful rounds and joyous dances that once a warmer sun had illuminated and the waves of the Nile had accompanied. Then they slipped back into their sealskin garments and returned to the deep, dark sea.

The youth still sat on the top of the cliff, staring dreamily down into the tide. He did not notice that the sun had set – later than in our German climes – and the gold had died out from the sea, nor had he seen the first pale, trembling moonbeam glide over the dark crests of the waves. The night wind gently rose, kissed his inclined brow, and danced over the waves of the sea so that the moonbeams scattered into a thousand glimmering sparks. Then came a sudden ocean roar that reached the dreamer's ear louder than before, right at the foot of the cliff. He leaned forward to see what caused the rushing sound.

Lo! The tales of his childhood had come to life. There was a rustling sound near the beach, and a huge selkie raised its head from the waves, glanced at the moon with its great round eyes, looked along the length of the beach, and then rose awkwardly out of the water. The next moment the selkie tossed aside his coat and presented to the astonished youth a tall and imposing form.

It was the king of Egypt! The unyielding pride inscribed on his dark brow told his rank more plainly than the robe of Tyrian purple, more than the golden headband or the ring of the pharaohs he wore on his right hand.

He leaned over into the surf to help another graceful little selkie up the steep bank. The newcomer gave a gentle shake, the shining skin fell off, and there stood on the strand, in the clear moonlight, the most beautiful creature that ever trod this earth. All the beauty that the youth had ever dreamed of or longed for he found in the features of her face and the radiance of those dark eyes. She lifted her milky white arms as if to assure herself that she was really free from the hateful sheath, and then she clasped them lovingly around the king's neck. It was Pharaoh's daughter.

They were still standing in a silent embrace, when again a rushing and splashing was heard, and the beach was covered with multitudes of seals. The smooth skins dropped away, and there they stood, the soldiers of the days of yore who had followed their king in his crimes, punishment, and death. White robes aflutter, bronzed arms agleam, they approached the king and his regal daughter, crossed their arms across their chests, and bowed their dark brows in greeting till they nearly touched the sand. Then they stepped back and began one of those strange dances of their native land in which they celebrated their feasts to the gods. But instead of the flames of the sacrificial fires, they had the light of the full moon; instead of cymbals clashing, they had the murmur of the sea as it broke against the cliffs.

The youth atop the cliff leaned far forward and looked over the edge, astonished at the strange scene below. Ever and again his eyes turned to the lovely princess, who sat sweetly nestled at her father's knee, resting in the sand and watching the dance of her courtiers. Her figure was as slender and graceful as the palm trees of her native land, and her sparkling dark eyes recalled legendary black diamonds. She rested her marble white brow on her hand, and her long black hair flowed in velvety waves over her braceleted arm and robe of shining purple. And every time the youth looked upon her, his eyes rested longer on this masterpiece of ancient beauty, and with every gaze he drank in a sweeter longing and deeper desire to have her for his own.

The dance seemed to be drawing to a close – he had to act if he hoped to succeed. Noiselessly, he glided from the rock, hidden from sight by the deep shadow of the overhanging crag, and then he stood on the dunes. Only a few steps from him sat the regal pair; right before him lay the sealskins, their only means of return to the underwater realm. He quickly bent over, seized the neat little skin that he had carefully noted, and, with it, climbed unseen to his perch on the cliff. There he carefully hid it in one of the numerous crevices and silently took up his old post again.

The full moon still shone, the strange forms still twined in bewildering mazes, but gradually the moonlight grew paler, and in the east a faint streak appeared. As it became stronger, the light of the stars dimmed, and the first faint, trembling glimmer of a new day sped over the dark waters.

Then the circle of dancers suddenly dispersed; they hastened to their sealskins, drew them over their bright garments, and, changed at once into beasts, plunged back into the sea and dove down into the ocean depths.

The king also rose and bent with a deep sigh to reach for the animal skin that, instead of his royal purple, was to clothe him for many days and rob him of his humanity. He threw it round his shoulders and in the next moment moved, a clumsy monster, to the water's edge. But before plunging into the surf, he turned his head toward his dearly beloved child.

She was not following him, as usual, to stay by his side in the ocean depths. No, she was hurrying anxiously along the strand, seeking the pilfered garment. It was not to be found. She ran to her father and in strange but melodious words told him of her misfortune. Never had the old king felt his sin and punishment more keenly than at this moment, when fate prohibited him from casting aside his own hated shroud and remaining on land to protect his darling child, who, robbed of her garment, could not return with him to the sea. Searing grief and deep despair in his eyes, he cast one glance at his daughter and then turned his head toward the east, where the first sunbeam was already darting from behind the morning clouds.

He dared not tarry longer. One more look of love and sorrow on the face of his only remaining child, and the next moment the waves closed over him. Once more he raised his head above the tide, moved, as in farewell, toward the shore, and then sank down to return, alone for the first time in thousands of years, to his ocean realm.

The king's daughter stood on the shore, gazing with clasped hands at the swirling eddies that formed above her beloved father, when she felt a hand laid on her shoulder. She turned in alarm and near anger, for hitherto none had ever dared touch more than the hem of her garment on bended knee.

"What are you doing here, fair stranger, on this lonely shore at this early hour?" asked the youth who had been on the cliff. He spoke as casually as he could, though his conscience smote him for the unwonted deception.

It never occurred to her that this youth with the honest blue eyes could be the cause of all her trouble, and so in a voice of wondrous sweetness she told him in broken words of her misfortune.

"Your garment will soon be found," he said soothingly. "We will both look for it in awhile, but come home with me just now. It is not far, and although it has neither much luxury nor comfort to offer, it will at least protect you from the gaze of the idle fellows who will soon be coming to the shore to fish."

Ah! He was right; she acknowledged this with a deep sigh. Mutely, she veiled herself in her robe of purple and gave her hand to the friendly youth, who, mindful of her tender, sandaled feet, led her to his cottage by the smoothest path he could find.

A thrill of delight such as he had never felt before filled his heart as her foot crossed the threshold of his ancestral home. Never, never should she leave it, if it cost him his heart's blood to make her forget her lost splendor. Carefully, he led her through the dim vestibule into the one comfortable room of the cottage, and then he brought forward the only piece of furniture of any pretensions that the house possessed: the leather-covered armchair that his sainted father had brought back with him from his last voyage. This he placed at the window that looked out on the sea, and then he fetched the softest sheepskins to make a soft, warm bed for her tiny bare feet.

The beautiful king's daughter accepted all these attentions as a matter of course, for she had been accustomed to homage and respect throughout long centuries, and while the young man bustled cheerfully about the hearth, preparing breakfast for himself and his fair guest, she put her head on her hand and gazed out in dreamy longing through the open window to the sea, now glowing gold and purple in the morning sun.

He chose the finest and rarest fish in his copious store and prepared them with unusual care, and with secret pride he offered them steaming on a shining pewter plate to the lovely maiden at the window. But she refused them – refused everything that his loving ingenuity could devise for her, and fixed her beautiful dark eyes, as before, in sorrowful longing on the sea.

He sat down disconsolately by the hearth; for him, too, the tasty meal was no longer tempting, and he stared gloomily at the fire and now and then cast a furtive glance at the graceful figure at the window. Plan after plan for winning her love and inducing her to remain here as his wife rose and then sank in his mind.

The hours went by in monotonous silence. The girl thought of her lost home, the youth of his ardent and yet quite hopeless love, and the cottage, usually quiet, was today even quieter, even though it boasted a guest. At last, at last the sun sank, and as its parting ray was quenched in the foaming waves that rolled once more in the pale moonlight, the king's daughter stirred, rose, and looked in silent entreaty to her companion. He nodded, smiling. If only he might once more talk to her and hold her milky white hand in his, even if he were obliged to refuse her the only wish she had expressed.

They stepped out together into the night, and when he saw how her tender feet shrank from the unaccustomed roughness of the path, he took her in his arms and carried her, as tenderly as a mother carries her child, all the way down to the beach. Then he helped her to search, in light and in shadow, in the pockets in the sand and the clefts of the rock. He did not look in the only place where the sealskin was to be found, however, but carefully kept her from climbing to the top of the cliff.

At length she clasped her hands in despair and sank exhausted onto the sandy shore. The moonlight gleamed on the tears that slowly fell from her silken lashes and trickled down her pale cheeks. The young man turned away; he could scarcely bear to witness her sorrow. Yet to lose her would be worse, and with that thought he overcame his pity.

"Come back to my cottage, fair stranger," he begged in his softest tones.

Marie Timme

"Rest on the bed of heather. In the meantime I will stay on the beach and continue the search, while you forget your sorrow for a few hours in gentle slumber."

She raised her beautiful eyes in gratitude, then rose and, placing her hand in his, walked back in silence to the quiet cottage. As the door closed behind her, he hurried back to the beach, not to fetch the magic garment but to drive it deeper into the cleft in the cliff. Then he filled the remaining space with seaweed and sand so that no moonbeam might disclose the hidden treasure. With a lighter heart he left the cliff and crept back to the hut. Had she been able to sleep in her sorrow? He looked anxiously through the window.

The moon sent its brightest rays into the little chamber to kiss the brow of the lovely king's daughter, who had so often admired its clear light through the ocean waves. The beautiful velvet black hair flowed almost to the pearl-embroidered hem of her robe, beneath which a little foot peeked out in a golden sandal. Her milky white arms lay under her head and, over her parted lips, a sigh of pain and longing trembled, even in her slumber. The young man gazed with clasped hands on this wondrous vision of beauty. No, he could not let her go; he loved her more than life itself. She must be his, even if he should have to contend with the mysterious powers of the ocean's depths to have her.

Many a night he wandered with her down to the beach and helped her seek what he had resolved should never be found. Her hopes grew fainter, but the hot tears flowed as freely as on the first evening, and when she crept back to the hut, exhausted with weeping, it was merely to change her waking sorrow for a short and broken sleep. The youth, who had attended her with constancy and patience throughout the day, lay like a faithful dog at her door and watched her slumber. At last she gave up hoping, and one evening, instead of going out to the beach, she sat at the window and watched, now the sparkling tide, now the industrious hands of her host, who sat at the loom busily plying the darting shuttle.

"She has yielded; she will stay with me!" hope whispered in his heart. He let the shuttle fall and sat down next to the maiden. She gave him a friendlier look than she ever had before, so that he took courage to tell her how ardently he loved her and that he could never, never leave her. He then entreated her to stay with him and choose his cottage and his island as her home, since she could never return to the magic kingdom of the deep. But, alas! It was a king's daughter he addressed, and the habits of thousands of years are not forgotten in a few days. Her eyes flashed sudden pride, and a hot flash of anger swept over her milky brow.

"Stay here!" she said at last in broken tones. "Stay here in this hut with the sooty ceiling! I, a king's child, brought up in the gold-adorned palaces of Memphis! Do you want the daughter of a land of palms to wither away on this desert island, without trees and flowers, without even a blue sky?"

"But my love will always surround you," argued the youth. "Are not the flowers of the heart unfading?"

"I know nothing of that," she said in a muted voice. "I love my father and his people; I love my home below the waves and that wonderful land we lost so long ago. Beyond these I can love nothing, and I desire nothing save these."

"But you will forget," replied the young man, whose hopes refused to die. "You will forget, and then you will listen to my entreaty."

"Never, never!" said she, shaking her dark head. "Never can I forget Egypt or the land below the sea! Oh, would that I could return to the ocean's depths! There, palaces of noble architecture raise their proud heads like the sunken halls of Memphis. Their walls are built of coral and rare shells, and the tides shine with golden light through the lofty windows of pure amber. And the pyramids of Egypt, the tombs of the kings in the desert – down there you can see them again, but this time built of costly pearls with the ocean's blue waves rolling round their gleaming walls. No, no; I shall never forget my home!"

There was now dreary silence in the cottage, and for some time there passed no more between the two concerning either the past or the future, but in the soul of the young man a faint hope still glimmered, while in the heart of the king's daughter it slowly faded. With it died her pride. Her father, her court, her palaces, all her wondrous treasures were impossibly distant, and nothing remained to her but the hut with the sooty ceiling and the young man with his true and profound love.

She sat as before at the open window, looking out on the sea. The evening sun shone on it, and one of its rays danced through the cottage window and played with her dark hair. But none of the pride of that other evening could be read in her eyes; she looked so mild and gentle that the youth once more found courage to woo humbly for her hand. And she said, "Yes." Not with the loud heartthrob of happiness but quietly, almost wearily. Still, it was a "yes," and to the young man it sounded more melodious than the hosanna of the heavenly host on the holiest of nights.

The next morning he readied his swiftest boat to carry his regal bride to the nearest island where the aged priest who would bless their union resided. He rowed, and she sat facing him in the bow of the boat. The morning sunlight sparkled in gleams of gold on the crests of the waves and kissed the shining bracelets on her milky white arms. She paid no heed to the beauty around her or the look of love and anxiety that the bridegroom fixed on her. She leaned over the side of the boat and peered down into the sea.

The ocean heaved below her, transparent as flowing sapphire, but her eye could not pierce the fathoms that lay between her and the coral palaces and the pyramids of pearl. Nor was this a misfortune, for had the sorrowing nation at the bottom of the sea suspected the nearness of their royal daughter, they would have come to the surface to greet her and lament, and the struggle in her heart and the youth's mortal fear would have begun afresh. Even as it was, he was filled with tormenting fears lest his happiness, so nearly reached, escape his grasp, and this made him labor with almost superhuman strength to gain the island.

The morning breeze took pity on him; it blew on the snow white sail and swelled it like the wings of a swan, and the light boat flew over the sparkling whitecaps as swiftly as an arrow. The little harbor lay close ahead – a few more powerful strokes, and the boat ran aground on the beach. The youth took his lovely, silent bride in his arms and bore her over the damp sand and rough stones to the door of the tiny chapel.

One evening sometime later, the moonlight stole through the cottage window to seek out its beloved king's child. It had known her long before it knew the bridegroom. It had gazed on her over thousands of years as she leaned by night against the pearl pyramids, looking up through the blue tide at its shining orb, or as she breathed the air of the upper world by her father's side on the sandy dunes. The moon felt it had a right to her and secretly called her "my own princess."

But could this be she? Those were indeed the same features of heart-stopping beauty: the same silken locks, and the eyes like black diamonds. But the graceful form was clothed with stuff such as the islanders make and wear, and the young husband at her side was proud of his handiwork, with which he now saw the radiant bride – his bride – adorned. She was kneeling before a brightly painted chest, laying in it her glistening garments and gold ornaments, the symbols of her former status. Now she would wear them no more, for she was no longer a king's child but the wife of a simple Shetland fisherman.

Her husband was standing beside her, watching the movements of her milky white hands attentively. As soon as everything had been carefully placed inside and the lid shut, he asked lovingly, "Will you now lay aside your memories of the past, as you have just done with your royal apparel, and be wholly mine?"

She looked up at him in sweet sorrow. "I will be yours in love and troth," she said. "But could you count on my fidelity if I could so soon abandon my dearest memories? I will be yours in love and troth, but I can never forget my home in the sea, my people, and my father."

And she kept her word. Quietly and industriously, she went about her household duties, caring for her husband gently and cheerfully. The hands that had once caressed the cymbal and played with pearls and diamonds now plied the needle and shuttle with graceful dexterity. It is true that she never returned her husband's caresses; still, she never shrank from them, and so he believed what he so ardently wished – that she loved him, and he hoped she would at last forget her old homeland, of which she never spoke.

One summer night of wondrous beauty, when the moonlight lit land and ocean almost as brightly as the sun, the young man suddenly awoke. His eyes sought his wife, but her bed was empty. Violent fear seized him; he hastily threw on his clothes and hurried out. The front door was ajar. With a sense of foreboding, he raced toward the beach and hurriedly climbed the cliff from whose perch he had first peered down. He looked cautiously below and discovered almost the same scene that months ago had riveted him to this spot. At the base of the cliff sat the king, but to the lines of pride on his dark brow were now added the furrows of deep grief. And with her head on her father's shoulder, and her arms around his neck, sat the youth's wife – the wife whose heart he had wished to be his, and his alone. She was not clad in the garment that his hands had made for her. The purple robe, which he had believed to be buried forever in the chest, once more adorned her lovely form, and the golden bracelets gleamed on her milky white arms. But this time there was no dance, no joyous commotion; the whole entourage stood in sorrow around the royal pair and listened in silence to their lamentations.

Although the man on the rock could not understand the words they spoke, he gathered from her broken voice and gentle sobbing that his wife was not his very own and that perhaps she never would be. With an aching heart he glanced once more at the mournful group, glided noiselessly from the cliff, and returned to his lonely hut.

It was late before his wife came home, and long her stifled sobs broke the silence of the night, but he never stirred. The next day, when he saw her going about more mutely than ever, with the traces of last night's turmoil on her sweet, pale face, he said nothing that could betray the fact that he had been witness to the scene on the beach. But he took care to lock the cottage door every evening, and he hid the key at his breast.

The years came and went, and from their bounty they showered on the couple gifts well calculated to banish the memory of the magic past. Two lovely children played around the former king's daughter, and when she looked into the clear blue eyes of her little ones, she thought no more of her former homeland. Her husband believed that all the more certainly, for she had never asked him about the locked door, nor had he, with all his watchfulness, ever been able to detect any desire on her part to return by night to the beach. He reasoned that this single visit must have been merely a farewell to her family and that his grief had been uncalled-for. She was now his own, wholly and forever.

His wife and children loved the sea, beside which they spent every leisure hour, and he thought he might safely gratify that desire; the more so, as the king's daughter never shirked her duty for the sake of this pleasure but remained as before – a dutiful housekeeper, an attentive wife, and a tender mother.

One lovely summer evening, when the day's work was done, the king's daughter went down with the children to the beach to await the return of her husband, who had taken the week's catch to the nearest island where fishmongers gathered.

She sat down at the base of the cliff where she had rested for the last time by her father's side, and her hands worked busily at a large net, while from time to time her beautiful dark eyes rested longingly on the heaving waters before her. The little ones played about her, picking up shells and pebbles from the sand, and then they climbed to the top of the cliff to build a splendid castle with their stash. The sun still stood high in the heavens, and its rays played on the azure tide, first gleaming on the foamy crests and then rolling down with them into the blue troughs.

The woman let her hands drop into her lap and gazed out on the ocean; the black diamonds of her eyes gleamed with tears, and in her heart awoke the dream of bygone centuries. "No, no, it can never be; it is in the past!" she murmured as she hastily dried her telltale tears. "My husband is loyal and good and worthy of my love." She rose, turned her back on the beloved ocean, and called her children.

"Oh, Mother," they begged, "please let us stay. Look! We're building a castle for you from shells and stones and seaweed!"

She blinked back her tears once more. "Then finish it," she said, "and come home. In the meantime, I'll get supper ready."

She returned to the cottage and busied herself about the fire. Then she set the table, for her husband would soon be home, and that evening she longed for his coming, so that a quiet conversation might once more restore her peace of mind. Her children's merry voices sounded from outside. Surely their father must have come ashore, and they must all be coming home together. She hastened to the door to welcome the arrivals.

But lo, it was not her husband; instead, the little ones ran joyfully up from the beach, the boy in front, his face beaming with joy, holding something in his arms. "Just look, Mama," he cried while yet far off, "what we found way up on the cliff hidden in a crack! Just look at this beautiful, soft, shining skin!" As he spoke, he ran up to his mother and proudly laid the found treasure in her hands. She stared dumbfounded at the familiar garment she had once sought so eagerly but in vain.

"Well, Mama," cried the little fellow. "Say something! Just look how soft and shiny it is. It will make a splendid rug for your feet in winter when it's cold. Say, are you not pleased?" Pleased? She still looked at it in stunned silence, but in her soul the old song surged. In silent entreaty she turned her eyes on her children, as if a look at their beloved countenances might break the spell that more and more captivated her soul.

Alas! The little ones could not understand, and she pressed her aching brow against the soft, cool skin that lay in her hands. But as the magic garment touched her face, the present, with its claims and duties, faded, and the ocean kingdom stood before her in the shimmering colors of the bygone time. She heard again the waves rushing past the coral palaces and the gleaming pearl-studded pyramids at the bottom of the sea; she saw her beloved father sitting lonely and grieving on his golden throne, stretching out his arms to her and calling her by the old, endearing names.

"I am coming, I am coming, Father!" she cried, as she looked up. Before her stood her little ones, anxiously watching their mother's strange behavior. She knelt and pressed them to her under a shower of tears and kisses.

"Farewell, my darlings, farewell! Would that I could take you with me!" she sobbed. "Farewell! Do not forget your mother, and bid your father farewell for me!" At that she leapt up, seized the skin, and raced toward the beach. She had to hurry, for her husband might return at any moment, and then he would certainly hold her back.

Scarcely had she vanished round the bend when her husband approached the hut from the other direction. He had made a successful sale and in exchange for his fish brought all sorts of presents, hoping to please his wife and children. When the little ones heard their father's footsteps, they rushed to meet him, frightened and weeping, and before he could ask where their mother was, they told him what had just transpired.

Although their telling of events was incomplete, he understood its import at once and shot like an arrow to the beach. He arrived just as his wife was about to put on the magic garment and return to her ocean home.

"Stay, my darling, stay!" he cried in despair. "Do not forsake your husband who loves you so dearly and your helpless little children." At these words full of love and anguish she stopped and turned her head toward her husband. The look of despair in his eyes moved her, and for a moment she seemed to hesitate, but a great white wave came rolling to her feet – it seemed to be a message from her father – and she tarried no longer.

"Farewell!" she called tenderly. "Farewell, and may your life be filled with good fortune! I have been yours in love and troth, but I have loved my father and my home yet more." He saw her beautiful face but a moment longer. The next her magic garment veiled her, and she plunged into the sea and returned to her watery realm.

The king's child, the daughter of palms, was once more in her old home, in her beloved father's arms. Instead of sooty ceilings, the halls of the royal palace now arched above her head. A purple robe and golden bracelets again adorned her graceful form; instead of the cold air of the bleak island, the gentle waves of the sea once more caressed her cheek. No gray fog veiled the sun; its beams drifted in full splendor through the blue waves and streamed in golden light through the lofty arched windows of transparent amber. All loved her, all did her homage; and yet, the next time she ascended to the upper world, even though it was far from the place where she had been bereft of her magic garment, she quietly stole from her father's side as the dancing began and hastened with winged feet away from the shore. It pained her tender feet, to be sure, but she did not heed the pain; instead, she hastened further until she reached the familiar path. In another moment she stood before the door of the cottage. It was now unlocked and opened easily. Softly, the king's daughter stole through the dark entry and noiselessly entered the little room.

All were asleep. No one stirred. A moonbeam slipped through the window and crept along the walls, curious to see what its princess would do. She went up to the children's bed, where they lay with folded arms in sweet and peaceful slumber – they did not yet know what it would be to go through life without a mother's love. For one short moment she looked at their lovely faces, and then she bent and pressed tender kisses on their rosy lips.

Then she turned to where her husband lay and bent on him an anxious look. The moonbeam followed her, as if it guessed her resolve and hoped to show her its urgency. Softly, it glided over the sleeper's face, and the king's daughter now saw how pale and sorrowful it had become. Love and repentance overpowered her; she knelt at her husband's side, threw her arms round his neck, and whispered tenderly, "Awake, awake, my beloved; I am with you again, never to leave you."

The husband opened his eyes and gazed as in a dream upon the sweet face that bent over him and looked into his eyes with a tenderness he had never seen before. "If it be a dream," he murmured, "let me dream on forever!"

"No, no," she said, softly. "You are not dreaming, my beloved. I have really come home, never to part from you again. When I was back again in the kingdom I had longed for, when I had embraced my father, greeted my people, and satisfied my gaze with the old splendor, longing for all of you awoke in my heart. Then I felt what I had never felt before – that I belong to you, that we have become one. And tonight, when I ascended again with my people, this longing became so powerful that I slipped softly from my father's side and hastened here. Now I will stay with you and my children; I will be yours forever in love and troth, and yours alone, as you once entreated me to be. Even if your island is a desert without blossoms, still the flowers of the heart grow here in unfading bloom."

TRANSLATED BY JEANNINE BLACKWELL

The Glacier King with Almansor. From Elisabeth Ebeling,
*Fantaska. Gesammelte Märchen, Legenden und Sagen von E. Ebeling. Mit 6
colorierten Bildern von Prof. Hosemann* (Berlin: Wincklemann
und Söhne, [1869]), facing 120. Reprinted with permission of the Sammlung
Hobrecker, Universitäts-bibliothek Braunschweig, Signatur 1007–3632.
Dr. Peter Düsterdieck, Bibliotheksdirektor.

Elisabeth Ebeling

1828–1905

Elisabeth Ebeling was an extremely prolific writer of fairy tale literature, including plays, novellas, poems, and anthologies. Little is known about her life: the daughter of a merchant family, she traveled extensively in Turkey, Egypt, Tunisia, and Spain. Together with her close friend Bertha Lehmann-Filhés, Ebeling wrote her first literary texts to generate income for a charity to clothe poor children. From that time on Lehmann-Filhés and Ebeling continued their collaboration for another forty years, producing several frequently staged fairy tale plays for children. Their *Dörnröschen. Ein dramatisiertes Märchen* (Sleeping Beauty, a dramatized fairy tale) was put to music by Engelbert Humperdinck. Despite the great number of works Ebeling produced, they are almost nonexistent in libraries in the United States and Europe today.

"Black and White" is one of the extremely rare examples of a fairy tale that problematizes race relations: the truly handsome and virtuous black prince is rejected by the princess as a possible suitor. Embedded in the narrative of the competition for the bride is a thoughtful critique of prejudice and the realization that denying who you are is the first step toward loss of the self. The story also reflects Anglo-European theories in Ebeling's time of the sources of racial difference. The author shows that trying to be what you are not must eventually fail and that being true to yourself will lead to happiness.

Although Ebeling doubtless knew two tales featuring the legendary Arabic wise man Almansor (or El Mansour) by Heinrich Heine and Wilhelm Hauff, she chooses to make him blacker, more like Shakespeare's Othello, to introduce the romantic love element and to feature the marriage test for her hero. Some related and contrasting tales include "The Princess's Hand Is Won," which present tests to suitors; "The Princess Who Never Laughed," which has a marriage riddle solved by an unlikely suitor; and "East o' the Sun, West o' the Moon," which has a similar quest of a lover who is helped by supernatural forces to find her way through overwhelming natural forces (see nos. 851–53 in Aarne and Thompson, *The Types of the Folktale*). "How the Summer Queen Came to Canada" depicts the supernatural conflict of the hard-hearted and murderous Winter King and the life-affirming Summer Queen (in Phelps, ed., *Maid of the North*). Finally and more significantly, Ebeling's Ice King and the unloving, callous princess have affinities with the title character of Hans Christian Andersen's "The Snow Queen."

Elisabeth Ebeling, "Schwarz und Weiß," in *Fantaska. Gesammelte Märchen, Legenden und Sagen von E. Ebeling. Mit 6 kolorierten Bildern von Prof. Hosemann* (Berlin: Wincklemann und Söhne, [1869]), 106–29.

Black and White

A Fairy Tale

1869

B ACK IN THE DAYS when the fairy tale roamed the earth and, in the form of a lovely maiden with mysterious and alluring eyes, traveled from land to land conjuring up miracles and waking secret powers from their sleep, there lay deep within Africa a great kingdom of Negroes whose king was named Selim.

A mighty and brave ruler, he had conquered all his neighbors during his long reign and had recently even taken captive the king of a people who lived far to the north as that king had sailed past Selim's coast, attempting a military attack. The latter had bought his freedom by paying a ransom but was required in addition to provide a ship full of gold every year to the victor, Selim.

The time had now come when this tribute was first to be exacted, and in order to collect the precious payment, Almansor, the eldest son of King Selim, undertook the trip to the distant land in the company of his large entourage.

After a successful journey, the prince landed on the coast and left the ship with his company to seek out the palace of King Odo, set high on a mighty mountain. The colorfully and richly attired knights made a splendid sight as they slowly rode toward the heights. A magnificent milk white Arabian stallion reared proudly as he carried Prince Almansor, and he was justly prideful, for the prince was as handsome as the night and as strong as a tree in the forest. His skin was as black as night, broken only by the ivory whiteness of his teeth, his blood red lips, and the whites of his eyes. A crimson cloak enveloped the prince's massive form, and a white turban, decorated with fluttering feathers and secured with a priceless diamond brooch, covered his woolly hair.

The newcomers' gaze swept over the scene, and eagerly they sought to glimpse the white people of whom they had heard so much. Yet the land was all but deserted; they saw no living thing, and only up on the heights could they hear lively, resounding music from the palace.

Arriving at the high gate of the palace, Almansor bid his herald blow into the horns of elephant tusk, and their frightening bombast so overwhelmed the fanfare resounding inside the gate that the music immediately fell silent. The doors were then thrown open, and a stream of astonished people received the Moorish heralds. A well-dressed knight approached and inquired what they desired.

"We come in the name of Selim, our mighty and sublime master, to demand tribute and duty from King Odo, the ruler of this land," was their response. The knight doffed his helmet as he heard these words, and the whole crowd stepped respectfully aside to admit the foreign prince, whose arrival had been awaited with trepidation. The procession once more set in motion and burst into the courtyard of the palace, which offered another astonishing and splendid sight. The broad courtyard, surrounded on three sides by buildings and ending in a garden, had been transformed into lists for a tournament. Colorful banners waved from the countless palace towers, fragrant garlands were draped from window to window, and thousands of knights practiced before a high dais covered with red velvet. There could be found the ladies of the court, clothed in festive garments, and in their midst sat the queen of the day, the lovely Princess Obstinata.

Everyone gazed in astonishment at the black guests who had so suddenly appeared in their midst, and they in their turn could not feast their eyes enough on the exotic white figures before them. The same knight who had addressed the heralds now asked Almansor to dismount and follow him to the king, who sat next to his daughter on the dais. The prince had climbed the few steps and was about to begin his speech, but when he saw Obstinata, he lowered his gaze, silent and awed. And truly no one could blame him for this, for she was as beautiful as the day. Her skin was white and rosy, and her dark blue eyes sparkled like stars in her glowing face, encircled by a wealth of golden curls. Almansor thought he had never seen anything more beautiful than this maiden, and thus his speech to the king was by no means haughty, as one might expect from the son of the victor, but rather gentle and ingratiating, as if it were a question of obtaining a favor. The king answered in the same tone and kindly invited the prince to stay with him as a guest and to grace his daughter's birthday celebration with his presence. The prince accepted this welcome invitation with immeasurable joy. He immediately joined the thousands of knights, and soon all of them had to yield before his superior strength and declare him the victor. He therefore was awarded the prize at the conclusion of the tournament, a white rose, presented to him by the princess.

Proudly, as if it were a precious jewel, he received it on bended knee and attached it to his turban. Yet he did not see the sneering glance of the king's daughter, who whispered scornfully to her ladies, "When he sniffs that, we will get to see the miracle of the black rose."

Day had barely broken the next morning, and all the palace inhabitants were still in deepest sleep, when Almansor awakened his servants and was dressed. He had decided in the night to ask for the hand of the princess and was much too impatient to wait for the old king to arise. The king was dreaming sweetly when his chamberlain entered the room, trembling and hesitant, and yanked his regal nose, for this was the only way he could be awakened. The king sat bolt upright in indignation and asked irritably why he was being disturbed in his most pleasant slumbers.

"Majesty," stammered the chamberlain, "His Black Excellency insists on having an audience with you immediately."

"Ah, Prince Almansor!" cried the king and threw his clothes on so quickly that he pulled his velvet robe on backward and his wig sat askew. The chamberlain helped with his wardrobe as much as the king's impatience would permit, pushed into his pocket the snuffbox without which the king never held an audience, and admitted the waiting prince.

The prince went straight to the purpose of his visit and asked for the hand of Princess Obstinata. In return he promised to waive all requirement of tributes. Odo was visibly embarrassed by his proposal and took one pinch of snuff after another before he finally answered.

"Most Royal Highness," he began. "The proposal that you make me brings me great honor and would be accepted for my part with a thousand joyful thanks, if my daughter were not so choosy."

Almansor's brow darkened at these words; taking note of it, the king hastened to add, "Not, of course, that she could take the slightest exception to the external appearance of Your Majesty. It is merely that I had to give her my word that I would never force her into a marriage, and for her part she is absolutely determined to marry only a man whose bravery and intelligence have been proved to her."

"No one can doubt my bravery," cried Almansor.

"Certainly not," responded the king. "And your intelligence will also prove to be brilliant, if you follow my request and stay here until winter, when the contest for all my daughter's suitors will take place. There and then I will give my daughter's hand to the one who can most quickly answer the riddle she poses."

"Agreed," cried Almansor happily. "I accept this invitation, Your Majesty, and will become your son-in-law, if Fortune decides to smile on me!"

The summer passed in banquets, festivals, and hunts. Not for a moment did Almansor regret staying at the court of King Odo, for the lovely Obstinata seemed to grow more attractive every day; he could hardly wait for the moment when the contest of suitors was to begin. Along with him, many rich and powerful kings' sons competed for the princess's hand; none, however, had attained any special advantage in wooing her. Occasionally, it seemed as if she favored the one or the other, but he could then be certain that he would be treated all the more heartlessly in the next moment, for the good princess stood in the thrall of an evil fairy named Moodina, and the suitors bore the brunt of this spell all too often. In spite of this, they held true to their purpose and were blind enough to consider it a delight to win the hand of the lovely but capricious maiden.

Finally, the day of the riddle contest arrived. Obstinata had declared it to be the third day before Christmas and invited the entire court as well as the suitors to gather in the throne room, where the contest was to take place. The princess and the king sat on raised thrones under a gold filigree canopy at the far end of the ornately decorated hall. Behind them stood their entourage, and at either side stood two heralds with furled flags. At the lower end of the hall the suitors formed a half-circle, and in their midst stood Almansor in festive regalia. Each of them tried to look as clever as possible, which proved to be so difficult for some that Princess Obstinata compared them under her breath to a herd of sheep.

Presently, three trumpet blasts gave the sign for the contest to begin, and the princess rose from her seat. A breathless hush fell over the vast hall while she spoke the following words:

> *I seem a trifle to most men,*
> *A tiny drop in one day's space.*
> *And then I stretch, with pain extend*
> *Into forever's fearful face.*
>
> *A few there are who use me well,*
> *And yet the man who once has held me,*
> *Him I'll help his dreams fulfill.*
> *He'll become both great and wealthy.*
>
> *I die before I'm barely born,*
> *My life, a short and passing dream.*
> *And so I pass you unadorned,*
> *And you see not my fleeting stream.*

After she had finished, Obstinata sat down by her father, and a herald announced that the suitors had a time limit of five minutes to consider the riddle posed. The time passed in deep silence. The contestants blanched, then blushed; most had beads of sweat on their brows. Some looked at the ceiling, others at the floor, some secretly wrung their hands. Almansor alone stood peacefully among them and seemed convinced of his own success.

Soon the time was up. The princess rose again and gave the sign that she was now ready to hear their solutions. But alas, the outlook appeared grim! None of the suitors seemed to have found one, for no one rose from his place except Almansor, who stepped forward with a calm and proud gait, bowed respectfully, and asked permission to put his own answer in the form of a riddle – a charade in three verses.

Sneering scornfully, Obstinata agreed to the request, and the prince began in the following way:

The last two words are stars that gleam
Which never stood in heaven's night
And which when those others beam
In heaven disappear from sight.

The first, a child of those two suns
That flashes like a mirror of the soul.
Grace to him who keeps it pure
Without a blemish, clean and whole.

All three parts, glimmering brightly
Could fulfill my heart's deep sighs,
And it would be – if I guess rightly –
My loveliest Moment – in the blink of your eyes.

At this, the flags were unfurled with sounding trumpets, and the word "Moment," embroidered in crimson letters on their white background, revealed to all that Prince Almansor had found the right solution. A loud cry of joy greeted him. The king left his throne, congratulated him, and led him to his daughter, who seemed in no way happily surprised by these events. She stared with horror, sat on her chair with pale cheeks and a frozen gaze, and stretched out her hands in rejection as her future bridegroom bowed on bended knee before her. In vain the old king tried to excuse her strange behavior as a case of nerves, but Obstinata interrupted him immediately and cried out with all the stubbornness of a spoiled child: "No, Father, I am not sick; I will never ever agree to marry this prince. I only allowed him to participate in the contest merely to make fun of him, and unfortunately he is more clever than the others."

Horrified at her impoliteness, which really exceeded all bounds of propriety, the king and the court looked to Almansor, who stood like an ebony statue.

"But my child, my dear Obstinata, think what you are saying," Odo finally said. "You allowed the prince to take part, and you promised to take as husband the one who solved the riddle, and you must therefore keep your word."

"No, I don't have to, and I won't ever do it!" shouted the princess. "I have been afraid of chimney sweeps since I was a little girl, and I will not agree now to marry a Moor, to accept a man whom I will always be tempted to wash off, and yet who will still never be white. No," she cried loudly and clearly. "If Prince Almansor cannot shed his color and become as white as you and I are, I will never give him my hand. I swear that as my name is Obstinata!"

The princess thereupon swept out of the hall and left her father and the whole court in the greatest consternation and poor Prince Almansor in the deepest despair. His sadly disappointed hopes of winning Obstinata were compounded by bitter feelings of embarrassment caused by the other suitors. They had at first envied him, but now they glanced scornfully over their shoulders at him and ridiculed him for his misfortune.

The old king was the first to compose himself. He asked the prince so pitifully not to take revenge on him for this insult that Almansor did not have it in his heart to reject the old man. He assured him most cordially that he was not angry with him, only very sad that the princess had refused him her hand.

"Why don't you give a try at becoming white, my prince?" asked the other suitors derisively. "There are examples of a Moor being washed white, and so perhaps that trick will work for you as well."

"Yes, do try it," said the king excitedly. "Then my daughter would have to submit and accept you as her husband."

"Yes, I will try," cried Almansor. "I will seek out all the forces of nature and the realm of magic. I will wander the whole earth to lose this hated color that is so repugnant to the lovely princess."

"Oh, my prince," responded the faithful old servant his father had given him. "Consider what you are saying! It is the color of your parents, the color of your whole people that you are ready to abandon!"

"But it is not the color of Obstinata!" the prince interrupted, and then he gave short, hurried orders to his entourage: they were to leave the next morning for their homeland without him and without the tribute, for since he had not given up the hope of becoming the princess's consort, he had revoked the demand. King Odo presented him with a magic ring by which he could understand the language of animals and lifeless objects, and thereupon he left the palace and began his pilgrimage to become a white man.

The stars sparkled brightly in the dark heavens as Almansor wandered sadly in the quiet night. Enviously, he gazed at the ash white moon that bathed every object in a ghostly white shimmer and, head hanging, trudged on deeper and deeper into the countryside. Finally, fatigue overcame him, and he sought out a refuge for the night. He found a sheep pen with its door standing open, stepped inside to lay down among the sleeping animals, and fell asleep himself. Soon he was awakened by the bleating and stamping of the waking herd, who were carrying on the liveliest of conversations. Almansor gazed at the snow white sheep in the moonlight and turned his magic ring so that he could ask them where he could obtain a color like their own. Hardly had he done this when an old ram with great curved horns, the finest of the whole herd, turned to him and said, "You are no doubt Prince Almansor, of whom the shepherd spoke with the shepherdess, for we are the royal sheep, and today he has been up to the palace."

"Yes, Sir Ram," replied the prince. "I am Almansor."

"Please, my title is Bellwether," answered the ram and then turned to his flock. "You now understand, my dear Misses Sheep and Monsieurs Mutton, and you young whippersnapper lambs, that my assumption was correct. When I saw this black man here in our midst, I did not consider him to be a charcoal burner but, rather, Prince Almansor." A widespread humble bleating was the answer to his speech; the honorable Bellwether then turned back to the prince and inquired, while shaking his beard ceremoniously, whether he could be of any service.

"Possibly, Sir Bellwether," replied Almansor, and he asked him for advice about how he should go about obtaining a color as white as the lambs' wool.

"Nothing could be simpler," retorted the old ram. "Our shepherd knows of a magic plant that he uses to bleach the black sheep, and if you were to ask him, he would make your skin just that white and bright as the sun. And you wouldn't get just that one advantage from it either. Once you use that plant, you will not only change your color, but your resemblance to us will be even greater, for you will take on the character of a perfect sheep."

Almansor quickly left the pen. He had heard enough, and he smiled at the thought of returning to the clever Obstinata with the brains of a sheep. At daybreak he walked on, ever onward into the wide world.

It was already toward the end of the third day since he had left the palace. Suddenly, the sky darkened, black clouds moved in, and large snowflakes began to fall. As they sank to earth, dancing and twirling, they sang:

We play, we twirl,
We jump, we whirl
In beautiful shimmers,
In opulent glimmers.

We fly, we heave,
We work, we weave
On earth in the fall,
Cloaks of stars over all.

The flakes grew thicker and thicker, their dance ever wilder. Soon the dark evergreens were covered with the brilliant snowflakes, and the mossy floor of the forest was transformed into a white blanket. Then Almansor quietly whispered his question: "How can I become as white as you are, you light, airy spirits whom I have never seen before?"

Immediately, he heard a harmonious ringing and singing, and the snowflakes answered him:

Ever higher you must climb
Where pure air wafts with dreams,
Where the splendid eagle nests,
Where rivers flow down into streams.

Where avalanches thunder,
Where ageless winter has domain,
Where the ancient Glacier Master
Majestic, has his lonely reign.

While they whirled and blew around him, sleep overcame Almansor's tired eyes. He lay himself down on the soft snow, and the falling flakes covered him up and hid him under their thick blanket. He dreamed of distant Asia, where the mountains soar up to hide in the clouds, where the mighty peak of the Himalayas raises its hoary head above all the others. When he awoke, he knew where he must journey to reach his goal.

He wandered a long, long time and patiently bore the burdens and dangers of the distant journey. He fought with bands of robbers and wild animals, he bore hunger and thirst, yet never did his courage flag. He wandered to the border of Europe, crossed the rough mountains of Caucasia, and finally reached the land he longed for: Asia, the land of Hindustan, where the sacred Ganges flows, where the lotus blossom perfumes the air and the Indian kneels before Brahma. One evening as he wandered there, nearly dead from exhaustion, he turned his eyes heavenward, and there he gazed on the object of all his trials. He stepped out of a stand of palm trees into a clearing and saw with astonishment the chain of mountains before him, towering up to the sky. He saw the gigantic forms and shuddered, for he thought of the difficulties they would cause him. Then, up on the heights, he saw a shape like a cloud of infinite clarity and purity. And as he gazed in astonishment at it and admired its pristine whiteness, its color changed to rose and became ever redder until it was the darkest crimson. All the mountaintops shimmered and glowed, the flowers in the valley smelled sweetly, the palms gently waved their huge fronds, and the birds sang. Everything was jubilant and praised the heavenly beauty of the place of light, the palace of clarity, the dwelling of the Glacier King, which arose there in complete majesty and grandeur. Then Almansor took courage anew, and after the night had strengthened him, he began his journey with fresh energy, climbing ever upward.

First he came to a luxurious tropical stand of palms where the colorful hummingbirds fluttered around like winged diamonds, the panther's glowing eyes shone, and the rattlesnakes hid themselves among the flowers. Climbing higher, he reached a great and splendid forest of oak and beech, shaped like a chapel, and then he scaled the heights where the pines and firs raised their evergreen heads and the ground was covered with a carpet of moss. Then these, too, disappeared, and only dwarf beeches and twisted shrubs crept along the ground, until finally all tree growth ended. But in its place an indescribable beauty blossomed and greened all around. For here the magic of the heights was to be found, the enchanted alpine world. Far above the underworld reigned a hush and peace in splendid solitude that quieted every anxiety in one's heart and made one bow before the wondrous majesty of nature. Other than the darting chamois goats, who rushed past like shadows, no other living things were here.

Almansor called to the goats and asked them to lead him to the palace of the Glacier King, which rose up in dizzying heights before him. They led him along the edge of terrifying abysses where thundering avalanches had plunged down and past rushing mountain streams into the realm of Eternal Snow. There all life was frozen: the carpet of flowers changed into a white shroud; the ice soared up into gigantic blue and green waves. There stood the palace of the Glacier King in its brilliant majesty.

It was a mighty ice grotto of glowing, transparent ice crystals, refracted by the sunlight into a thousand colors whose overpowering splendor the naked eye could hardly bear. Here Almansor left his adept guides behind and walked alone into the great open hall where his fate would be determined. It was wondrously beautiful inside. The blue sky shone in everywhere, and the sunbeams filled the space with such brightness that it seemed the cradle of the dawn, but the ancient man who sat in the middle of the grotto was terribly solemn and majestic. His face was as pale as snow, and his silver white hair cloaked him like a mantle; his powerful eyes glowed with a haunting threat, peering darkly as if they wanted to judge and destroy a guilty man. Devastated by this gaze, Almansor knelt and was about to stammer out his request when the King of the Ice interrupted him and, with a voice as powerful as an avalanche, spoke thus: "Silence, youth, your wish is already known to me before you speak it, and if the sanctity and majesty of the region you have traversed have not taught you the folly of your request, then my explanations will also be fruitless. Therefore, let your will be done. Freeze solid and turn pale," he said as he touched him with his icy finger, "and, turning pale, become a white man!" Then a horrid, deathly coldness crept through the prince's veins, the life froze ever more out of him, his limbs lost their flexibility and turned to ice, but he retained consciousness and feeling.

Days, weeks, and months rushed past as Almansor was in this state, unchanged in his horrible position, robbed of every movement, and constantly under the scornful stare of the Glacier King. Finally, the king raised his icy finger and guided one of the sunbeams trapped in the grotto to the prince's heart. It began to beat gently, and his body, which had been shackled for so long, began to come to life again. Almansor tried to move his hands. He raised himself from his knees and shouted with glee like a child when he could use his limbs again.

"Your wish is granted," said the Glacier King. "You are as white as the day. Leave me now and spare me your thanks."

Almansor did not dare reply. He left the ice hall and the realm of Eternal Winter and climbed back down to earth again to the inhabitants of the lower world. Arriving there, he greeted the flowers and trees with glee and hurried without pause to the court of Odo and the homeland of Obstinata.

A full year had passed since Almansor had first entered the palace of the White King. The birthday of the princess was again being celebrated with fife and drum, jousting, and waving banners. A colorful crowd filled the courtyard, and joy and merriment reigned wherever one looked. As before, Obstinata sat on a high platform and received all the accolades brought her. Suddenly, a strange murmur spread through the gleeful crowd, and everyone stared in horror at a tall, manly figure that suddenly stood in their midst. No one knew where he came from or who he was.

And who was this pale man in the exotic costume of a Moor? Why did he press forward through the crowd so insistently and have eyes only for the princess? Finally, he stopped directly before her and grasped her hand. She gazed at him and cried loudly and scornfully to him who had borne so much for her sake: "My heavens, Prince Almansor, white as snow and uglier than ever!"

The king had also taken note of the newcomer and hurried to greet him, but the prince had finally come to his senses. Obstinata's contemptible words had opened his eyes: he disdained her now as much as he had loved her earlier. And now, as she held a mirror before his face to ridicule him even further, he saw a white Negroid face with large lips and flat nose staring back at him. He turned his back silently to her and, ignoring the king's pleading, left the palace, never to return.

He went to the shore of the sea and lamented his deep sorrow to the waves and grieved about his misplaced quest and its foolish beginning. Then he took the magic ring that Odo had given him and had it returned to the palace by a swallow that nested there. He signed on as a sailor with a ship that was about to sail to his homeland. In a few months it brought him to the African coast, where he departed to hurry home to his father's kingdom. Soon he spied the tall pyramids that rose behind the tent city of his father, he heard the rushing waters of the Nile and the roaring of the tame elephants, and he knew he was home again.

Only a few more steps would take him to his parents, and he could find solace in their loving arms for the suffering he had endured. Then some children who were busy feeding a tame ostrich saw him. Almansor smiled at them and gave a friendly greeting, but they covered their eyes and cried in horror: "The Devil is coming, the Devil is coming!" and fled from him into their tents. Drawn by the screams of the little ones, their parents rushed up, and they too stared at the prince and made gestures of disgust and cried, "Yes, it is the Devil who wants to destroy us!" And everyone, men, women, and children, fled before him and sought refuge in the king's tents, which rose so magnificently above the others. Speechless and stunned, Almansor followed them. He did not understand at all; he had no notion that this fear and flight had to do with him. He pulled back the silk drapes covering the entrance to the king's tents and saw his father in the midst of the terrified Negroes, who knelt before him and begged for protection from the persecutions of the Devil.

"My father!" cried Almansor and staggered toward the father he longed for, covering his hand with kisses.

"Why are you here, White Devil? Do you want to annihilate my people, as yours have killed my son and made me a childless old man?" cried Selim with horror, and he tore himself from him. But Almansor embraced him again and said tenderly, "My father, your son is alive! He is standing before you. Do you not recognize me?"

"You claim to be my son?" cried the king. "You are a liar; you blaspheme! My son was as black as ebony and as handsome as the night. You are pale as the Devil and a horror of ugliness. Leave me and flee, before my warriors seize and kill you!"

"Have pity, father!" cried the unhappy prince. But Selim had no sympathy; he pushed him away and ordered him again to leave the tents on pain of death and never again to show his face in this kingdom. Almansor obeyed with a bleeding heart. He walked out of the tent as if in a trance and stood, confused and despairing, not knowing where he should turn. "My people flee from me, my father has banished me, and the white men abhor me," he whispered. "Where shall I turn, poor unhappy man that I am?"

He felt a hand placed gently on his shoulder and heard a soft voice say, "My son, my poor son!" He turned and found himself in his mother's arms. She had seen him from a distance and recognized him; in spite of his white color and his different attire, her mother's heart had recognized him when all others fled. Maternal love alone welcomed him home. They embraced each other silently for a long while, and then the queen took the prince into her tents, where he was for the moment safe from Selim's rage. Here she heard his tale and considered with him what his next actions should be. He could not remain with her, for she feared her husband's wrath. So she sent him to a wise friend from whom he could obtain advice about winning his father's heart again.

The wise man, Cyril, lived in one of the ancient tombs of the kings that were hewn into the rock on the banks of the Nile. It was a great cave painted with strange hieroglyphics, and the waves of the Nile swept past it, wailing and gruesome. Almansor entered it the next day. The mysterious twilight that reigned there gave the room a horrid and ghostly appearance. Mummies of humans and animals lay about; a giant snake with distorted feet, hewn of stone, slithered along the wall. In the darkest corner cowered a being of supernatural appearance. A huge ancient Moorish figure with white hair and a long white beard, old enough to be an image of the past, squatted there and read a yellowed papyrus roll by weak torchlight.

At Almansor's approach, some night birds and bats rushed through the air with heavy wing beats. The ancient apparition rose and approached the newcomer.

"Who are you and why do you disturb my solitude, unbroken for decades by humankind?" he asked with a voice from the grave. Almansor told him who he was, who had sent him, and why he had come. He told him everything and asked for his advice and help. Thereupon Cyril shook his head and said solemnly, "You acted like a child. True love makes every sacrifice that doesn't contradict law and reason, but at no time should one allow himself to be swayed by the moods of a woman, and no man should ever scorn the gifts bestowed on him by nature and try to change them simply to acquiesce to a girl's wishes. This serves you right; you deserved this punishment. I cannot help you, but I will advise you: you are disdained by blacks and whites alike, and so you should flee into the desert, into solitude, and work there for the good of your people. Thereby you will accomplish at least this one thing: inner peace."

He then presented Almansor with a vial of miraculous water that possessed the power of refilling itself every day and a basket with three dates that was replenished by magic every day so that he would not perish in the barren and dry desert. In addition, he provided him with a spade and showed him where to go to dig out the most precious treasure that desert travelers have ever known – water. Almansor then left the wise man Cyril and went into the desert, into the glowing solitude of the sea of sand, where the sun rays burn like fire, where no branch, no tree interrupts the eternal monotony, where the fleeing ostrich and the timid antelope are the only living things, speeding past like spirits.

At a heap of bleached camel and human bones, Almansor began his weary work, digging by the sweat of his brow while suffering hunger and thirst, for the water and the fruit of the wise man sufficed only to keep him alive but not to fill his belly.

While he dug and worked for his brothers who had rejected him, he became peaceful and happy. Despair left him, and inner peace came to him. For a long while, the rocky, parched soil resisted Almansor's efforts. Hot winds blew the work of many weeks back again, and a hundred times he had to begin the difficult work anew. In spite of that he never let his courage flag, and his persistence was not fruitless. Finally, the sand became wet and wetter, a few drops of water sprang forth, the loveliest pearls for the digger. And then it happened. One more push with the spade, one more powerful thrust, and he had reached his goal, the jewel had been found: a clear spring sparkled back at him. He raised his hands in gratitude to heaven, and then he sank down and bowed down before the precious element that he had won, ready to slake his thirst with the cooling waters.

But what was that? Was it deception or reality that looked back at him from the water's surface? A proud and handsome Moor's face smiled back at him. He had lost his white color; the desert sun had darkened him and transformed him again into a Moor. He sprang up as if reborn, and in the distance he heard a thousand-voiced celebration coming toward him. He saw his parents leading all the people, who greeted him as son and prince. His mother had not rested or tarried but had worked steadfastly for her child, had assuaged his father and convinced him that it was really his son whom he had repudiated. She had calmed the people, freed them from their foolish fears, and then led them all out into the desert, where she had been sent by Cyril, to bring her banished son back home. They arrived at the happy moment when he had reached his goal and had found the treasure for which he had been digging.

All the people were jubilant and welcomed him as their prince, he who again wore their color and who had created this fountain in the desert for their benefit. His parents wrapped him in their arms and were glad with all their hearts that he was like them once more, the image of the night.

They then accompanied him with fanfare back to the tent city, where he led his life from that day on as he deserved. The spring in the desert was planted with fruit trees and soon came to be a lovely, verdant, and blossoming island in the parched, sandy ocean of the desert. Thousands of travelers quenched their thirst in the clear waters of the Almansor fountain, as the oasis was named.

Soon after the spring had been dug, a strangely formed stone, similar to the face of a weeping woman, was found standing close to the edge, so close that it was reflected in the crystal waters. No one knew where it had come from; no one knew who had brought it. But the swallows who flew every year from north to south, from the kingdom of Odo to Africa, had certainly heard of it and often twittered about the story of the willful Obstinata, who had continued to treat her suitors with the greatest capriciousness and had finally been punished. For it happened that a powerful king, the favorite of a fairy, had asked for her hand, and she had scorned him because of his crossed eyes and called him King Walleye. This had outraged him so that he had asked the fairy to avenge him with the princess, and she had granted his wish. To the bitter pain of the princess's father, who did not live long after this misfortune, the fairy changed Obstinata into a stone statue. She placed it in Africa at the oasis that had been dug by Almansor, the prince whom Obstinata had so cruelly mistreated. Here she was cursed forever and always to see her own distorted face in the water and to hear every traveler who came past sing the praises of the man whom she had despised.

And Almansor earned this praise in every respect. He reigned after the death of his father with goodness, might, and wisdom, for he had learned to see that the color of one's skin is not important and that it does not matter if you are black or white, as long as you are wise.

TRANSLATED BY JEANNINE BLACKWELL

Hedwig Dohm. Atelier Hanns Hanfstaengl, Berlin.
From the S. Fischer-Verlag Archive, Schiller Nationalmuseum
und Deutsches Literaturarchiv, Marbach.

Hedwig Dohm

1833–1919

Hedwig Dohm was one of the strongest early voices for women's emancipation in Germany. Author of several plays, novels, and essays, she is best known for her novella collection, *Wie Frauen werden. Werde, die Du bist* (How women become: become who you are, 1894), and a direct attack on the demagogues against the women's movement, *Die Anti-Feministen* (The antifeminists, 1902). In addition, Dohm contributed to a variety of socialist and artistic journals. One of eighteen children, she was raised in Berlin but traveled widely in Europe with her husband, Ernst Dohm, intellectual leader and founder of the satirical journal *Kladderadatsch*. Hedwig Dohm is also known as the grandmother of Katja Pringsheim, the wife of Thomas Mann.

Her two fairy tales are found in collections: "Lotti Sorehead" (in *Märchen für die lieben Kinder* [Fairy tales for sweet children, 1883]) and "The Fragrance of Flowers" (in *Märchenstrauß* [A bouquet of fairy tales]). This tale presents a princess isolated high on a sterile, cold mountain who longs for living things, beautiful flowers, and the wonderful scents of a blooming garden. When she finds such a garden among the poor people at the bottom of the hill, she falls in love with the young gardener. Only the smell of his flowers can revive her to life, and, against her father's wishes, the gardener wins her hand. The king dies of grief at this mésalliance; the couple lives happily ever after. This critique of class relations begins the socialist fairy tale tradition, associating the working class with blossoming organic nature, the exploitative classes with sterility and withered isolation.

Other tales to read with this piece include the anonymous "The Red Flower" in this collection and Susan Wade, "Like a Red, Red Rose" (in Datlow and Windling, eds., *Snow White, Blood Red*).

Hedwig Dohm, "Blumenduft," in *Märchenstrauß. Eine Sammlung von schönen Märchen, Sagen und Schwänken. Gesammelt von Jul. Hirschmann, Verf. von Guckkastenbilder, Histörchen, Mädchenspiegel, Blüthenjahre u. s. w.* (Berlin: Winckelmann und Söhne, [1870]), 165–72.

The Fragrance of Flowers

1870

H AVE YOU EVER, my child, put your little nose to a flask full of rose or violet oil? It's very fragrant, isn't it? Almost more so than the rose in the garden or the violet in the field. Would you like to know, my child, how it came to be that they pressed that delicate essence out of the petals and throats of the flowers? Well, listen to this tale!

Once upon a time there was a king's castle on a cliff high above the sea. Everything around it was barren and desolate, and only the ocean waves crashed with dull claps against the cliffs. Neither flowers nor trees grew on the barren soil; even the king himself didn't really prosper, for he was a sullen, gloomy old man, and the poor queen closed her gentle blue eyes for eternity shortly after she had brought a daughter into this world. The people said she was glad to die, because the king had treated her harshly.

Only a single, delicate blossom flourished in the castle on the cliffs, a blossom that combined the charms of all the other flowers. It was Lila, the little princess, who was slender as a lily, vibrant as a peony, and sweet as a forget-me-not. Lila was bored in the dreary castle. Of course, she had a garden, but the flowers there were artificial ones of silk and velvet, and they had no fragrance. Lila had a private tutor and ladies-in-waiting, and neighboring little princesses and countesses were invited to play with her, but still she was bored. Her playmates always sat so stiffly in their taffeta dresses, drinking hot chocolate and hardly daring to move for fear their tiaras might slip off their heads. The countesses sat just as still because they didn't want to be less stiff than the princesses.

Lila didn't like her tutor at all; he always looked so serious, and that annoyed her. Once she had seen a Negro in a picture book. "Papa," she said to the king. "I want a Negro as a tutor." At the king's command the tutor had to paint himself black as night. That was so amusing that for two whole days the princess couldn't stop laughing. But it was the ladies-in-waiting who had the most difficulty with her. If it were raining and she couldn't ride her pony in the courtyard, she wanted to ride around indoors. The stoutest of the ladies had to pretend to be the horse. Lila climbed on her back, and the other ladies-in-waiting had to spur the chubby lady on with dainty little switches. The princess didn't do this out of nastiness but, rather, out of boredom.

If you climbed down the cliffs the castle rested on and went a bit farther into the valley, you came to a charming little cottage surrounded by flowering gardens. A gardener lived in the cottage with his son. Egbert – that was the son's name – had raised all the glorious flowers that grew in his father's garden himself. He loved them above all else. He could be seen working in the garden from morning till night; he watered the flowers, freed them of weeds and annoying insects, chatted with them, and before he entered the cottage in the evening always said to them, "Good night, my darlings!" And every time the flowers turned their little heads toward him, nodded, and whispered softly, "Good night, good night!"

One day, when the princess was walking up and down in her silk flower garden, she was more bored than usual. "I want to run down the mountainside for once," she said to the ladies-in-waiting. They were alarmed. "A princess," they said, "never runs down a mountainside."

"Well, we'll just see about that!" replied Lila, and she ran as fast as she could down the mountainside and didn't stop until she stood before Egbert's garden. Astonished, stunned, enchanted, she looked around and sucked in great whiffs of the sweet scent streaming from the flowers. Everywhere there were trees full of golden fruits, everywhere living flowers of never-before-seen magnificence. She thought she was in fairyland.

Egbert had noticed Lila through the lattice and at first thought she was an angel who had just descended from Heaven. She really did look indescribably charming in her snow white shift with golden shoes and a sky blue ribbon tied around her blond curls, but when she reached out her dainty white hands toward the red cherries, he realized that she couldn't be an angel but that she must be a princess instead. After awhile Lila became aware of Egbert's dark eyes watching her.

"Let me into the garden, boy!" she commanded.

Egbert opened the gate, and she entered. Entranced, she wandered among the flower beds and couldn't take in enough of all the glories. Egbert picked her strawberries, sweet cherries, and golden apricots, but just as she was engrossed in her snack, the corpulent ladies-in-waiting appeared, panting and out of breath. Her pleading was to no avail: Lila had to return immediately. Egbert gave her a large, fresh rose in parting. That was her consolation in the old castle, which now seemed even more barren and gloomy to her than otherwise. She studied the rose, kissed it, put it next to her bed that night, and even dreamed of it. But the next morning the rose was wilted, the petals lay on the floor, and the scent was gone. Lila wept. "I want another rose!" she cried and stamped her dainty feet. The ladies-in-waiting, fearful that Lila, in her fit of pique, might tell the king what had transpired, finally gave in and agreed to climb down with her into the valley again.

Egbert was working as usual in the garden. He, too, was not as cheery as otherwise. He sang no jolly tunes but thought instead of the little princess and wondered if she would come again. And there she stood in front of him and gave him a big smile. Egbert blushed with pleasure. From that day on Lila came to the garden every day. The ladies-in-waiting no longer opposed her, because ever since the princess had been spending time with the young gardener, she was the best-behaved child in the world and didn't pester anyone.

While she played with Egbert, the ladies-in-waiting lay under trees and napped. But Lila didn't always just play, she also worked with Egbert, so that bright pearls of sweat ran down her white brow. She watered the flowers, she plowed, she hoed and weeded, she climbed in the highest trees with huge shears and pruned away the deadwood, she gathered fruit in baskets, and she braided wreaths. When the workday was over, they lay, Lila and Egbert, arm in arm under a tree, exchanging confidences and eating fruit; at home, she secretly gave her chocolate to the cat. When she was in the garden, she tossed aside all her jewels and braided evergreen sprigs into her curly locks; on her finger she sported a ring of daisies and wore ripe cherries on her ears instead of earrings. Lila looked like a darling little flower fairy. The flowers soon knew her as well as Egbert, because when she took her leave, they always turned their heads toward her and whispered, "Adieu, adieu!"

The children grew to love each other so much, so very much, that Egbert swore to the princess that she and no other should become his wife, and Lila threw her arms around his neck and said, "You and no other shall be my husband!" And the flowers nodded so enthusiastically that they practically fell off their stems, and they whispered, "Congratulations! Congratulations!"

One day, as Lila was weeding especially energetically, the ladies-in-waiting overslept, and since the princess had to hurry home so quickly, she forgot to wash her hands at the well. At the castle she exuberantly ran up to her morose father and, without thinking, reached out her hands to him in greeting. The king looked in shock at her otherwise lily white hands. They were black, black as soot. "What's this?" he thundered. "How did my royal daughter get sooty black hands?"

Pale with fright, the ladies-in-waiting fell to the king's feet and confessed everything. Then they fainted. The king ranted and raved, and when the ladies-in-waiting came out of their swoon, he meted out a terrible punishment: they had to let themselves be painted black as soot and for a week were to have nothing other than rhubarb, horseradish, and salt to eat.

Poor Lila was imprisoned in the castle. She gazed longingly out the window, but she could no longer see the garden where she had strolled hand in hand with Egbert. She couldn't hear the birds singing, she couldn't breathe in the fragrance of the roses, and she couldn't gaze into Egbert's dark eyes. It was unbearable, and indeed, the princess couldn't bear it. In her grief she grew sicker and sicker, and soon she looked like the whitest lily in Egbert's garden. Doctors were summoned, sorcerers were consulted, but when they asked the princess what she lacked, she only answered: "The fragrance of flowers! The fragrance of flowers!"

When they brought flowers from all corners of the land to the castle on the cliffs, a smile brightened Lila's pale face, and she seemed to breathe a sigh of relief. But when the flowers wilted the next day, Lila's smile faded. Eventually, she couldn't get out of bed, and the king grew terribly worried, because Lila was the only heir to the throne; if she died, where would they find a ruler? A people without a ruler – the old man shuddered at the thought. In desperation, he let it be proclaimed throughout the land: whoever could cure the princess with the everlasting fragrance of flowers would have her as his bride and become king. But since no flower could bring itself to bloom longer than a day in the raw air of the castle on the cliffs, no one was able to cure the languishing Lila.

In the meantime, news of the princess's illness had reached Egbert. He almost died of worry and could think of no solution. He showered the flowers with his tears. "Lila is dying because of you," he told them. "Sweet flowers, help her and me, because if Lila dies, Egbert will die, too!" You could see the flowers growing under the shower of tears, and they became even more fragrant than before.

Egbert's sorrow kept him from sleeping in his cottage at night, so he went out into the garden, bid the flowers a melancholy goodnight, and fell asleep in their midst. But hardly had he closed his eyes than there was a magical rustling in the trees and bushes. Egbert awoke, amazed to see little fairy heads peeking out of the flower calyxes. They swayed back and forth and whispered to one another, pointing to Egbert. Eventually, a fairy floated out of a rose calyx; she wore a gold star on her lilting curls and crimson butterfly wings on her shoulders. She flew directly to Egbert and motioned him to follow her.

Marveling, he got up and followed the lovely apparition. She led him to

a rose, wrapped her arm around his neck, and said, "Look into the calyx!"
He did so. A magical scene appeared before his eyes: minute golden ladders
leaned against the inside of the rose petals, and dainty, tiny elfin creatures
hurriedly scrambled up and down the ladders. In their hands they held delicate bowls of ruby red alabaster. What were they doing on the ladders? Why
were they working so fast and furiously? At first glance Egbert couldn't make
any sense of it all, but after awhile he noticed that they were using their delicate fingers to press something from the rose petals. As they squeezed, drop
upon drop trickled from the petals into the alabaster bowls, from which an
incomparable perfume arose.

"Do you see the nectar in the bowls?" said the rose fairy. "That is the everlasting fragrance of flowers," and she grabbed his hand and led him from
one flower to the next. In every calyx he saw golden ladders, elves, and ruby
bowls. "Oh, if only I had a single bowl of that fragrant oil!" Egbert cried out
in dismay. At that a little elf tossed a full bowl into his face, and, startled,
he reeled back. When he looked over again, everything had disappeared:
the elves, the rose fairy, and the moonlight, and bright morning light swept
over the flowers and into his drowsy eyes. Egbert would have believed it all
a dream, had not the broken alabaster bowl lain next to him; his clothes
were damp and were giving off the same perfume he had breathed in during the night. He mused about the meaning of the dream, and the answer
finally came to him. With a quaking hand and a sharp knife he approached
his fair blossoms. He felt like he was about to commit murder, but behold!
They stretched their little heads toward him, and they bowed their stems
and whispered, "Be brave! Take heart!" He snipped them off, carried them
into his cottage, and pressed the fragrant oil from their petals. Droplet after
droplet trickled into a crystal receptacle, which he carefully sealed. Then he
set out for the princess.

They didn't want to let the humble gardener's boy into the castle. "I bring
the everlasting fragrance of flowers," he said. Suddenly, the French doors
opened before him, and he saw Lila, like a little flower drooping after a
storm, resting on a white satin pillow, with cheeks even whiter than the pillow itself. As she saw Egbert, she reached her arms out to him and smiled
at him through her tears. Egbert opened the flask, and a heavenly perfume
wafted through the room, through the entire castle, over the cliffs and over
the gardens – yes, even the ocean was as fragrant as a bouquet of glorious
flowers.

Lila sprang out of bed, bright and hearty as a peony, and the king, the
ladies-in-waiting, and the ministers came, and everyone reveled in the perfume. They sprinkled the glorious essence on their clothes and handkerchiefs

and dabbed it in their hair; the ladies-in-waiting smelled like jasmine, the king like a rose, and his ministers like violets. Butterflies and bees, mistaking the room for a sumptuous garden, streamed in. An impertinent butterfly settled on the prime minister's nose and made him sneeze most indecorously, and a bee went so far as to sting the king in the left leg, so that for many a day he had to rule with a limp.

In the midst of all this merriment, everyone had completely forgotten the young gardener, but finally he stepped forward, genuflected before the king, and expressed the simple wish to be immediately wed to Princess Lila. Everyone, from the king to the stable hands, threw their hands in the air in astonishment, and the king in his rage might have choked on a piece of cake he'd just put in his mouth if one of his ministers hadn't quickly patted him on the back. When he was able to breathe again, he gave Egbert a piercing look and pointed imperiously to the door. The entire court pointed to the door, too. Stunned, Egbert fled from this terrifying scene, but in the doorway he shouted to the king, "Beware, Your Majesty, the revenge of the flower spirits."

The king had cleverly retained the flask, and he put it next to his bed at night to keep the ladies-in-waiting from stealing little dabs. He was already sound asleep when he was awakened by a strange sound. Frightened, he rubbed his eyes and noticed that the crystal flask had sprung its cork; a wispy, white mist was rising out of the bottle. It grew denser and denser. Fine outlines materialized, and the mist took on form. One flower after another emerged from the fog, and they grew bigger and bigger until they reached the ceiling, and these monstrous flowers crowded closer and closer to the king's bed. But he wasn't afraid and shouted, "Just wait, you silly flowers, I'll put an end to you." And he strode valiantly over to the rose. But alas! A gigantic thorn shot out of the stem, deeply piercing the king's finger. He attacked the lily, but a sharp sword glinted out of its throat and hovered threateningly above the king's head. Quickly, he took off his nightcap and put on his crown. "The sword will respect my crown," he thought. Then he approached the forget-me-not and attempted to snap it off. "That little flower," he thought, "has no defenses," but as he reached for it, two eyes stabbed at him from the forget-me-not's throat; they enveloped his chest like fire, and as he peered closer, he recognized them as the eyes of his long-departed wife. Trembling, he turned his head away, and when he finally looked around again, the flowers had disappeared, and in their place bees, mosquitoes, beetles, and flies were swarming around the room. They buzzed over to the king, who lost all sense of where he was. "Bzzzzz, bzzzz, zzzzz, zzzzz" rang in his ears, and soon he was so stung, scratched, and bitten that he was almost unrecognizable. He fell to his knees in exhaustion and begged for mercy.

"Wed Lila to Egbert," droned a fat bee.

"That will never happen!" the king exclaimed angrily, jumping up. The creatures disappeared, and the room became a lake. Every flower had become a wave, and the bees and mosquitoes were nasty fish who stuck their heads out of the water. The king was standing with bare feet in the water, and the water was ice cold. The waves rose, and the water swelled higher and higher.

"No! No!" cried the king. "I won't do it!" and he stamped his feet, causing the water to spray up. The water rose faster and faster, climbed to his neck, climbed to his chin, over his mouth, and in another moment he would drown.

"Stop!" he cried, his brow bathed in mortal sweat. "I approve the union."

The water disappeared, the fish disappeared, and the first glint of sunlight fell on the king's pale face. At the break of dawn he summoned Egbert to the castle and said to him, "My son, last night I thought things over; the person who claims to be king must keep his promises! My dear child shall become your mate."

Overjoyed, Egbert wrapped Lila in his arms, but the king continued in a contemptuous tone, "Of course, my dear boy, you'll first have to see to it that you find a castle worthy of a king's daughter," and he thought to himself, He'll never get a castle without stealing it! At that he bowed mockingly toward Egbert, took the weeping Lila by the hand, and left the room.

Saddened and deep in thought, Egbert remained behind, but as soon as he was in his flower garden again, his courage returned. Again all the flowers in his garden came under his knife, and he extracted the precious oils from their petals. Every morning, the flowers he had cut in the evening bloomed more beautifully and bountifully, and he worked the entire day in the garden. At night the elves helped him, and soon he had filled hundreds of flasks with the amazing perfumes. He traveled with them to various courts and offered the flower essences for sale, and he was paid in gold. Soon he was one of the richest people in the land, and he built a castle of extravagant beauty in the midst of his flowers. Then he went to the king and said, "I bring you salutations from the flower spirits. My castle stands ready."

The king was forced to agree to the wedding since he no longer had any excuse. So Lila became Egbert's wife, and you can ask the flowers – they'll tell you how happy they were.

That a gardener should become the king – the king did not endure this sorrow very long. He died of a broken heart. Shortly before his death he had his crown nailed to his head and his scepter welded to his hand. He went to his grave with them.

But Egbert, who had become king, didn't deliberate long: he had himself a crown of flowers made. It had the advantage of not being too constraining, and it also had a wondrous power: its flowers continued to blossom and never wilted as long as Egbert ruled well and wisely, but if he did anything unbefitting a monarch or treated his subjects badly, the flowers wilted and only bloomed again when he'd repented of his error and corrected it.

Every night, before Egbert and Lila went to bed, they went to the garden and spoke to the flowers, "Good night, my dears!" The flowers turned their little heads and whispered, "May the Lord protect you!"

TRANSLATED BY SHAWN C. JARVIS

The princess of Banalia discovers the lovers. Illustration by Hans
Anker. From Marie von Ebner-Eschenbach, *Die Prinzessin von Banalien.*
Ein Märchen von Marie von Ebner-Eschenbach (Berlin: Concordia
deutsche Verlags–Anstalt Hermann Ehbock, 1904), 63.

Marie, Freifrau von Ebner-Eschenbach
1830–1916

The highly prolific and beloved writer Marie von Ebner-Eschenbach is considered by many to be one of the finest critical realists of central European literature. Her stories capture the tensions of the landed aristocracy and its rural village subjects in the declining Austrian empire. A precocious reader, Ebner-Eschenbach learned about literature from a series of stepmothers and governesses. She married her cousin in 1848 and lived in Vienna after 1856. For years she tried to produce dramas and failed; encouraged by other writers such as Franz Grillparzer, she turned to prose and became both successful and lionized by the public, the women's movement, and other authors. She is best known for her stories and novels of unusual, strong, and unhappy women, her aphorisms, and several fairy tales.

The dramatic fairy tale "The Princess of Banalia" was first planned as a stage play, and it still has the markings of high drama and tableau in its presentation of the heroine's suicide. It is a poignant, harrowing tale of a good, well-behaved queen who has spent most of her life in unrequited love with a wild man.

Suggestions for related and contrasting tales are "The Fox Wife" (in Datlow and Windling, eds., *Ruby Slippers, Golden Tears*), the story of a wife who becomes wild and goes to live with the foxes; Mary Louisa Molesworth's "The Story of a King's Daughter" (in Zipes, ed., *Victorian Fairy Tales*) which depicts a woman who is kind to animals and the rescue of a prince from an enchanted forest to rule the land; and Cole's *Princess Smartypants,* the story of a princess who refuses all suitors.

Marie von Ebner-Eschenbach, *Die Prinzessin von Banalien. Märchen* (Vienna: L. Rosner, 1872).

The Princess of Banalia

1872

THERE WAS ONCE a mighty princess of Banalia who was courted by many a royal suitor. One after the other sought to win her love. One counted on his fame, the other on his intellect, a third relied on his handsome countenance, a fourth on his riches, but in vain; none of them was able to arouse the slightest interest in the princess.

One day ten kings rode dejectedly out of the castle, each at the head of his splendid entourage. They had been dismissed the previous evening and were departing at the first cock's crow, broken in heart and spirit. The princess, relieved to be rid at last of these tedious suitors, had already hurried into the garden at daybreak and gazed at the retreating train of rejects. Her bright, joyful laugh rang out loudly as she saw them grow smaller and more indistinguishable in the distance; she could no longer discern the colors of their waving banners and the flashing of their gilded spears. There was nothing but a cloud of dust, long and gray, and soon even that disappeared.

Only then did the princess begin to swagger. She leaped and danced about, not like a sixteen-year-old but a six-year-old, and not like a fairy tale maiden but like a common, everyday one. And yet she was so fair, just as a fairy child should be. She gazed on the world with eyes as blue as the sky and as deep as the sea. Her blond hair flowed around her like a silken mantle, majesty rested on her brow, and purity shone on her countenance. She wore a voluminous robe of white that had a little golden dagger, a gift from her mother, in its waistband. Her mother, a fairy of the third order, was permitted by the laws of the Diamond Fairy Decree, which must be carried out to the letter, to descend to earth to visit her daughter not more than once every three years, and then for precisely three days, three hours, and three minutes. Their last farewell had been the most painful to her dear mother; she had parted from the charming child with thousands upon thousands of kisses and tears, and in that final third minute she had pulled from her belt a dagger and laid it in her daughter's hand. As she floated away, she called,

"When it is thrown in anger or fear, it kills everything it hits – care for it well! Losing it will bring unfathomable ill – care for it well!"

At that moment the princess thought neither of her mother nor of her dagger. As happy as a young thing can be when she doesn't know why she is so blessed, she raced over the meadow as fast as an arrow, as graceful as a gazelle. Then she suddenly stopped in midgallop. Before her in the grass lay a young man asleep. The sun shone down on his dark face and unruly black locks, his lips were firmly closed, and there was a frown on his brow. He was dreaming, it seemed, of battle, or blows, or the hunt, for he stirred restlessly and clenched his fist as if holding his sword. Yet he did not wear one at his side; he had only a dull knife in a wooden sheath. A primitive bow and a quiver with arrows lay beside him. He wore rags of rough cloth.

"A real vagabond!" they would have said at court if they had seen him, and they would have turned away with scorn. But the princess stood there enchanted and gazed at him with awe and sympathy and curiosity. She liked the dark look on his face; he was a pleasant contrast to the eternal grinning of the courtiers. The sleeper did indeed look angry, or was it only his dream? Who knows, it is all really part of him in the end, she thought, and then she was gripped with fear. "O heavenly spirits, do not let him wake!" She wanted to flee but could not; it was as if she were rooted to the spot, as if she must stay for days and days. Something rustled in the grass. Silently, it came slithering up, silent and quick, and suddenly, a viper curled around the arm the young man had stretched out above his head. Automatically, he struck the ground to shake it off. It hissed and was already flicking its tongue, already lowering its head for the deadly bite, when the princess threw her dagger, barely aiming it. But the magic weapon hit its mark. The snake lay speared to the ground, and the princess ran back to the castle, breathless and with a pounding heart.

There everything was in a total uproar. Their mistress had been away five minutes longer than usual, and already the machinery of the state had come to a standstill. When the princess appeared, her loyal subjects sprang to life again. They surrounded her, each wanting to be the first to receive her orders, for each saw his own task as indispensable to the continued existence of the kingdom. On this day, the young monarch governed with confusion. She muddled the names, titles, ranks, and persons, and thus came about some very bizarre official appointments. But since in every well-organized kingdom the office provides to its appointee the requisite wisdom, the princess's absentmindedness had no terrible repercussions.

When she emerged from the council chambers after four deadly hours, exhausted and listless, to go to the Regal Brunch, her Mistress of Ceremonies

approached and announced that the Lady-in-Waiting on duty had been dismissed because she had forgotten – as had been duly noted with solemn
shock by several court officials – to attach the dagger as usual to her majesty's
waist, the last gift of her most esteemed mama.

The princess blushed a deep crimson. She wanted to explain to the old
servant what had happened to the dagger, but a feeling she could not fathom
held her back. She was overcome by a strange confusion that grew worse
by the minute. It seemed as though all eyes were on her, every face. "The
Lady-in-Waiting will stay!" she finally shouted and left the room.

There was no chance that day to pull herself away from her royal duties
and rush into the garden, much as she longed to. Only the next day, after an
anguished and sleepless night, was she able to return to the spot where she
had found the sleeper and lost her dagger – but more than her dagger! She
strode confidently toward the place she was sure she would find it, and she
did indeed take the right path, straight through the meadow. Here it was;
the trampled grass marked the spot where the stranger had rested, and the
dead snake lay close by. But she could not find her magic weapon, and, even
stranger, that profound and fateful loss seemed not to bother her at all.

She had merely fooled herself that she had come to find her dagger.
What did it matter? What if it bore future disaster? She suddenly believed
that everything she had wished for or feared until now had been childish
and pathetic; only now had something magnificent, something significant
entered her life, something worth celebrating, worth suffering for. She knelt
and brushed her hand over the grass where the young man's head had lain.
Her heart trembled as she remembered the mixture of fear and wonder she
had felt on seeing his impudent face; then she thought of his ragged clothes.
"He is poor," she murmured to herself. And thus her intense compassion
grew into an irresistible, all-consuming sympathy, that tyrannical feeling
that strikes the gentlest souls the hardest and makes them willing slaves of
those they pity.

Hours passed. The High Mistress of Ceremonies appeared and dared to
mention the dagger once more. The princess rose and said, "I've lost it." A
pitiful wail and great cry arose, and all leaped to the anxious search. The dust
of a century was stirred up; no stone was left unturned. When nothing was
found in the castle, investigations ensued in the gardens. All the subjects of
the land were out and about, searching in birds' nests, treetops, and moles'
burrows. All in vain, in vain! The princess watched the hubbub in silence
and did not betray her secret. She fell into a deep melancholy.

She almost never left her favorite spot in the garden. As the air turned
brisker, she ordered a temple to be built over the spot where she had en-

countered the sleeper. Golden columns bore a crystal roof through which the shining sun kept the grass fresh and green as if in eternal summer. There she rested and dreamed while the whole court was bored to despair.

And thus passed the saddest year that even the oldest of the Banalians could remember. Then, suddenly, some news flew through the capital that set everyone in motion. The order came that all the councilors of the court and the senators of the people were to assemble in the Great Throne Room. It was proclaimed with ceremony at the marketplaces: the princess would give an address at noon to which all her subjects were invited.

The crowd was, of course, extraordinary, and the tension was palpable. As the announced hour struck, the princess appeared. She was very wan, but all the court poets swore that she had never looked lovelier, and Almansor, the Court Sonneteer, compared her to a white rose, an image that the General Procurer of National Criticism pronounced both novel and accurate. Be that as it may, the princess had appeared. The jubilation of the crowd was all the more unbridled, since she had forbidden any loud show of joy at her first public reappearance. She mounted the throne and said, "Everyone great and small of my kingdom!

"My dear and true subjects!

"My good people!

"Your hard work in trying to find my treasure has been fruitless. Its loss threatens my welfare, and thereby your own. I have therefore decided to turn to more powerful means than ever to locate the dagger, and so I command: a thousand heralds are to mount horses and ride through the land. They are to announce in every town and in every village, at every lonely cottage, through forest and field, through valley and grove. Whoever brings me my dagger, even if he be the lowliest of all my subjects, I will receive him before you all. Dressed in all my magnificent glory, with the crown upon my head and the scepter in my right hand, I will kneel before him as my savior and the savior of my people.

"And whatever his heart desires, whatever his fantasy can imagine, it will be given him.

"To this I swear, and thus it shall be done!"

All the princess's daydreaming was now over and done. She roamed through the palace in feverish anticipation and climbed the tower twenty times a day to see if there were any sign that announced her messengers' return. She had a horse brought and then raced over hill and dale toward some purpose unknown to her and everyone else. Often she would bring her courser up short in midgallop, so that he reared up, and then she would turn around and ride home again slowly with her head hanging. Sometimes she sprang out of the saddle and threw herself on the ground, burying her head in the moss and weeping bitterly. Sometimes festivities would be organized, cheerfulness was to reign supreme, and music was to sound, but other times all the chambers of the castle had to be dead silent, for every sound was torture and pain to the princess. The stress on her entourage grew beyond measure; she exhausted to the last drop that most inexhaustible of all things – the patience of groveling courtiers.

As the court's despair reached its peak, the hour of salvation finally arrived. Before daybreak, pealing bells woke the palace residents from their sweet or sad slumbers. A flaming red ball floated in the air, a good portent of happy news for the castle warder. In a flash the whole city was alight, and the people were up and about. In the castle there arose a tumult that defied every description. A storm-tossed sea was the face of a sleeping babe in comparison with this ruckus. Soon the castle was draped in ceremonial grandeur. The gates to the Throne Room stood wide open. The marble stairs that led there were laid with purple carpets, and on each step stood two huge knights in golden armor, frozen like statues. An army of huntsmen, Moors, falconers, pages, and lackeys in splendid attire filled the vestibule. Thirty men from the regiment of the White Elephant Guard formed a cordon. Bands seated high on camels, each musician a world-renowned brass player, stood before the castle. The guilds came on foot, the students arrived on borrowed steeds, the professors rode on hobbyhorses from their own stables, and all of them were dressed in sparkling robes embroidered with gold, ornaments, and jewels.

And then, cymbals ringing and trumpets blaring, the princess left her chambers and entered the Throne Room. The ceremonial tones of the national hymn swelled mightily through the air, and as if it had waited until just this moment to send its glowing message to the festival, the sun blazed up on the horizon and flooded the earth with rays of its life-giving light. From the mountains the music came rushing back down like a crashing storm.

With waving banners, the heralds raced down on their dappled steeds, and behind them came thousands and thousands of mountain dwellers and people of the valleys. In front of them all a herald jumped and shouted, "The treasure is found, found by a beggar!" and the news spread from mouth to mouth.

"You call him a beggar?" thought the princess and glanced around. And all the splendor surrounding her, all the regal grandeur that shone in her house seemed to her a vain, empty show, too small to receive him in dignity, him – a beggar!

The train of heralds was already riding, merrily trumpeting fanfares into the avenue. At their head was a youth, acclaimed by the crowd, who stared mutely and balefully into the noisy horde. On arriving at the stairway, he sprang from his mount and lovingly stroked the neck of the noble steed, which he seemed loath to leave, but then he quickly climbed the stairs to the hall. Inside, in contrast to the cries and hubbub outside the palace, a breathless hush reigned. With the same indifferent glance at the shimmering company of courtiers, he strode calmly and steadily up to the princess, without hesitating or bowing his head. She was trembling, and her heart sang out, "It is he!" and her heart trembled, "It is he!"

At the throne, he pulled the dagger from his belt, saying, "Here is your dagger. I found it –"

The princess interrupted him. "Hush," she whispered. "I know where you found it."

"And was it you who killed the snake? Was it you?"

"It was I."

"Then many thanks."

"But accept my thanks first," she cried, rose from the throne, and knelt before him. "I promised to give this homage to you!"

The guard presented arms, all foreheads almost touched the ground in respect, but the one who was being so honored was utterly indifferent to it all. "Thanking me? Because I brought back that little plaything?" he asked. He turned and was about to leave.

"Stay!" ordered the princess. "Stay and answer me. Who are you?"

"I'm a man."

"And your parents?"

"I never knew them."

"Your name?"

"I have none."

"Where were you raised?"

"Don't know. Maybe a lioness in the desert or a roe in the forest suckled me."

"How do you live now?"

"I roam and I hunt."

"Where is your home?"

"Everywhere and nowhere."

"You don't live in a house?"

He laughed. "The world is my house, the forest my bed, springs quench my thirst, and date palms sate my hunger."

The princess's astonishment grew as she watched him. He was so strange, so different from all the others she had encountered before, and he wore this difference, this strangeness so well. He was so free and so proud that she sensed with shy and happy confusion that here was a man who needed nothing a princess could offer him. And she humbly beseeched him, "Do you have any wish?"

"No," he said quickly.

"Consider this well. No one is without some wish."

"Well, then," he said, "I'd like a sword like these men bear." And he pointed to the guards who stood motionless around the throne. The princess gestured, a sword was brought, and she handed it to him. Gleefully, he seized it and tested its shiny blade.

"You have asked for too little. Make another demand," she said.

"Too little?"

"Make another demand."

This time he did not consider long before crying out, "Give me that horse that the messengers let me mount when they found me, that great horse that brought me here!"

"It is yours."

He rejoiced, saying, "I thank you!" and then turned to leave. But she said, "You have a sword. Don't you want to learn to brandish it? You have a horse. Don't you want to learn the art of real horsemanship as is befitting a man?"

"Yes, I do! I want that!"

Radiance filled the princess's face. With a sweet and trembling voice she continued, "O homeless and nameless man, I will make a home for you. I will give you a name. You will be called Abdul. You take pleasure in the hunt, and so you will lead a party of well-armed huntsmen to hunt lions, tigers, and hyenas. You are pleased with your sword and steed – you will have the most precious weapons and ride the noblest horses. Look around you in my house: what is mine is yours. Choose it and take it. Command all those who serve me; you are now their lord!"

And then the princess turned to those standing nearby to say, "This day will be a day of rejoicing for all my people. My beneficence will reward every deed. Whoever shows me a desire I can fulfill, a service I can reward, and above all a pain that I can ease will not go empty-handed. Bring them! Bring those who suffer and languish! Every supplicant is my friend, every starving soul my honored guest. Let no one go away empty-handed and unconsoled! Let an outpouring of blessings proclaim to my subjects at the farthest reaches of my kingdom that their queen has found infinite salvation. Oh, if only my people had one heart so that I could fill it more quickly with delight." Deeds followed these prophetic words apace. All the hungry ate, and all the thirsting drank. Every poor man became wealthy, and whoever asked for consolation was consoled; the charity of the princess was unending.

Abdul was brought to the most splendid chambers of the palace, now his own quarters. He was clothed in priceless garments, and the most honored of dignitaries at the court sought his favor. He learned to fence and ride and soon surpassed all his famous teachers in those arts. What he did not learn, however, was to submit to the rules of etiquette: to listen to a speech, to receive visitors, to return a greeting, or even to sit quietly at table. When he grew tired of sword practice, he mounted his steed and rode into the forest, or he jumped into a small boat and was carried off by the swift current of the river flowing hard by the palace. Often he stayed away for days, even weeks, and the whole time he was gone the princess wandered about in a dream and feared for his life. When he finally returned, he remained aloof and soon disappeared again. The palace air choked him, the walls closed in on him. He did not even deign to glance at the kowtowing courtiers; he barely noticed all the inventive attentions of the princess. When he did notice them, they left him cold or incurred his wrath. She revealed her gentleness and grace to him in vain; the woman irresistible to all others had no influence over this savage child of nature.

As indifferent as Abdul was to humans, the more he loved animals. The less works of art and the splendor of riches affected him, the more he stood in thrall to the magic of nature. It seemed as if he was more deeply connected to it than normal human beings. A flower spoke to him through its fragrance and the storm through its raging. Small birds flew to him, and even the shy deer followed his tracks. Once he came home bleeding with a lacerated breast, carrying in his arms a small antelope that he had torn from the murderous claws of a tiger. Ignoring his wounds, he bound up those of the wounded animal. The princess saw him and thought, Oh, if only once a little share of the goodness and patience that he wastes on this dumb animal were given to me, I would be the happiest princess in the world.

She followed him on the hunt, just to be close to him for some hours. Here, too, he only attacked in self-defense. His aim was to save and to liberate, to wage a war for the weak against the strong; he went out to protect others. And he was victorious in that! His true arrow hit the eagle and the hawk in midair, a stab from his dagger laid the predator on the ground. The princess thought him even more handsome than ever in the heat of battle, in his daredevil bravery and death-defying lust for danger. Boundless love showed in her every glance, every gesture – her love and her pain. She did not complain, but she languished. Even those who most soundly condemned her foolish passion could not help but pity her.

Then another suitor appeared: the noblest king in the world, a prince as has never existed outside a fairy tale. Full of generosity and wisdom, modest because he was proud, gentle because he was strong, he was a brave hero and a kindhearted person. Good people honored him, the evil hated him, the clever admired him, and the stupid slandered him; in short, he had everything to glorify his name. The princess did not treat him as poorly as she had previous suitors. She soon saw that he loved her, not her riches or her power. Did it happen by chance or plan? She was never more friendly with the king than in Abdul's presence.

It happened that there was to be a great banquet to celebrate some festival in Banalia. The king sat at the right hand of the princess, who was quiet and withdrawn and responded with a forced smile to his attempts to cheer her up. Suddenly, she blanched and trembled. Abdul had entered. She had seen him leaving that morning in a canoe and had not expected his return today. A thought ran like a bolt through her body: does the king's presence disturb him? By the gods! What if he were to fear losing me, what if he was not so indifferent to me as it appears? Indescribable delight flowed through her, and, struggling to regain her composure, she showed him a place at the table across from her. She pulled together all her courage and strength and led a lively and merry conversation, her features aglow and her eyes sparkling. The king expressed his admiration in glowing terms – and how happy he was that they were kindly accepted! The happy mood of the regal couple spread to the groveling courtiers. Everyone smiled. Meaningful glances were exchanged, as one whispered to another, "She likes him; he's winning her over! Bless us! Soon we'll have a king and a little highborn prince!" Only Abdul remained unaffected. The High Mistress of Ceremonies, who had held him in particularly biting scorn, though it was well hidden until this moment, could not deny herself the satisfaction of croaking at him in her froggy voice, pointing at the king: "He's going to be our lord!" The princess's fine ear picked up these words, and shyly she glanced at Abdul. But alas! She saw only his calm face, which did not betray a trace of concern. The High Mistress of Ceremonies was not satisfied. "What do you say to that?" she continued. "Well, that I'm happy about it," he responded, unruffled, spitting out the seed of the date he had just eaten (for he never touched another dish) with such speed and accuracy that it broke the pheasant feather on a lackey's cap in half.

The princess ended the meal abruptly. She felt unwell; she wished to be alone. Despondent, the king withdrew, and the courtiers lamented aloud – though of course not in her presence – about the discourteous way in which he was dismissed.

Relieved to be able to give her tears free rein, the princess stepped out onto her terrace. It was a lovely, starry night. The moon hung over the mountains, their fantastically shaped peaks gleaming like molten silver raised above the dark blue horizon. Not a single cloud floated in the sky, not a leaf trembled in the trees. All of nature was still – no noise, no echo, only the rolling of the river over its cascading riverbed, like a heavy breath in the majestic stillness. The princess sank into long, quiet thought and finally opened her eyes to the starry heavens. "Silent stars," she said, "is that what they call you? Oh, you have voices, voices that wake longing! If only you had the power to still that longing! But you are powerless in your majesty – a human eye has more power than your millions of blinking lights. One glance could do what all your brilliance could not – give me consolation. My pain is more infinite than you. The boundlessness that you hint at is carried in my own breast. Alas, the burdensome question: these worlds were created – for what? Cast into space – toward what goal? All of creation, why so divinely beautiful, if in it," the princess lamented, "hearts are breaking?" Suddenly, a footstep sounded in the sand. Quick, light footsteps approached from the garden, footsteps she would have known from a thousand others.

"Abdul!" she cried as he stood before her.

"What is it? Why are you crying?" he asked as he sat down beside her. He pulled her hands from her face and asked her gently and tenderly to tell him her woes, a thing he had never done before. But when the princess just sobbed harder, he became impatient. "Why did you call me if you don't have anything to say?" he said angrily, about to stand up. She wrapped her arms around his neck.

"I am crying because I am hurting."

"Who has hurt you? Tell me who he is. Whoever hurts you should not be allowed to live. I will kill him."

She had to smile through her tears. "That would be the worst thing you could do, for I love him."

"How can you love the one who hurts you? How can that be?"

"I don't know how it can be, but it is so. And the one who is hurting me and the one I love – is you."

"It is me?" He nestled her head on his chest and kissed her brow. "Oh, you foolish princess, stop crying. If you love me, then I will love you, too."

"Do you want to, Abdul? Just as I do, deep in your heart? Forever?"

"What do you mean, in my heart, forever! Just burning and hot!" And he embraced her with such wild passion that she trembled deep inside. She struggled from his grasp, only to sink back into his arms again.

"Tell me once more that you love me," she begged, "that I will be yours my whole life through, you my husband, my lord!"

"Not your husband, not your lord – I am your friend, your lover."

"Not my husband? You don't want to belong to me before God and the people, you don't want to be king?"

He chortled. "No, I don't want to be king!"

"Why not?" she asked anxiously. "Abdul, why not?"

"Because I can't bow to your customs, I can't walk your streets, I can't breathe in your rooms, I can't sleep under your roofs. Because I have to be as free as the eagle in the sky, as free as the lion in the desert!"

The princess rose and stood, a vengeful goddess, before him. Her eyes flashed fire, bitter scorn twitched on her lips. "Be honest with me," she commanded. "You do not love me. Admit it, and let us part." The full light of the moon fell on her tall figure. To the man she looked magnificent in her anger, in her bravely suppressed pain.

"Us part? Oh, no, no!" he cried and leaped up. They faced each other with pounding hearts and burning cheeks, she, angry at him for the first time, he for the first time captivated by her magnificent beauty.

The princess turned. "Stay!" said Abdul, pleading but proud, and as she kept walking, he repeated: "Stay!" and pressed her with force to his breast. She broke away from him.

"Get back!" she ordered with a dark look and disdainful gesture. But he held her all the more ardently.

"Stay!" he cried. "Stay with me! . . . Did I not already tell you – if you love me, I will love you in return?" Her anger and pride melted under his kisses.

"I was a fool to think – for only a moment – that I could ever pull myself away from you! Do you love me?" she said. "Then know this, even if you did not love me, I would still be yours. You see, I will not chain you or hold you, but you have control over me. Be free, and let me be your slave."

Did he hear her words? Did he understand her? Did he know what she had promised him? As clearly as the storm understands the language of the palm tree that it breaks in thoughtless abandon.

Hoping and despairing, waiting, longing for days and weeks, then a fleeting glance, a quick kiss, an ardent embrace that was too often followed by a cold parting – and then again hoping and despairing, waiting and longing: that was now the life of the princess.

The king, just as unhappy as she, had repeatedly given his entourage the command to depart and then repeatedly revoked it. The princess was incapable of hiding her love for Abdul. She never even tried. As soon as the king realized this, his first thought was to withdraw and yield the field to the favored rival. Yet he soon saw how little Abdul valued his own good fortune. How long could she delude herself? The moment would have to come when she would wake from her delirium. Should she then look around helplessly, unconsoled, finding no arm to support her, meeting no eyes in which she could read sympathy? His pity for her overcame his self-pity, and he remained.

The courtiers' disgruntlement about her badly chosen favorite increased daily and spread ever wider into all classes of the people. Dissatisfaction became common, and the heavens lay heavy over Banalia. The only one who remained naively unaffected by all this confusion was its cause, Abdul.

During those confusing days there awoke in the Court Sonneteer an irresistible urge for action. One could see from the stubborn wart glowing redder than ever on his famous nose that his soul was heavy with the gift of great thoughts. And so it was. He had decided on nothing less than bringing Abdul himself to use his influence to convince the princess to marry the king. He wrote a powerful address in which he described beyond all doubt the glory and majesty of the act to which he aimed to inspire his protégé. Moreover, he issued a free pass to immortality for the doer of this deed. As soon as Almansor had captured his outpourings on paper, he seized the moment. As Abdul entered the palace, he followed him into his chambers, the manuscript under his arm.

He found the youth busy with an abandoned bird's nest in a straw basket, putting bread crumbs soaked in milk into the gaping beaks of the peeping, unfeathered brood. Since Abdul was standing close to the window, making it impossible for Almansor to face him, the Sonneteer resigned himself to a view of his back and began the address. At first Abdul took no notice of him, but as the Sonneteer raised his voice ever louder, he gestured in a manner that said precisely this: "Get out! You are bothering me!" The imaginative Sonneteer, however, interpreted it as a somewhat awkward attempt at applause, and, elated by this apparent approval, he fell into a yearning tone that strangely moved even Abdul's imperturbable spirit.

Abdul took a few steps back, and Almansor took the opportunity to rush into the window niche. Unfortunately, he flourished the manuscript dramatically with his hand at just the wrong moment and flung the basket with the nest off the window sill. Abdul immediately grabbed him by the throat, and in a flash the Sonneteer was tumbling through the air, following the bird's nest down with such a powerful curse echoing behind him that he no doubt heard more angels singing than in the entire heavenly host.

Several of his disciples, apprised of the Sonneteer's great plan, were waiting under Abdul's window, and they sent up sighs of ecstasy on hearing their master's voice. But suddenly, they saw him flying through the air in a beautifully executed arch, landing in the middle of the river. They ran with haste to pull him out of the drink and found him wet and stiff with fear, robbed temporarily of speech and almost deaf but otherwise unharmed.

The accident caused a great hubbub. The sonnet-loving crowd in the capital felt that they themselves had been defenestrated with their Sonneteer. His loyal disciples rushed off to court and entered a charge of attempted murder against the royal favorite. Only a countermand by the princess could hinder Abdul's immediate arrest, and although her action surprised no one, everyone disapproved. The princess, of course, tried everything to cool the heated atmosphere. At her command the Court Doctor, the Apothecary, and the Royal Litter were put at Almansor's disposal. The highest-ranked Royal Actor was required to read aloud to him his own sonnets, which visibly speeded his recovery. The princess herself attended his bedside and brought him a decree in which she named him the First Salaried and Truly Literary Meteor in the Heavens, in recognition of his long, if involuntary flight. She instructed the guilty party, Abdul, to avoid the castle until she was able to stop the trial against him. Ignoring this request – or perhaps just to thwart it – he appeared the very next morning to check on his birds, who had been seriously wounded in the fall. First he tried to get food for his patients in the Royal Kitchen. He entered and saw the whole staff gathered around the Royal Chef; one of the boys was holding a turkey in obvious pain between his knees while another was forcing its beak open, allowing the Royal Chef to funnel steaming red wine down its gullet. The gathered crowd seemed to be enjoying the procedure tremendously, laughing, hooting, and clapping.

Abdul stood by, pale as death. "What is going on here?" he thundered at the servants with a powerful voice that shook the casseroles from the walls and caused the great iron stove to wobble. The whole crowd stared at him frozen in fear; no one dared to speak. "What is going on here?" Abdul repeated. "We are preparing the roast for tomorrow," stuttered the Royal Chef and automatically grabbed for the roasting spit next to him. In a flash Abdul grabbed it from him and stuck it deep into the fat body of the turkey torturer, who fell gasping to the ground. With undiminished anger Abdul started in after his accomplices.

"You vile swine!" he cried. "You laugh when a helpless animal that has never hurt you is being tortured?" and he struck down one after the other with mortars, skillets, and every weapon that this scene had to offer. A few of the braver members of the kitchen staff tried to defend themselves, and a fight ensued, accompanied by the most terrible racket, which eventually roused the castle servants and the guards. Abdul fought through the swarm and ran directly into the chambers of the princess. He heaped accusations on her about the cruelty she allowed to happen. He raged, he stormed; it was impossible to quiet him and impossible to understand his incoherent speech. There came a loud wailing from the horde outside the palace who stood making threats below the princess's windows. The Captain of the Palace Guards came and announced the death of the Royal Chef, who had died with the words "Adieu, ragouts!" on his lips.

Sad yet true, it must be reported: the Royal Chef enjoyed a popularity beside which that of the Court Sonneteer paled in comparison. He had enriched thousands along with himself, and they had hoped he would keep enriching their lives. Thousands admired his art, and thousands of his disciples were spread throughout the land.

The princess stepped onto the balcony and tried to placate the mob with her words, but the crowd interrupted her with whistles and jeers. She heard insults whose denigrating meaning she sensed but did not understand. Shuddering, she covered her shamefully crimson face with her hands. Then the king appeared at her side. "Hurrah! Vivat!" resounded, and then again cries for revenge.

"Not revenge!" cried the king. "You will have justice, and the princess vows it through me, her spokesman."

"Pledges, we want pledges!" cried a few voices that swelled to one voice from the crowd.

"Is the word of the princess herself not pledge enough?"

"No, give us your own!"

The princess wanted to die. Is this where she stood now? None of her people believed in her? "I refuse to give my word to anyone who does not believe the word of the princess," said the king, and furious howls went up from the crowd.

Then Abdul broke loose from the guards who had tried to restrain him and rushed to the balcony. A roar of rage greeted him. "What are you doing making deals with these mangy beasts?" he cried to the king. He had barely finished when a well-aimed stone came flying toward him; he dodged quickly, and the stone hit the princess's brow. She collapsed, a river of blood gushing from the wound. The king gathered her in his arms and ordered the guards to take Abdul into custody. They did, in spite of his desperate resistance, and brought him bound and foaming with rage into his chambers, threw him on his couch, and barricaded the door – he was a prisoner. The mob camped before the palace had made it clear from its horrible shouts that the people would not budge until their enemy had been delivered to them.

From her faint the princess had sunk into a feverish sleep, in which dream images mingled strangely with her realization of what was happening around her. It seemed that a figure was bending over her, asking her questions. Then she heard the Court Doctor's voice clearly saying, "She is sleeping calmly and deeply." Then a second voice whispered, "Make sure that she does not wake before it is all over." All over? she thought. What was supposed to be all over? Like a flash it struck her that Abdul was in great danger. She fell into a stupor; she wanted to get up, to speak, but it was impossible. Her limbs felt like lead, and though her lips moved, no sound came out. She listened. There came some conversation she did not understand, then the whispered words: "The guards have been won over, they will hand him over to the people. Even God Almighty cannot save him now." That was the Royal Mistress of Ceremonies speaking, and the one to be delivered was Abdul.

In mortal fear the princess struggled for strength to overcome her stupor. She lay quietly for a while, then opened her eyes dramatically and, declaring that she felt fine, ordered the Court Doctor and her Ladies-in-Waiting to leave. In anticipation of future orders, they asked to wait in the adjoining room and then removed themselves. As soon as she was alone, she rose and dressed, put her dagger in her belt, and went to the large, arched window. The marble niche above it was decorated with delicate golden arabesques, and the princess examined them carefully by the flickering lamplight; she seemed to be looking for something. Then she touched the calyx of a fantastic flower; slowly, silently the wall slid open, a small stairway in the wall became visible, and the princess entered it, closing the niche behind her.

While the mob raged outside the palace, demanding Abdul's surrender, he slept peacefully on his cot, as if resting in the cloak of God. He was wakened by a gentle touch. The princess's hand lay on his lips, and she whispered to him, "Say nothing and follow me." She unchained him and led him, still drunk with sleep, silently feeling along the walls through the dark chamber. It seemed to him that the room had enlarged endlessly, for they walked and walked and still did not come to the exit. "Where to?" asked Abdul. "To freedom," replied the princess and pulled him along with her. Still the deep darkness and a damp, dank air surrounded them, as if the path led through a narrow stone-walled space. They climbed a wooden stair with hundreds of steps and then another passageway as if cut through rock; still the night grew darker, the air ever danker. Abdul barely breathed. "Your path to freedom is too far," he gasped occasionally from his constricted breast.

After long wandering, they suddenly saw a narrow ray of light far off in the distance. "Daylight!" cried Abdul and rushed forward. "It is not daylight," said the princess. Gradually, the ray of light became a beam, broadening as they approached it. Two huge gates retracted even farther into the walls of the passage with each step the princess took toward them. As she stood directly before them, they had completely disappeared.

So the princess, accompanied by Abdul, stepped into a high, vaulted hall whose walls were built of shimmering stones that cast their glow all around, chalky and white like the moonlight. A shiver passed over the two young people. The princess embraced her beloved and said, "I am breaking a holy vow, my darling Abdul, by bringing you into these mysterious halls. No human has ever set foot here other than the kings of this land. The secret of the halls' existence is passed on from one ruler to the next. Here the kings found protection in times of extreme danger; here they communed with the spirits who once lived, thousands and thousands of years ago. The spirits erected this palace for the founding father of my race, himself given life by one of their leaders. Here many of my forefathers ended their lives in ghostly silence, weary of battles and daring deeds. Far from life's intimacy, distanced from every mortal urge, they sleep here a dreamless sleep. They do not think, they do not feel. They live their death." Abdul shuddered. He said not a word; he held the princess's hand in his own and hurried forward.

The silent, empty, eerie hall seemed to extend and grow longer under their feet. The farther they went, the farther the room stretched before them. Suddenly, there rose before the wanderers four rows of majestic alabaster columns. They led to a large rotunda in whose midst stood a monument of the purest, most transparent crystal. On it rested the body of a king in pure white robes with a marblelike face and glazed eyes, a crown on his head and a scepter in his hand. The princess and Abdul passed on, and the same spectacle repeated itself countless times; surrounding them was unending brightness and unending death. They walked on, their steps making no echo, their bodies casting no shadows; they spoke, but their voices made no sound. They huddled together but felt no contact. They lost all sense of time; they felt no hunger and no fatigue. The princess was calm; her eyes never left Abdul, who walked on, dark and despairing, at her side.

Finally, the scene in the halls changed: a colorful glow streamed down from cupolas of jewels, and broad staircases led to richly decorated temples with golden doors that sprang open as soon as the princess touched them. The rooms became increasingly smaller and darker, and a strange tremor shook the ground and the walls. Abdul turned around. The brightness was extinguished; the miraculous palace had sunk away without a sound. The princess spoke, and now her voice could be heard. "The secret of my fathers has come to an end, because I have betrayed it."

"That is good," shouted Abdul. "That horrible magic does not belong in a free and happy world! Away!" he insisted. "Are we almost at the end of our journey?" Thick darkness surrounded them again; there was yet another long trek through labyrinthine passages, a steep climb upward, and then the sound of a spring and a whiff of refreshing, breezy air. What ecstasy! Abdul rushed ahead, and the princess followed. The entrance to a cave opened before them, and soon they walked through it to the open air, trees rustling above their heads. They were seized by crushing exhaustion as they approached the forest. They did not ask how long their journey had taken; they did not care what time of day it was. It was as if their very breath stilled their exhaustion. They sank silently, incapable of moving, into the soft moss and, soon, into the silence of deep sleep.

A violent pain woke the princess early the next morning. Her wound was burning, her pulse was feverishly beating, she felt numb and ill. Her robe was heavy with dew, and her loosened hair was damp. Slowly, she rose from the ground. There Abdul lay before her, a blissful smile on his face. How wonderfully he slept! How freely his chest rose and fell, how robust was his whole being, a blossoming image of ecstatic inner peace! He seemed to feel it in his sleep: "I am home, in my own element!" The princess looked at him long and lovingly, and the happiness that seemed to fill him flowed over her own soul. It was her doing that his eyes would behold this day, that he would live it in freedom and joy; she had beaten back fate.

Gradually, life began in the forest; the treetops rustled softly and the birds flew about, landed on branches, and twittered each other a morning song. Roes and gazelles frolicked in the thicket, peeking out with curiosity and then shyly butting their heads together, as if telling each other important news. The princess stepped back a few paces to a spring pouring out of a nearby cliff to cool her burning lips and her painful wound.

Meanwhile, the creatures of the forest dared to approach the sleeper. The birds perched on his shoulders and chest; a little rabbit sat across from him on a broken log and wiggled its long ears as if in greeting. One deer licked Abdul's hand, another his foot, and a gazelle even dared to touch his cheek with her cold nose. He awoke, looked around, and with a cry of delight spread his arms as if he wanted to embrace all of nature. He kissed the earth, he pressed the trees and grass to his heart, he lovingly stroked the pelts of the animals and the feathers of the birds. "Greetings!" he cried. "Green forest, clouds, and breezes! Greetings to all you creatures of the wilderness! Abdul is with you again, Abdul dreamed a horrible dream, you know, about a castle and a princess and evil and cruel people . . ." He turned and saw the princess at the spring, and a cloud darkened his brow. "It wasn't a dream?" he asked and sighed in pain. "It wasn't a dream – I lived it all?" The princess approached him, her folded hands ready to plead. "Forget, my darling

Abdul," she begged. "Forget what you have suffered. You should forget all the things that tortured you. It is all past – look, you are home, you are breathing freedom, love surrounds you. Here we can lead a happy life –"

"We?" interrupted Abdul. "You are not returning to your own people, to your house, your homeland?"

The princess blanched. "Part from you?" she cried. "Do you think I could do that?" He did not answer. When he saw that she was determined to stay with him, he built a hut of twigs and moss, and this became their home. Their food consisted of forest berries, their bed was made of dry grass. The princess's clothes slowly disintegrated into rags, and she often suffered from hunger and cold. But what did that matter? That was not what clouded her happiness. What angered her and gnawed at her heart was that Abdul cared less and less about her, that he undertook outings ever farther away from her, for ever longer periods, with ever shorter moments of return home.

Once, when she was tortured by longing and worry, she ventured deep into the forest to look for Abdul. Thousands of times she called his name with all her strength but heard only startled birds screeching and branches rustling in the wind in response. It began to get dark, and night fell. The princess thought that perhaps Abdul had taken a different path back to the hut than the one on which she had gone. She wanted to turn back but could no longer find her way; she was in a totally unknown part of the forest and had lost her bearings. The moon stood covered with clouds in a dusky sky, and the howl of wild animals sounded uncannily in the distance through the quiet night. The princess reached for her dagger – it had been her true friend in her deepest despair!

Bravely, she walked on. As long as her feet would carry her, she kept on going, calling with an ever weaker voice the name of her beloved. Finally, she sank down exhausted under a huge tree whose branches hung completely down to the ground and covered her. She lay there, sleepless, with her heart racing until the morning dawned.

A reddish glow in the east heralded the sunrise when a long mating call, a call that she had so often heard from Abdul, sounded in the princess's ear. It was he! It was Abdul! And he was calling her, he was perhaps seeking her as desperately as she him. She struggled to her feet and took a deep breath to give a loud and happy cry in return when the same tone sounded from the opposite side of the forest. And now the cries quickly alternated with each other, repeating each other ever closer. The princess listened in astonishment and terror. Who besides her knew this sign of Abdul that he gave upon his approach? Who besides the two of them lived in this wilderness, untouched by any other human? She retreated closer behind the trunk of the tree, hiding deeper behind its protective branches, and listened. A light, rapid footstep approached her hiding place and stopped directly before it.

Even though the leaves covered the princess, they did not prevent her from seeing what was happening around her. Turning cautiously to the side from which the steps approached, she saw a girl, petite and slim, barely out of childhood – a girl with dark skin, flashing eyes, and full lips, with lively and lambent features that were, however, not beautiful. A piece of colorful cloth hung over her partially bare breast, another was slung around her loins. Her arms and legs were naked. Curly locks of dull black hair twined around the head and nape of the young troglodyte.

Suddenly, the girl broke out in a wild, gleeful laugh and greeted Abdul. He stepped from between the trees, ran to her, picked her up in his arms, and kissed and caressed the wild creature. At first she pushed him away but then returned his stormy caresses no less wildly. Seeing this, the princess felt her heart twist inside. Rage, disgust, and hate filled her soul, a soul that had never opened to any but the most noble emotions. With a cry of crazed anger, her dagger held high, she rushed to attack the murderers of her happiness. Self-defense – and despair – drove her. Beside herself with pain, she threw her fateful weapon. A mortal blow struck Abdul's beloved, who sank into his arms. He knelt beside her, lifted her head to his breast, and called to her with the sweetest names. A last tremor crossed her face, and it was over. Abdul covered her body with kisses, wept, and lamented.

The princess did not move. She shuddered with horror at herself, at the deed she had committed: horror and the pain of hell – regret. With an insane gaze, she stared at the pair at her feet. She had murdered this girl, this child whose heart streamed out a river of blood. She! She was a murderer. How could that be possible? She apparently had committed a crime that was unthinkable to her.

"No!" she cried suddenly. "Not I; I did not do this!"

These words woke Abdul from his unfathomable pain, and he raged against the woman who had caused it.

"Accursed wretch!" he cried. "To your crime you add your denial of it; that is just like you! Away with you! Get out of my sight, I despise you! Why did you force yourself into my life? I have been miserable since the moment we met; every hour I lost on you has meant pain to me. I never knew pain before, just as I did not know happiness, until she taught me!" He threw himself on the corpse and sobbed anew. "Oh, my darling, you are lying there so still, and now you are gone. Never again will we roam the forest, never again rest hand in hand, never again race together against the deer, never again sing to spite the birds. Oh, my joy and my delight! I loved you, and you knew how to love me. Laughing you ran into my arms, and laughing you have left me. You did not ask, 'Where to?' when I left you and not 'Where from?' when I returned to you. Oh, my love! What can I give you now? A grave in the cool shadows, under flowers and branches." He stood up, lifted the body gently from the ground, and carried her off in his arms like a sleeping child.

The princess sank to her knees. "Abdul, do not damn me!" she cried with such desperate grief that he was gripped by it in spite of his own despair.

"Can you bring her back to life?" he asked. She groaned. "I would give the last drop of blood in my heart to do it!" She wrung her hands and pressed her face into the dust of his footsteps.

In the next moment they heard horses neighing and horns sounding. Separate voices could be heard calling to each other; the crackling of underbrush sounded in the otherwise quiet forest. Abdul stood still. "Do you hear your people coming?" he said. "They have been looking for you for a long time. They are coming to take you home to your golden prison. Go to them; they are your own kind."

"Never!" cried the princess. "I can never return to my home, laden with sin and shame as I am. Reject me, desert me, but do not deliver me up to them. Hide me. Have pity on me! Hide me!"

He did not deign to look at her or to speak to her again. Quickly, he continued on his way with his sad burden and soon disappeared behind the trees.

Deepest despair reigned in the capital of Banalia. The rumor had spread everywhere that the king, who had set off on horseback with a large entourage several months ago to search for the mysteriously missing princess, had returned but had brought back only the corpse of the unhappy monarch. He had found her dead, it was said, in a dark forest populated by monsters and beasts of prey, and the people came in hordes to the palace, for their grudge against the princess was long past. They demanded, weeping and wailing, at least to be able to see the remains of the dear departed. The king stepped out onto the balcony, thanked them for their loyal sympathy, and explained that the young sovereign was not dead but lay in a deep stupor. Nothing had succeeded in waking her.

And thus it remained.

Paralyzed and pale, with closed eyes, the princess lay on her bed. Only a feeble beating of her heart betrayed that she was still alive. Her Ladies-in-Waiting stood by, weeping, and the king leaned in a corner of the room sunk in grief and kept his eyes riveted to the ailing princess.

The day that the kingdom regained its princess was the same day that her immortal mother was due to return. The final hour of the third year since her last visit to Banalia had sounded, and suddenly the fairy stood at the bedside of her daughter.

Her face enraged, she stood and dismissed all the courtiers so that she could be alone with the king. He knelt before her, and with a gesture toward the princess he cried, "Save her, save her for me! Free her from the terrible spell an ungrateful wretch has cast on her! Ignite a spark of feeling in her heart for me, and I will make her life peaceful and good, a life for the blessed."

"My son," replied the fairy, "I can command a withered tree to blossom and a dry spring to flow and flood. I can wake the dead, but I cannot spark love in a human heart. I can unfetter and shackle the elements, destroy armies or lead them to victory. The face of the earth transforms when I command it, but I cannot break the magic spell that holds this girl in thrall. Even the Almighty Ones are powerless against it. Yet it may be that you yourself can do what you demand in vain of me. If your love for my unhappy daughter is greater than her love for Abdul, if you do not shrink from the thought of taking her, desecrated as she is, into your blameless life, perhaps you will be able to make her forget the one she now belongs to body and soul."

"My life would have no meaning for me if I could not dedicate it to her," said the king.

"You are making an enormous sacrifice," warned the fairy. "Consider well, my lord, your faultless name, your renown, your honor."

But he answered, "Do not speak of sacrifices! Love knows no sacrifice. My honor? No one but I alone can exalt or endanger it. If my name is blameless, I am blessed! For it will all the better protect the one I share it with."

"Very well," spoke the fairy. "Go and fulfill your destiny and your own desire."

She bent down over the princess, who opened her eyes. Slowly, her daughter regained consciousness and stared blankly at her mother. She struggled to get up, but her head fell back into the pillows. But though her strength failed and she was not able to move, the paralysis was fading, and a soft whimper escaped her breast as her mouth grimaced in pain. She suffered; she was alive.

All at once, as if overcome with complete awareness, she cried aloud, "Mother! O Mother!" and, wringing her hands in unspeakable anguish, she begged, "Give the dead girl back the life I took from her! Do not leave me a murderer!"

The fairy pulled a mirror out of the folds of her robe, breathed on it, and held it before the princess's eyes. She gazed into the glass. The mist cleared, and on its shining surface there appeared ever clearer an image of the forest.

Ancient trees hung thick with vines, and an open grave at their feet held the dead girl, who lay on a bed of flowers. Abdul knelt beside her and kissed her cheeks, her mouth. And suddenly something like a warm, gentle ray of sunshine gilded her pallid face, her lips took on color and opened, her rigid arms loosened and embraced Abdul. With speechless delight he took her in his arms and pressed her to his heart, for she was given back to him. The princess buried her face in her hands. Heavy teardrops gushed through her fingers – tears of unspeakable joy, of unspeakable anguish.

"I thank you, Mother," she said finally. "You have lifted the curse that burdened my soul. I thank you. Abdul is happy again, and now I can die."

"Cowardly creature," chastised the fairy. "You are not to die, you will live – a new life, one purged of the shame of the past. You shall raise yourself up out of your deep degradation. You can do it, for a generous helpmeet has offered his aid. It is my will that you accept it."

The king approached. "Entrust me with your cares," he pleaded, gentle and solemn. "Entrust me with the care of shielding you from future sorrow. Let me try to reconcile you with your fate. I ask for your hand; do not reject me. Since I can do nothing else but love you, give me the license to love you."

"My lord," said the princess, "turn your affections to a worthier object than me. I have already belonged to the one I love; I cannot be your wife."

The king replied, "You were in the thrall of an evil spell, and it numbed your spirit and paralyzed your will. I have nothing to forgive you for, but if it were my place and you had committed some sin, it would already be forgiven. Be mine. I will love and honor you as if you had never known Abdul."

He held out his hands to her and then left the room. The princess fell to her mother's knees, bathing her feet in tears, but the fairy remained unmoved. Preparations were made for the wedding. Three days later the princess stood at the altar, pale, cold, and indifferent. The fairy was deeply pained and moved. The king was solemn and withdrawn. It was a sad marriage feast.

Three years passed – happy years for the Banalians. The king ruled with both might and forbearance, and success crowned his every deed. If ever a monarch was worshiped, it was he. The queen glided at his side like a trans-figured reflection of his greatness. She had borne him a son who was the apple of his father's eye and the hope of the people.

Again it was the day of the fairy's return. All around, festive preparations for her reception were being made. Midday, when the sun stood at its high-est point, was her usual moment of arrival, and anticipating this moment, the king and queen stepped out of the castle. She led a boy by one hand and rested the other on the arm of her husband. His eyes lighted lovingly on her face, and her glances and her words exuded her deep and intimate respect for him.

The king stepped back into the castle to give orders, and the queen walked onto the terrace alone with her child. She leaned on the railing and looked down into the rushing current of the river. Her poignant loveliness exuded incomparable enchantment, but the soft lines of suffering around her mouth betrayed the pain she had known. She did not seem happy but reconciled and at peace.

Her little boy played at her feet. How lovely this child was! His rosy face had the king's features, but his wonderful eyes were like his mother's. He shouted with joy at each wave as it crested and rolled past. The queen smiled at him, and her hand rested on his blond head as she pressed him tenderly to her. Suddenly, the little boy cried, "Look! The birds! So many of them!" And it was true: there came flying across the river a long, dark, unending flock of birds, every kind on earth. They seemed to be flying in pace with something floating on the water. They sang loudly and twittered and peeped, yet the tone of their cries was mournful. Often they flew down low as if they wanted to lap something from the waves, and then they rose again to lament in the skies, lamenting more sadly than before! Meanwhile, on the shore ran deer, gazelles, antelopes, and all types of timid forest creatures who normally hid themselves shyly from human eyes. Like a leaderless herd they ran along the banks, bleating and mewing, crowding together and then running apart again. They gazed into the river and continued on their way, breaking out in fresh lament. Ahead of the whole procession a majestic eagle soared peacefully with outspread wings.

They came ever nearer. The queen saw what the animals had accompanied so mournfully: it was a corpse. It lay half naked, borne up on the waves, a powerful, slender male figure. The head, thrown back, rested on an arm, the other lay across his breast. His eyes were closed in the deepest of slumbers. His loose locks hung heavily about his dark face. And then a scream came forth from the queen's mouth, a scream of despair and joy, insane hurt and jubilant delight. "Abdul! Abdul! You have come? You have come back to me?" And she plunged with outspread arms down into the river.

A few moments later the king stepped onto the terrace, and the fairy stood before him, enveloped in a rosy light. She gazed down; the waves had softly washed the bodies of Abdul and the queen onto the wide lower step of the marble stairs. The little boy had climbed down, snuggled up to his mother's body, and called her with loving little names. Yet she did not answer; she held her beloved in a tight embrace. In the sublime grandeur of death, her face wore a look of divine joy, one that the two people staring down at her had never seen on that dear face before.

The king stood like a stone statue. The fairy's eyes filled with tears; even the Immortals must sometimes weep. "My Lord," she finally said. "Have pity; do not damn her."

"She was my only joy; I loved her," the king replied. He walked down the stairs, took the child in his arms, and pressed it to his heart.

TRANSLATED BY JEANNINE BLACKWELL

Dramatized fairy tales. Cover of Henriette Kühne-Harkort, *Kinder-und Puppen-Theater Nr. 1–10. Dramatisierte Märchen. Nach Grimm, Müsäus, Hauff u. a. Mit Winken und Unterweisungen in Bezug auf Ausstattung und Aufführung* (Leipzig: Otto Spamer, [1894]). Reprinted with permission from Thiel College Library.

Henriette Kühne-Harkort

1822–1894

Almost nothing is known about Henriette Kühne-Harkort's life other than that she was the daughter of an engineer and soldier of fortune who immigrated to America and that she married Friedrich Gustav Kühne in 1841. Kühne-Harkort was the author of a small oeuvre of children's literature; a list of her publications suggests that she used the canonical fairy tales of Romantic authors (the Grimms, Johann Karl August Musäus, Wilhelm Hauff, and Richard Leander) as the basis for numerous reworkings. Her works, with titles like *Sleeping Beauty, Snow White,* and *Undine,* consist mainly of puppet plays and children's plays designed for performance at home or school.

Kühne-Harkort's play *Snow White,* based on Musäus's "Richilde," with "tips and instructions for staging and production," grew out of the tradition of the fairy tale play as part of the salon culture. The work presented here is a clear example of the kinds of fairy tale plays popularized by the Kindergarten movement in Germany, where the memorization of parts and the performance became an integral part of the child's education. What is especially interesting about this version of the Grimms' classic tale is Kühne-Harkort's treatment of the dwarfs. Although she lists seven in the cast of characters, she actually has eight dwarfs bearing names of various minerals and elements; their lines explain the natural world to the performers and audience. In addition, her version also noticeably lacks the original's horrific punishment of the queen (here a countess). Besides naming the dwarfs long before Walt Disney gave life to Dopey and Sleepy, Kühne-Harkort's piece develops clear personalities for the various characters. Her work also suggests that adapters of fairy tales were already toning down the more brutal elements of the Grimms' tales for younger audiences long before the educational reform movements of the twentieth century.

Other interesting versions of Snow White to read with the piece include "Snow White" from the Merseyside Fairy Story Collective (1972, in Zipes, ed., *Don't Bet on the Prince*) and no. 53, "Snow White," in the Grimms' 1857 edition. The Walt Disney film also provides an interesting contrast.

Henriette Kühne-Harkort, *Schneewittchen. Frei nach Grimm*, in *Dramatisierte Märchen. Nach Grimm, Hauff u. a. Mit Winken und Unterweisungen in Bezug auf Ausstattung und Aufführung. Kinder- und Puppentheater*, vol. 1, no. 10 (Leipzig: Otto Spamer, [1877]), 249–80.

Snow White

Freely Adapted from the Grimms

1877

CAST OF CHARACTERS

Richilde, countess of Brabant
Snow White, her stepdaughter
Prince Kunimund of Flanders
Count Courtly
Count Heartafire
Count Languor
Gunderich, the countess's gatekeeper
Brigitta, his wife
Ursula, the countess's nursemaid

DWARFS
Granite
Sodium
Carbon
Iodine
Soda
Sulfur
Quartz

TIPS AND SUGGESTIONS FOR THE PRODUCTION

To the Director
The staging of this fairy tale is not complicated, although care must be taken in making the dwarfs; such gremlin figures are, however, not difficult to make. The dwarf Granite should have an especially long white beard. The other characters should have medieval-looking costumes.

Backdrops

Boulders and bushes. Flowerpots. A table with seven place settings, a smaller table. A bier for Snow White out of gray cardboard. The window needed at the dwarfs' house can be suggested with a curtain of white silk paper on a side backdrop; a small table and a vase of flowers should be situated close by so that the scene between Snow White and Richilde is obscured. It is best to make two Richilde figures, one beautifully attired and the other in a simple dress with a little basket.

Props

A mirror. A small basket with apples.

ACT I

Room at the house of Gunderich the gatekeeper. Gunderich, Brigitta, later Ursula, lastly Snow White.

GUNDERICH: At last, at least a short repose.
    The city gate awhile is closed.
    I'm coming to you, O wife of mine
    For a bit of gossip to pass the time
    While they're all sitting at the square.
    Such toil and trouble I've had there!
BRIGITTA: You poor dear man, you have my pity.
    It's a terrible time for you in the city.
    How oft have you opened the gates today?
    More than fifty times, I heard you say.
GUNDERICH: That's just about the number!
BRIGITTA: Why preparations so intense?
    The number of guests is just immense.
GUNDERICH: You ask me that and are so smart?
    The mistress's beauty plays its part.
    It lures them all, like honey the fly,
    Like sticky traps the sparrow on high.
    The suitors come from far away
    To sing the same tune every day.
    I'm only puzzled they never grow tired
    Of the same old tune, so uninspired,
    In which they all their love evince.
    I just let in Kunimund, a prince,
    A knight from blessed Flanders.

BRIGITTA: Is the countess the one to whom he panders?
GUNDERICH: It may well be, for all I care!
BRIGITTA: He's certainly got a special air!
    I'd hate to see him in a mess.
    To see him's to love him, I must confess.
    Most noble and grand, he's quite a gent.
    The finest of manners, 100 percent.
GUNDERICH: You act as if he's well renowned,
    Though he's just arrived in Brabant, our town.
BRIGITTA: As he rode into town, that handsome knight,
    I stood at the window with Snow White.
    There I watched him with great care
    As he came to her window and then stopped there
    To doff his feathered cap to Snow White
    As befits a lady, when one's polite.
    That greeting, I thought, would never end
    So long to her did he attend.
GUNDERICH: That's no surprise. Is that child so dear
    Not lovelier than all in the castle here?
    Is she not higher born than all the others?
BRIGITTA: But is kept much plainer than no other.
    Oh, if the blessed king, now in his grave
    Saw that, oh, how he'd rant and rave!
    Poor thing! Not a year without the mother
    Her father began to woo another.
    A stately, pretty wife he wed
    Who's got nothing but vanity in her head.
    And when he died a short while later
    The new mother began to hate her.
    The child hindered her everywhere,
    So soon she came into our care.
    The years passed by and as time whiled
    By and by she forgot the child.
    The thought of it just makes me weep.
GUNDERICH: It's not that bad, if I may speak.
    Snow White we both have loved and treasured.
    Yes, riches and splendor have been measured.
    She stayed away from sumptuous feasts
    But learned contentment with the least.
    And even if fate has dealt hard blows,

In adversity she is composed
And has even blossomed like a rose.
BRIGITTA: But it's a shame she's so hidden away.
GUNDERICH: Just wait, she'll see the light of day.
BRIGITTA: Yes, strange things happen under the sun.
As if it just was, I recall what's done.
It's well nigh sixteen years we've observed
Since the departed countess I did serve.
Before Snow White came into being
The countess at her hoop was seen
Sewing and stitching as she longed for the child.
The icy wind outside blew wild
And hurled great flakes against the glass.
Her highness jumped from the storm, aghast
And stabbed herself in the finger, so deep,
That soon red blood began to seep.
And as she opened the window wide
Some drops of blood then fell outside.
The red blood shimmered on the snow,
Whereupon the countess said, aglow,
"Brigitta, look out there, below
As red as blood, as white as snow,
As black as here my ebony frame.
A child like that I'd proudly claim."
A few days later she held in her arms
The sweet young thing God kept from harm.
Never was there a prettier sight,
Hair so black, skin snow white,
The delicate cheeks like blood so red.
But soon the mother lay pale and dead,
And they lowered her into a snowy grave.
Snow White's the name the girl they gave.

Ursula enters.

URSULA: It's me, breathlessly aflit.
I have to catch my breath a bit
And spend some time with both of you
To chat a bit and share some news.
I stole away, away did dart,
It weighs so heavy on my heart.

The news today, the whole long tale
I have to tell in great detail.
The castle in gold is so ablaze
It outshines the sun on its brightest days.
Ladies and knights in the castle teem.
Set for a hundred, the table's agleam.
Today from pure gold they all shall dine –
Who else has riches so very fine?

BRIGITTA: Why the splendor at this banquet?
The reason is special, I will bet.

URSULA: Yes, my friend, and that's just why
For this heart-to-heart I've stopped by.
I've spied awhile in the countess's court.
Today she'll choose her new consort!

BRIGITTA: It can't be so! Her vows disparage?
She'll bow again to the yoke of marriage?

URSULA: Bow? Not she! Her ladyship
Is the one who here will crack the whip!
The *man* will bow into the yoke.
He, not she, in chains will choke!
Whomever she deigns to grace as a bride,
He'll just have to take it all in stride.
Isn't she known by each sycophant
As the loveliest lady in all Brabant?

BRIGITTA: She the one who knows it most –
It's the stuff of her every presumptuous boast.

URSULA: Her mirror repeats it day after day,
So often she doesn't hear the parley.

BRIGITTA: She views herself by far most fair
But needs it confirmed, truth or dare.

URSULA: My friend, you haven't even a clue!
What the mirror says is always true.
Keep this secret for just you two –
The mirror's glass gives a special view.
From a sorcerer in a far-off place
It once was brought here by Her Grace.
She holds it in the highest esteem
And with it only she can scheme.
Through the keyhole, once, at quite close range
I attended to their daily exchange.

In answer each time to her command –
"Who's the fairest in all the land?"
The mirror echoed each time from the wall,
"The countess is the fairest one of all!"
She finally grew weary of the tired refrain.
Farewell, I'm off to the castle again,
There the countess's train to fold.
Keep to yourselves what I have told.

BRIGITTA: By the saints, what tales she did recite!

Snow White enters.

URSULA: Hush, hush! Here comes Snow White,
To me, the fairest of them all.
The purest white of a fresh snowfall,
The blushing cheeks, as red as blood.
Protect her well, our sweet rosebud.
If the countess finds out, to the tower she'll go,
The poor little thing in the dark below!
Make haste! Don't tarry long!

Exit.

SNOW WHITE: Oh, Aunty dear, might I come along
Just once to see the throng
Of proud ladies and the noble knights?

Curtain falls. Scene change. Hall in the castle. A mirror on the wall at the right. Richilde surrounded by guests: Counts Courtly, Languor, Heartafire, later Prince Kunimund of Flanders.

RICHILDE: Ladies and gentlemen, all so dear,
Who've come today from far and near,
I greet you all as precious guests.
Let our feast today now please you best!

COURTLY: From your praise I'm set aflame.
Brabant's most fair, I thee acclaim!

LANGUOR: 'Tis I who pay you all respect
O, you should, you know, I'm quite abject.

HEARTAFIRE: Searing hot, like molten ore,
Love's ardor rends my very core.

RICHILDE: If every heart here for me blazes,
Let it be so, then sing my praises!

And now, until it's time to dine,
Let's play some games to pass the time.
Show your eloquence most sublime.
So fight a battle of the wits,
What's my rival, what's counterfeit?

COURTLY: The only comparison to you that's right
Is the diamond, Countess, ever so bright,
That sparkles by day and in night's dark veil.
Makes flowers and stars in the heavens seem pale.

RICHILDE: 'Tis true, to you I'm truly known,
My heart's most certainly made of stone.

LANGUOR: Hardly a kinship that overwhelms!
Your beauty extends to many realms.
You, the ecstasy of all creation,
Like you's the sun, in my estimation,
Quickening, enlivening all you touch.

RICHILDE: And for many a man often simply too much!
My essence, Count, you rightly evoke.
But please! Take heed! Beware sunstroke!

HEARTAFIRE: Howe'er a probing intellect
Should try your equal to select,
He'd have to search the whole world through
To find such thing, Madame, like you.
For naught – you're beyond compare!

RICHILDE: Now, Count, your praises are profuse,
But you've wriggled too quickly out of the noose!
What says the prince of Flanders?

HEARTAFIRE: Distracted, while his glance meanders,
As if he hoped a happenstance
Produced a quick retort, perchance.

RICHILDE: Prince Kunimund! Your contribution?
Let's hear the wit of your solution!

KUNIMUND: *Distracted.* My contribution? I've nothing to add.

RICHILDE: *Aside.* He stands there aloof. That makes me mad!
Aloud. You've heard nothing of the war of words?

KUNIMUND: Oh, yes, indeed! I think I heard
The discussion how, beyond compare,
The sun sears hot. One must take care
To avoid sunstroke. It happens fast.

RICHILDE: *Aside.* The impudence! My rage is vast.

Aloud. My, my! Such absentmindedness!
But now, it's time for us to sup.
Sirs, please lead the ladies up.
Your arm, my prince, I take your lead.
Aside. It's manners you're wanting; my teaching you'll heed!

As everyone walks offstage, the curtain falls. The same scene.
Richilde, then Ursula.

RICHILDE: Ha, at every move I feel my pulse,
　　Seething with fury, my veins convulse.
　　The day for me is out of hand –
　　I, the fairest in the land,
　　Used to doting and serenades –
　　But from the one whom I find grand
　　I cannot wrench such accolades!
　　Despite my frequent coy advances
　　Detached, Prince Kunimund hardly glances.
　　To any quip or query I pose,
　　He just replies with yes's and no's.
　　I'm about to die from irritation!
　　Hasn't he come for my adoration?
　　Why's he so distant? Am I no longer fair?
　　Did he see another
　　Who stole his heart from me?
　　What a thought! Who could it be?
　　Tell me, mirror on the wall –
　　Who's the fairest of us all?
THE MIRROR: Till late you were beyond compare.
　　Today Snow White is the most fair.
RICHILDE: Snow White? I can't believe my ears!
　　I haven't thought of her for years,
　　And I've completely lost sight of her.
　　Has she slowly become a beauty so pure
　　That her beauty could be my saboteur?
　　I'll sniff her out to the ends of the earth.
　　Woe to her, if the mirror has told the truth!

Ursula enters.

RICHILDE: *Aside.* Here comes the nursemaid. That suits me fine!
　　I'll loosen her tongue with punch and wine;

She owes me now a full explanation
Of Snow White's beauty. I want information.
URSULA: I have to check on that darling of mine!
RICHILDE: So, nursemaid, pray tell, how tasted the wine?
URSULA: You ask me yet? (To her taunts I'm resigned.)
To your health I've emptied a few.
Your eyes are like the storm's preview,
Like lightning that streaks through the inky sky.
RICHILDE: Enough! Has the gatekeeper his wine supply?
And some for Snow White, that lovely child?
URSULA: How kind of you! I'm quite beguiled!
She has blossomed like a rose.
I'd often feared her you'd oppose
If her beauty to you were known.
Quite dazzled was Kunimund, as he stood alone
Before her window on his steed
And stayed there half an hour.
RICHILDE: Preposterous!
URSULA: No matter if people gossip and pry,
Relax – she hasn't your piercing eye.
RICHILDE: Enough idle gossip! That gatekeeper of mine –
Summon him here. I'll give him the wine.
Aside. I gave him the child that I detest,
Now let him rid me of the little pest!
URSULA: I'm going now, dear.

Exit.

RICHILDE: No time to lose.
Snow White, your fate is sealed.

Curtain falls. End of Act I.

ACT II

Wild forest scene. Gunderich, Snow White.

SNOW WHITE: So, tell me, Gunderich, my dear,
Where do you take me so far away here?
It's deserted and I'm filled with fear.
Were you not here, my terror'd increase.
I'm certain here lives the wildest beast.

309

The wind, it howls, the owls awaken,
This place is utterly godforsaken!

GUNDERICH: *Aside.* Alas! The plan I must convey
Will fill the child with such dismay.
She meets her fate; her moment has come.
If only the pact could be undone!
How could I escape? My lady's endeavor
Beguiled this fool with means most clever.
She threatened with dungeons most forbidding
If I tarried at all in doing her bidding.

SNOW WHITE: What's that you say, Gunderich? What's your travail?
Whate'er it may be, it makes you quite pale.

GUNDERICH: Snow White, asunder it tears my heart!
Alas! This world you must depart!

SNOW WHITE: Help, merciful Heaven! What's happening here?
Why for my life should I have to fear?

GUNDERICH: It's a secret I'm not allowed to betray –
I'm supposed to dispatch you without delay.

SNOW WHITE: O Gunderich, friend most kind and dear,
To whom did I fail myself to endear?
On bended knee I'll make my plea.
It won't happen again, I guarantee.

GUNDERICH: It's nothing you've done, quite blameless you'll die.
Accept your fate: quick death. Indeed,
As token your heart will have verified
That you no longer live but rather died.

SNOW WHITE: It's true, not just a frightful dream?
I'm still so young, not quite sixteen.
So much to see, so much to do,
And now surrender my life to you?
Oh, have mercy on me, I beg you, do!

GUNDERICH: Yes, even the stones would take pity on you.
Still, I must perform the dastardly deed.

SNOW WHITE: Oh, please, don't kill me! Hear me plead!
If I fill someone with that much hate,
That killing me they contemplate,
I'll leave from here, shan't hesitate.
After wandering long I'll far away be,
As far away as my feet carry me.
Seek shelter in caves, eat berries from vines –

I'll eke out my food, drink from streams crystalline
If only my bit of life you'll spare!
GUNDERICH: All right, Snow White, I'll mull the affair;
Will you swear on a Bible stack
That to the castle you'll never come back?
It would bring us both to wrack and ruin,
And together we would meet our doom!
SNOW WHITE: May a sunbeam never caress my face
If I return and bring disgrace.
GUNDERICH: So, flee, my persecuted thing;
Let Heaven its blessing on you bring.
An angel, I hope, has shelter prepared.
SNOW WHITE: A thousand thanks for the life you've spared!

Exit.

GUNDERICH: She's off, as fast as her feet can run.
How tell I the countess what's not been done
When she asks for the heart she wants, bar none?
I'll secretly take a lamb to slaughter,
The heart she'll take for that of her daughter,
Since both are pure and innocent!

*Curtain falls. Scene change. Room in the dwelling of the seven dwarfs.
In the middle of the room a table with seven place settings and
all kinds of foods. Snow White, later the seven dwarfs.*

SNOW WHITE: Thank Heaven I've found a place to stay
After running and searching the whole long day.
Amidst thorns and rocks I had to crawl,
Arms and legs, 'bout broke them all!
About to drop, so tired I've been,
I knocked and knocked. No one let me in.
So in I came, without permission.
I hope it's not an imposition.
It's so tidy and cozy here,
And the table speaks of such good cheer.
The table for seven places is laid –
I'd like to try the dishes they've made.
My stomach's growling, do I dare
Nibble from all those dishes there?

Just snatch a bite from plates so small,
No one will miss a bite at all!

She goes around the table.

From each glass a little taste.
It runs through my veins like fire apace.
Dear Lord, I give you many thanks
For what I've eaten here and drank.
I'd be lost, if not from you blessed.
Now let me find a bed to rest!

Goes to the door of the adjoining room.

Now what do I see, seven beds there.
Some tiny guys must share this lair.
The beds are too short, but since I am so tired
I'll lay right across them, that's all that's required.

*Exit to adjoining room. The dwarfs enter: Granite,
Sodium, Carbon, Iodine, Soda, Sulfur, Quartz.*

GRANITE: Greetings all, my brothers, friends!
Here we are together again
In our cozy mountain, safe within.
We, the dwarfs, all seven kin.
So let us seven tell our tale
Of what we've done, of our travail,
And praise to him who was so wise
And used time well for our enterprise.
Although we here are deep below,
The humans of us never know.
We're here to work for all their sakes;
The Lord commands our shares to take.
And while the lords on Earth do sleep
We're hard at work in the earth so deep.
So, salty lad, tell of your deeds
Give your report – did you succeed?
SODIUM: I knew quite well the humans to serve
And replenished again their salt reserve.
They need me oft to spice their meal;
Without me food has no appeal.
GRANITE: And Carbon, now, you sooty chap,

What good feather's in your cap?

CARBON: Today I stoked the volcano's blaze
And heaved my brothers into sunlight's rays
So that on Earth coal always stays.
My matter I let crystallize
So diamonds from it can arise.

GRANITE: I ask you, Ferrous, sturdy lad,
Have you harnessed that brawn you've always had?
Been pious and meek, was that your goal?
Were you of help to each mortal soul?
On paths unsafe I've oft you found
And had to urge you turn around.
Is the tempest in your heart now tamed?
Isn't iron with blood bestained?

FERROUS: Lo, Father Granite, I'm not to blame.
'Tis not I who fans war's flame.
I'm just a useful element.
But when man's anger must be spent,
When neighbors each cannot abide,
What's left to me but fratricide?
Isn't it they and their human failing
Who've used you all for their assailing?
But today I conquered the world in peace
And plowed the fields so crops increase.
I hammered and tapped till late in the night,
Stitching with needles without respite.
And many a maiden, pale and weak
I helped with powders back to her feet.

GRANITE: So Iodine, my brother tan,
How've you done the Lord's command?

IODINE: In Kreuznach's waters I took a swim
To ease the pain in human limbs.

GRANITE: And Soda, spunky little guy,
What tricks were yours? Don't act so shy!

SODA: Today my hands were full with work.
Ne'er a second I had, my duties to shirk.
Scrubbed pots and pans, did laundry in piles,
The pharmacist crammed me into vials.
They boiled me into foamy soap,
So I'm quite tired, you know, I hope.

GRANITE: And Sulfur, you with that sallow face,
Your duties for us, them please retrace!
SULFUR: My tasks today were a success –
I sprang where hot springs effervesce.
Who questions my talents? Who's in doubt?
There's no better cure if you've got the gout!
GRANITE: And Brother Quartz, I ask you now –
You've aided the world, but pray tell, how?
QUARTZ: In sweltering ovens, by the heat of my brow,
They tortured me. Then my maltreaters
Compounded me with some saltpeter
That Phoenician glass might be repleter.
And so I'm blown laboriously
Into vases, flasks, glass fantasies.
GRANITE: You've all had good and useful days,
And now I'll heap you all with praise.
I, the eldest, have earned my rest.
For eons I've watched with interest.
As the Creator uttered his "Let there be,"
Earth's very bones he made from me.
It's quite a burden. I wonder whether
My own old bones will hang together!
So let our deeds in the Lord's eye shine,
And, above all else, now let us dine!

They all turn to the set table.

SODIUM: Who has eaten from my plate?
CARBON: Who dared a craving here to sate?
IODINE: Who used my bowl?
SODA: Who dunked my roll?
SULFUR: Who from my glass has dared to sip?
QUARTZ: Who used my spoon to take a dip?
GRANITE: Who took a bite of my fine roast?
It seems to a stranger we've been host.
Now let us search each little nook
Until we find the nasty crook!

They all begin to scurry around.

SODA: *Approaches the door of the adjacent room.*
It's not a crook. Now just look here –

It's a beautiful girl! My, how dear!

All crowd into the doorway.

GRANITE: There she lies sprawled across the bed.
   Don't wake her! Let her sleep instead.
   She's sleeping almost like she's dead.
   Let's let her sleep till dawn's first red.
   Perhaps she came in an hour of dread
   And didn't know where to rest her head.
   Let us stand guard and do our best –
   We must protect our little guest!

Curtain falls. End of Act II.

ACT III

*Wild forest scene, as at the beginning of Act II. Prince Kunimund
and Gatekeeper Gunderich, later Richilde.*

GUNDERICH: Here's the spot among the trees
   Where, pleading, Snow White fell to her knees
   And begged me to spare her poor, young life.
   I couldn't take it with my knife.
   I swore to the countess I'd done the deed.
   My post as gatekeeper I've had to cede,
   For had she asked her mirror the truth,
   To her he'd tell the tale, forsooth.
   And my reward would now await me –
   Around my neck the noose would be.
   So wife and I, in the dead of night,
   Under cover of darkness, we took flight.
KUNIMUND: And on the run, you came upon me.
GUNDERICH: And I confessed why I had to flee.
   My heart is lighter, it almost seems
   As if all were forgiven, those shameful schemes.
KUNIMUND: The poor child! How I'm overcome.
   She trembled here 'cause her time had come.
   Here she set out, with no helpmate,
   Toward her most uncertain fate.
   Who knows where now, with wounded feet,
   What malice of strangers she will meet.

And lonely, pale as death and spent,
The fate she'll suffer – what torment!
What if, before our rescue comes
To death's repose Snow White succumbs?
Oh, darling girl, disappeared from sight,
I'll never rest till I hold you tight.
Since first I saw your image sweet
It's filled my soul, made me complete.
Let's off! Let's seek the poor one lost –
My soulmate – now at any cost.
For her I'll risk both life and limb,
To be her savior, hero, friend!

> *Both exit. The stage remains empty for a few moments,*
> *then Richilde appears, disguised as a peddler.*

RICHILDE: Here's the entrance to the mountainside
Where the seven dwarfs now reside.
The dwarfs with whom Snow White has stayed,
As the magic mirror to me betrayed.
I'll find her now to wreak her ruin.
Without mercy I'll send that girl to her tomb!
The gatesman lied with every breath,
Deceived me 'bout her presumed death,
Escaped through flight his sentence of death.
Now I trust none, no one but me.
I want the messenger of death to be!
Snow White alone, she bears the blame,
That the prince never tried to gain my acclaim.
Not till she from this life is banned
Am I the fairest in the land.
So let her die, now at my hand.
These apples here will bring her doom.
A tiny taste will mean the tomb.
Soon enough she'll breathe her last.
The apples' poison is strong and fast,
And yet they're pleasing to the eye.
Snow White, resist? Don't even try!
Before sun's set in the western sky,
Too young, perhaps, but . . . you shall die!

Snow White

Curtain falls. Scene change. Scene at the home of the seven
dwarfs, as in Act II. A set table in the middle of the room,
a small table with flowers at the window. Snow White,
then Richilde, finally the seven dwarfs.

SNOW WHITE: I've cleaned up all the things I can.
All's neat and tidy, spic and span,
So that my dear old dwarfs, those seven
Will think they've died and gone to heaven.
The soup I've made is awfully good,
Of roots and herbs picked in the wood.
I think it's turned out mighty fine,
This roast of mole with crust divine.
And when they're pleased, the dwarfs' happy voices
Make my heart sing as it rejoices.
I love them dearly for everything
They've done while taking me under their wing,
And still they tend me with concern.
Where else have I, poor child, to turn?
What would happen to me I cannot say.
I'm not allowed in the light of day.
I could be happy here, content,
But being alone I often resent.
I'd like to gossip just a bit,
But those old guys are opposed to it.
Their warnings 'bout visitors have been stern,
As if danger lurked at every turn.
What e'er became, I'd like to know
Of that fine man, who gazed at me so?
His eyes seemed so intent on me.
Might he and the countess wedded be?
Those were my last happy times.
I like to think of it sometimes.

A knock.

A knock? Who's stumbled on this place?
Who's made it up the steep rock face?

She goes to the door.

Who's there? Whoever you may be,
Move on. You can't come in with me.

317

RICHILDE: *From outside.* Long I've toiled up steep stairs
  To bring you treats beyond compare.
  I've pretty apples here to buy.
  Reward my trials! Give one a try!
SNOW WHITE: For you I cannot open the door,
  But come a bit closer so I can see more.
RICHILDE: *At the window.* Have you ever seen such apples as these?
SNOW WHITE: They look so tempting, sure to please!
  The dwarfs will praise me for my buy.

> *Richilde pushes the little basket with the apples inside.*

RICHILDE: So hurry now, give one a try!
  Here, this piece is quite a treat –
  Nothing has ever tasted so sweet.

> *Hands Snow White a little piece.*

RICHILDE: *Aside.* Death shall come, he will not pause!
  Now he has you in his claws!
SNOW WHITE: What's happening? I'm all adaze!
  My throat is burning, I'm in a haze.
  I'm spinning, and I can hardly see!

> *She slumps to the floor.*

RICHILDE: *Exiting.* It's working – I've silenced you eternally!

> *Exit. A few moments later the dwarfs enter.*

GRANITE: So quiet? Snow White's not singing a tune
  And isn't bounding across the room.
  Has she taken ill? That makes me fret.
  This morn she was her sweet self yet.

> *Notices Snow White lying on the floor.*

She's on the floor! Her face so pale!
Come hither, my brothers, she doesn't look hale.
Is she now dead or simply supine?
Come, sharp Sodium and stinging Iodine.
Beside her lips take up position
To check and see to her condition.

> *All surround Snow White.*

For naught! Both cold and mute she stays.

318

Let's search and look around the place
If there is not some tiny clue
To explain to us this sad to-do.

Some scurry around, others stay next to Snow White.

GRANITE: What apples are these, so gold and red!
O, woe! They're why Snow White is dead.
The tiniest morsel of one will suffice
That a child of man forsakes her life.
Steeped in poison these apples have been.
Woe to the culprit should I find him.
I'll take him to task, I'll even kill him,
Oh, how I want to crush that villain.
Our sweet rose bowed, oh, sorrow, despair!
That my old eyes this sight weren't spared.
Let us, dear brothers, together unite,
And with hot tears our sorrow requite,
Let, like a brook, our many tears flow
So that they through our realm will go,
And that they reach the rockiest cleft.
Come, start the vigil of the bereft!

*Curtain falls. Scene change. Moonlight, rocky glen. In the
background Snow White on a bier surrounded by flowers, so that
only her face can be seen. Flanked by the dwarfs, Granite at the
head of the bier, later Prince Kunimund and Gunderich.*

GRANITE: Oh, if only we'd been here!
Flow, you fountain of tears!
Like a stream that swells its vale
And washes over hill and dale.
So let our mournful keen
Resound through the ravine,
And howl from the mountainside,
Because our rose has perished and died.
Apple of our eye and all our pride,
Fresh spring breeze, and joy besides.
This world for eons I did know
Because my ribs, my jagged rocks,
Have formed the Earth's firm bedrock.
I saw glaciers come and go,

319

Saw in hourly fleeting parade
Flowers blossom and then fade.
Forever changing this Earth has been.
Many calamities were in my ken –
The means that malice employs,
How man himself destroys,
How passions and fury blind
Wreck joy, and to evil incline.
I've heard wailing and lamenting
But never seen sorrow so unrelenting.
So let our tears, as a river flows,
Bring fresh water to our sweet rose.

Loud sobbing. Funeral dirge by the dwarfs.

When the pilgrim weary
Ends content his journey,
Shuts his eyes, tired from life,
Softly we weep, he has ended his strife.
But when a life so young
Into death's maw is flung,
On the grave fresh roses pour,
Let the bitter wailing roar,
While we cry and ask, "Wherefore?"

Loud sobbing. Prince Kunimund and Gunderich enter.

KUNIMUND: What's going on? Such loud laments,
Loud sobbing, and such great torment!
A funeral here, my grief's addressed –
Pray tell, who's being laid to rest?
For whom are meant these fervent words?
Whom is it that this tomb inters?

He approaches the bier.

What do I see? Cruel fate! Alas!
Snow White lies dead! My fortune's passed!
Beloved, so I thee behold?
GUNDERICH: How could it be? Let it be told!
GRANITE: She ate an apple from a deadly brew!
GUNDERICH: Only you, Richilde, this deed could do.
Methinks I saw that woman's face.

She just ran past in extra haste.
I'll send my men for a quick look-see.

Exit.

GRANITE: *Calling after him.* It's the abyss for her, if it be she!
KUNIMUND: Were we united in eternal sleep,
　　I could with Snow White my vigil keep.
　　Give me, my friends, her earthly shell
　　So that at home in my citadel
　　For the dear departed, heaven-sent,
　　I might erect a monument
　　And shower her grave with tears besprent.
GRANITE: Brothers, take now the wreaths, on my order,
　　And carry our darling with them to our border.

　　　　*The dwarfs gather closely around the bier so that it is
　　　　completely concealed; a little cough is heard. The dwarfs
　　　　move aside so that Snow White's head becomes visible.*

GRANITE: We must take leave. It's come to this!
　　Let's place on her lips just one last kiss.

Snow White sits up.

KUNIMUND: Why are you stopping? What's going on here?
GRANITE: A miracle, sir, she's sitting up now.
　　She's spit out that poison apple somehow
　　Her eyes are glowing, her cheeks are pink.
KUNIMUND: Snow White, you're alive! Just a word! Please, one blink!
　　Speak. Do you recognize me?
SNOW WHITE: Prince Kunimund!
KUNIMUND: And do you love me? O beloved, say!
SNOW WHITE: I've thought of you every hour each day.
KUNIMUND: May I pledge as your spouse my life to you?
SNOW WHITE: Can it be true?
　　I thine, thee mine?
GRANITE: Gone is all sorrow, all torment.
　　May your union be solid as a rock's cement.
　　But, pray tell, what brought you back again?
　　Did Sulfur's strength breath life into limbs
　　That were so long to death forsaken?
　　Did Sodium's kiss now you awaken?

Did Ferrous put color in your lips?
Did Soda release you from death's grip?
Did Carbon fan life's flickering flame?
Pray tell, which brother this deed can claim
So that by men his name be extolled.
SNOW WHITE: Each of them played his part, all told.
What gave me strength through and through,
Awakened me to life anew,
What pierced my soul and set it afire
Was the power of love, our hearts to inspire.
GRANITE: Hail love, that the dead to life can restore,
Be it on Earth or in the mountain's core,
Three cheers for LOVE!

Curtain falls.

TRANSLATED BY SHAWN C. JARVIS

Queen Elisabeth of Rumania.
From *A Real Queen's Fairy Tales by Carmen Sylva*
(Chicago: Davis, 1901), iv.

Elisabeth of Rumania

1843–1916

Queen Elisabeth of Rumania was born princess of Wied-Neuwied, a small principality in the Rhineland of Germany. The great-granddaughter of the poet Marie zu Wied, she came from a family of artists, writers, and musicians, and she herself studied piano with and was a friend of Robert and Clara Schumann. After a childhood of much suffering (the slow death of a young brother, the death of her father, and an epidemic of typhus in her hometown), she was married in 1869 to Prince Charles of Hohenzollern, who was named king of the newly created kingdom of Rumania. After the death of her only child as a toddler, she turned with devotion to charitable work, learned Rumanian fluently, and organized orphanages, hospitals, and art galleries. She also supported the Rumanian folk arts and professional artists and revamped the school system. She began writing patriotic lyrics during the War of Rumanian Independence in 1877 and continued by translating folk legends and tales into German, as well as writing her own stories and poetry in both German and French. Among her many works translated into English are *A Real Queen's Fairy Tales* (translated by Edith Hopkirk, illustrated by Harold Nelson and A. Garth Jones [Chicago: Davis and Company, 1901]) and *Pilgrim Sorrow* (translated by Helen Zimmern [New York: Henry Holt and Company, 1884]). After the king's death in 1914 in the midst of the turmoil and deprivation of World War I in the Balkans, her own health declined, and she died of pneumonia at the age of seventy-three.

"Furnica, or The Queen of the Ants" is an almost surreal tale. It is the story of a girl whose virtue and diligence are so exemplary that she rejects human contact, with all its inherent problems, and becomes queen of the ants. Yet as time passes, she becomes a captive in their earthen anthill. The story can be read as the legend of an actual mountain in Rumania that bears the name Furnica, but it might also be read as an autobiographical statement of a too-virtuous queen held in her conventional place by a domineering and regal Prussian husband, as well as a demanding population. This dreamlike story prefigures later central European surrealism as seen in Franz Kafka's stories "The Metamorphosis" and "The Burrow." Its summoning of a virtuous woman to an underground setting can be compared to Amalie Schoppe's "The Kind and Diligent Housewife" in this collection and to Sibylle von Olfers's early-twentieth-century stories about the *Wurzelkindern* (root children).

[Elisabeth, Queen of Rumania], "Fornica," in *Pelesch-Märchen von Carmen Sylva. Aus Carmen Sylva's Königreich* (Stuttgart: Alfred Kroner, 1904), 29–46 (first edition, Leipzig: Wilhelm Friedrich, 1883). This translation is based in part on "Furnica," in *Legends from River and Mountain by Carmen Sylva (H. M. the Queen of Roumania) and Alma Strettell. With Illustrations by T. H. Robinson* (London: George Allen, 1896), 55–67.

Furnica, or The Queen of the Ants

1883

T HERE WAS ONCE a beautiful maiden named Viorica. She had hair like gold, eyes like the blue sky, cheeks like carnations, and lips like cherries, and her body was as lithe as the river rushes. Everyone rejoiced on beholding this fair maiden, not so much because of her beauty as her great diligence. When she went to the spring with her pitcher on her head, she carried her distaff in her belt and spun the while. She could weave, too, and embroider like a fairy. Her blouses were the finest in the whole village, wrought with black and red stitches and with wide seams of Altitza embroidery on the shoulders. She had adorned her skirt and even her Sunday stockings with flowers wrought in the same way. It seemed as though her little hands could never rest. In field and meadow she did as much work as in the house, and all the lads turned their eyes upon the fair Viorica, who would someday be a renowned housewife. But she never turned her eyes toward them; she would hear no talk of marriage. She had no time for that, she said, and she had to care for her old mother. Hearing this, her mother would furrow her brow and say that she thought a stalwart son-in-law would be an additional help. But this troubled the daughter, who asked if she were of no more use at all then, since the mother seemed so set on having a man in the house.

"The men do little but make more work for us," said she, "for we must spin and stitch and weave for them as well as ourselves, and then we will never find time to finish working in the fields."

Then the mother would sigh and think of her dead son, for whom she had made so many fine shirts and washed them so dazzlingly white that all the village maidens stared their eyes out looking at him. It had never been too much trouble for her. But then, what will a mother not do and never get weary?

The hour came when Viorica had to admit that her mother had been right to wish for a son-in-law. It seemed as though something had warned her mother that she was not much longer for this world. She began to fail, and all her daughter's love was powerless to hold her on earth. The fair maiden had to close her beloved mother's eyes, and then sit all alone in the little house. For the first time her hands lay idle in her lap. For whom, indeed, should she work now? She had no one left.

One day, as she sat upon her threshold and gazed out sadly, she saw something long and black moving across the ground toward her. Behold! It was an endless procession of ants. It reached so far into the distance that no one could have told how far the creeping host had traveled. But now it halted, forming one great circle about Viorica, and a few of the ants stepped forth and spoke.

"We know you well, Viorica, and often have we admired your industry, which we liken to our own – a thing we seldom see among humans. We know, too, that you are now alone in the world, and so we invite you to come with us and be our queen. We will build you a palace, finer and larger than the largest house you have ever seen. Only one thing must you promise – that you will never return to dwell among humankind but stay with us your whole life long."

"I will stay with you gladly," replied Viorica, "for I have nothing more to hold me here except my mother's grave; but that I must still visit, and bring flowers, wine, and cake, and pray there for her soul."

"You will visit your mother's grave, but you must never speak to another person on the way, or else you will be unfaithful to us, and our revenge will be terrible."

So Viorica went with the ants a long, long way until they reached the spot that seemed most fit for building her palace. Then Viorica saw how far the ants surpassed her in skill. How could she have raised up such a building in such a short time? There were galleries, one above the other, leading into spacious halls, and farther yet, into the innermost recesses where the pupae, or infant ants, dwelt. And these were carried out whenever the sun shone and brought quickly under shelter again as soon as there was a threat of rain. The chambers were daintily decked with the petals of flowers, fastened onto the walls with pine needles, and Viorica learned to spin cobwebs, out of which canopies and blankets were made.

Higher and higher the building grew, but the chamber that was prepared for Viorica was more beautiful than any vision of her dreams. Numerous passageways led to it, so that she could receive communications from all her subjects with the greatest speed. The floors of these passages were laid over with poppy petals, so that the feet of the queen should rest on nothing but crimson. The doors were of rose petals, and the hinges were spiders' threads, so that they could open and shut noiselessly. The floor of the room was covered with a thick, velvety carpet of edelweiss, into which Viorica's rosy toes sank softly down, for she needed no shoes here; they would have been far too clumsy and would have trampled the flower carpets to pieces. The walls were hung with a tapestry cleverly woven of carnations, lilies of the valley, and forget-me-nots, and these flowers were constantly renewed, so that their freshness and perfume were always entrancing. The ceiling had a tentlike covering of lily blossoms stretched across it. The bed had taken the diligent little ants many weeks to prepare; it was made completely of flower dust, the softest they could find, and a piece of Viorica's cobweb spinning was spread over it. When she lay there asleep, she was so lovely that the stars would have fallen from heaven, could they have seen her. But the ants had built her room in the most secret recesses and guarded their beloved queen jealously and well. Even they themselves never dared to look upon her in her sleep.

Life in the anthill could scarcely have been made happier or fairer than it was. They took pride one and all in doing the most they could and trying to surpass each other in pleasing their industrious queen. They were as quick as lightning in carrying out her every command, for she never gave too many orders at once, and never unreasonable ones, but her gentle voice sounded as if she were only giving friendly advice or an opinion, and her eyes expressed her thanks in a sunny glance. The ants often declared that they had the sunshine dwelling within their house and exulted over their good fortune. They had made a special terrace for Viorica where she could enjoy the air and sunlight when her room grew too confined, and from thence she could observe the progress of the building, which was already as high as many a mountain.

One day she sat in her room embroidering a dress, upon which she had sewn butterflies' wings; she used threads from a silkworm that the ants had brought in for her. None but her dainty fingers could have accomplished such a task. All of a sudden there was a tumult round about her mountain; the sound of voices rang forth, and in a moment all her little kingdom was thrown into alarm, and her subjects came breathlessly crowding about their queen, crying, "They are destroying our house; evil men are trampling it down. Two, nay, three galleries have fallen in, and the next is threatened. What shall we do?"

"Is that all?" asked Viorica calmly. "I will bid them stop their actions, and in a few days, the galleries will be built up again." She hurried through the labyrinth of galleries and appeared suddenly upon her terrace. Looking down, she beheld a splendid youth who had just dismounted from his horse and was engaged with some of his followers in turning up the anthill with sword and lance. But when she appeared they all stopped short, and the noble youth stood shielding his dazzled eyes with his hand as he gazed upon the radiant figure in its shimmering raiment. Viorica's golden hair curled to her feet, and her eyes shone like stars. She lowered them for a moment before the young man's glance, but soon she raised them again, opened her rosy mouth, and cried in ringing tones, "Who are you that have laid such rude hands upon my kingdom?"

"Forgive us, fairest lady!" cried the youth. "And as surely as I am a knight and a king's son, I will henceforth be your most zealous defender! How could I guess that a fairy – no, a goddess – reigned over this kingdom?"

"No, thank you," answered Viorica. "I need no other service save that of my faithful subjects, and all I ask is that no human foot step into my kingdom."

With these words she disappeared as though the mountain had swallowed her up, and those outside could not see how hosts of ants were kissing her feet and escorting her back in triumph to her chamber, where she calmly took up her work as though nothing had happened. Outside, before the mountain, the king's son stood as though in a dream and for hours could not be prevailed upon to remount his horse. He still kept hoping that the beautiful queen would reappear – even though it were with angry word and glance, he would at least see her once more! But he saw only ants and yet more ants in an endless stream, busying themselves with all diligence in repairing the mischief that his youthful exuberance had occasioned. He could have crushed them underfoot in his anger and impatience, for they seemed not to understand or perhaps not even to hear his questions and ran quite boldly in front of him in their newfound sense of security. At last he dejectedly mounted his steed. Plotting and planning how he might win the loveliest maid his eyes had ever beheld, he rode on through the forest till nightfall to the great discontent of his retinue, who wished both anthill and maiden to go to the devil when they thought of the supper table and the bumpers of wine that had long been awaiting them.

Viorica had gone to rest later than any of her subjects. It was her habit to visit the nurseries herself, to see to the infants and feel if their little beds were soft enough, so she glided about, lifting one flower curtain after another, with a firefly clinging to her fingertips, and looked tenderly after the little brood. Then she went back into her room and dismissed all the fireflies who for many hours had been lighting her about her work. She only kept one little glowworm beside her while she undressed. Normally, she fell at once into the deepest and quietest sleep, but this night she tossed restlessly to and fro, twisting her hair about her fingers, sitting up and then lying down again, and all the time feeling so hot – oh, so hot! Never before had she sensed a lack of air in her kingdom, but now she would gladly have hurried outside if she had not feared being heard and corrupting others by her bad example. Had she not already, though under much pressure from the others, been obliged to pass many a harsh sentence, to banish some ants from her realm because they had indulged in forbidden wanderings, no, even to condemn some to capital punishment and, with a bleeding heart, to see them ruthlessly stung to death?

The next morning she was up earlier than any of the rest and gave them a surprise by showing them one of the galleries that she had built up all alone. Doubtless she herself did not know that while doing so she had cast several glances toward the forest and had even stood listening for a few moments.

She was scarcely back in her chamber again before some of the ants hurried to her in terror, crying, "The bad man who came yesterday has returned and is riding around our hill!"

"Let him be," replied Viorica the queen, quite calmly. "He will do us no more harm." But the heart of Viorica, the sweet maiden, beat so fast that she could scarce draw breath.

A strange disquiet had come over her. She roamed about far more than was her habit; she was always thinking that the baby ants were not enough in the sunshine and carrying them out herself, only to bring them in again as quickly, and now she often gave contradictory orders. The ants did not know what had befallen her and doubled their efforts to do all their tasks quickly and well. They surprised her with a splendid new vaulted hall, too, but she gazed at it with distraction and gave it miserly praise.

The sound of horses' hoofs circled their mountain day and night, and for many days Viorica never showed herself. A desperate yearning for human beings, which she had never yet felt, now grew in her. She thought of her native village, of the garden, of her little house, of her mother, and of her mother's grave, which she had never again visited. After a few days she announced to her subjects that she had decided to visit her mother's grave, and at this the ants inquired, in alarm, whether she were no longer happy with them, since she had begun to think of her home again.

"Oh, no," replied Viorica. "I only want to go for a few hours and be back among you before nightfall."

She refused all escort, but one or two ants followed her, unobserved, from afar. Everything looked greatly changed to her, and she thought she must have been away a long time. She began to reckon how long it could have taken the ants to build the great mountain wherein they dwelt and said to herself that it must have been years. Her mother's grave was no longer to be found, the spot was so overgrown with grass and weeds, and Viorica wandered about the churchyard weeping, since here too she was nothing but a stranger. Evening drew on, and still Viorica sought for the grave she could not find. Then close beside her she heard the voice of the king's son. She tried to flee, but he held her fast and spoke to her of his great love with such gentle and moving words that she stood still with bowed head, listening to him. It was so sweet to hear a human voice once more and to hear it speak of love and friendship. Not until the night had grown quite dark did she remember that she was no forlorn orphan but a queen forgetful of her duties, and that the ants had forbidden her to have any contact with humankind. Then she broke away and fled in haste from the king's son. But he pursued her with endearing words to the very foot of her mountain. Here she begged and implored him to leave her, but he would only consent when she promised to meet him again the following evening.

She glided noiselessly in, feeling her way along the galleries and looking fearfully behind her, for she fancied she heard the sound of hurriedly tripping feet and whispering voices all around. No doubt it was but the anxious beating of her heart, for as soon as she stood still, all was silent. At last she reached her chamber and sank in exhaustion on her couch, but no soothing sleep fell on her eyelids. She felt that she had broken her promise, and who would now hold her in respect, since her word was no longer sacred? She tossed fitfully; her pride revolted against any secrecy, and yet she knew the ants only too well: their implacable hatred, their cruel punishments. Many times she raised herself on her elbow to listen, and always she seemed to hear the hurried tripping of thousands of little feet, as though the whole mountain were alive.

When she felt that morning drew near, she lifted one of the rose petal curtains to hurry out into the open. But to her astonishment she found the doorway completely stopped up with pine needles! She tried another, then a third, until she had tried them all. In vain – they were all filled in to the very roof. Then she called aloud, and oh! The ants appeared in hosts, creeping through countless tiny, invisible openings.

"I must go into the open," said Viorica in commanding tones.

"No," replied the ants. "We cannot let you go, or we will lose you."

"Do you then no longer obey me?"

"Yea, in all things save this one. Crush us underfoot in punishment if you like. We are ready to die for the good of our community and to save the honor of our queen."

Viorica bowed her head, and tears gushed from her eyes. She implored the ants to give her back her freedom, but the stern little creatures were silent, and all at once she found herself alone in those dark halls.

Oh, how Viorica wept and wailed and tore her beautiful hair! Then she began to try and dig an opening with her tender fingers, but all she scooped out was filled in again as quickly, so that finally she threw herself on the ground in despair. The ants brought her the sweetest flowers and nectars and dewdrops to quench her thirst, but all her laments remained unanswered.

In the fear that her wailing might be heard outside, the ants built their hill higher and higher, till it was as high as the peak Vîrful cu Dor, and they called their mountain Furnica, or "the ant." The king's son has long since left off riding round the mountain, but in the silence of the night one can still hear the sound of Viorica's weeping.

TRANSLATED BY JEANNINE BLACKWELL

"Take heart!" From Emma Adler, ed., *Neues Buch der Jugend* (Vienna: Ignaz Brand, 1912), 32. Reprinted with permission of the Staatsbibliothek zu Berlin, Preußischer Kulturbesitz, Kinder- und Jugendbuchabteilung, Signatur BIX 1, 778 So.

Anonymous

The workers movement in Germany already had vigorous proponents by the time of the failed 1848 German revolution. Not only Karl Marx but also many of the men and women of Young Germany – among whom are counted Bettina von Arnim, Fanny Lewald, and Louise Dittmar – were strong proponents of a liberated republic. Each revolutionary had a plan, a special project to tackle: the economic oppression of Silesian weavers, the denial of civil rights to assimilated German Jews, the exploitation and disenfranchisement of factory workers, or the abuse of the beleaguered children of the proletariat. Already in the 1840s came the beginning of Friedrich Fröbel's Kindergarten movement: a plan to raise the children of the poor in gardens where the mind and spirit could grow, observing nature and playing with the beautiful forms and primary colors of classical antiquity and the aesthetic sublime. Playing with beauty was to make them free people, capable of growing into citizens of a free land. The Kindergarten movement was stymied after the failure of the Revolution; many proponents went into exile, and the Kindergarten was prohibited in 1851 in Prussia as atheistic and revolutionary.

The Kindergarten was again legalized in 1860, and the workers movement continued; with both of them went a movement for the protection and education of working-class children. Radical Kindergarten proponents such as Lina Morgenstern (founder of the soup kitchens of Berlin) began to appropriate the fairy tale for programmatic, didactic social purposes. It was not long until radical women socialists and first-wave feminists joined the ranks, producing fairy tales for proletarian children, culminating in the socialist fairy tales of the 1920s by the literary-political avant-garde in Berlin (for example, tales and illustrations published by Hermynia zur Mühlen, John Heartfield, and Georg Grosz).

Emma Adler, Anna Ausfeld, and Hedwig Dohm are foremost in the group of socialist-feminist intellectuals who answered this call from the 1880s to the

335

outbreak of the First World War, compiling moving anthologies and composing some less than convincing fairy tales for the lower classes. Soon, however, writers from the proletariat themselves began to write anonymously, as did many other supporters of the socialist movement.

"The Red Flower" is such a tale. It is taken from the anonymous *Märchen-Buch für Kinder des Proletariats* (Fairy tale book for children of the proletariat) of 1893. It is not certain that the author of the tale was a woman, although most of the proletariat anthologies are very closely aligned in gender with respect to authorship, main characters, and themes. The character of Maggie is so poignantly drawn and so in keeping with the tenor of the other heroines in this anthology that she deserves a place in *The Queen's Mirror*. The story's sad yet hopeful message gives an intentional slap in the face to the German Romantic tradition by making the center of indescribable longing not Novalis's blue flower but a red one. Romantic poets sought the blue flower, the symbol of unfulfilled longing for the sublime, in the passive inspiration of an idealized female muse. For Maggie, the red flower symbolizes a new and fairer world for both men and women in which the sick are healed and wealth is shared.

This tale can be read in contrast to no. 153, "Star Coins," in the Grimms' 1857 edition; "The Pied Piper of Hamelin"; the "anti–fairy tale" in Georg Büchner's drama *Woyzeck;* and Hans Christian Andersen's "The Little Match Girl." Compare it to John Ruskin's "The King of Golden River, or the Black Brothers" (in Zipes, ed., *Victorian Fairy Tales*) or "Hunter Maiden" (in Phelps, ed., *Maid of the North*), in which a young girl takes on a task (the hunt) traditionally carried out by men to provide food for her starving family.

"Die rote Blume," in *Märchen-Buch für Kinder des Proletariats* (Berlin: Hans Baake, 1893), 74–96.

The Red Flower

1893

THE RAIN FELL in buckets, and the cold wind blew as fiercely as if it were the middle of autumn instead of the height of summer. Indeed, it was no weather for staying outdoors on the street except in an emergency. But apparently the people standing gathered before a stately home did not think so, for they stood getting drenched while satisfying their curiosity.

The sight was, to be sure, not an unusual one in the great city. A scene was taking place that happens every day. Tight against the wall of the house but insufficiently protected from the rain by the overhang stood a bed frame with a straw sack in place of a mattress amongst no less sparse and pitiful furnishings. On the straw sack lay a pale, emaciated woman, embraced by a sobbing girl.

"Evicted – set out in the cold," some bystanders called to each other, and then came all sorts of other comments.

"How on earth can they – such a sick woman – in this kind of weather – that scoundrel up there." Someone shook a fist at the first floor of the building. "Ought to throw a brick through his big fancy window."

And so the comments flew back and forth, but none of the people acted on their words. They came and went, and the rain drizzled down and soaked through the old blanket the woman was wrapped in and through her ragged, thin clothes all the way to her ailing body. Finally, someone came, and who should it be but the stout doorman of the house, who in fine weather usually stood before the entrance, carrying a walking stick with a golden grip. "Move on along," he thundered at the woman. "There is nothing more for you here. And if you don't disappear with all your rubbish, I'll call the police." He did not have to carry out his threat, for a policeman was just then forcing his way through the crowd. "You are making too much of a ruckus with this riffraff," he said to the doorman and turned to the sick woman. "So, leaving anytime soon? March, march! Up with you and out of here!"

"Have mercy!" begged the woman. "I cannot walk, I'm deathly ill, and where am I supposed to go? I haven't a spot in the whole world to call my own."

"Things will take care of themselves," shouted the officer. "For people like you there are still police custody and shelters for the homeless, but if it takes much longer, it will mean the workhouse. Understand?"

He was about to put his words into action, grabbing the woman by the arm and yanking her up from the bed, pushing the child to one side. She had thrown herself screaming over her mother, as if to protect her from the rough assault. Then an old lady hurriedly pushed her way through the crowd, stepped up between the policeman and the sick woman, and said, "Stop with all that. I have a place for the two of them to stay; I'll take them along with me." The man was not unhappy to see the situation resolved so quickly. He raised a few objections, asked some questions, and jotted down all sorts of things before he left, muttering to himself. Then the woman waved to some boys standing nearby, and they sprang to work, two of them taking the bed frame with the sick woman on it, the others the furniture and household goods. They formed a little parade with the old woman in the lead, and they reentered the same house where the scene had begun.

Where the kind old woman was leading her brood was no magnificent palace but, rather, a former horse stable. She had been assigned this as living quarters behind the house where the outcasts had lived in the attic. All but one of the little windows were covered over with paper, and through one of them ran a little stove pipe, so that the smoke could be ventilated out, and since the pipe did not fill the window opening completely, wind and rain found their way inside through the gaping hole. Her furnishings were sparse, but still one could call it a shelter, and Brigitte, the resident, was happy and thankful that they had given it to her and that she could take in these poor outcasts.

Brigitte had been permitted the free use of the horse stable in recognition of her long and loyal service, as well as in lieu of an old age pension. She had first served as a nanny for the grandparents of the present owner, then for his parents, and finally for the owner himself. She carried over from one generation to the next, and all of them knew that they could depend on Brigitte, that she was untiring and would even sacrifice her own night's sleep when the children were ill. Once she had had a good offer of marriage, but she had refused it so that she could remain with her dear masters. When she entered the service of the present master of the beautiful, spacious house, she was no longer young, and as the children grew up and left their ancestral home one after the other, she became a tired old woman, but she could still make herself useful and oversee the other servants.

The mistress, however, decided that it was high time the old staff left. The master said he would provide fully for Brigitte in her old age, but he hated having such old wrinkled faces about the house. It got on his nerves, and in general it was not a good idea to keep such servants in the family for so long – they would get uppity and think up all sorts of things. In short, old Brigitte had to leave.

The mistress wanted simply to dismiss her with a good reference, but the master decided that wouldn't be right, for she would never find another post at such an advanced age, and what would people say if she were put abruptly out in the street? Finally, someone thought of the old horse stable, which had stood empty for some time because a newer, fancier one had been built. That would be just the place for the used-up old workhorse. "She should be happy and thankful," asserted the mistress, "for not every employer does so much for his people." An old iron stove and broken-down furniture from the attic were placed there, as well as the bed Brigitte had used during her service, and as an extra kindness, they gave her all the family's darning and sewing to do. "Free quarters and an easy, productive way to earn money is what we've given her," they said proudly to their friends. No one needed to know that her quarters were a stable and that her needlework paid half as much as the rate elsewhere.

And thus Brigitte came to be in the stable. She had lived there quite a long time alone when she took in the ailing Mrs. Werner and her child. She had been very afraid of dying alone like a dog abandoned by its master after a life of loyalty and sacrifice, but now she was no longer by herself. On the other hand, hunger and bitter want had come creeping into her wretched home. How would she be able to support the child with the thirty pennies a day that she earned in unending labor, even if she did it at night? Mrs. Werner needed very little, to be sure; she was getting ever weaker and more ill, and her end seemed near. Little Maggie pleaded with the poorhouse doctor so long that he finally came to make a house call, but he prescribed no medicine. "The woman needs dry, well-ventilated quarters, a good bed, and nourishing food, a bit of wine, and other stimulants," he said. "Then she might have a chance at recovery, but as it stands . . ." He shrugged his shoulders, quickly left, and never returned.

Maggie was inconsolable. "I am going to lose my mother," she sobbed with a breaking heart. "They will carry her away in a black box like they did our neighbor, when we lived up in the attic. And I have to watch her die; I can't give her a thing that could save her. All the shops are filled with wine and chickens and roast venison and other good things, but my mama is going to die because I can't even buy an apple or a glass of wine."

With a heavy heart she went to school every morning, for her mother wanted it so – with a heavy heart and an empty stomach. But when school was out, the barefoot child in the hand-me-down dress ran all over town. She went up the back stairs to the servant girls and asked shyly if they had any work – she would do it gladly. She could shine shoes, run errands, watch over the smaller children. She never found anything; she was always turned away. Then Maggie slouched sadly back home, hanging her head, and sat darning socks at her mother's bedside until it was quite dark, and she had to put away her work. They didn't light a candle; that was too expensive for Brigitte, and she knitted on in the dark. Maggie wasn't adept enough to do that, and so she sat quietly holding her mother's wizened hand until she crawled with her into bed. So it went day after day, night after night, and the sick woman became weaker and weaker while Maggie's hopes faded evermore.

One day on the way home Maggie came across a busy street. There she saw an old blind man with an unsteady gait, groping his way across the street with his cane directly in front of a coach that was rushing past on the thoroughfare. In the next moment he would have been run over, but Maggie jumped out in a flash, pulled the man to the side, and led him out of the path of traffic. "Where are you trying to go, old man?" she asked kindly. "I'll lead you there, but you can't walk here alone!" The trembling blind man named a far-off street on the outskirts of town and described the house where he lived. "Yes, please lead me there, my good child," he said. "I used to have a loyal guide, my dog, Sultan, and I could get everywhere with him. He's dead now, though, and I must go alone in eternal darkness."

They walked slowly through the streets and alleys, and Maggie told him how her mother had supported them with washing and cleaning after her father's death, but how one day she had come home sick from work, and as a result hunger and misery had moved into their attic room. She told of them being evicted from those quarters and how Brigitte had taken them in at the stable. "And now my mother is going to die," the child ended, weeping. "And I don't want to live anymore either. I will only be a burden to Brigitte."

"Don't say that, child," admonished the blind man. "Your mother might still get well. Describe her illness to me; I might be able to give you some cause for hope. I know many things that are hidden to others."

Maggie shook her head sadly, for she already knew what her mother needed and that she could not provide it, but she told the blind man everything that she knew of her mother's malady. In the meantime they had arrived at his quarters, a pathetically bare room. The old man offered Maggie the only chair, and he sat on the edge of his bed.

"Listen," he said. "I hope I can give you some consolation. Anyone who has studied the secrets of nature for half a century and gone blind doing it, as I have, has learned a few secrets that remain a mystery to other mortals. And a person who is denied vision of the physical world can sometimes see with his mind's eye deep into the beyond. From this book here" – and he pointed to a large, strange-looking folio volume with clasps that lay on the table – "I have learned much. And so I can say to you that there is a cure for your mother, for you, and for the kind Brigitte, for everyone who suffers in innocence and is trampled in the dust by the mighty. There is a cure, yes. Most certainly the time has come when everyone will rise up free and strong, and you, my child, you may be called to bring this time to fruition. Listen to what my book says about it: 'It shall be a child of the poor, a child of pure heart and chaste will, who follows its goal straight as an arrow and shies away from nothing, lets nothing lead it astray or seduce it from the path.' Tell me, do you feel yourself to be so pure and brave?"

"I am a child of the poor," said Maggie, "and I don't know about any sins I've committed. If I failed, it was out of ignorance. And if I can hope to make my mother healthy again and other poor people who suffer as we do, then nothing will be too hard for me, nothing will tempt or frighten me away from the path. Just tell me quickly what I have to do!"

"Yes, I believe you have been called," said the blind man, his face beaming. "Well, then, listen. Far away from here there blooms a wondrous and beautiful red flower that has no equal on earth. You must find it and pick it, for its fragrance is salvation and life. This scent awakes to new strength whatever has withered in weakness. It fills the downhearted with new hope. Evil men cannot bear the fragrance; they flee from it as far as they can run. They cannot live within its reach."

"And where will I find this blossom?" cried Maggie breathlessly.

"It blooms," replied the blind man, "in a breathtakingly beautiful garden that is growing larger every year, and soon it will fill a whole realm and grow ever larger until it covers the whole world. And then all people of goodwill who can bear the fragrance of the flower will become citizens of this happy new realm and live peaceably with each other in freedom and equality. Oh, my dear, child of the poor, I can see that flower. It trembles, it bows its head on the vine, and you are the one who shall pick it." The blind man rose up with outstretched hands and upturned eyes, and he was called back to reality only by Maggie's voice.

"I'll get that red flower," she cried with glowing cheeks and beaming eyes. "Tell me, Master, where to look for it."

"Go straight toward the sunrise, look neither to the left nor the right nor behind, and whatever may threaten you or lead you into temptation, do not let it deter you from the path. If you are asked, however, who you are and what you are doing, always say, 'I am a child of the poor. My mother is sick, and I want to make her well with the fragrance of the red flower.' You see, that is all that I can tell you and advise. No talisman will protect you; no guide will lead your steps. You have only your deep need and desire to be your guide and stay. Have you committed my words to memory?"

"Yes, I have," said Maggie. "And now I must go to my mother, for I will leave her early tomorrow. But Master, what if she dies before I return home? If I arrived with help too late and could not be with her in her last hours? Oh, I cannot leave at all; I cannot leave her. It would be too terrible if I did not find her when I returned."

"You can venture out assured," said the blind man and gave her a small flask. "Look at this elixir; a few drops of it suffice to retain a fragile and fleeting life for weeks and months. Tell Brigitte that she should give your ailing mother a few drops every morning; they will replace food and drink for her and put her into a slumber from which she awakens only sporadically. That way she will be spared her pain at separation from you and worry about you."

"Oh, thank you, good Master!" cried Maggie, and she ran out to return to her mother as quickly as possible.

Her mother had already begun to fret about her long absence and was sicker than ever, but when Maggie told her about her encounter with the blind man, she listened with full attention and compassion. Maggie's goodnight kiss was more loving than ever, for it would be the last for a long time. As her mother fell into slumber, Maggie explained everything to Brigitte, gave her the flask, and asked her to administer the elixir to her mother every morning.

Maggie stayed awake and dressed the whole night, and as morning broke, she went once more to her mother's bedside, kissed the sleeper lovingly, threw a last glance at Brigitte, and strode out. Outside, her gaze sought out the rising sun, and she walked toward where she saw the day star emerge from its crimson shroud. "I am a child of the poor," she said to herself. "My mother is ill, and I want to make her well with the fragrance of the red flower." She said it to commit the words to memory but also to raise her courage; it was the first time she had been away from her mother, and she sensed that many dangers awaited her.

As noon approached, the city and all its paved roads lay far behind her, and she found herself on a rough, stony path. Weeds and wild brambles grew all around, and no tree or sparkling brook was to be found. The sun burned hot on the little wanderer's head. Maggie could barely walk farther on her bare little feet, but she fought back the pain and kept going straight ahead, always straight ahead. Thistles and thorns clung to her dress and hindered her progress, and finally she saw before her a thorn hedge that seemed impenetrable.

"I am a child of the poor, and I want to make my sick mother well," Maggie murmured and pushed ahead. Oh, how it hurt! The sharp thorns bored into her flesh and tore at her uncovered hands, face, and feet. But she pushed through, even though she was bleeding from a thousand wounds. "Nothing's gained without a fight," she said bravely and pulled the thorns out of her face and hands as she went on.

The road improved somewhat. Between the sharp stones there were some stretches carpeted with a lawn of moss or soft grass, but if these patches were not directly on Maggie's path, she kept on the stone path without paying any mind to her aching feet. She did not seek out the shadow of the trees that multiplied around her, unless her path happened to go directly past them. Soon she saw something shining between their branches, and after she had gone a little farther, she stood on the bank of a rushing river. "Oh, no," she cried. "How shall I cross? You waves, listen to me: I am a child of the poor, and I want to make my sick mother well. Move to one side so that I may go my way." But the waves roared and rushed even wilder than before, as if they wanted to say, "Go back, you foolhardy child!"

Maggie did not have to think long before she ran as fast as she could into the waves, which crashed above her head. "Mama!" the child cried and lost consciousness. Yet the same blustery waves that had pulled her down into the drink now lifted her up in their powerful arms, brought her to the light, and tossed her light body onto the opposite shore.

"Oh, think of the time I have lost!" cried Maggie as she was awakened by the sunshine. "Now onward!" The ruin of a castle stood to one side of her path; she had to enter through its decrepit gate, walk through the overgrown courtyard, the rubble, and the crumbling walls. Suddenly, two knights in armor stepped into her path. They rattled their terrifying weapons, aimed their spears at her, and cried with hollow voices from the grave, "Go back, go back, child of the present! Why do you disturb the peace in our castle?" And as Maggie tried to push the spears to one side and hurry on, the knights held her back by force.

"Leave me alone," cried the girl. "I am a child of the poor. My mother is ill, and I want to make her well with the fragrance of the red flower."

"A child of the poor?" cried the knights. "And you dare to approach this holy place? Arise, my legionnaires, awake from your slumber and help us to drive this blasphemer from our sanctuary." One of them blew a horn, and in a moment a countless horde of night birds swirled up. They encircled Maggie and fluttered with their great wings around her head; they hacked at her eyes and deafened her ears with their uncanny shrieks and caws. "Mama, Mama!" cried Maggie and ran with closed eyes through the middle of the flapping, shrieking flock until she broke free through a crack in the farthest wall of the ruins.

Oh, just to rest, just for a moment! Maggie thought, but then she saw off in the distance a high cliff jutting up, and it seemed to her that she had to go there without stopping, as if the garden with the red flower lay beyond it. She dragged her feet as she approached the mountain, but as she stood before it, she saw that it was very steep and had a face as slick as glass. "But I have to get up there," she thought, and she tried to scale it with her hands and feet. Then the wounds made by the thorns all opened up again and began bleeding; but the clotting blood helped her hands and feet to find a grip on the slick rock face of the cliff, and thus she climbed higher and higher.

"What are you doing there, child?" a voice suddenly intoned in her ear. A little figure sprang toward her. It was a gnome, which Maggie had heard described as one of the little dwarfs who guard the treasures in the bowels of the earth. "If you have come here to rob us of our gold and jewels," he said, "I'll throw you down into the abyss so that you can never dare such presumption again."

"No," said Maggie, climbing ever higher. "I'm not after your treasures. I am a child of the poor, and I left home to get the red flower from the lovely garden. It will make my mother well. Don't get in my way."

"Abandon your task," said the dwarf. "You are dead tired, and even if you arrive at the peak of the mountain, your sore feet will carry you no farther. You have undertaken a task that exceeds human ability."

"And if I die doing it," said Maggie, "I shall know that I have done every-thing possible to save my mother. Let me climb higher; get out of my way."

"I see that you are convinced of your path, and I respect that," said the gnome, stepping to one side. "But at least rest with us, gather your strength, and if you want to go on after that, we will send along the most magnificent treasures with you. Then you won't even need the red flower. You can return immediately to your home, and your mother will get well soon, when she is rich."

"But there are others, hundreds of brothers and sisters in need of the red flower. I have to keep thinking about the welfare of them all."

"Well, at least take a look at what we want to give you," cried the gnome as he put his finger to his lips. In the next moment a host of little gnomes crawled out of a crack in the stone that Maggie had not noticed before. Each carried on his head a basket filled with sparkling jewels, and the little fellows gathered around Maggie, as if the slippery precipice were solid ground, and, giggling, they showed her their immense treasures.

"Come with me," said the leader of the dwarfs again. "You may have all this and more. You will be richer than the richest person in the world."

But Maggie gave no further response. She just climbed farther, with failing strength perhaps, but ever steady. The gnomes tried to topple her down the slope, but the blood on her hands and feet was strong glue, and she could hold on.

It was still green below in the valley, but up above on the peak lay snow and frozen ice. Staggering, the exhausted child pushed on while thick snowflakes swirled around her and an icy storm blustered. "I can go no more," Maggie finally stuttered and sank to her knees in the cold snow. A sweet drowsiness embraced her, and she wanted to close her eyes. But suddenly the words of the old blind man came to mind: "No talisman will protect you. Your own strong, driving will must accomplish it. You have only your deep need and desire to be your guide and stay." Her own desire, her will! Was it not about to slacken and to give up the fight? Quickly, she sprang up and pushed on, and soon she found herself before a shining castle whose walls and battlements seemed to be made of diamonds.

Yet as she came nearer, she saw that the whole castle was made of ice. It was the palace of the Ice Giant. And again she encountered knights, this time in icy suits of armor, and they blocked the entrance with icy spears. Even the Ice Giant himself, a frightening man who carried a heavy ice cudgel in his hand, forbade her to enter, but as Maggie uttered her little watchword, her breath melted the armor and the spears, the Ice Giant retreated, and the dungeons opened to release the harbingers of springtime, which had up to then been held captive. And as there was merely one more stubborn ice wall between the little girl and the open air, she used her warm heart to melt that away as well.

The ice palace had stood on the highest peak of the mountain, and so now the path descended. Once she thought that she had arrived at her goal, for she stepped into a blooming garden, and sweet voices rang out of all the bushes: "Stay here in the enchanted garden! Live in the fairy castle, you darling child!" but soon she saw that the red flower did not grow there. The fragrance that blew her way was the scent of roses; little winged children hovered about to escort her into the fairy palace, holding bouquets and garlands filled with roses. "What do I need with these flowers?" asked Maggie, as she strode through the garden. "They are not the one I am seeking." As she entered the castle, a wondrously beautiful woman came to meet her, took her by the hand, and said, "I am the fairy Amarantha, the mistress of this castle. From my servants, the winds, I heard about how many hardships you have suffered, poor child, and how steadfast you have been. All this misery would now end, if you chose to stay here as my own dear daughter. What do you need with earthly life? Your own mother will not tarry there much longer, and then you would be quite forsaken and abandoned to misery. But here you would find everything your heart desires, and if you wanted for anything, I would acquire it for you. Look around you! Is there such splendor anywhere on earth?"

They walked through a long, long series of halls, each more lovely than the last. There was an entire hall filled with the most delightful playthings, another with picture books. One was stuffed with marzipan, the paneled walls and the parquet floors made of chocolate and barley sugar, the furniture of rock candy – it was unbelievably beautiful. In another room there were gathered the most splendid clothes and hats, and so each room contained something new and magnificent. Maggie saw and admired it all, but she was not swayed for a moment. Finally, in the last room, the fairy said to her, "Now, my child, you will stay with us, won't you? Surely you do not want to return to the poverty of human existence?"

Without hesitating, Maggie replied, "Good fairy, it is very lovely here, but I may not tarry at this place. I am a child of the poor, and I want to get the red flower for my mother, for it will make her well. Allow me to go through the gate, I beg of you." The fairy wanted to lead Maggie back with gentle insistence into the inner chambers of the castle, but she broke free and ran to the portal. A quick tap with her hand, and the bolt sprang back. Maggie was suddenly in the open air in a beautiful rose arbor.

She continued walking a long way in its fragrance, and then her surroundings became wilder and drearier. She was happy about that, for the scent of the fairy roses had numbed her senses, and as her daze dissipated, she noticed that her strength was completely sapped. Wild berries grew at her feet, and wild red plums shone on the trees as she approached. She would have gladly stopped and refreshed herself with them, but she did not dare to interrupt her journey, for she sensed that then she would not be able to lift her feet again. Suddenly, it seemed that a faint and delicate fragrance began to waft toward her from the distance, one she had never encountered before. "The red flower!" she said to herself. "There it is, that's it!" And with her last ounce of strength she pushed on. But a raging storm arose and seized the small figure in its clutches, trying to toss her out of the way. Maggie struggled with all her might against the gale, but in vain. The storm was stronger than she. She had to let herself be buffeted about wherever the storm threw her until, deathly tired, she sank down and lost consciousness.

A strong, indescribably lovely fragrance awakened her. She lay on a velvety soft lawn, and, so close by that she could touch it with her outstretched hand, she saw something tall and glimmering, from which the lovely scent came. The red flower! Golden pollen filaments cascaded out of its large, bell-shaped calyx, which swayed on a slender stalk. The flower was so wondrous that no flower on earth could ever equal it, and Maggie, who all at once felt no hunger, weariness, or pain, went up and picked the flower, holding it carefully in her cupped hands.

The garden was larger and lovelier than that belonging to the fairy Amarantha, but Maggie did not tarry a moment there. She was anxious to return to her ailing mother. And lo! Everything that had made her path difficult on the way here now revealed itself to be subject to her will. Unhindered, she crossed the fairy garden, and as she arrived at the peak of the mountain, the wind, which had treated her so roughly before, took her in his strong arms and carried her to a cloud that sailed down below.

"Take her, she has the red flower," said the wind, "and carry her safely back home." And the cloud did so. When it arrived over the right street, however, it called to a passing swan, who took little Maggie on her back and set her down on the bank of the river flowing through town, for of course the cloud could not descend all the way down to earth.

As Maggie hurried through her old courtyard, many children were playing there, including some of the ones who lived in the main house. Three of them were the grandchildren of the owner, paying a visit to their grandparents, and when they sniffed the fragrance of the flower, they ran after Maggie into the stable. There they saw how the sick woman sprang out of bed, healthy and strong, after Maggie held the flower out to her; they saw how her daughter embraced her with tears of joy. And then they heard as Maggie said, "Now all our suffering is past. We will enter the splendid garden, the realm of the future, where we will all be safe and sound."

Children are always curious, and so they pressed around Maggie and bade her tell them all about it – their grandfather's harshness, the old, blind scholar, and the trip to the garden of the red flower. And then Brigitte began to tell of the long, long years she had sacrificed all her energy for their family, and how she was now happy to have a roof over her gray head, even if it was the roof of a stable; she spoke of earning her dry bread by the sweat of her brow.

With what astonishment the children listened to her! With what outrage did they react against their grandfather, against the whole world in which such awful things could transpire! In the end, they asked if they, too, could come along into the new realm, for they no longer wanted to remain where everything was so unfair. They no longer wanted to wear fine clothes and eat tasty foods while others who worked more diligently and commendably lived in stables, wore rags, and suffered want. A new spirit blossomed in these children, and this may have been the doing of the fragrance of the red flower. They certainly did not shy away from telling all their parents how they felt, and one can only assume that the parents were not delighted about it, especially when their children explained that they wanted to be residents of the new realm.

After the first joys were past, and Maggie had rested and refreshed herself, she went with the red flower to see the blind scholar. As he heard her approaching footsteps, he recognized her immediately. "It is you, my girl," he cried happily. "And you bring salvation with you. I can sense the fragrance of the flower. Blessings on you, dear child!" Maggie stood before him and touched his blind eyes with the flower. Suddenly he could see, and this joy made him young again. As the two of them strode out of his door to go to Maggie's mother, they were suddenly surrounded by a large crowd of children. Maggie's neighbors had told all of their friends of the red flower, and these had then told their own friends, and so the number of people had grown quite large. All of them declared that they wanted to become citizens of the new realm, and they meant it with all their hearts.

The next day the owner's grandchildren were not to be found, and all the neighbors sought their children in vain. Many other houses in the city had the same problem, and many mistreated servants and workers were also missing from their posts. The scent of the red flower had permeated and transformed everything: here it clarified something previously unknown, there it gave someone courage to fight the good fight, in yet another place it encouraged flight from unbearable conditions. The house owner, who well understood that this movement had begun in the very stable he had assigned to his old faithful servant, was absolutely outraged and sent people to throw the "scum down there" into the street, lock, stock, and barrel. But the stable was empty. Its inhabitants were already on their way to the garden of the red flower, and with them went the young people of the city and the countless number of the dispossessed who were now enlightened. All of them followed the fragrance of the red flower and awaited salvation from it. It was a long, long procession. At its head walked the scholar with his book and Maggie, holding the red flower, then followed Mrs. Werner and Brigitte, then the children and all the others. But although they distanced themselves farther and farther from the city, the flower's fragrance was left behind in the city walls and kept on working its magic.

TRANSLATED BY JEANNINE BLACKWELL

Ricarda Huch with friends Emma Reiff and Hedwig Waser
at a Mardi Gras party on 1 February 1896. Photo from the private
collection of Ms. Ursula Hildbrand-Wehrli.

Ricarda Huch

1864–1947

Ricarda Huch, considered by many to be one of the most significant female authors of the twentieth century, was an accomplished writer in numerous genres, from drama, lyric poetry, fiction, historical and literary criticism, historiography, biography, philosophy, and theology. Her groundbreaking studies on German Romanticism (*Blütezeit der Romantik* [The golden age of Romanticism, 1899] and *Ausbreitung und Verfall der Romantik* [Diffusion and decline of Romanticism, 1902]) influenced both literary criticism of the period as well as "romantic" lifestyles in her contemporary society. Huch was one of the first German women to earn a Ph.D. (in Zurich), and her professional and public life was crowned with success, including induction as the first woman into the Preußische Akademie der Künste (Prussian Academy of the Arts). Huch's personal life, however, was fraught with tragedy and disappointment with the early death of her parents, her two failed marriages, and other personal setbacks. Like Benedikte Naubert a century earlier, Huch intentionally wrote in genres that had been the bastion of male authors: the historical novel, philosophical treatises, and literary criticism.

"Pack of Lies," like many of Huch's other short stories and novellas, is typical of neo-Romantic prose – the fragmentation of the narrative through dreamlike interactions and the devilish mix of irony and mockery. The age-old tale of the water sprite who yearns to have a human soul and the youth who longs to attain the magical powers of the siren's song, Huch's story critiques Fouqué's *Undine*, Hans Christian Andersen's "The Little Mermaid," and a host of other water sprite stories. "Pack of Lies" weaves a complicated web of illusions and half-truths that leaves the reader wondering just who comes out on top. A careful reading reveals the betrayal of the magical realm but no gain for the human.

Other stories to read with this piece include the other water spirit tales in this collection (Marie von Olfers's "Little Princess" and Marie Timme's "The King's Child"), as well as a score of other mermaid stories, most importantly, Hans Christian Andersen's "The Little Mermaid," and the Walt Disney film of the same name. Fanny Lewald's "A Modern Fairy Tale" in this collection also makes interesting comparison reading. The mermaid's self-destructive quest has affinities with Joanna Russ's "Russalka, or The Seacoast of Bohemia" (in Zipes, ed., *Don't Bet on the Prince*) and Doris Lessing's "How I Finally Lost My Heart" (in Park and Heaton, eds., *Caught in a Story*).

Ricarda Huch, "Lügenmärchen," in *Die Zeit* (Vienna, 1896; reprinted in *Teufeleien,* Leipzig: Haessel, 1897).

Pack of Lies

1896

A YOUTH HAD READ in an old book about water sprites and their immense beauty, but this had not impressed him as much as the other information he discovered in the same book. It said these nixes could sing with such exceptionally sweet voices and exquisite skill that they were able to coax the soul out of any being. It happened in this fashion: as the soul listened, it strained so longingly toward the singing force that it laid itself bare and revealed itself without resistance. This might befall not only humans and other creatures but also plants and mute and inanimate objects in nature. This enormous magic charmed each thing to reveal in its own way what its essence was. To the young man this seemed the most curious and glorious thing in the world, and he daydreamed incessantly about how the stars in the heavens would heed his command, and the pebbles on the path and the greenish gold beetles that crawled before him on the sand would make themselves known to him. He would simply know, without understanding how, which is something a person can claim only when he is totally aware of his entire being and at the same time can express everything he knows. In short, he imagined it would be as if every speck of them would become completely transparent in body and soul before him.

He read the book from cover to cover to find out more about all of this, and it reported that such mermaids did indeed confer this skill on mortal men to whom they had taken a fancy but only in return for the utmost sacrifice, which no mortal would ever make. From that point on the youth brooded incessantly about what kind of sacrifice it could possibly be that was too great for such a gift – one that, so it seemed to him, offered humans the most sublime ability they could possess.

Soon enough he was to learn what there was to all of this, because one evening, as he lay sleepless on his bed, he heard – quite softly, as if it were intended only for ghostly ears – a sweet melody that seemed to rise up from the sea. He was instantly seized body and soul by such a mellifluous yearning

that he could not resist long, but instead he rose, clothed himself, and followed this incomparable music. Arriving at the seashore, he beheld, bathed
in moonlight on a rock half-submerged in the surf and radiant from afar, a
woman of such incredible beauty that he was immediately certain it could
only be a nix.

She smiled as she caught sight of him, dipped her finger into the water,
and splashed a few drops in his face. They flew through the air like milky
pearls and, eerily cool, brushed his cheeks. Although at first he felt uneasy,
he nevertheless was still unable to elude her allures and swore that he must
die and perish on the spot if he could not partake of her love. And lo! she
took him in her arms, and as his head lay on her breast, he heard no heart
beating in her silent bosom, but the yearning in her glimmering eyes and the
restless smile on her sly lips enveloped his senses so completely that he threw
caution to the winds. They pledged to meet again every moonlit night, and
from that moment on all the youth's endeavors were fixed on her teaching
him the magical means by which she could coax from all things the secret
of their existence.

In the meantime, the nix also had her own designs and desires for the tender union she had entered into with the young man, for alive in all heathen
water demons is the longing for an immortal soul, which they can obtain
only by eating the heart of a mortal man, which the selfsame must willingly
proffer out of love. She hoped to beguile the young man with her rapturous
charms, so much so that he would not withhold this gift from her, and, with
exquisite skill in unfurling love and lust, she fanned the flames of his passion
to an ever mounting frenzy. This gave the youth the greatest pleasure, to be
sure, but brought him in no measure closer to his goal.

Once, when he asked her to give him a sample of her magical singing, she
declared herself prepared to do so but added that if people were awakened
by it and were lured to the spot, she would have to vanish and would never
be allowed to return, whereby he, of necessity, had to abandon his request.
But the opportunity to express his most ardent wish presented itself one
evening as the water nymph, in order to come closer to her own goal, began
to speak of the sorrowful fate of her people, who, like she, certainly lived
many centuries but still not eternally and were in general limited to the life
of the flesh, whereas for her, the most pleasurable form of life imaginable
would be the unfettered floating of a soul in endless blue space. The youth
consoled the disconsolate nix by telling her that a lifetime in the caressing
waves and the companionship of diverse fish and other water wonders was
certainly the most entertaining of all and that she could also amuse herself
with the precious art of her song, which men, despite their immortal souls,
had to do without.

The water sprite listened intently and said that if it were nothing more than that, she would be happy to teach him her art of song. Alas, she couldn't do it for nothing; he would also have to render her a service, but it wouldn't cost him all that much. Nothing more or less was required than that he give her his heart, willingly and out of love. After delighting in his heart, she would partake of an immortal soul, just as humans did. She threw her arms around his neck and kissed him tenderly and let her damp beauty shimmer all over him, and she said that it was in essence a small token insofar as she herself had no heart, nor had she ever had one, but that she had nonetheless always felt well and content.

That notwithstanding, the notion gave the youth pause, because it seemed dubious to him that he would continue to thrive without a heart, since he had from the very beginning been equipped with one that served all sorts of useful purposes. Indeed, his beloved suggested to him all sorts of magical aids by means of which he could remove his heart from his breast without difficulty or pain, yet he did not completely believe these statements. And, as blissful as her caresses were, he still asked himself if she really felt genuine and true love for him, and if she wouldn't embrace any old scaly sea creature just as intimately when his cadaver rotted on the silty ocean floor.

The more he thought about it, the more firm became his decision not to relinquish his heart, which he believed he could not spare in this lifetime; nonetheless, he was certainly not willing to do without the siren song of the nix. Instead, one evening he asked his beloved to give or tell him the means by which he could take out his heart without too much hardship, whereupon she appeared the next time with a pointed, transparent little blade, saying her mother had fashioned it out of fish teeth. It would glide into flesh with an agreeable ease, more pleasure than pain. She also offered her services to do the deed herself forthwith, but the youth feared she might miss the mark because of the vague light of the beclouded moon; he swore, however, to appear the next evening with the precious token.

Since moonrise the mermaid had been sitting on her rock, stretching her glistening body in sweet anticipation and singing softly to herself so that the waves rolled in from afar, dancing a little ring-a-rosy around her and joyfully spouting their foamy souls into the air and swallowing them up again in turn. The young man did not leave her waiting long but appeared holding in his outstretched hand a beautiful, still bleeding heart. It was, forsooth, not his own but, rather, that of a young calf that he had contrived to procure from a slaughterhouse.

After the curious nix had feasted her eyes on it, he asked if he should perhaps light a small fire and roast it, for it was absolutely superb to eat that way; she replied, however, that she would prefer to eat it raw and immediately bit off a large piece with her sharp, barbed teeth. The youth watched as she ate, especially how the color of her eyes danced from a limpid light green to a smoky dark green and then back again, as if they were not eyes at all but rather waves reflected in a delicate crystal, dreamy and mysterious to watch.

After she had completely consumed the heart, she asked her lover with great tenderness how he was feeling and if the little blade had rendered a fine service, whereby he quickly answered, blushing a bit, that it was exceptionally effective and that he would like to request that he might keep it. He was actually a bit exhausted, though, and would have stayed in bed if he had not imagined with what anticipation she had awaited him. At the same time he could not deny that he was now eager to be initiated into the art of magical song. Hereupon the water nymph laughed a charming laugh that leapt high into the air like a fountain of crystalline tones and trickled back down and asked if he hadn't already tried it. She no longer needed to teach him anything, because he now possessed the art as well as she. The youth did not exactly know what to make of this remark and stared dumbly and uncertainly at the nix; she, however, pressed a lingering kiss on his open lips and said, "You should know, my love, that our magical singing is due to the fact that we have no heart. I couldn't teach it to you, but at that very moment when you became bereft of your heart for my sake, the talent developed in you, so that the reward evolves naturally from the sacrifice. Just go ahead and try singing a little tune, and we will see what effect it has on the turtles and mussels lying there curled up in the damp sand."

This suggestion put the youth in a frightful predicament, but he regained his composure and said cleverly that he recalled how she had warned him how singing aloud could lure people, and their trysts would have to come to an end if they became known. The nix praised his prudence and took hold of him with her bare, trickling arms to kiss him. As she embraced him and his heart beat on her cool breast, she sat up and said, "If I had not just partaken of your heart, I would swear I heard it beating in your chest." The youth replied that he had put a tiny hammermill in the empty spot so that no one would ever be unpleasantly surprised by the silence in his chest. Of course, he had to take it out from time to time and rewind it; that was the very reason why he had asked her to be allowed to keep the little blade. Pensively, the nix kissed the spot where it beat and was especially fond of doing so every time they celebrated their trysts. Often she would remark that it was really true that humans, because of their immortal souls, were capable of truer and more selfless love, since they were willing to rob themselves of their hearts to enrich their loved ones. The youth replied that it was for that very reason that he was so happy to know that she, too, now had such a soul that put her in a position to love him, not with only a heathen carnality as before but instead truly and earnestly.

"How wonderful it will be," she said, "when we float through eternity together."

"Yes," he said, "and when we sing together, even the Holy Spirit, present in the form of a dove, must reveal his essence to us, not to speak of all the millions of human souls we encounter. Knowing and loving one another is the essence of eternal bliss."

"And we are enjoying it already here on Earth," said the smiling nix, and she kissed the youth on both eyes.

TRANSLATED BY SHAWN C. JARVIS

Wedding day. From "Von der Brautschaft,"
illustrated by Gisela von Arnim. Reprinted with
permission of the Stiftung Weimarer Klassik,
Arnim Bestand GSA 03/995.

Epilogue
Wedding Day
1853

Dear Achim,

Last night the old lady was here again, and she thought long and hard about what story she would tell me. Finally, she asked me if I would like to know how she had looked as a bride. "Oh, yes," I said. "Well," she answered, "I was dressed magnificently; when my groom came and wanted to give me a kiss, I had such a big hoop skirt and such a large bouquet that he couldn't get close to me.

"After church my girlfriends ate fruit at my house, and the young men held their plates. They acted as if they had such tiny mouths that the cherries had to be tapped in with a spoon. Then one of my girlfriends fell into a faint because she noticed that she had been sitting on a fancy green embroidered pillow, and she thought she had caught a cold from it. There was a great hue and cry, and she was considered to be very high-strung."

And then I really had to laugh, and the ghost fled, so quickly that I don't know at all if she will return. But I think she will, for she will want to get back that bracelet, now that I have laughed. So we will just see how it turns out tomorrow.

TRANSLATED BY JEANNINE BLACKWELL

From the Cradle to the Grave

Reading These Tales

Shawn C. Jarvis

ONCERNED WITH CREATING a world where everyone lives happily ever after, fairy tales chart a trajectory along the path of maturation to reach that end. The stages from the cradle to the grave drive the fairy tale world: childhood, the first tentative venturing out from home, the search for a partner, marriage and its aftermath. Those way stations in the tales we have collected here are similar to those of the "standard" or "classical" tales from the Grimms, Hans Christian Andersen, and Charles Perrault, but the paths to that happy end, the interactions between the characters in that pursuit, even the definition of what constitutes a happy end (and if one is possible) come into sharp focus against the backdrop of traditional tales. How the various authors in this anthology examine life's way stations reveals many of the characteristics of German women's fairy tales that make them a tradition unto themselves.[1]

THE IMAGE OF CHILDREN

In contrast to many of their counterparts in "standard" tales, the children in these fairy tales do not stumble into the clutches of voracious witches or rely on the Rumpelstiltskins of the world to get them out of a fix. When on the horns of a dilemma, they take the dilemma by the horns and are active, resourceful, and often self-aware. The girls in Sophie von Baudissin's "The Doll Institute," for example, actively oppose the king's decree, organize a demonstration, and successfully plead their cause to the king through well-reasoned and clever arguments. Little Maggie in "The Red Flower" is no shrinking violet match girl doomed to death à la Hans Christian Andersen but is instead an activist proletarian child who scorns the aid of misleading magical helpers and continues on her solitary quest. Little Princess in Marie von Olfers's tale finds ways to explore the life she longed for as a real princess and then return to her former existence without dire punishment or great sacrifice, weary but wiser.

Many of the protagonists in this collection are either prenubile or coming of age, an important moment in fairy tales when characters on the cusp of adulthood leave home. These tales (as do the "standards") suggest that the first journey from home is different for males and females. Bold and manly characters typically set out on a self-initiated adventure full of exploits to seek riches and glory (and maybe even a princess to boot). Female protagonists are more likely to have been cast out; from this initial involuntary motivation, their journeys lead inward as they undertake a voyage to greater self-awareness.[2]

On their self-initiated adventures, male characters typically experience some hardship to be withstood, as Frederick's brutal abuse at the hands of the black princess in Anna von Haxthausen's "The Rescued Princess" or Johannes's shipwreck in Amalie Schoppe's tale. The adventure may also happen simply from the desire to see the wide world and what it holds, as in the case of Catherine the Great's Fewei and Amalie Schoppe's Johannes. In our collection, the male characters' journeys are like those of their traditional peers, but the outcomes are profoundly different. Classical heroes rarely return to their home base, while the heroes in our tales come back to their beginnings in their original families, where they reflect on their actions and the wisdom of them. Johannes loses all he has and returns home as a pauper to seek his wealth there, "for the tastiest bread is always homemade," and Fewei returns with greater wisdom so that he might be a better king. In these tales, the journey out leads the characters back to solidification of hearth and home.

In contrast to a hero's quest, a heroine's journey out is rarely a self-initiated pilgrimage; more likely, she has been torn from home and forced to fend for herself. Benedikte Naubert's princesses in "Boadicea and Velleda" set off on an imposed adventure, Agnes Franz's Rosalieb finds herself spirited away to a tower, and Maggie in "The Red Flower" is evicted from her home. In such circumstances, heroines in traditional tales usually cannot by themselves effect any change in their status and must instead rely on the indulgences of magic helpers and/or the kindness of strangers (princes, dwarfs, men in general). Heroines in these women's tales work independently, become self-aware, sharpen their wits, gain skills for their survival, and possibly even accomplish a higher purpose, such as little Maggie effecting the salvation of all workers and people who suffer. The daughters of Boadicea in Benedikte Naubert's tale learn the ways of magic through the sorceress's tutelage and prefer their lives of female community and freedom to the constraints of society. The outcome of the female protagonist's development is rarely material gain but, rather, maturity of mind achieved through diligence, reflection, and self-discovery. Agnes Franz clearly outlines this process in "Princess Rosalieb: A Fairy Tale" when the protagonist learns to spin and weave as well as to read and ultimately even to write her own life story.

THE PARTNER QUEST

For nubile characters, the next milestone on the fairy tale road is the quest for a suitable partner. Some stories in this collection explore the classical bride quest (a standard motif in fairy tales since the Middle Ages), while others contemplate this moment as a much more problematic event. Henriette Kühne-Harkort's version of "Snow White" overtly follows the Grimm model and has the bride sought and saved by the prince, but the other bride quests in this anthology – Elisabeth Ebeling's "Black and White" and Louise Dittmar's "Tale of the Monkeys" – are doomed to failure. Although the authors present the seekers as sympathetic characters, they also expose their quests as misguided. The potential groom in "Black and White" discovers that the object of his desire is not worthy of his wooing. Almansor learns how much he is willing to sacrifice and how much of his identity he can betray in order to follow his bride quest to its bitter end. In "Tale of the Monkeys," Juste Milieu's quest to find the woman who will adore him unconditionally also fails because his goal is unattainable, inasmuch as he himself is an unworthy partner. Milieu's quest is closely related to those of other heroes who inadvertently stumble into an alliance because of some other overarching, hubristic desire: a youth's quest to "see" the essence of things by gaining the siren's song enters him into a duplicitous union with a water nix in Ricarda Huch's "Pack of Lies," and Sophie Tieck Bernhardi von Knorring's Leonhard in "The Old Man in the Cave" unexpectedly discovers the chimerical maiden only love can make real while on his ill-fated quest to see his own thoughts.

The stories that focus on the female character's search for a mate are more complicated and more foreign to the traditional fairy tale. Often the heroine is not even on a partner quest but nevertheless finds herself confronted with a potential mate. In Anna von Haxthausen's "The Rescued Princess," for example, the bewitched heroine simply wants disenchantment, but she ends up with a husband whose resolve (and longevity) she tests through merciless abuse. Often female characters are torn between duty and desire. Marie von Ebner-Eschenbach's princess of Banalia must unhappily settle for the fairy tale king, because the actual union she longs for can only happen in death. Karoline von Günderrode's "Temora" presents a tragic twist to the partner quest. The complication of loving the man her father has wronged and then killing him to avenge her father's murder is hardly the making of a happy end. Elisabeth of Rumania's "Furnica, or The Queen of the Ants" is perhaps the most chilling tale in this complex: the ants immure the heroine for contemplating a fairy tale romance with the prince and thereby deserting her duty to her subjects. Ricarda Huch's "Pack of Lies" lays bare the entire farce of the partner quest: neither the nix in search of a human heart nor the youth seeking the magic of the siren's song accomplishes the desired end.

TO WED OR NOT TO WED

Once the partner quest is complete, the sealing of the vows and the move to the happy ending take center stage. While traditional fairy tales often implicitly suggest that the happy ending is matrimony, our tales problematize that holy state. Some tales overtly damn the whole sorry state of affairs. Elisabeth of Rumania's heroine, Viorica, tells her mother she'd rather not marry at all, because all husbands do is make more work. Sometimes the experience of the female community outside traditional society has a greater appeal, as in "Boadicea and Velleda," in which six of the Iceni princesses choose death over life in servitude as mates to the Romans. The seventh, Boada, pays with her life for betraying her virginity, and only Velleda retains her autonomy and, perhaps for that reason, her life. Other tales explore marriage as a union entered into because of true love, as Lila and Egbert's marriage across class lines in Hedwig Dohm's "The Fragrance of Flowers." Marie von Ebner-Eschenbach's "The Princess of Banalia" explores the tension between affinities and responsibilities in the princess's desired union with the noble savage, Abdul, and her correct marriage with the good and kindly king; her passion for the wild man eventually drives her to abandon the perfect fairy tale of marital bliss and choose death instead. These tales also explore how marriage involves resignation and loss, as in the case of Marie Timme's king's child, who relinquishes her selkie heritage to return to her husband and children in the upper world.

Sometimes the bonds of wedlock bring unexpected complications, especially when the partner turns out to be an ogre. The theme of the monstrous husband, either through bad genes (as in "Bluebeard") or bewitchment (as in "Beauty and the Beast"), is a standard of traditional collections, and it appears in our anthology as well. In traditional tales, heroines wedded to Bluebeards wait, wringing their hands, for their brothers to arrive and save them; in women's tales, the heroine facing such a fate springs into action and demonstrates her resourcefulness and sagacity. In "The Giants' Forest" the protagonist uses every wile in her repertoire to avoid marrying her ogre fiancé, but the exigencies of the situation also require her wits (and a little dose of magic in the form of a wishing cap). The treatment of the bewitched spouse needing disenchantment – the fairy tale cipher for the redeeming power of love – stays close to its classic roots in Ludovica Brentano Jordis's "The Lion and the Frog" with the disenchantment of the lion brother and his froggy girlfriend, but it takes on a modern, ironic twist in other stories. In two tales the potential spouses gain the ability to "see" what it is they would disenchant; in Louise Dittmar's "Tale of the Monkeys" the prospective husband, Juste Milieu, sees behind the facade of his future brides-to-be, while Fanny Lewald's "A Modern Fairy Tale" endows the Sunday's child with the ability to see her suitor for the cold fish he truly is.

FAMILY RESPONSIBILITIES

Although the standard fairy tale often culminates with the consummation of the marriage, many tales in this anthology explore the dynamics of the family unit and move to resolve problems that plague the family's happiness. Rather than evil (step)mothers abandoning children or sending them off to certain doom, mothers and other family members in these tales typically strive to preserve or restore family—hence the sister seeking and disenchanting family members in Ludovica Brentano Jordis's "The Lion and the Frog" or the spectral mother encouraging the father to right past wrongs and forgive his daughter in Sophie Tieck Bernhardi von Knorring's "The Old Man in the Cave." The queen in Bettina von Arnim's "The Queen's Son" persists in finding her lost son and reconciling him with his brothers, and the Moor queen in Elisabeth Ebeling's "Black and White" plays a vital role in the family's reconciliation when she sends her son to the wise man and then brings the king and court to the desert to find him restored to his former self. Karoline von Günderrode's "Temora" explores the tension between duty to the family honor (the princess's need to avenge her father's murder) and her desire for the perpetrator that can only end in the lovers' final, fatal embrace. In Amalie Schoppe's "The Kind and Diligent Housewife" Mistress Mary assures the family's happiness with the elixir that restores the father to health, and Johannes returns to understand his mother's teachings and that his wanderings have been foolhardy; his rightful place is at home. Perhaps one of the most poignant texts in this collection valorizing the family is Marie Timme's "The King's Child," in which the selkie, faced with returning to her father and the magical world below the sea, recognizes that she has become one with her Shetland Island fisherman and their children. Similarly, the merchild in Marie von Olfers's "Little Princess" chooses life with the family above the waves in the decrepit mill over the sterile, loveless splendor at the bottom of the sea.

MATURITY AND OLD AGE

An especially significant marker of women's tales is their multigenerational nature, and a number of the tales in this collection explore the end of life's journey. Whereas standard tales often demonize powerful older women and compel them into mortal combat with their younger, more beautiful rivals or leave them lying in wait for scrumptious children to happen along, the tales in this anthology present mature women in the role of family historians and wise mentors. Loving protectresses of their protégées and the generations following them, older women initiate girls into the ways of magic, as do the fairy giantess in "The Giants' Forest," Velleda in "Boadicea and Velleda," the prophetess in "Temora," Gisela von Arnim's ancestral ghost lady, and Aunt Renate in "A Modern Fairy Tale." Even the punishing fairy godmothers of Karoline Stahl's piece and Amarantha in Agnes Franz's "Princess Rosalieb" always have the best interests of their wards in mind and teach them about the magic in the everyday.

The authors of our tales also examine the roles of older men, but they are not always as uniformly positive as those of their female counterparts. Wiseworth in "The Tale of Fewei," Cyril in "Black and White," the eponymous old man in the cave, and the aged sage in "The Red Flower" are important mentors, although the last two ultimately need the help of their protégés for their own redemption. Father figures are a motley crew ranging from loving but fearful fellows (as in "Boadicea and Velleda"); vengeful or simply misguided men standing in the way of their daughters' happiness (as in "Temora," "The Fragrance of Flowers," and "The Godmothers"); or relatively passive, powerless creatures (like Pharaoh in "The King's Child"). Curt in "The Kind and Diligent Housewife" and the king in "The Rescued Princess" typify the most problematical father figure: he is the cause of all the family's woes and yet is powerless to resolve the situation. These characters rely on the women or the kindness of strangers to get them out of a difficult situation.

The reader will have to determine if the writers of these tales intended the messages that we, the editors and fairy tale scholars, impute to them and if the tales are emancipatory or prescriptive, confining or liberating. It is certainly true that these stories often promote a catalog of traditionally feminine virtues for female characters: kindness, devotion to family, self-sacrifice. But they also blur the gender lines between "correct" behavior for men and women and present powerful, positive females and kind,

concerned males. They chart new psychological territory in sibling, parental, and spousal relationships unknown in the standard tales. They stress
the importance of education, not only for men but equally for women. They
even present happy endings other than marriage.

Ultimately, these tales inscribe in the German fairy tale record the stories
of self-reliance and community that today's women and girls long for. They
existed all along – we just did not know where to look for them. They were
always there, hiding in the folds of someone else's cloak, locked away in
secret chests, just inside the mirror. On the trip from cradle to grave, we
remember a girl's rite of passage, a moment of reflection some readers will
recall from their own youths: the investiture ceremony of the Brownies. With
it, we end our story and turn it back over to you.

Twist me and turn me and show me the elf.
I looked in the water and saw – myself.

NOTES

1. Many other features of the fairy tale deserve attention in these tales, such as the
role of the magic helpers; the treatment of standard motifs like physical beauty; the
function of talismans; the system of punishments and rewards. These stories are also
replete with recurring images and motifs (e.g., cave imagery, "special vision," sequestering methods and purposes) that bear greater scrutiny. Studies of narrative
perspective, use of language, speech acts, and stylistics could also prove fruitful.

2. See Abel, Hirsch, and Langland, eds., *The Voyage In.*

BIBLIOGRAPHY

Aarne, Antti, and Stith Thompson. *The Types of the Folktale: A Classification and Bibliography.* Helsinki, 1928 (FFC 74). 2nd ed., 1961 (FFC 184).

Abel, Elizabeth, Marianne Hirsch, and Elizabeth Langland, eds. *The Voyage In: Fictions of Female Development.* Hanover NH: University of New England Press, 1983.

Auerbach, Nina, and U. C. Knoepflmacher, eds. *Forbidden Journeys: Fairy Tales and Fantasies by Victorian Women Writers.* Chicago: University of Chicago Press, 1992.

Baader, Renate. *Dames de lettres: Autorinnen des preziösen, hocharistokratischen und "modernen" Salons (1649–1698).* Stuttgart: Metzler, 1986.

Belcher, Stephen. "Framed Tales in the Oral Tradition: An Exploration." *Fabula* 35 (1994): 1–19.

Bernheimer, Kate, ed. *Mirror, Mirror on the Wall: Women Writers Explore Their Favorite Fairy Tales.* New York: Anchor/Doubleday, 1998.

Bertuch, Friedrich Justin, ed. *Die blaue Bibliothek aller Nationen.* 12 vols. Weimar: Industrie-Comptoir, 1791–96.

Blackwell, Jeannine. "Fractured Fairy Tales: German Women Authors and the Grimm Tradition." *Germanic Review* 62 (1987): 162–74.

———. "German Fairy Tales: A User's Manual: Translations of Six Frames and Fragments by Romantic Women." *Marvels and Tales: Journal of Fairy-Tale Studies* 14 (2000): 99–121.

Blackwell, Jeannine, and Susanne Zantop, eds. *Bitter Healing: German Women Writers, 1700–1830, an Anthology.* Lincoln: University of Nebraska Press, 1990.

Bolte, Johannes, and Georg Polívka, eds. *Anmerkungen zu den Kinder- und Hausmärchen der Brüder Grimm.* 5 vols. (1913–32). 2nd ed., Hildesheim: Georg Olms, 1963.

Bottigheimer, Ruth B. *Grimms' Bad Girls and Bold Boys: The Moral and Social Vision of the Tales.* New Haven CT: Yale University Press, 1987.

———. "Silenced Women in the Grimms' Tales: The 'Fit' between Fairy Tales and Society." In Ruth B. Bottigheimer, ed. *Fairy Tales and Society: Illusion, Allusion and Paradigm.* Philadelphia: University of Pennsylvania Press, 1986.

Byatt, A. S. *The Djinn in the Nightingale's Eye: Five Fairy Stories.* New York: Random House, 1994.

Carter, Angela. *The Bloody Chamber and Other Stories.* London: Gollancz, 1979.

———. *The Old Wives' Fairy Tale Book.* New York: Pantheon, 1990.

Cole, Babette. *Princess Smartypants.* 1986. New York: G. P. Putnam's Sons, 1991.

Datlow, Ellen, and Terri Windling, eds. *Black Swan, White Raven.* New York: Avon, 1997.

———. *Black Thorn, White Rose.* New York: Avon, 1994.

———. *Ruby Slippers, Golden Tears.* New York: Avon, 1995.

———. *Snow White, Blood Red.* New York: Avon, 1993.

Doderer, Klaus, ed. *Lexikon der Kinder- und Jugendliteratur. Personen-, Länder-
und Sachartikel zu Geschichte und Gegenwart der Kinder- und Jugendliteratur.*
3 vols. Weinheim and Basel: Beltz, 1975.

Düsterdieck, Peter, et al. *Die Sammlung Hobrecker der Universitätsbibliothek Braunschweig. Katalog der Kinder- und Jugendliteratur 1565–1945.* Munich: K. G.
Saur, 1985.

*Enzyklopädie des Märchens. Handwörterbuch zur historischen und vergleichenden
Erzählforschung.* Berlin, 1975–.

Feen-Mährchen zur Unterhaltung für Freunde und Freundinnen der Feenwelt.
Braunschweig: Bei Friedrich Bernhard Culemann, 1801. Rpt. Hildeshem: Olms,
2000. Ed. Ulrich Marzolph.

Früh, Sigrid, ed. *Die Frau, die auszog, ihren Mann zu erlösen.* Frankfurt: Fischer
Taschenbuch, 1985.

Galloway, Priscilla. *Truly Grim Tales.* New York: Delacorte, 1995.

Gilbert, Sandra, and Susan Gubar. "The Queen's Looking Glass." In *The Mad-
woman in the Attic: The Woman Writer and the Nineteenth-Century Literary
Imagination.* New Haven CT: Yale University Press, 1979. 3–44.

Göbels, Hubert. *Hundert alte Kinderbücher 1870–1945: Eine illustrierte Bibliographie.* Dortmund: Harenberg, 1981.

———. *Hundert alte Kinderbücher aus Barock und Aufklärung: Eine illustrierte
Bibliographie.* Dortmund: Harenberg, 1980.

———. *Hundert alte Kinderbücher aus dem 19. Jahrhundert: Eine illustrierte
Bibliographie.* Dortmund: Harenberg, 1979.

Grätz, Manfred. *Das Märchen in der deutschen Aufklärung: Vom Feenmärchen zum
Volksmärchen.* Stuttgart: Metzler, 1988.

Grimm, Jacob and Wilhelm Grimm. *The Complete Fairy Tales of the Brothers
Grimm.* Translated by Jack Zipes. Toronto and New York: Bantam Books, 1987.

Haase, Donald. "Feminist Fairy-Tale Scholarship: A Critical Survey and Bibliography." *Marvels and Tales: A Journal of Fairy-Tale Studies* 14 (2000): 15–63.

———. "German Fairy Tales and America's Culture Wars: From Grimms' *Kinder-
und Hausmärchen* to William Bennett's *Book of Virtues.*" *German Politics and
Society* 13 (1995): 17–25.

Hamilton, Virginia. *Her Stories: African American Folktales, Fairy Tales, and True
Tales.* New York: Blue Sky Press, 1995.

———. *The People Could Fly: American Black Folktales.* New York: Alfred A.
Knopf, 1985.

Hay, Sara Henderson. *Story Hour.* Fayetteville: University of Arkansas Press, 1992.

Hobrecker, Karl. *Alte vergessene Kinderbücher: Nachdruck der Ausgabe von 1924.*
Edited by Hubert Göbels. Dortmund: Harenberg, 1981.

Jarvis, Shawn. "Trivial Pursuit? Women Deconstructing the Grimmian Model in
the *Kaffeterkreis.*" In Don Haase, ed. *The Reception of Grimms' Fairy Tales:
Responses, Reactions, Revisions.* Detroit: Wayne State University Press, 1993.
102–27.

Bibliography

————. "The Vanished Woman of Great Influence: Benedikte Naubert's Legacy and German Women's Fairy Tales." In Katherine R. Goodman and Edith Waldstein, eds. *In the Shadow of Olympus: German Women Writers around 1800.* Albany: SUNY Press, 1992.

————, trans. "The Rose Cloud," by Gisela von Arnim. *Marvels and Tales: Journal of Fairy-Tale Studies* 11, nos. 1–2 (1997): 134–59.

————, trans. "The Wicked Sisters and the Good One: A Fairy Tale," by Caroline Stahl. In *Marvels and Tales: A Journal of Fairy-Tale Studies* 14 (2000): 159–64.

Klotz, Aiga. *Kinder- und Jugendliteratur in Deutschland 1840–1950. Gesamt-verzeichnis der Veröffentlichungen in deutscher Sprache.* 5 vols. Stuttgart: Metzler, 1990.

Kord, Susanne. *Ein Blick hinter die Kulissen: Deutschsprachige Dramatikerinnen im 18. und 19. Jahrhundert.* Stuttgart: J. B. Metzler, 1992.

Park, Christine, and Caroline Heaton, eds. *Caught in a Story: Contemporary Fairytales and Fables.* London: Vintage, 1992.

Phelps, Ethel Johnston, ed. *Maid of the North: Feminist Folk Tales from around the World.* New York: Holt, Rinehart and Winston, 1981.

Rölleke, Heinz. Anhang und Nachwort. In *Kinder- und Hausmärchen der Brüder Grimm.* 3 vols. Stuttgart: Reclam, 1980.

————, ed. *Kinder- und Hausmärchen der Brüder Grimm.* 3 vols. Stuttgart: Reclam, 1980.

————. *Märchen aus dem Nachlaß der Brüder Grimm.* Bonn: Bouvier, 1977.

————. *Unbekannte Märchen von Jacob und Wilhelm Grimm. Synopse von Einzeldrucken Grimmscher Märchen und deren endgültiger Fassung in den* KHM. Cologne: Eugen Diedrichs, 1987.

Rose, Ellen Cronan. "Through the Looking Glass: When Women Tell Fairy Tales." In Elizabeth Abel, Marianne Hirsch, and Elizabeth Langland, eds. *The Voyage In: Fictions of Female Development.* Hanover NH: University of New England Press, 1983. 209–27.

Rowe, Karen E. "To Spin a Yarn: The Female Voice in Folklore and Fairy Tale." In Ruth B. Bottigheimer, ed. *Fairy Tales and Society: Illusion, Allusion and Paradigm.* Philadelphia: University of Pennsylvania Press, 1986. 53–74.

Rush, Barbara, ed. *The Book of Jewish Women's Tales.* Northvale NJ: Jason Aronson, 1994.

Schoof, Wilhelm. *Zur Entstehungsgeschichte der Grimmschen Märchen: Bearbeitet unter Benutzung des Nachlasses der Brüder Grimm.* Hamburg: Hauswedell, 1959.

Schulte-Kemmingshausen, Karl. "Annette von Droste-Hülshoff und Wilhelm Grimm zeichnen ein Märchen auf." (Volksüberlieferung aus dem Nachlaß der Brüder Grimm.) *Westdeutsche Zeitschrift für Volkskunde* 33 (1936): 41–50.

Schulte-Kemmingshausen, Karl, ed. *Märchen aus deutschen Landschaften: Unveröffentliche Quellen.* Vol. 2, 1963. Aschendorff: Aschendorffer Buch-druckerei, 1976.

Seifert, Lewis. *Fairy Tales, Sexuality, and Gender in France, 1690–1715: Nostalgic Utopias.* New York: Cambridge University Press, 1996.

Bibliography

————. "The Time that (N)ever Was: Women's Fairy Tales in Seventeenth-Century France." Ph.D. diss., University of Michigan, 1989.

Sexton, Anne. *Transformations*. Boston: Houghton Mifflin, 1971.

Tatar, Maria. *The Hard Facts of the Grimms' Fairy Tales*. Princeton NJ: Princeton University Press, 1987.

————. *Off with Their Heads! Fairy Tales and the Culture of Childhood*. Princeton NJ: Princeton University Press, 1992.

Walker, Barbara. *Feminist Fairy Tales*. New York: Harper Collins, 1996.

Warner, Marina. *From the Beast to the Blonde: On Fairy Tales and Their Tellers*. New York: Farrar, Straus and Giroux, 1995.

Wegehaupt, Heinz, with Edith Fichtner. *Alte deutsche Kinderbücher: Bibliographie 1507–1850. Zugleich Bestandsverzeichnis der Kinder- und Jugendbuchabteilung der deutschen Staatsbibliothek zu Berlin*. Berlin: Kinderbuchverlag, 1979.

————. *Alte deutsche Kinderbücher: Bibliographie 1851–1900. Zugleich Bestandsverzeichnis der Kinder- und Jugendbuchabteilung der deutschen Staatsbibliothek zu Berlin*. Stuttgart: Dr. Ernst Hauswedell, 1985.

Wesselski, Albert, ed. *Deutsche Märchen vor Grimm*. Vienna: Rohrer, 1938.

Yolen, Jane, and Heidi E. Y. Stemple. *Mirror, Mirror: Forty Folktales and What One Mother and Daughter Found There*. New York: Viking, 2000.

Zipes, Jack. *Fairy Tale as Myth/Myth as Fairy Tale*. Lexington: University Press of Kentucky, 1994.

————. *Fairy Tales and the Art of Subversion: The Classical Genre for Children and the Process of Civilization*. New York: Methuen, 1983.

————, ed. *Don't Bet on the Prince: Contemporary Feminist Fairy Tales in North America and England*. Aldershot, England: Gower, 1986.

————, ed. *The Outspoken Princess and the Gentle Knight: A Treasury of Modern Fairy Tales*. New York: Bantam, 1994.

————, ed. *Victorian Fairy Tales: The Revolt of the Fairies and Elves*. New York and London: Methuen, 1987.

————, ed. and trans. *Beauties, Beasts, and Enchantment: Classic French Fairy Tales*. New York: Meridian/NAL/Dutton, 1991.

————, trans. *The Complete Fairy Tales of the Brothers Grimm*. Toronto and New York: Bantam Books, 1987.

R\M